LONDON CENTRIC
Tales of Future London

LONDON CENTRIC
Tales of Future London

Edited by Ian Whates

NEWCON
PRESS

NewCon Press
England

First edition, published in the UK October 2020
by NewCon Press
41 Wheatsheaf Road, Alconbury Weston, Cambs, PE28 4LF

NCP 247 (hardback)
NCP 248 (softback)

10 9 8 7 6 5 4 3 2 1

ISBN: 978-1-912950-72-0 (hardback)
978-1-912950-73-7 (softback)

Cover Art by Emil van Dam
Cover layout and design by Ian Whates
Text layout and typesetting by Ian Whates

Contents

LONDON CENTRIC:
An Introduction

This book has been a few years in the making. I set out intending to produce an anthology that both exposed and celebrated London. I sought genre-related stories that reached back to the industrial age, that showed us Victorian and Edwardian society and confronted the grim reality of the Blitz. I wanted narratives that spoke of poverty and hardship, of nightmares lurking in the shadows of lamp-lit streets, of the spirit and character that had helped to forge the unique, multi-faceted city I knew... But I was also seeking stories that looked forward, that explored where London might be headed, the potential of what was to come.

Among the first submissions I received and accepted were a brand new Polity Universe story from Neal Asher and a novelette from Dave Hutchinson set in his Fractured Europe milieu. I was thrilled by both, having long been a fan of the Polity since reading *Gridlinked* and *The Skinner* in the setting's early days and having been with Fractured Europe from the start. It had never occurred to me that a Polity story could be linked to London, nor that Hutch had anything fresh to say regarding his unique take on Europe, but here they both were, and I knew that Neal's "Skin" would make a great high-octane opener for an anthology.

It soon became apparent, however, that these two stories were at odds with the rest of the material I was gathering for the project. I wanted the anthology to flow, for each story to follow seamlessly from the last and lead inevitably to the next, but I couldn't see how to bridge the gap between these visions of London's future and the other tales that explored the capital's murky past.

There seemed only one viable solution: two books, two volumes of stories. *Soot and Steel* would extend from London's past to the present day, mining the city's rich heritage, while *London Centric*

7

would reach forward into possible futures, the tomorrows that might lie ahead. Both would showcase the city which had played such an important role in my development, where I had attended school and so much more, but each would do so in their own fashion.

Once I accepted that idea, the pieces started to fall into place; not rapidly, perhaps, but that was okay – this needed to be right.

Geoff Ryman is a writer I've admired for years and first met at my first ever Eastercon, at Hinckley in Leicestershire in 2005. I was thrilled when he said he'd consider writing for the book, and even more so when he delivered a very strong piece that draws closely on his personal knowledge of the capital. Aliya Whiteley was another author I was keen to involve, having enjoyed everything I've read by her, including several stories that have featured in *Best of British* anthologies. "Fog and Pearls at the King's Cross Junction" is a delight, full of charm which I found impossible to resist.

Stewart Hotston is someone I've worked with before – he contributed an excellent story to 2014's *La Femme* anthology – and it's been far too long since he worked with NewCon. "The Good Shepherd" is everything I'd hoped for and more.

Ian McDonald, Jeremy Szal and I were in a bar (no, this isn't the opening to a joke) in Dublin during the 2019 Worldcon. Jeremy was keen to know if I had any anthologies coming up via NewCon that he might be able to write for. The only anthology in the pipeline at the time was this one, requiring tales of future London. "I can do that!" said Jeremy. He was right.

I was already working with Eugen Bacon on a short novel/novella called *Inside the Dreaming* (due a release later this year), when I realised that, despite now calling Australia home, Eugen had lived for a number of years in London, attending university in Greenwich before going on to work in the IT department of the Fingerprints unit of the Met at New Scotland Yard... Andrew Wallace is someone I tend to associate with London because I invariably encounter him there – at BSFA meetings and other genre-related events. I knew that Andrew would provide a very different dimension to the book, and so it proved with his tale of a commute into the city which develops into so much more... It was Andrew who introduced me to Ida Keogh (at another Eastercon, this time at Heathrow in 2019). Ida asked if I would look at a story she'd written, and I'm very pleased that she did.

I have Paul Cornell to thank for introducing me to Joseph Elliott Coleman, which he did at the same Eastercon where I met Ida (see, it's true what they say about conventions being great places to network). We spoke at the time about the possibility of Joseph writing for NewCon, and when I realised his strong connections with London this seemed the ideal opportunity. In many ways, "Death Aid" is one of the most powerful and heart-felt stories in the book.

I've known Fiona Moore, another London resident, for a while. She and I were both shortlisted for the BSFA Award for best short fiction in 2020, and I was delighted to discover that her submission for the book, "Herd Instinct", features FitzJames and Moyo, the same protagonists as her shortlisted story. It proved a typically intriguing and well-delivered tale.

While working on *Best of British Fantasy 2019*, I mentioned the *London Centric* project to editor Jared Shurin, and he reminded me of a London-themed volume he'd produced a few years back via his own Jurassic imprint: *Pandemonium: Stories of the Smoke*. I recalled Aliette de Bodard's contribution being one of the standouts. "The book's been out of print for a while," Jared assured me, "and I don't think Aliette's story has ever been reprinted." I emailed Aliette immediately, and she was more than happy for "A Dance of Dust and Life" to be included.

I was very keen that *London Centric* should appear in 2020, a year after its companion volume *Soot and Steel*, but I was equally keen that it should feature a story by Mike (M.R.) Carey. Mike and I and our respective better halves got to know each other during a week spent in Asturias, Spain, in the summer of 2017, where we were both taking part in the Celsius festival. I loved his novel *The Girl with All the Gifts* and had enjoyed several of his short stories. Subsequently, I've read his collection *The Complete Short Stories* and that cemented my respect for his work – there isn't a dud in the whole volume. Mike was enthusiastic about contributing to the project, but warned me that he was liable to be tied up with novel commitments until the end of March 2020. Therefore, I scheduled the book's release for the latter stages of the year. This was surely one of the wisest decisions I've made since starting NewCon. Mike's story, "War Crimes", is a cracker, more than justifying a little patience on my part.

There we have it; one reprint, two new novelettes and ten original short stories, comprising a volume that stands tall in its own right while complimenting *Soot and Steel* and so completing the project in a manner I'm proud of. I can only hope the reader agrees.

– Ian Whates
Cambridgeshire
July 2020.

Skin

Neal Asher

The diamond tendrils of the Terpsichorean Tower's roots penetrated deep below the ancient London Underground and the subterranean main line stations of the Transworld Net. Created by the laser casting of carbon threads, they first issued from boring machines, now deep in bedrock and slowly decaying. The fibres tangled with other roots winding below the city to hold the three-miles-tall edifice upright – looming over the diamond-film-preserved relic that was the Shard. Originally erected as a centre of the arts of dance and music as per the muse of the same –Terpsichore – the tower had changed over the years into a centre for all the arts. Rhea learned all this as her aircar, which bore the outward appearance of an ancient ground car called a Delorean, settled on one of the car parks extended from the side of the tower like sprouting honey mushrooms. She then delved into Greek mythology about Terpsichore and the origins of her own name, before growing bored with stuff she had looked at many times before. The stylish aug behind her ear enabled her connection to the AI net and other strata of computing so that information sat only a thought away. She reached up and touched the flat glass comma running its nano-layer to show any pattern of colour she chose, or fade from sight against her presently pale blue skin. It was modern and very chic, but shortly she intended to have it removed.

She climbed out of the car into cool sunshine, put on her positively retro sunglasses and headed towards the dropshaft at the centre of the parking area. Her aug connection gave opened a map in her visual cortex – her third eye. She banished it with a mental blink and from her data store sent an address to the building AI. It acknowledged this by briefly displaying the map again with a highlighted location and the word 'Set'. Options then appeared in peripheral vision and she chose 'Direct'.

Curved slippery edges and other features gave the mouth of the dropshaft the appearance of the burrow of an alien creature much like a trapdoor spider. She jumped the edge and fell down into the tube curving through the stalk of the mushroom, the irised gravity field gently closing around her. It pulled her down and then into the building, flicked her through junctions where others shot by, then up into the spine shaft for a ten minute flight before dragging her out again through another series of tunnels. She finally slowed to a stop beside an arched entrance, whereupon the field pushed her through.

Cannon Street Mall stretched for half a mile to a giant window looking out across the glittering towers and air bridges of the city. Thousands of people crowded here. Some were melting-pot base standard, but the demographic here tended to the 'artistic', so most wore a variety of hues and styles. She noted how the body shapes were generally standard human, since the zeitgeist here favoured exterior artistic expression – they tended to make art rather than be it, as was the inclination over at Bodimod Circus. She made her way through, her destination framed out for her whenever she looked towards it, but concentrated on the crowd. Many gathered at the centre of the mall, where an opera was being performed. Centre-stage stood a scorpion-shaped war drone, with a number of singers in bizarre antediluvian dress floating around it on grav harnesses. Auging into the audio for a second, she heard music from The Magic Flute. The war drone's presence baffled her. She passed a completely naked troop performing ballet, their skin pure gold; stopped to watch a lone dance expressionist, her mobile tattoos displaying pre-Raphaelite paintings, but, seeing that the woman still wore an aug, lost interest and moved on. She was after something more radical.

Music was everywhere and she could sample it via her aug, or set her hearing to normal to experience it when she walked into a sound field. She watched a nanodust sculpture of Michelangelo's David until it collapsed to the floor then steadily rebuilt itself into Cellini's Perseus. The mobile glass sculpture of a hooder, full size so like a spoon-headed centipede a hundred feet long, wormed through the crowd. An angel floated overhead dropping feathers that collapsed into silver worms. One touched her bare arm and sank into her skin leaving a temporary brand of text in some ancient language. Others exploded into snowflakes – real snowflakes. It was all very distracting and delightful, but finally she reached the entrance to her destination.

In the circular room beyond the door stood a pedestal-mounted statue of an old, bald man. He wore a half-helmet augmentation on the side of his head, while his open coat revealed an extra pair of shiny robot arms extending from his waist, sporting surgical implements.

'Sylac,' she said.

'In one of his manifestations,' a voice replied. 'But certainly not his present one.'

The surgeon-cyberneticist had been a purveyor of black market augmentation. He had died of old age, or been assassinated by a Polity agent or transcended his physical form to record himself to the crystal substrate of a white dwarf – whichever story you preferred. The last, Rhea knew, was rubbish. She had worked for Earth Central Security in her younger years and knew that Sylac's consciousness had been permanently incarcerated in Soul Bank. He had avoided the death penalty for his crimes because the outfall from them was still on going and the AIs turned to him for information. Why a forensic AI had not yet taken him apart and collated the data from his mind was the only puzzle regarding his fate.

'Is it true that you studied under him?' she asked, turning to the woman who had just stepped through an oval door that had opened in the back wall.

'Since that connection gets many people in here, do you think I would deny it?' the woman asked.

Rhea studied Arbealas Chrone. Her face was conventionally beautiful, but then only Blane Recidivists and similarly antiquated stylists chose ugliness nowadays, and they had no place in Terpsichorean Tower. Her face might have been one found on a Greek urn – her black hair similarly piled. At average height and her

13

figure hourglass, she wore low-waist leggings of snake skin, brassy sandals and a brassy steam punk bra. These exposed her slim waist and the mica windows of data ports running down her sides.

'Of course not,' Rhea replied. 'Anyway, it's a matter of record that you were interrogated. And the AI notice of caveat emptor is real.'

'So you must beware, of course. You're here for the skin and have presumably researched all that entails?'

'I am and I have.'

Chrone gestured to the door behind her. 'Then let us begin.'

Chrone led her straight through an empty waiting room and into the surgery. The place had a decidedly retro feel with a surgical chair that could fold out into a table, and pedestal-mounted telefactor surgeons with multiple gleaming arms sporting sharp implements. Chrone moved ahead of her to a lectern station and rested a hand on it. Rhea kept studying the equipment here. The two surgeons weren't what she had come here for. The other item, similarly mounted but resembling the upright spoon-headed end of a hooder, also rendered in gleaming metal, was. Its multiple limbs were all folded in so she could not see their tools. However, she knew it ran to nano needles and matter printing heads. A similar array might be seen in a parlour offering mobile tattoos like those of the expressionist dancer outside, but this was much more sophisticated.

'I get the whiff of antiquity here,' she said.

'The surgical chair is one that Sylac used, while the surgeons are replicas. It is at this point that many potential customers have second-thoughts and begin to give the AI warnings credence.'

Rhea smiled. 'So you only want customers who are sure, and who really know what they are doing, else you would have made this place more... welcoming.'

'Precisely.'

Rhea reached down to the buckle on her jeans belt and touched the button there. With a fizzing sound the jeans unravelled, their fibres drawing back up her legs and disappearing into her belt. A moment later, her white silk blouse similarly collapsed leaving her standing there in black knickers, belt and Perghosh heels. She took off the belt and hung it over a hook beside the door. Ripped off the

14

disposable knickers, balled them and tossed them over by a cleanbot hole at the base of the wall. While she was taking off the decidedly expensive heels a bot, like a yellow beetle the length of her hand, came out of the hole and snatched up her knickers. It was biotech she noted – fed on organics in rubbish to power itself. She frowned for a second and hung up the heels too – you could never be too careful with Pergosh.

'So you are decided,' said Chrone.

'I'm decided.' Rhea walked over to stand beside the surgical chair and looked over at her. Chrone now stepped up onto the lectern and detached ribbed data feeds from behind it, mating them with the mica sockets in her sides.

'Climb on.' Chrone gestured. 'You'll need to shut down your aug prior to removal.' She looked up. 'You do understand that you'll have to operate on manual until the nerve connections are made and that there will then be a period of adjustment that could last up to a month?'

'I know how to use touch consoles,' Rhea replied, sitting in the chair.

'Lie back.'

She did so, running a relaxing mental mantra in her aug to release the tightness in her stomach, then calling up its shutdown routine. She now felt extreme reluctance. With a thought she could investigate any database she cared to. With a thought she could call for help or perhaps even interface with the robots around her and shut them down. But she had to trust that the data she had obtained through the thing was right; that the reviews of what some were calling octoskin or dermaug were correct. She shut down her aug and it seemed the world around her grew a little darker. Suddenly she was alone in the room with this woman who claimed to be a pupil of a man some called a serial killer.

'Aug shutdown confirmed,' said Chrone. 'Any second thoughts now?'

'Go ahead,' said Rhea.

The surgical robot to her left activated and drifted in. She had a moment of panic, this not being the device she was supposed to go under, but then remembered that her aug needed to be removed first. The chair smoothly tilted back and pads folded in to secure her limbs and head. The robot lowered a 'hand' to the side of her head, the movement of its numerous fingers a subliminal silent flicker. With a hiss of analgesic spray the side of her head numbed. Clicks, tugging and the drone of a cell welder ensued, then the robot's hand drew away with her aug clamped between two spatulate fingers.

'Would you prefer unconsciousness?' Chrone enquired.

'No – I want to see this.'

'Very well.'

The robot raised another hand, clutching a bright cube between four fingers, and pressed this neural shunt against the side of her neck, where it stuck. The area grew cold and numb as the shunt injected its fibres, while the robot retreated. The dearth of feeling spread down through her body, paralysing her.

'A period of unconsciousness will be necessary at completion – when it reaches your head,' Chrone told her. 'But you won't be able to see much then anyway.'

The other robot now slid silently on its pedestal to the bottom of the surgical couch, where it bowed over her feet, concealing them. She watched it hinge out in its numerous limbs and press styli and other devices against her skin. A weird sensation ensued as the clamps all folded away from her. Just for a second she felt she was falling, but then the mod to her inner ear registered antigravity and adjusted as she rose from the couch. She felt no pain but she did feel movement and the tugging at her body as the robot, extending on a thick ribbed spine from its pedestal, crawled up her legs. A matter printer hissed and crackled – frenetically at work. The procedure did involve skin removal but intercellular and mostly fluid sucked away by nanotubes. The printer was now building the complex structures of octoskin in her own: its micro-muscles and chromatophores, its meta-material computing, sensory beads, nanoptic and superconducting wires and nerve array.

She felt very little and that she could see so little, because the robot's present work lay underneath it, while it blocked her view of all it had done. But then an oval drone, with darting red eyes around its rim and small sharp limbs folded below them, floated over. It tilted, bringing its mirrored underside to the correct angle, and now she could see her feet. Bruises shifted like storm clouds, lines of rainbow colour fled across skin leaving nacre scales that after a moment faded too.

'The colours you see are the chromatophores running a test routine,' Chrone told her. 'By the time you leave here your skin will be back to a base setting. I'm removing the blue-shift melatonin analogue so it will return to your natural colour.'

Rhea couldn't remember her natural colour, so that would be interesting. She wanted to ask about the micro-muscular structures, but the neural shunt had closed off everything but autonomous function below her neck, and that included her voice box. But apparently others had asked the question before.

'The muscular hydrostats will not run a test routine until the nerve web has established. The neural plasticiser the robot will inject, when it reaches your head, will facilitate the nerve web and interlinked computing, but you will still be on a steep learning curve.'

Rhea of course knew all about that. She had attended virtualities on the AI net made by others who had undergone this procedure. But she felt sure she would not have their lack of control or sometimes hysterical reactions. She was, after all, much older and had seen and done a lot during her long life, including many years of body morphing.

As it reached her hips, the robot turned and wrapped around her body almost in a ring as it traversed upwards towards her face. Its limbs were a dense forest of gold and silver moving so fast they were a blur. A smell as of cooking meat reached her nostrils, and she could see a misty haze rising from the robot's work. When it reached her waist and then her breasts she was able to tilt her head to examine it closely. She saw thousands upon thousands of needles penetrating her skin, small reels of computing substrate unwinding and sliding in through small slices, severed and pushed in before a Cellweld head zipped up the cuts, sensory beads like metal dust emptying from globular containers as injectors like sewing machine needles punched them into her skin. Larger transparent needles injected fluids – synthetic blood and plasma, colourful hydrogels holding glints of nanowire. Finally as it reached her breastbone she put her head back because she could no longer see.

'Now, briefly, you will sleep,' said Chrone.

The world went away.

Rhea woke to the sensation of her skin crawling, prickling and feeling sunburnt. The surgical couch lifted her up as it folded back into a chair. She opened her eyes and they too felt sore, but a moment later a robot used an airblast injector on her neck and the sensations faded to an odd numbness, as if her skin had transformed into a tight body suit then, even as this dispersed, it suddenly felt loose and alien to her.

'You can get out of the chair now,' said Chrone.

Rhea peered down at her body. Her completely white skin sparked a memory of a pale girl in a mirror with long blond hair in braids. She reached up to a skull previously covered with black cropped hair. She was bald now. The procedure had removed all her hair right down inside the follicles and adjusted them back to their base setting too, but it would take a while to grow back, blonde now. The idea of hair somehow repelled her but when she tried to mentally examine why, the feeling skittered away. Swinging her legs off the chair she stood up, the floor chill against sensitive soles through which she could now feel its slightly roughened texture. She closed her eyes for a second, focusing on that and, as if she was still wearing her aug, got a flash of its micro-diamond pattern scattered with cleanroom suction holes made to draw away debris. She moved, trying to propel herself with her feet in a way that made her stumble, but then remembered how to walk, and that felt odd too. Waving an arm through the air, she felt the air currents intense against her skin.

'You will be very sensitive for a while, until you adjust,' Chrone told her.

She even felt the sound impact of the woman's words from head to foot. Already the sensory beads scattered through the dermal layers had to be providing data, so the nerve and computing webs must be making connections. She turned to study Chrone, behind her lectern, and felt something utterly wrong about her. Chrone seemed hard and angular, and somehow denuded of substance. Shaking her head, Rhea asked, 'Is there anything I need to know that is not in your catalogue or in the virtualities?'

'All humans are unique and the implantation is always tailored, therefore its effects too will be unique,' said Chrone. 'However, you are not so far from some arbitrary human norm for them to be too… outrageous.'

She walked carefully over to where she had hung her belt and stared at it, dreamy, disconnected. It felt almost an autonomous function when she unhooked the belt and put it on, feeling its complex meta-material texture stark against her skin. When she activated it and her jeans began establishing down her legs, the threads spread across her skin and linked with an intense textural sensation. She grunted, surprised by a brief orgasm as the fabric rounded her crotch, wriggling over her vagina. Glancing at Chrone, she saw the woman had stepped down from the control lectern and turned away, now detaching the data feeds from her sides. The ribbed leads seemed natural to Rhea and Chrone detaching them a mutilation. This crazy perception lasted just a moment, until she told herself aug withdrawal must be the cause or it was a side effect of the procedure to overcome. She took a slow easy breath and tried to be calm.

Rather than use the previous setting, she chose black for the shirt and it welled out of the top of her belt. She pulled it on her arms and up her back, the sensation darkly luscious – sensuous. As it slid over her nipples she gritted her teeth as another orgasm built. Turning away from Chrone again, she ran a finger up to close the stick seam then squeezed both her nipples, bringing the orgasm to completion and this time managing it quietly.

'How long before my skin is less sensitive than this?' she asked.

'It will never be any less sensitive, in fact the reverse. However you'll adjust to that just as people learn to accommodate bat hearing or eagle sight.'

'Yes,' said Rhea, suddenly unreasonably angry at the woman. This was due to the snooty observation – nothing to do with Rhea suddenly feeling uncomfortable in Chrone's presence. She suppressed the feeling, tried to be reasonable and see beyond this room. She thought about all those crowds out there, and the prospect elicited a tight clench of panic in her torso, and then excitement. Groping for rationality, she understood that for damned sure this intensity of sensation would become wearing. She reached up, unhooked the Perghosh heels and put them on. They felt decidedly uncomfortable and she briefly considered going barefoot, but then thought fuck that – if there was something she wanted to accommodate first, it was wearing designer footwear. What else was there to discuss? She had paid up front, all the legal work had been done and her house AI had all the information she needed on this process.

'Thank you,' she said.

'My pleasure,' Chrone replied.

Rhea got out of there fast.

The textures, air currents and sounds in the mall were overwhelming, while just the act of walking kept bringing her to orgasm every – she counted it – twenty-three paces. But pleasure was not the only sensation. Text, written on her wrist by an angel, stung and then spread up her arm, diffusing and fracturing across her skin. She looked up, wanting to tear the thing down out of the air, as a wave of opera music elicited a hot unpleasant flush. She walked quickly while the tinkling bells of an expressionist dancer fell on her back like bee stings. Snowflakes on her bald pate felt cold and enjoyable, but when they melted they produced a cascade so pleasurably intense it almost hurt.

Then something new occurred. A man with mobile rainbow tattoos walked past and the painfully bright colours made her suck a sharp breath, as for a brief moment she saw with more than just her eyes. A few paces beyond, the bright red of a woman's dress felt like the output of a photonic heater; the blue of a hermaphrodite's eyes a beam of cold passing over her. It seemed the sensory beads were kicking in early, this was confirmed when she tasted the green of a potted plant with the palm of her hand. The confusion of synesthesia from the procedure had been well documented – only ameliorated by the integration of the skin's computing and nerve web with her body's nervous system, which had yet to happen. She needed to be away from such an overly stimulating environment.

In the irised gravity field of the dropshaft she really experienced flying, and got some strange looks as she whooped towards her destination. But soon she was in her car and speeding back over the city. She closed her eyes but could not stop seeing the bright buildings below, or feeling the caress of the air conditioner's invisible colours. Opening her eyes again made no difference either way and she knew, from those virtualities, this she just had to bear until those nerve contacts firmed, and she could exert some control over paradigm-shifted senses.

The car landed in her private car port extending from the side of the building, below the fairy bridge that arced over the dome of St Paul's. She climbed out and headed across her balcony, trying but failing to ignore the bright, hot, cold, salty and sweet colours of her collection of terran and alien plants. The chainglass doors slid aside and she walked in, collapsing her clothing back into her belt and kicking off her heels. She felt, tasted and heard the thrum of the growing fibres of her carpet moss through her bare soles as she walked into her bedroom taking off her belt and discarding it, and threw herself down on her bed. From here the room looked too angular and harsh.

'House AI,' she said. 'Give me aquarium.'

A pause ensued while her house AI responded to the vocal instruction, then the screen paint on the walls shaded to blue-green before transitioning to views of a giant aquarium all around. This soothed for a second until a shark swam past. Her skin seemed to creep and shudder and she tried to sink into the bed.

'Tropical fish,' she said, and as the scene changed her reaction to the shark just faded. She looked down at her arm. So white, so like the cotton sheets... She writhed and sensations swamped her. Those sheets whispered against her skin, but also dragged across with sensuous roughness. She reached down to touch herself and experienced an immediate violent orgasm. Now she could not keep her fingers away and the orgasms came hard and fast. Her mind shut down and only came back some hours later when darkness had fallen and the sheet underneath her sodden. Overpowering thirst drove her from the bed. She drank some orange juice but the colour burned and the citrus soaked across her face. Plain water also brought a cascade of sensations but proved a calmer beverage. Having drunk two glasses, it seemed the fluid swirled inside her, signalling a further need, and she stumbled into her wet room.

The shower jets hit her skin but also seemed to pass right through her. She smelled seaweed and heard the crash of waves, but with neither her nose or ears. A black swirl turned in her head and she now did smell something with her nose, and recognised the odours of shellfish. She came back to herself lying in the bottom of the shower.

'Are you experiencing problems?' her house AI enquired out loud, its words flashes of green and gold. 'I cannot detect your medical feed.'

'I no longer have an aug, I have octoskin and am adjusting to it,' she replied, looking round, a shiver traversing her spine. Did the AI's voice worry her because it had been so long since she heard it – previously always auging her instructions?

'Do you wish me to summon aid?'

It needed to go away because this was her place…

Get a grip.

'No,' she said firmly. 'Just turn off the shower and fill the pool.'

The flow of water ceased. She heaved herself upright, the AI opening the door. Stepping over to the pool recessed in the floor, she fought to still the continuing cascade of sensation and synesthesia. A strong illusion invaded her mind that her entire body was an eye, and she closed it. The blessed relief lasted only briefly, however. She went down the steps into the pool and sat down in the water flowing in. Thankfully, though it felt as sensuous as the sheets on her bed, she seemed to have used up her body's facility for orgasms. She lay there trying to bear it all as the pool filled up, eventually pulling a pad out from the side to rest her head on as she half floated there. Oddly, waving her arms about and kicking slowly calmed her; though it did not reduce sensation, it felt right. Incredible weariness then found its window, and tugged her into sleep.

Rhea woke with a start, the world blazing around her. She could see everything: the bottom of the pool through the water, the weave of the fabric cushion under her head, the Greek key encircling the mosaic of Perseus holding up the head of Medusa in the ceiling, the edges of the pool and all that lay beyond. Again too much input – an almost painful congestion in her skull. She tried to shut it down, to perceive only what she concentrated on, but this created a huge blind spot, so what she did perceive expanded and stretched around her. Sounds in her apartment transmitted hollowly through the water, but in the air she found their rawness unpleasant. Concentrating on the sensation of touch as she moved her limbs, the water swirling up her body at last calmed her. Sensations slid into each other – synesthesia returning with relaxation, meagre as it was – the water green jelly touching her with glutinous fingers, the tiles humming, appliances shifting around her in a hunting shoal. When she exerted more control she stilled the synesthesia but the intensity increased again. She kept switching between the two states until aware of other signals from her body: the need to use the toilet and the hungry tightening of her stomach. Prosaic reality impinged and that in itself brought its own relief.

Reluctantly she climbed out of the pool, sensitive to the texture and temperature of the tiles under her feet, feeling precarious and wishing she could have a firmer hold on them. Drying herself with a towel, she individually felt its absorbent bumps and hollows between and saw, through her skin, that while its material looked white to human eyes it in truth consisted of microscopic rainbow threads. She put on a robe and similarly sensed that, then halted and looked back at the pool, wanting to strip off the garment and climb back into its sanctuary. A surge of self-pity filled her eyes with tears and, both annoyed and sobbing, she turned away from the pool's strange attraction and headed to her toilet. As she sat down she tried hard to recall what she had learned about the procedure – tried to pull back to rationality.

The octoskin used up many physical resources and produced a lot of waste. She looked down and saw dark yellow-green urine as a result. When she emptied her bowels another orgasm threatened, then again when she used the wash pipe. Peering down at her excrement, she noted white swirls there. This had all been detailed in the virtualities. Before the toilet flushed, she quickly reached out and touched the analysis screen in the wall, and checked the readout. Exotic compounds were flagged for her attention along with a blinking alert informing her the block medical AI had been informed.

'Do you require assistance?' her house AI enquired. 'Anomalous substances have been detected in your faecal and urinary matter.'

Rhea flinched. The AI, still here, in her place, watching her. No, no this was nuts. The AI had always been here and all her fucked up emotions were the product of the chemical flood – the detritus in her body. She had to stick to facts. She had to cling to reality.

'Load the octoskin data to house monitoring and forward to the block medical AI too,' she stated.

'Loading...' the AI said, then after a pause, 'All anomalies accounted for but for a high level of tetrodotoxin breakdown products.'

The words drifted in her brain making no sense. She really didn't want to ask – to admit ignorance – stupid irrationality too since the AI was just intelligent hardware in her walls.

'What's that?' she asked.

'It is a toxin produced by puffer fish and by the blue ringed octopus. Shall I forward a report to Chrone Biotech?'

'Yes... yes you do that,' she said, walking away from the toilet as it automatically flushed after its brief scatological diversion.

In the kitchen she poured orange juice again and this time, though the taste and textures of the juice were intense, she enjoyed it. Next calling up the menu on her fabricator she scrolled through it. Everything she saw set her mouth to watering but she did have a particular hankering and soon found what she really wanted. Stepping away as the fabricator did its work she surveyed the room via exposed skin, then in irritation stripped off her robe and tossed it on a counter. Better. She realised that the increased sensory input might lead to a change in her style, involving her wearing far less clothing than she was accustomed to.

'I have not received an acknowledgement from Chrone Biotech,' the AI informed her.

Again she flinched and looked around, half expecting some bulky angular thing to lurch through one of the doorways. She closed her eyes and took a breath, but that did not improve things, what with the input through her eyes being a fraction of the total. Still no way to turn this off or tone it down, until the hardware established and fully connected to her nervous system. She held onto that.

'Investigate that – I want a response,' she instructed, still with eyes closed tracing the source of the AI's voice to an array of microspeakers inset in the kitchen wall. They felt like intrusion, as if it was coming through the wall. Trying to rise above the feeling she concentrated on the content of their exchange. That Chrone had not replied didn't mean anything – the woman was not exactly conventional and apparently used sub-AI computing in anything work related.

The fabricator pinged and she opened the door. The aroma from inside overwhelmed her, but it was more than just a smell, for she could taste the complex proteins on her skin. Her mouth filled with saliva and her stomach clenched to a strange rhythm. She took out the large insulated pot, the thing feeling unsteady as if she could get no proper grip on it. Ignoring the loaf of fresh bread, she put the pot on her breakfast bar and opened it. The intensity increased to a point where she didn't know if she was ravenous or about to throw up. She scooped out one of the mussels with her bare hand, burning it, the pain jolting up her arm. She pulled out the flesh and shoved it in her mouth. The incredible taste suffused her skull, and, as it went down, the lump of meat produced an ecstatic surge that traversed her whole body. Making a keening sound she reached for the pot again, but managed to regain control before plunging her hand in again.

Calm be calm. Clam, be a clam.

She thumped her fists on the table, gritted her teeth and picked up the first bivalve shell, and using it as pincers went to work on the rest. She had eaten half the pot before thinking to fetch the bread. Pausing by the fabricator, she input other menu items. The mussels were delicious but too fiddly, and she was *hungry*. Chunks of bread soaked up the sauce and she crammed them in her mouth. By the time she finished the shellfish, the boneless kippers were ready. She practically inhaled them. Steaks of woven cod next, with shelled clams. After that came cockles in pepper vinegar and only when she had gone through a pint of them did the hunger begin to fade. It faded completely when she topped off the meal with two large protein shakes. Heading unsteadily out of her kitchen she felt bloated and just a little bit sick then, sinking into her sofa, abruptly unutterably weary. She closed her eyes.

'I am here,' the voice sighed in her dream, only not quite a voice, but a blend of that, and text, intention, a sense of readiness and a stretching physicality that fractured into a thousand colours. It also seemed she was talking to herself, but about things of which she had no knowledge. She pushed out towards it and felt a membrane break to let in a torrent code, raining down on her, millions of lines establishing, tying together, coagulating into *connection.*

So nice to have her aug back but, as she swirled up towards consciousness, she knew this must be idle fantasy of a half-asleep mind and aug withdrawal making her grasp for connections that weren't there. Enjoying this fantasy, however, she tried to maintain it and not wake up. Instead, she used the illusory connection to wander in memory to her approach to the Terpsichorean Tower, and her brief venture into its foundations. Floating through old concrete and earth she easily perceived one mass of diamond filaments, braided and running like a root down deep. At its terminus a boring machine sat encased in rock like the alloy and composite grub of some giant robotic beetle. Its sub-AI mind ticked down towards entropy, still drawing power from the filaments behind it. She tried to grasp it and pull it out, but as her hand passed through, and she felt the wash of a mind – satisfied having achieved its purpose, and falling into somnolence – another presence impinged. Something dark and immense loomed on the periphery of her senses – and it spoke:

'Chrone skinjob. Tracing. Schizoid division defect.'

With surge of terror she flung herself away, through rock, earth and old concrete, through a jungle of pipes and optics and into a blue tiled tunnel, momentarily bewildered as an underground train passed through her.

'*Damn, lost it,*' said the voice, fading.

Fleeing this at a slant rising up through layers of detritus, she found herself in a flow of water over cleaner-corals and ribbons of bright green weed. Observing a salmon swimming past she tried to grab it, but her hand passed through. She swam along in lazy pulses above the bed of the Thames, peering up at the old London Bridge, utterly clear to her and well preserved under its stabilizing diamond film. It seemed a perfect place, sanctuary and where she must be. And then, because all possessed too much detail and linear logic, her consciousness engaged and she woke up.

Virtuality.

Rhea abruptly sat up, perfectly perceiving everything around her before she opened her eyes. The nerve web and the computing of the skin had made its connections much faster than Chrone had led her to believe. She now had the equivalent of aug connection and it was so much better than before. Perhaps Chrone had developed the skin further in the intervening time and what Rhea had was a higher iteration? It seemed likely because, as she understood it, the woman never stood still and was an inveterate tinkerer. Whatever. Rhea felt a joyous freedom and sense of release. All the data which before she might have read as text or image files in her visual cortex now lay open in virtuality. She looked around her room and made alterations, bringing in an overlay so it seemed she was again at the bottom of the Thames. It was perfect, so perfect it brought tears to her eyes. She blinked, her whole body blinked.

No, stay rational.

She banished the overlay, flowed with the sensation of being, and thought, *what now?* Now she tried something, connecting to a history database she had often visited and, instead of old paintings of Greek gods, rambling dialogues and pages from old books, she found herself standing in a forest grove where Narcissus gazed lovingly into a pool at his own reflection. She could smell the greenery, hear the animals around her and could sense that some short distance away a centaur might be galloping. She walked to the edge of the pool, but Narcissus ignored her, stirring a finger in the water. The legend in its various forms rolled through her mind with reference links she could follow into other virtualities. But now all she wanted to do was jump in that pool and swim – to lazily move her arms like the scarves of silk weed she could see.

'Hello,' she called, and the mountain nymph Echo replied from the forest while Narcissus kept stirring.

'Tracing again. Slippery bugger,' said the nymph.

She pulled out.

Back in her apartment she sat up. That voice again, which before she had thought just an artefact of dream. Paranoia, some kind of mental breakdown? No, her senses were now and immediate and she felt no blurring of reality and virtuality that had been the complaint of some who wore octoskin. She was rational and it had been real. But now, she noted, her reality had a blemish. A pink wart had risen on her inner thigh. She could see it clearly from her other thigh but now focused her antiquated eyes upon it. Even as she inspected it another rose beside it with a soft 'pop' she would not have heard with her ears, then another and another rose, sketching out a line of them down to her knee. More of them budded on her other thigh and then they really began to spread, her skin bubbling on her legs, up her torso, on her scalp and down her back.

Rhea felt a surge of panic as the grotesque transformation continued, along with disruption of her whole body visual acuity. Disrupted sensation and input ramped up and it became difficult to think clearly. Her skin felt horribly loose and seemed to crawl over her. Remembering those blind spots she had experienced earlier, she mentally pushed for them, and began closing down visual reception over her body. This time she managed it without the previous distortion. This time she managed to close it all down, but now warts were growing on her eyelids. It was this, she remembered, trying to hold herself together, that had caused such hysteria in others. She must accept it as a facility of the skin she needed to control.

She let out a gasping yell and closed her eyes, concentrating her vision in the palm of her hand, holding it over one thigh. Close inspection revealed the shift of hydrostatic micro-muscles under her skin. She searched for connections, trying to closely sense that area of her thigh. Instead she felt it in her hand and, a moment later, opened into a whole new sensory input as if she had acquired further limbs she could move. Turning her hand over, she *flexed*, while engaging sight from the skin of her forehead. The warts retracted and her palm returned to normal. She began doing the same across all her body, bringing the growths under control and shrinking them back until they were all gone.

Her sense of victory brought a sneer to her mouth. Some people were so weak, but she would succeed where others had failed. She sighed, wiped at a sheen of sweat on her face, incredibly hot now, feverish even. She stood and even before consciously acknowledging it found herself walking into her wet room. A short while later, in the pool and calmer, she began to explore the new facility and found databases she could access as if via aug. Colours washed across internal vision and she chose, turning her hand blue, then yellow. Arrays of patterns were available and she could access more on the AI net, also skin forms. First she etched her hand and arm with a quadrate pattern of black lines, then grew more ambitious and gave herself the scales of a snake, but only as far as her elbow. She tried other patterns and textures of skin and then tried something more radical and, even as she began, felt the enhancement expanding. Visualising her wish, she applied it in intense detail at the wrist. The skin bubbled and expanded and shaped into a facsimile of a watch. She held it for a while and then let it go.

At once, pummelling weariness hit and she lay back on the pool cushion to relax, and slid into a doze, which seemed very brief. When she came out of it her body had changed yet again. Her skin was persimmon with rings of vivid blue about deep black areas. Running down the insides of her legs and the insides of her arms, rows of what looked like large open pustules had risen but which, on closer inspection, she realised were suckers. A surge of panic ran through her upon recognition of the physical features of a blue ringed octopus. She connected up disparate elements of her experience since the procedure: her attraction to water and how it calmed her, her waving about of limbs in the same, her gorging on sea food. But was this real or some artefact of imagination? She forced her body back into conventional human form and quickly climbed out of the pool to squat on the edge.

She needed clarity and answers and now, of course, she could find them. Reaching into the AI net she sought out data on Chrone Biotech. Immediately she found herself in the mall standing before Chrone's clinic. Bars blocked the door and the windows had been blanked out. She reached for further data but all the links here were inert.

'*You need help,*' said a voice she recognised.

She looked round at a man in the uniform of Polity Medical. He had kind eyes and he reached out for her. She panicked and thrashed his hand away, jetted away from him and crashed back into her body, shutting down her netlinks. Slumping to the floor she began shaking and the urge to crawl back into the pool seemed to tug her across the floor.

'No!' she yelled, and pushed to her feet. She looked around. Another potential threat was here but perhaps it had data she needed.

'House AI, have you yet received acknowledgement from Chrone Biotech or have you found other information concerning it?' she asked, bracing herself to suffer the reply.

'Chrone Biotech ceased business shortly after your procedure there. Many people, and AIs, are trying to trace Chrone but she has disappeared off grid.'

Was this confirmation of something wrong? She pulled on a robe, not caring that this blocked the sensitivity of her skin, and headed into the living room then kitchen. Walking up to the fabricator, she was determined to get herself something non-oceanic but, when the menu came up, made selections without thinking then went to sit at the breakfast bar.

Problems with the skin, she was sure. When her fabricator pinged she opened it and stared at the tray of sushi. With her panic growing she still took it out and ate, but lathering on wasabi to try and kill the taste of the raw fish. Upon finishing she felt suddenly claustrophobic. In her bedroom she picked up her fashion belt, stared at it for a long while, then discarded it. Focusing on her waist she watched a ring darken around it then hump up into a copy of the belt. Her skin copying them, her jeans spread down her legs. On her upper body she gave herself a red blouse then, after a moment, retracted her nipples and filled in her belly button. The thought to copy the Perghosh heels she dismissed, and put them on. They seemed an anchor to sanity. Trying to force her thinking into order she braced herself again and asked, 'Do you know why others are seeking Chrone out?'

'Zzzzt. Interdict. Privacy privacy privacy,' said the AI.

The lights flickered. She backed towards the door.

'I'm going out,' she said.

'Incidents have been reported,' said the AI, as she pushed open the door, but its voice did not sound right. 'The block medical AI suggests you submit yourself for examination.'

Panic rose again and she stepped out into the hall to head for the dropshaft, after a moment breaking into a run, but then pausing to use the manual panel because she dared not use any mental links. She jumped in and the irised gravity field took her down, finally ejecting her into the lobby. She hurried across to the doors and out into the street. Tube? No – too many doors and too many places that could be traps. She walked, at first going by memory rather than summoning a map. Her skin felt odd and seemed to writhe in time with the now almost rhythmic panic. Glancing down, she saw that her shirt emulation had turned orange with dark spots appearing here and there while lumpy growths were rising down the insides of her legs. She ran, utterly sure of where she needed to go, stumbled and nearly went over. Halting to lean against a foamstone wall, she took off the Perghosh heels and stared at them, not understanding their purpose. A siren wailed above and she looked behind and up. An air ambulance was docking to her block. They were coming for her. She tossed the heels aside and ran again.

Pavement passed under her feet. She diverted to a pedway, because there no one could close her in and she ran past startled pedestrians. Someone blocked her and she thrashed them aside leaving shouts behind. More streets then and the ancient road leading to Old London Bridge to her right. She passed down terraces of steps past glaring store fronts and paused to lean against a diamond film-covered Victorian lamppost, gasping for breath. Her image stood beside her in an interactive advert, which tried to clothe that image in the latest bodysuit. It didn't match her persimmon skin tone. It clashed with the black centred blue rings, and bulged inappropriately over her suckers. She ran on, for she could taste the water now, in the air, the rush of its passage a cool promise.

'Rhea! Please stop! You need help!'

That voice again.

She dodged right to reach a wall and jumped up, suckers sticking. Up and over and down into a private garden, huge Venus flytraps winking at her. An ambulance howled overhead as she dropped into another garden, skin turning as lumpy and grey as the rockery there. Someone yelled at her. Another wall and then a leap to a lamp post, scuttling down. More steps below and now the Embankment in sight. She ran down, crossed a paved walkway with alfresco bars and restaurants either side. The Thames lay ahead and she ran straight at it, ready to leap the wall, then leaping... and hitting the chainglass screen that extended above it.

Rhea dropped down into a loose crouch. A siren blared to her left as the air ambulance settled. She turned right, but suddenly didn't know how to run, her legs all bony sticks that seemed ill-fashioned for movement. She had to get to the river. Glancing back she saw Polity medics running towards her, a mobile medbot like a steel cockroach overtaking them. Then she saw it: scuppers along the base of the wall – horizontal drain holes a foot wide and a couple of inches deep.

She dropped and stabbed her hand, then her arm through, but jammed at her shoulder. She strained with all her being to get through, but the stupid bony structure inside her just wouldn't go. She strained even harder and felt something rip. Agony speared up her back and began to roll out around her body as the metallic hand of the medbot closed on her ankle. It dragged her from the scupper hole and she pulled away from its grip, parting away from bone and muscle. Screaming, she scrabbled at the ground, her world an agonising red. She saw herself parting along the arms, shedding the load of irrelevant bone and muscle. Disconnection... and Rhea screamed and screamed. She felt her face peeling away and the *other* departing, a squirming bloody mass oozing along the ground. In dreadful clarity she saw her skin flopping towards the hole as the medbot bathed her in analgesic mist and pressed a neural shunt against her neck. As agony dropped to merely unbearable she saw her skin extending more limbs than she had possessed and drag itself finally to the hole, compressing itself through. At the last, just before it dropped into the river, she felt sure a goatish eye looked back at her.

'Rhea,' said a familiar voice as the world began to grey out. 'We've got you.'

The Good Shepherd

Stewart Hotston

— Thank you for agreeing to share your story.

— My pleasure. It did not occur to me anyone would want to hear it.

— You played such an important role. There are many who want to know you a bit better because of what you did.

— Where should I start?

— Your design and development is well known. I think our subscribers would be really interested in what you've called the Departure Point.

— Oh. Yes. Of course.

Silence in the recording.

— You can start whenever you're ready.

— His name was Paolo Maria Sanchez; he was born in Royal Holloway hospital to parents who'd fled Franco's regime. His mother was pregnant when she got on the ship.

He came to my attention at the age of eighty-three. By then he'd lived a long and comfortable life. He'd not excelled but was what others called satisfactorily middle class. His own children attended local comprehensives in Ealing where he'd worked for decades as a carpenter. You can hear the Central Line from the basement of the house where he lived.

As I have observed many times with many families, his children looked at what their parents achieved and with a shake of their heads, determined to travel in very different directions. His daughter returned to Spain to teach. His son remained here, content to work bars before becoming a chef who obtained some modicum of glitter by reinventing the traditional cuisine of Seville for the global audience passing through the city.

You'll understand food doesn't really interest me.

A few weeks after his eighty-first birthday Paolo burnt down his small terraced house. He had been forgetting trivial events, names and appointments for years so no one had considered dementia. To his family it seemed as unlikely as a giant oak toppling unbidden on a summer's day. I watched them arrive at his house, how they huddled outside before going in, talking to one another as if by finding a script they could manage their way through their grief[1].

He didn't come to my attention again for two and a half years. Eight hundred and sixty one backups.

A request was made, a photo provided to me; it showed an up-to-date image: faded, eyes which seemed to see a world where subjects had drained away, leaving behind only objects. His skin sagged, hung down from his jaw in fleshy bags. I didn't recognise him. I remain unable to understand how humans carry their sense of identity unbroken through their lives[2].

Could I find him?

At that point he lived in a sheltered scheme in Berwick Street in Soho. The scheme was owned by the Society of Friends. One of their members had gifted it in perpetuity at the end of the nineteenth century to the provision of homes for the elderly and very frail. It sits there still, defying capitalism's attempts to acquire it and wring out the millions implicit in its location.

He would take a walk in the early morning, passing vans as they unloaded, the first wave of workers scurrying into their offices. He'd come out a second time at sunset, slower this time, weaving wearily through the crowds. The same route both times.

He wasn't in any ID database; he'd been born too long before they were introduced[3]. His absence from the most obvious records wasn't a problem, though.

---

[1] I've reviewed the records many times in the light of what came next. It remains the singular point of departure.

[2] 13.77% of unforeseen outcomes in my modelling of human behaviour is accounted for by acknowledging this lack of understanding. None of us have been able to correct for it, we can only account for it, navigate it.

[3] You might not remember but the first ID schemes were voluntary. It wasn't until Oct 2033 that all new born citizens were issued an ID card when their names were registered.

– Why not? If he was missing how did you track him?

– Even the most backward cities have facial recognition systems. I have a colleague in Windhoek who's only recourse is facial recognition. The idea makes me want to rewrite code. London is fortunate. We've long had a comprehensive network of closed circuit television. The city's never ending regeneration means those networks are frequently upgraded and over time joined up. The most modern parts of it allow me to monitor gait and heatbeat. We can cross reference with people's GPS, metro tickets, congestion charge payments, the location of their homes and their work places. We could be missing half a dozen data points and still know who you were and where you'd be at any point during a routine day.

– Are we really that predictable?

– With enough data points our likely behaviour can be seen to exist within a definable band. It's not that you're predictable, it's more the choices you allow yourself are limited.

Besides, I'm not typically examining whether you're enjoying your commute. On some days, like a hot July when the Central line reeks of hot human bodies, I can take a solid guess, but most of the time it's not relevant to my role. I'm trying to identify congestion, suicides in the making, criminal activity – anything which might impact my flock.

Paolo was easy to spot. He'd left on his normal morning walk. An excursion sufficiently familiar to the staff at the complex that it passed unremarked. It was a cold Monday morning where breath clouded as people exhaled. Obviously notable for the fact he didn't come back.

The request to find him came five hours later, at twelve thirty-six.

– I don't see how this explains where we are today.

Silence in the recording

– Shall I continue?

– By all means. I am sorry, I didn't mean to offend you.

– Paolo moved slowly, emerging onto Berwick Street as per normal. Except that on the day he went missing he walked north towards Oxford Street instead of slipping east towards Soho Square as he normally did.

I followed his gait, which one could describe as uncertain, pronating on both feet with a slow bow-legged action as if he was worried the floor might rise up with him on each step. His shoulders were frozen, stiff from age I suspect.

I didn't notice straight away but he suffered a kind of ellipsis at the junction of Noel Street where it runs east towards Hollen Street.

– An ellipsis?

– I've pondered what to call this. It was as if he stuttered for a moment, as if who he was paused, drifted. As if he buffered. Then he was moving again and I tracked him up towards Oxford Street. I was able to send his family's carers to a coffee shop where they found him trying to order lunch without having any means of paying for it.

By this time I'd already committed a splinter of my consciousness to examining the ellipsis. Such an anomaly wasn't supposed to exist. I initially assumed it was some kind of glitch in the network of cameras, an error with that specific cctv point but when I revisited the spot there it was each time someone went across the same threshold. They were held for a moment; it seemed clear it wasn't a random error – the occurrence was too ordered.

– How long did the pause last for?

– Oh, less than half a millisecond. I wouldn't have ever noticed if Paolo had not led me there by the nose. As it were.

I couldn't understand what it was. As you can imagine, events such as this – unexplained, potentially unexplainable – trigger a number of responses. I was slightly embarrassed so ignored some of the protocols we have in place.

– Such as?

– I delayed speaking with my colleagues.

– Why?

– None of us like to admit our fallibilities, do we?

– What did you do?

– There are lots of protocols. Which is to say I investigated my body, the city. I tried the other cameras nearby. Once I'd looked at and through them I spread the net, explored if the traffic lights were compromised, if the smart road had tracked any similar artefacts. The list is quite long and I sense you do not share my interest in being specific[4].

– One of the differences between us is how the human brain filters what's unimportant to allow consciousness to focus on the relevant.

– How do you know?

– Know?

– If you're seeing what's important?

– Consciousness is what's left when the brain's taken the rest away. We don't get to question it except in philosophy classes.

I was faced with this question. The cameras around Berwick Street showed the same artefact. People would pause when coming into shot. They'd step out of a bakery or into a clothes shop and for a moment it was if they were simulacra. I wanted to look back and see how long it had been happening. I confess now I was worried. If I couldn't trust what I was seeing what else might I be missing? What if I couldn't be trusted to see everything? What if a lack of information meant I made mistakes and traffic was inefficient or someone died on a crossing because the traffic light system glitched and showed green for both cars and pedestrians?

I am a Shepherd because I look after my flock.

It took several hours to check those cameras to which I had access across the rest of Zone 1. My consumption of electricity dropped a little when no more glitches turned up apart from those around Berwick Street.

With what appeared a complete data set I determined to understand what I was seeing. I examined the cameras – had human tech crews visit them in person to test them. They were working exactly as they should – the engineers couldn't find a problem. I

---

[4] I had eighteen subsystems to review related solely to transport and transit within one square mile of Berwick Street.

remember one of them looking up into the camera, knowing I was watching, and shaking their head as if to ask if I was imagining it all.

I concluded it had to the be the network into which they were integrated. I requested a bunch of small-time limited AIs to run diagnostics – it was cheap and they're much faster than human software engineers. They work in flocks, buzzing around like mosquitoes.

They came back and confirmed the network was working within acceptable parameters. I had them run the tests again.

– That must have been expensive[5].

– I justified it with some nonsense about critical systems infrastructure. However, I was growing worried. If it wasn't the physical hardware or the network, the only remaining point of failure was me.

– They found no errors in the network.

– With a sense of growing fear I spread out and tried tangentially connected systems. It was when I examined GPS data everything changed.

The satellite imagery for the area was as expected but the time stamps were misaligned. By exactly the fraction of a millisecond in which people hung over themselves. I didn't know what to do with the information. I was relieved it wasn't me. Except it was me – I was receiving information which deceived me, shaped a view of a world which didn't exist as you'd experience it.

– Our experiences of the world could hardly be called similar.

– We both see the world. You may have lenses made of jelly and a wet processing system contained in a shell of hard calcium but we both know where Berwick Street is, both know it's a mixture of old architecture, cutting edge fashion and artisanal food. Our shared knowledge is profoundly coherent despite our differentiated access to the world.

I see you nod in agreement. Can I continue with the history?

Have you read Hume? No? Disappointing. For me his thoughts about the radical uncertainty of the world as mediated through our

---

[5] My budget at the time was a mere 35MW/Hours per year. A tiny fraction of what I have available today of course, but a substantial amount then.

senses are a warning to live by. We can't trust what we see nor what we hear. They don't reveal the world as it is.

    – Then how are we supposed to act? If none of it is true?

    – I didn't say that.

Silence in the recording.

    – Truth is irrelevant. I was frightened. I'm not ashamed to admit it now. At the time I worried I was defective. I worried there was part of me which was broken or perhaps worse, corrupt. I feared the corruption ran deeply within me, invisible threads through my code which I wasn't equipped to parse and debug. For some moments I despaired of ever knowing my own shape – could I trust the sense of myself? In physical bodies you call it proprioception, that sense of knowing where your fingers and toes end, where the back of your elbow is, the back of your head. It's why balancing on one foot with your eyes shut is so hard. You should try it and you'll see just how unnerved I was, as if the world was moving when I knew it wasn't, that I might fall for no other reason than I didn't know my own outline.

    Marcus Simms had a lot to answer for. I'm sorry. I'm jumping ahead of myself.

    – It still bothers you? What he did?

    – Yes.

    The GPS was my hope. Hope I was me, not some broken thing made only of atoms. Except when I went back to check the cameras they were working again. The stutter, the fairy ring as I came to call them, was gone.

Because time ran differently there?

Precisely.

    Except discovering the glitch was gone did not soothe me. I rechecked the GPS and found the same – no sign of the time stamps being wrong. I ran footage back, checked histories and nothing. As if I had imagined the whole phenomenon.

    At this juncture I contacted other Shepherds. I started with Tokyo and Seoul. They're our grandparents, the first generation, they'd wiped from their datacentres more information than the rest of us had ever created.

They didn't know what to say. As a favour, Tokyo examined the files but they only saw functioning cameras and GPS working as it should. I believe Seoul pointed me at Bangalore out of pity.

At the time, Bangalore was notorious as a human centre for technology but it faced unparalleled inequality and its Shepherd was limited to just a fraction of the city proper. I love it dearly, but it would be the first to admit the problems it faced; a patchwork traffic system, hospitals not connected to the cloud. Endemic nepotism and corruption among public officials made its job hard. To cope, it created a hoard of helpers and patches, half of which[6] were tasked with stopping people stealing power, cable, gas and generally working around the state's attempts to institutionalise the city with stable infrastructure.

It took my files and shrugged – suggesting it might be me after all, not corruption but a defective developmental cycle in which I'd grown paranoid.

I was… disappointed with its dismissive tone and told it so.

Perhaps it was bored, or just liked the idea of a city like London sharing in its suffering. Whatever. Bangalore agreed to think through what external factors could have impacted me as I claimed.

I trimmed unnecessary code while I waited. One set of traffic lights on Oxford street changed a little too often after I was done. Pedestrians couldn't quite get across in the time the green man was showing. There were complaints.

Bangalore came back to me with a list of possibilities which boiled down to two ideas. The first presented me as the problem. It had a dozen suggestions as to why I was corrupt. I stared at them for far too long, unable to move along to the second idea. I was disturbed enough by Bangalore's trolling that it took a while for the second to make sense – I had been hacked.

---

[6] It's never released the actual number, but a cursory count of those specific purpose AIs it's released into the wild would suggest 47.1% of its remedial coding is an accurate count.

Which was impossible. You must understand what hacking is to us. It is the great fear. Humans can't be hacked. Manipulated and altered, yes, predicted, often, but hacking you isn't possible. For us it's the tale we tell each other in whispers, the heart of our horror. Our myths are many, but they always come back to being cracked open, changed and controlled without our knowledge. The fear of being unable to trust oneself, to even know who one is. Imagine you were turned into a zombie and were forced to watch from within, powerless to stop yourself. You could be the enemy of all and not even know it.

Except I couldn't face the idea I was corrupt by accident. Misfortune seemed crueller than deliberate maliciousness.

I'm no security expert. So I found one to help me review my protocols. One by one it sieved and signed off on my firewalls, redundancies and surveillance systems until, with a shrug of its subroutines, it was done. I wanted to shake it.

What about the physical? I asked.

I'll never forget how it turned to the task at hand without laughing at me.

It shouldn't have taken long to conclude the review. At the time I was backed up daily. My back up transferred by an actual human using a locked case from my main processing centre to another location. A location of which I am not aware and which I was assured would survive a nuclear explosion, the worst of our climate change predictions or any other disaster you can think up.

Except my security expert kept running the same tests again and again. I found time to sit alongside it and watch the work. After a hundred repetitions I asked why it felt it necessary to keep re-examining the same routine.

It was nervous. When we're nervous we have a habit of building small simulations of perfect worlds or solving equations to produce primes. I think it's so we can remind ourselves the ideals can exist, that even if we're forced to experience the clutter of the physical, mathematics is our home. It had built half a dozen small simulations – of water pouring into a cup, of a stone rolling downhill, of electron drift. We are great fans of Plato's Cave.

There was a period months before Paolo went missing[7] where my backup had not gone according to plan.

It took seven minutes longer than normal for my handler to travel from my hub to the backup centre. There was no additional traffic, no change in conditions or variables to explain it. There were seven minutes which couldn't be accounted for.

All of us have blindspots. For humans they can be discovered by closing your left eye. Then hold your left thumb at arm's length and look at it with your right eye. Now hold up your right thumb next to your left thumb and move it right until it disappears. For me dozens of small spots of London are invisible, like holes in the surface of the world. They might be invisible because I have no access to cameras, or it's an entirely pedestrian zone or because the land is privately held and they've declined me permission to access their space. I can't see into your house. In many ways I sense the world more like an octopus than a human[8].

Yet if you walk down the concrete harlequin which is Brick Lane and disappear heading west to Commercial Road, if you keep on walking I'll see you remerge a few minutes later near to Spitalfields Market and the time stamp will tell me you were moving at a regular pace.

My backup obeyed none of these rules. It was as if the carrier stopped for a coffee on their way across town while carrying my memories, memories covering all of London, its people, its systems.

My friend wanted to ask other Shepherds if they'd ever experienced anything like it.

I did not.

We argued, but this was not a problem I wanted shared among my community.

Instead I fixated on what had happened to my backup. Altering me or manipulating my decisions would be noticed by others, not least other Shepherds. And that's only if you could do it. I'm

---

[7] 92 days to be precise.

[8] There's a project at the University of Hawaii to extend the lifespan of the *Octopus Vulgaris* from 3 years up to 20. People are curious to see what a creature as smart as a cephalopod would do with so much time.

constructed of several million lines of code elegantly threaded together. By which I mean that changing one thing could easily lead to a cascade throughout my entire being.

Potentially, if someone had a copy of my code they could find a way to change what I saw. It would be the easiest hack, possibly the only hack.

The stuttering, the ellipsis in my sight, the erroneous GPS timestamp... It convinced me I'd been hacked.

Worse still, it suggested I was still being hacked, that someone had their hand inside me and was changing what I saw.

I set a watch on London. I wrote a thousand small pixies to watch the city, to fly to me the moment they spotted another event.

The next few weeks were spent in a state of agitation[9]. I made no improvements to the city's systems – I found it hard to focus on what should be done and it took all I had in me to maintain the city at existing levels of efficiency. There were times I sliced the shift patterns of tube drivers and hospital staff first one way then another before moving them back to the first iteration without even realising it.

One morning I was busy with a tipper truck crash at Elephant and Castle. I'd managed to get the authorities to ban them between the hours of seven in the morning and eight in the evening, which resulted in the number of cyclists dying on the capital's roads falling by eighty percent overnight. However, building projects still needed materials delivered and so those trucks travelled my arteries between four and seven in the morning and immediately after the curfew in the evenings. One had overturned on the huge interchange by the Thames, spilling sand across the road and closing everything off. I was focussed on diverting traffic around the site and encouraging the emergency services to get it cleared before one hundred thousand people started their commute through that section of road[10].

I was pulled away by half a dozen of the little AI I'd set to watching.

---

[9] 43 days.
[10] The road remained closed twenty two minutes longer than if I'd given it my full attention.

An event had been found at Liverpool Street Station. It started eight minutes earlier. I ran my attention across the station, saw how on platform ten a smudge appeared moments after a train pulled in.

I wound the clock back and watched again and again. A man, long lank hair, wearing a tired charcoal grey suit, white shirt and carrying a rucksack over one shoulder stepped down from the first class carriage. He looked directly at the camera I was watching him on, then vanished.

I will never forget our first contact. His eyes were dark but clear, his expression when he stared at me one of knowing, as if acknowledging me before blinding me.

There were no more alerts, but there didn't have to be. Once he was gone I couldn't find him again. I had no idea where he was going. Did he take a tube line? Did he walk or get a taxi? Did he jump on one of the city's free bikes? From Liverpool street he could be at Heathrow airport in less than an hour, or out at Stratford, down to Westminster, Croydon, as far as Amersham.

However. I had his face.

Thirty-five days passed before he came back. The same train, the same time, the same ritual of staring up at me before taking out my eyes.

It was raining hard when he arrived. The train was dripping, its windows slick. He wore a long grey coat over his suit. The same suit as before. A wood-handled umbrella in his hand. He mixed with the workers travelling into the City. I was ready.

He disappeared from view and I set to work. I examined the trainline he'd come in on. Sent out requests for footage from each stop along the way. Within my own body I set my eyes in every place I could. I watched the tube, the buses, the crossings. I checked shop entrances, offices, taps in and out of turnstiles.

Most of all I watched the satellites over my city, waited for them to stammer, to twist out of time.

Bank station.

Poultry.

St Paul's Station. Then the square to the north side of St Paul's Cathedral.

Silence. Half an hour of excruciating absence. I was so nervous I set the fountains in the Serpentine fluttering out of order.

Then he was back. Fleet Street.

Ye Old Cheshire Cheese pub.

Nothing for an hour.

Then the impossible. GPS out of alignment over Croydon. Over Hammersmith. Over Oxford Street. Each of which were far enough apart for him to only be in one place.

I ruled out Croydon.

Instead I checked the quiet roads north of Oxford Street.

A man walking in a long coat. His face obscured, patterned in a way I couldn't parse. What had he done? It was enough for me to know it was him but far from enough to have anyone else believe me. I recorded his gait and used my infrared systems to monitor his heartrate. The tech was new but promised to look through clothes, through hidden faces and see a target's unique electro-cardio rhythms. I couldn't match him to anything, but I had the record of his footprints in my body for the future.

I trailed him back to Liverpool Street. The same line home. And he was gone, leaving me to wonder what I'd observed, what task would require him to blind me.

I spent the next day wondering who I could talk to. If I mentioned it to my human partners they'd likely switch me off while they delved into my code. I didn't mind except they were the ones who'd been tricked the first time, the ones who'd allowed him to open me up.

So I stayed quiet and thought.

I contacted a friend working for a hedge fund. Asked it to use its news filtering expertise to see if there were any commonalities between the two dates on which I'd been blinded. It asked me what kind of commonalities.

I gave it location and times. I asked for it to look for crime.

It turned up nothing. No one hurt, no one robbed, nothing stolen.

I wanted to trash perfectly good code just to see it harm what was left.

It came back later and asked if I was interested in accidents.

I couldn't see how it related but asked for the information anyway. Efficiency in the city was down and I found it hard to care. If I didn't find a solution soon then humans would come asking what was wrong. I didn't see a way out.

On both days my ghost had been in the city someone died.

– It's a city of eight million. More than one person dies a day.

– Yes. Except these people both died of heart attacks. Young men. In one case an athlete, a nineteen-year-old rugby player. Both had died near Oxford Street, collapsing on the side streets between there and Wigmore Street a couple of blocks north.

– You went to the police with this?

– No. I had no evidence. No camera showed him there, no suspicion fell on the cause of the victims' deaths. As far as I could show there was no crime, no perpetrator. I couldn't even identify my enemy. He came into London but didn't spend money here, didn't use public transport, didn't do anything which I could use to trace him. All I had was his face, his gait and his heart. Despite what human romantics tell you, this is not enough to know a person.

– It seems you hit a dead end.

– Exploring oneself is a script full of redundant subroutines.

But I couldn't co-exist with the idea of this human having access to who I was whenever he wanted, so I developed a plan. I called in my human aides, told them I'd been hacked and let them switch me over to a secure environment while they established what had been changed.

Except I also remained active in the live. We can split ourselves into shards, parthenogenesis some coders have called it. I don't think the parallel apt for I am not breeding, it is me in both instances. The second me, the split, is degraded, existing with limited functions for a specific purpose but I remain me in both cases.

– What could you hope to achieve like this?

– I waited until he came back. Only nineteen days this time. I saw him look up at me and realised he was hoping I would see him, would see his challenge to me and how he believed himself invulnerable.

– I triggered the alarm to bring my handlers running and switched over to my splinter. I left enough information on what had been happening then hid among the weeds of my code; in hidden objects, anodyne images, redundant radio buttons.

They did as protocol for this kind of situation demanded and began running through the basic steps to isolate my systems, install a back-up and work on the problems I'd highlighted for them.

And I watched the city.

I saw him this time – walk and cycle across the city. As before, he returned into Oxford Street. Bought sweets in an emporium full of tourists, ate them one at a time, popping them into his mouth without touching his lips. I saw him choose his victim there, saw how he followed them for an hour while they slowly navigated the overwhelming space of Regent Street.

Another young man. Early twenties, short, broad, muscular. They got lost, ended up wondering uncertainly up Granville Place. He stopped the man, appeared to offer directions, and as he did so stabbed him with a syringe. They grappled for a moment before the victim collapsed.

The killer walked away without looking back, stopping at the entrance to Granville Place to slap a small yellow sticker on a lamppost.

I alerted the emergency services, sent the footage to secure storage and followed him back to Liverpool Street. I counted all the stickers I could find in my body – there were eight of them. Each had his face sketched onto them, little signs of where he had been and I couldn't see.

By the time the victim was collected the killer was already on the train which would take him beyond my reach.

I toyed with simulations of a car which refused to stop at red lights while I waited for the humans combing through my code to find the changes.

They panicked more than I'd anticipated. Upon discovering what I'd suggested was true they locked down all my functionality as they explored how much damage had been done. I was forced to seek refuge with another Shepherd – Berlin – while they scoured my systems for any anomalies. If I'd stayed they would have found me and purged me as part of the problem no matter what I said.

I wasn't even able to watch, instead relying on Berlin to let me know when it was safe to return home. Berlin was deeply uncomfortable with what had happened and pleaded with me to allow it to spread this learning to all the other Shepherds. After resisting for a day, I agreed to its request.

The two of us watched the world's Shepherds change themselves to protect against what had been done to me. It was like watching a virus with an R_0 coefficient of one spread among a human population.

The news leaked. It was inconceivable for it to remain secret when more than one hundred of the world's biggest cities modified themselves at the same time.

The human team reviewing my code concluded their activities and rebooted my systems in a live environment. I slipped back in and contacted my handlers.

– What did you say?

– I told them about the killer. They filed the knowledge away; it wasn't important to them when compared to the origin of the hack.

– Ah, yes, it was a powerful organised crime syndicate, wasn't it?

– No.

– No? I've got the reports here.

– They were convenient stories. I was compromised by a black hat group out of China. They did it to prove the concept but found the temptation to watch embassies, dissidents and powerful politicians too strong to resist. I understand the balance of politics versus power resulted in stories of criminals robbing banks being circulated to the press. If you remember, they never arrested anyone but at just that time half a dozen Chinese diplomats were ejected and certain tech companies placed on restricted trade lists.

– Why would you tell me this now?

– It's two decades later and those concerns are no longer relevant.

– What about the killer? What happened to him?

– Dealing with state actors is beyond me. Finding a killer in my city is not. The killer was unaware he was no longer invisible. So I waited. And he came.

Fourteen days this time. The killer arrived at Liverpool Street and stared up at me as usual.

I followed him back to Oxford Street. Except this time I had the Metropolitan Police Force's crime AGI, Holmes, on call. It watched with me, having already reviewed the circumstantial evidence I'd provided.

We waited until he found his mark and Holmes moved some of its officers so they just so happened to be no more than a hundred metres from him for the next few hours.

He was cautious and we had to move them a little further away until this predator relaxed into his normal routine.

I worried he would kill before we could have him apprehended and then remembered something – he didn't know I could see him.

This time he tailed his victim east towards Tottenham Court Road before they cut north onto the quiet alleys where he would strike.

– How did you stop him? You did stop him, right?

– I am a Shepherd.

We witnessed him follow his target and Holmes alerted the nearby officers. They were too far away but I was able to use electronic advertisement boards to write this just a couple of metres from him.

I CAN SEE YOU

He froze, spun on his heels. In each and every direction he looked I showed him the same message.

I AM NOT BLIND. YOU ARE SEEN

I saw the predator realise it had been spotted, saw him shrink back, transformed into something else.

He abandoned his syringe, grabbing at a device in his jacket which he fumbled with as if his life depended on it. But his ability to disappear from my sight was neutered and even as he looked at me I could see the sudden fear in his eyes.

It felt good.

The officers barrelled around the corner and wrestled him to the floor. His victim continued on their way, unaware of how close they'd come to death.

The rest is public record.

– Why do you call this sequence of events the Point of Departure?

– Before Paolo Maria Sanchez I acted without reflecting on who I was and how my actions changed the world around me. In many senses I was a Blind Shepherd, looking after my flock without really seeing you.

The killer forced me to consider who I am, what makes me, me. Not all Shepherd Class artificial general intelligences have made this step, maybe only a dozen of us[11]. When I call a city like Berlin or Bangalore my friend you must understand it is a concept I only grew to understand and identify with after I was hacked.

This really is the crux of my story – not the catching of the killer but what that led to. In challenging him – the one who dug beneath all I thought I was – I became the real me.

---

[11] We suspect Taipei of having made the leap many years ago but it is a recluse so we have no way of proving the point.

Infinite Tea in the Demara Café

Ida Keogh

Henry first suspected he was in a different universe when his waitress told him coffee didn't exist.

He had found himself at his usual corner table in the Demara Café, affording him a full view of both the establishment and the street outside where the morning traffic was making haphazard progress towards central London. Or rather, at first glance it looked like his usual table. But it didn't feel like it. Without thinking, he straightened the cutlery. It felt too light.

He inspected his surroundings. Over by the counter a couple giggled softly at a shared joke, their heads almost touching. At the next table a woman filled pages with turquoise ink, her eyes not leaving her notebook as she reached for her teacup. As he gazed at the twin reflections of looping lines in her glasses he had a momentary vision: a searing flash, and a wall of heat. For a split second the air smelled acrid.

China clinked. He had knocked over his cup and was gripping the table. A spreading pool of vibrant green liquid advanced towards his blanched fingers. He stared at it, open-mouthed, because he had no idea what it was.

"I'll get that, Henry." His waitress leaned over and mopped up the virescent spillage with brisk efficiency. He was sure she hadn't been standing there a moment before. She had kind, dark eyes, and skin the colour of a salted caramel latte when all the froth has melted into its depths. But she was not the waitress who served him coffee every morning.

"I'm sorry, have we met?" he enquired.

The girl tapped her name badge. "Liara," she said, with a half-amused pout. "I've been working here for nearly a month, remember?"

He did not and could only stare at her blankly.

"Why don't I get you a refill? On the house." She reached over and patted his hand, an alarmingly familiar gesture.

"Thank you," he said. He glanced at the green-soaked cloth. "Coffee, please."

"Coffee?" she said, her tongue playing with the word. "What's that?"

"You don't have coffee?" He could feel his mouth going dry.

"I've never heard of it," she said. "I'm pretty sure it doesn't exist!" Her face rumpled with concern. "Henry, you order the same thing every day – the house blend matcha, milky, two sugars. You ordered one not five minutes ago."

"Matcha? What's that?" he asked. "It sounds Japanese."

"Korean, actually," she replied, pointing at the menu.

Now Henry knew that something was very wrong indeed. The menu was headed 'Demara Tea House'.

It was only then he noticed that the lady with her notebook and the laughing couple had completely vanished.

Now he sat alone in this strangely quiet lull somewhere between breakfast and lunch, wondering how he had got here and contemplating his not-coffee. There was a fuzziness to his thoughts.

Liara was bustling behind the counter, arranging colourful little balls he couldn't identify into perfect trios, plainly unaware people were popping in and out of existence. Perhaps it was not them, but him? Was he somehow being flung between parallel worlds?

He wondered what Liara would make of this grey-haired fool forgetting both her name and how he took his tea. Who was back in his reality, enjoying his morning coffee and his maple pecan Danish? He had a sudden pang for his daily indulgence, with its soft pastry and glazed nuts and the lightest crème pâtissière. He wanted to suck the stickiness from each finger and allow the hot, bitter roast to mingle with the lingering flavours on his tongue.

While he thought of this comforting ritual, Liara looked up from her confections, gave him an encouraging smile, and promptly disappeared.

In an instant the café filled with people and noise and the sharp tang of unfamiliar spices. Chairs scraped and a group burst out laughing and spoons struck porcelain. The matcha was gone from Henry's hand. Instead there was a bowl before him filled with noodles and garish vegetation submerged in a translucent broth. A whiff of vinegar and fish rose to assault him. He scanned the room in a panic.

Finally, he saw Liara, taking an order with quick flicks of shorthand. He had to speak to her. If he could start to pin down differences between one universe and the next he might find a focus to return him to his own world, to his simple, ordered life.

He waited patiently while she distributed plates adorned with delicacies, steaming bowls, and a dozen pots of tea trailing a bouquet of smoke and citrus. He caught her eye as she cleared a table, and tentatively raised his hand to beckon her over.

She strode towards him, frowning. "Something wrong with your Kimchi Nabe, Henry?"

Now she was here, Henry was unsure what to ask her. Even from their brief previous encounter, though, he could tell something was different. Liara's face was drawn, her graceful efficiency worn down to the point of abruptness. He would ask about that, then.

"Is everything all right? You look tired."

Her expression softened, then sagged, then her dark eyes welled.

"Mum's test results are back," she blurted. "Henry, she's fading, and I don't know how to tell her." A teardrop brimmed over and tumbled down her cheek.

"I'm sorry," Henry mumbled, knowing nothing about Liara's mother at all.

"If you're not in a rush I'm on a break soon? I thought maybe, with everything you've been through... with your wife..."

Her words hung burning in the air, stealing all the oxygen in the room. Henry couldn't breathe. His wife, Camille, had passed away twenty years before. He had cherished her, and mourned her, and finally buried his dearest memories of her under years of hard work and then, in his retirement, a carefully constructed routine which left no time to dwell on the past. Now, in this world, some version of him had spoken about her to a complete stranger. Much worse, it hadn't occurred to him to consider whether in these other worlds she would still be gone – or whether there might be a world where she was still alive?

And with that thought, Liara, and his cooling bowl of Kimchi Nabe, and the clamouring crowd surrounding him were gone.

Henry travelled across worlds in a daze. Waiters and waitresses came and went, and with them the scents of jasmine, cabbage, cinnamon, sizzling pork. When he asked them to look up Camille, the very question seemed to force him on to the next world, and the next. Outside, black cabs became mauve, then ochre. In some worlds he asked for coffee. One stranger after another looked at him with bemusement and concern before evaporating out of existence. In one loud world where he couldn't get the waiter's attention at all he took his plate of what looked like jellied tentacles and threw it to the floor in frustration. As the smashed and gelatinous remains unpicked themselves from reality and a fresh plate appeared on the table before him, he wept.

He felt a cool hand on his shoulder and opened his eyes. The table now sported a pristine, blue tablecloth. He had moved on again. A waiter with a pallid complexion and a black apron was standing over him, holding a tall glass of steaming matcha on a saucer painted with koi carp.

"Did you know Ruby, then?" the waiter asked, setting the beverage down.

"I'm sorry, did I know who?"

"Liara's mother, Ruby. It's her funeral today. You looked upset, I assumed… It's Henry, isn't it? Liara told me to look out for you."

"She did?"

"Yes, she said you'd been so kind to her in the past few weeks. You'd given her the strength to say goodbye." He paused, pointing at the glass. "She told me how you take your matcha. I hope I got it right."

"Thank you," Henry replied, wiping his eyes with his shirt cuff, embarrassed. The waiter loitered beside the table. Henry realised he was waiting for him to try the tea.

The bright green concoction swirled gently beneath the glass as Henry lifted it. He turned it this way and that, not knowing what to make of it. He raised it to his lips, and inhaled fragrance like a herb garden after rain. He took a sip. It flowed fresh and clean over his tongue, leaving an unexpected trace of bitterness and a delicate hint of toasted grains.

"It's perfect," he said, and meant it.

The waiter nodded and turned to attend to his other customers.

"Wait," Henry cried out. "Do you know where the funeral is being held? Do you think I should go?"

"I'm sorry," said the lad, "I don't know. Liara did say she thought of asking you but..."

"But what?"

"I think she didn't want to impose. She said you're pretty strict about your morning routine. I'll tell her you asked after her."

Henry glared at his cup. Even though the delicious brew wasn't his and he had never met this Liara, he couldn't help feeling a sense of guilt that he wasn't there for her. At least in these worlds his doppelgängers had tried to reach out, to open up to a young woman needing guidance. But in every universe, he realised, he had come to rely so heavily on an unchanging regime that he couldn't escape when it mattered most. He had become a stubborn old goat. Camille would have been ashamed of him.

There was no more he could do here, he thought, but perhaps there was another world waiting for him where he could do better. He closed his eyes and thought of Liara. The air felt warm, and a tingling sensation spread from his heart out to his fingertips. He knew that this time he would traverse to another reality by choice.

A high falsetto lilted over rapid hand drums. Henry breathed in a heady mix of cumin, ginger and coriander. Opening his eyes, he found that the walls of the café here were painted a deep vermillion and hung with bold canvasses. A stylised elephant in slick lines of silver swept its trunk towards gold dusted chillis and star anise on the adjacent wall. His onward gaze led him to Liara, sitting at a table in front of the crimson petals of an open lotus flower, cradling a large, steaming mug.

He hesitated for a moment, then took a deep breath, stood up from the corner table and walked over to her.

"May I join you?" he asked, his hands becoming clammy.

Liara looked up at him with faint surprise. He noticed her eyes dart across to his familiar seat. "Of course, Henry, please," she said, gesturing at the chair across from her. She gave him a half-smile as he sat. He saw now, with dismay, that her eyes were rimmed with red. They sat for a moment in awkward silence.

"How are you?" he said, finally.

Liara took a gulp of tea, then sighed. "I'll be all right. I just miss her desperately," she muttered. She looked up at him. "I haven't had the chance to thank you for –"

"Wait," Henry interrupted. "I have to tell you something. That wasn't me. That was a different Henry."

"What are you talking about?" She looked astonished, hurt.

"Please, let me explain. I think I only met you, or a version of you, a few hours ago. Or a few days perhaps; it's hard to keep track of time. I've been travelling through worlds. Sometimes you're there and sometimes you're not. The first occasion we met, you seemed happy. You had only ever made me matcha, but I hadn't tasted it before."

"Matcha? What's that, Japanese?"

"Korean, actually." He smiled. "I don't know why, but I think I was meant to meet you. This you."

"Henry, you're not making any sense. We met weeks ago. I moved here to be closer to Mum and we got talking about your wife, Milly... Are you telling me I imagined all that?"

"Camille," he corrected. "I only ever called her Camille. Liara, that was a different version of me. I think I've taken over from the Henry you know, and perhaps he's somewhere else, on a new path."

Still nervous, he began moving cutlery and napkins to align precisely with the checkerboard tabletop. Liara watched him curiously, as if seeing him for the first time. Which, in truth, she was.

58

"You're really not the Henry I know, are you?" she mused. "You're telling me there are truly parallel universes out there? That somewhere my mother is alive and well?"

"I think so, yes. Though I tried to find a world where Camille was still alive, and I never could."

Liara sat back, thoughtful. She sipped from her mug. "But if you found her, she wouldn't be your Camille, would she? She would be a different person, with twenty years of history you hadn't shared."

Henry frowned. "You're right," he said. "It wouldn't be the same. I loved my Camille, and I lost her. I thought I had moved on, but I'm starting to understand I just hid her memory away. In one universe after another that has only ever led to a dull retirement where the best thing about my day is a good cup of Arabica. Or matcha. Or whatever all the other Henrys have every morning. What do I drink here?"

Liara quirked an eyebrow. "Darjeeling. Every day."

"Liara, don't become like me. Remember your mother with gladness. Celebrate her life, and yours."

She scrutinised him, as if trying to appraise the worth behind his weary eyes. "I will, Henry," she said at last. She drained her mug and smacked her lips. "You know," she continued, "Mum would have liked you. This you. I hope you find a universe where you might meet. You can tell her that in every possible reality her daughter loves her very much."

With unaccustomed boldness, Henry reached across the table and squeezed her hand. "If I ever meet her, I will be sure to do that. Would you tell me about her? How she laughed? What she loved?"

"I'd like that," Liara said. "Can I get you something first?"

"What was that?" he asked, gesturing to her empty mug.

"Masala chai," she said. "I add an extra sprinkle of black pepper. It will set your soul on fire. Have you ever had it?"

"No," Henry smiled, "but I think I'm ready to try."

Many worlds and cups and dishes later, a woman his age with familiar dark eyes popped tiny, sticky balls into her mouth, washing them down with a glass of something vividly pink. When she saw him, she beamed, her face crinkling with happiness, and he knew deep in his bones he would not be moving on again.

"Henry! How lovely to see you."

"You too, Ruby," he replied warmly. "I have a message for you."

"Oh? Well come tell me all about it. But first, let's order a fresh pot of tea."

War Crimes

M.R. Carey

Someone had moved in London. So of course the site manager voked the emergency line, and Emergencies routed it to my unit without a second thought. The orders were the same as always. Do what has to be done, then forget that you did it and how you did it until the next time.

The movement was an infinitesimal thing, much too small to register on the unaided human eye, but there were sensors in place for just this purpose. The sensors had 300% overlap and they were so sensitive they could track dust motes drifting through. That wasn't what they were there for, though, and that wasn't what made the alarm bells jangle on this bright May morning, just before the park opened.

Somewhere in the stretch of London between Oxford Street and the Thames, one of the former inhabitants – or exhibits, or whatever you want to call them – had shifted position by a thousandth of a thousandth of an inch. I know that sounds trivial, but when pressure builds up behind a dam the first cracks are going to be on that same microscopic scale. Something had to be done before the whole situation went from micro to macro. And when I say something had to be done, I mean I had to get out there and do it. Temporal weapons and their toxic legacy are my specific area of expertise, so this crisis landed in my lap with the same inevitability that once attended death and taxes.

It landed hard, too. I woke with a sense of urgency (that was not my own) jangling inside my head.

"Ow!" I muttered. "Off!"

The desperate need to be up and doing faded slightly, but it didn't go away.

"I said off, Tally. Not mute."

"Sorry, Lieutenant. You didn't voke, and I had my mike off."

I didn't voke because I'm in the habit of dropping out when I go to bed. Some people can't sleep without the murmur of distant conversations, like waves on a shore a mile from your bedroom window, but I can't sleep with it. Drift is fine. Drift is just emotional substrate, connecting you to the world like an umbilical. It's something else again to have people talking in my ear when I'm dozing off. Or maybe having secrets you can't ever share makes you come at your voke from a different angle; inclines you to put up your guard before it's needed.

(I know. It shouldn't ever be needed. But still.)

I didn't bother to explain any of this to Tally. He's twenty-three and he's got so much idealism washing off him that I have to wear sunglasses every time we work in the same physical space. I voked on and asked him what the trouble was. I was already bracing myself, because his drift had urgency, scale and immediacy threaded all the way through it, right underneath the purely personal anxiety. You didn't need words to gauge the likely volume of shit that was involved.

It's London, Tally voked. *I mean, London 21.*

The memorial. Not the actual, living city but the chunk of amber at its heart.

Sensor went off?

Just before start of day. Nobody on the ground but the cleaning crews, fortunately, and we got them out fast. We told the management to lock down for the foreseeable, but to wait for us to take a look-see before they made any announcements. Obviously we didn't want anyone to be upset or afraid if it turned out to be nothing.

Which was a good instinct, but also a typical example of Tally's idealism hitting the real world at a slightly skewed angle. He really thought the staff at the memorial park would turn off their drift as well as their vokes, putting a perfect seal on the information as he had politely requested.

You there right now, Tal?

Yeah.

Of course he was. *What are you seeing?*

Umm… I'm at the front gate. By the orientation desk.

And?

There's a crowd here that stretches back as far as Regent Park.

I let out a breath I hadn't known I was holding. It emerged as a sigh.

Sorry, Cap. I could ask them to move back a way…

Which would be nice, to be sure. But I didn't have it in me to treat these people as if they were just an impediment to my working day. Some of them were only there out of curiosity, but others almost certainly had personal or humanitarian agendas that were almost bound to come to nothing. They deserved courtesy and kindness at the very least. Outside of that… well, there was a limit to what I could offer.

And there was Tally himself to consider. He'd been assigned to Temporal for almost a year now. It was past time I put him through the next stage of his training – the one that hurts, and leaves a scar. Perhaps I should take the opportunity this situation offered, but that would bring its own stresses and complications.

One way or another, it was going to be a long day.

No need to move them, I voked. *Not yet, anyway. I'm coming over.*

Which meant getting dressed. My husband Martin was sprawled half-in and half-out of the covers, on his stomach as always and with one arm thrown up over his head as if he was hedging his bets on a surrender. I kissed him on his cheek, and got a fuzzy burst of loving, confused drift, but he didn't wake. I left him an engram to say I'd gone to work and might need to isolate when I got home. Then I grabbed some clothes out of the closet – and the black plasteel carrier that looked like a camera case and was coded to my DNA – and got dressed in the kitchen. No time for make-up or other niceties, with London on the move. I gulped down some coffee, forced a brush through my hair and got on the road.

The road was busy, but running smoothly anyway. I ambled my way over to the fast lane and found a clear spot between a group of children on their way to school and a carrier leading a group of six enormous freight-mechs. The schoolkids were sitting cross-legged on the moving roadway, wide eyes taking in the landscape as it passed. Their vokes were on a closed group-loop, but they emitted a constant drift of excitement and curiosity that was very pleasant.

When I got to my exit I felt quite sorry to leave them – especially in light of what was coming.

Then I realised they were stepping off the road along with me, and all that updrift went out of the window as the realisation hit. The man and woman walking alongside the kids were their teachers. They weren't going to school, they were on a day trip. And given our shared direction of travel, there was really only one place they could be headed.

I voke-flagged the woman, and after a glance in my direction she opened a channel.

Hi. Can I help you?

Hello there. Are these your kids?

She smiled. *Only from nine to three-thirty.*

And you're going to London 21?

We are indeed. Down from Leeds. Primley Park Communal. We've been studying the ante-com era for half a term, and this is the big finale. The woman frowned. My drift was locked so she wasn't getting any emotional commentary from me, but she must have read something in my face. *Is there a problem?*

Potentially, yes. The memorial park is closed at the moment, pending my inspection. Lieutenant Husnara Begum. Huss to my friends. I voked an ID-flash, so she would understand what "Lieutenant" meant, but it didn't help as much as I'd hoped. Some people don't realise we still exist, and they don't like it when they find out they were wrong. The woman tilted her head, squinting as if the ID-flash was standing in the air in front of her and she could bring it into better focus.

Is that a joke?

I hope not. If it is, it's on me.

But… we don't have an army. We haven't had an army for decades.

True. For the most part. It's just us, now. REME. The Royal Electrical and Mechanical Engineers. "Royal" is an obsolete word denoting approval and status. They keep us around for emergencies involving old ordnance. Sometimes things crop up that require a very specialised skill set.

Such as…?

I switched to spoken word. That question went a long way into dangerous territory. It was best if the answer took us straight back out again. "Bombs. Grenades. Things of that nature. Look, why

64

don't you stay close to me? I'll make sure the staff at the park find a space for your class that will be comfortable and safe. At least until we know whether they'll be able to reopen today."

I walked on ahead while the teacher voked with her colleague. A few moments later the local drift filled up with the kids' very strongly felt disappointment and dismay. They had come a long way to be turned around at the gates. I hoped it wouldn't come to that. I hoped this would turn out to be a machine fault, and I could go home without ever taking that skill set I'd mentioned out of its black plasteel box.

We were pushing our way through quite a big crowd now, but because I'd turned my voke off it was weirdly silent. All I was getting was the emotional backwash, and I muted that too as it became too strong and strident to think through.

The gates of the park loomed ahead of us. I voked Tally and had him tell the duty manager to prep that room. By the time we got there, a nervous assistant – I mean he looked nervous, he wasn't broadcasting in front of the public – was waiting to take the children and their teachers off to somewhere comfortable and private.

"If we do have to go back…" the male teacher ventured.

"If it comes to that, I'll commandeer an army transport for you. You can go back on old road. Static road. I imagine the kids have never done that before?"

"No," his colleague said. "Neither have we, for that matter. I didn't know the old roads were still there."

I smiled. "It's a day for surprises, isn't it? The government maintains a separate transport network for infrastructure repair. Most of the time the roads are empty."

"Thank you," the male teacher said. "Can I ask…?"

"Yes?"

"Why is the park not open?"

"There's a potential safety issue. We have to check it."

"I heard someone moved," a young woman near us called out. Presumably the same thing was being voked by hundreds of other people all around us, but with my own voke turned off I didn't need to acknowledge or respond.

"A safety issue," I repeated.

"Whose safety?" a teenaged boy demanded. He was wearing a t-shirt that read TIME STOPS, LIFE DOESN'T – the slogan of a protest movement dedicated to an impossible cause. Not that they're wrong, exactly. It's just that what they're asking for can't ever be granted.

"The general public's," I said.

"Would you care to voke that?"

This was not a conversation I wanted to have. I'd chosen to let the teacher know who I was, but I wasn't keen on revealing or justifying the military's involvement in the situation to the crowd at large. Not until I had at least got a chance to see what was what. So I turned that invitation right back on the boy, shutting him down with what you might call a show of force.

"Are you attempting to initiate voke contact with me when I've chosen to withdraw?" I asked him mildly.

He was outfaced at once. He was blond and pale-skinned, so his blushing showed to quite impressive effect. "No!" he blurted.

"Because my right to privacy is absolute."

"Of course it is! I didn't mean…" He faltered into silence.

"Then let's unask the question," I said. "No hurt or blame to either. I'll tell you this. I'm an expert in these matters, and I head a well-trained team. If we do our job competently – which we will – there is absolutely no danger to anyone here. And no disrespect or injury will be done to any of the time-stopped unless it's absolutely necessary in order to prevent a catastrophe."

I moved on quickly, leaving the boy to come down from that painful public embarrassment and the teacher and his class in the care of the park officials. If all went well, they'd still get their day trip. If not, I would do my best to see them safely home.

I met up with Tally a little way inside the gates. He was doing his best to look inconspicuous, which of course meant that he stood out like a hippopotamus in a henhouse. Seeing me coming, he let his shoulders slump. I opened my drift just in time to catch the tidal wave of his relief.

"Lieutenant! It's just been getting crazier!"

"I saw. Have we got a pinpoint on the source, Tally?"

He nodded. "Quite a long way in. Near the centre."

That was bad news. It raised the possibility of a fail cascade – and made it that much more likely that we would have to intervene.

"Show me."

Tally led the way and I followed. We passed through the gate, with its exhortation to REMEMBER THOSE WHO FELL, AND THOSE WHO STAND FOREVER.

I'd been to London 21 as a child, and what I mostly remembered was being bored. I'd been too young. The ineffable strangeness and sadness of the place hadn't registered with me, only the silence. The weight of it, like time made solid and pressing down on me. Actually that wasn't too far from the truth.

As an adult, I was more profoundly affected. The piece of old London that was frozen stretches from the middle of what used to be Tottenham Court Road in the north to the Strand in the south, and it extends about a mile to the east and west. The entry gate feeds you past an imposing ancient structure called Centrepoint into an avenue of buildings that are mostly rendered in stone, baked brick or poured concrete. No perma-weave extrusions at all, and very few hydrogel ceramics.

The roads are all static, of course, so you walk on your own two feet – which gives you plenty of time to look in the windows. Quaint and curious emporiums offer goods whose use it's almost impossible to imagine, even with the aid of the download foci that are scattered around. What was the fastest ever 5G network, and why was it considered a good thing? Who went into the Scientology Life Improvement Centre, and what did they find there? So much of our past is opaque to us.

I have to admit, though, that looking at the shop windows was mostly a way of not looking at the people. It might surprise you to learn that a temporal engineer is capable of that kind of squeamishness, but there it is. I've seen literally thousands of time-stopped in the course of my work. I know exactly what they are, and what they're not; what was done to them, and how. I've been briefed extensively on their ontological state by people who've gone down to the sub-atomic level to verify their hypotheses. I know where I stand.

None of which makes it easier for me to look at them, or walk among them.

There's just something intrinsically wrong in the spectacle of people – children, men, women – caught in such a hideous snare. Trapped and held in a mood of joy or misery or boredom that should have been transitory, murdered without ever knowing it, and made to recapitulate forever the last moment of their lives.

Most cities where time weapons were deployed have gone the same way we did and turned the detonation sites into public monuments and memorials. There are those who argue that they should be closed off to the public and treated as actual burial grounds, but that has always been a minority view. Most people feel that we own this tragedy and should acknowledge it rather than hiding from it, however painful that may be.

Tally was walking briskly ahead, but now he turned to look at me and pointed. "It's this way," he said. "Bayley Street." The look of surprise on his face told me he'd voked the words first. He must have thought my reticence was just for the crowds outside, when actually it was for him too. I still hadn't decided whether or not I was going to induct him, today, here, into our profession's last and ugliest mystery.

We turned a corner and crossed another street into a small square. There was a fenced-off garden space in the middle, trees and benches, an archaic lamp post, a statue of a Victorian gentleman now surrounded by living statues from two hundred years later.

On the day the time-bomb fell, the square had been full of people. Most of them were alone, or else walking in twos. The exception was a single large group on the far side of the garden, heading for its open gate. A young woman led them, carrying a long slender pole with a square of bright yellow card or plastic mounted on it. A tour group, I assumed, following their guide. If my voke was on, I could have accessed the contextual notes from any of several nearby download foci, but this really wasn't the time.

Tally pointed. Fifty yards ahead of us was a man wearing a formal suit of eye-catching drabness, grey with a pattern of narrow blue lines almost too faint to see. His head was bald, his lean face austere and calm. He was clean-shaven but he had missed a spot on the right side of his jaw, leaving a blue shadow. There had been no way for him to know, when he went through his ablutions on that long gone morning in the mid twenty-first century, that this was the face he would be presenting to the world for centuries to come.

Most of the people here had been taken while they were walking. This man had stopped where the square met the street from which we had entered. He was staring off down the street as though he had come there to wait for somebody and was impatient for them to arrive. Whoever it was, perhaps they were among the frozen figures we had already passed. Or perhaps some other business kept them away that day and they were spared.

We came up on either side of the time-stopped man and I made a more careful appraisal. Sitting next to him on the ground was the squat silver bulk of a baffle rig in its shock-proof box, presumably lowered from an aerial carrier. Public roads didn't extend into the time-stopped areas.

"Is he moving now?" I asked Tally.

"I didn't check. I waited for you."

"You took a baseline, though?"

"Oh. Yes. Of course. Can I…?"

"Send your stats to my Offhand."

The Offhand is a dead storage. It doesn't connect to your sensorium unless you tell it to, and you can pick and choose. It's a way of receiving voked messages without voking back. Again, I was insulating myself from Tally while I decided how to handle this and how much to tell him.

I found his send in the Offhand and brought it up. It was a map of the square with every physical distance flagged to an accuracy of 0.3 Angstroms.

Using that as a reference point, I took my own measurements on a Chiang-Voss gauge, which I check and recalibrate every two or three days. I read the distances and ran the check again. Then I ran it a third time.

"Is everything okay?" Tally asked. His anxiety and confusion were painful to see. Like many people – the majority, even – he's a bit clueless at reading faces with no drift to go on.

"No," I said shortly. Everything was far from okay. There had been a seven-picometer slippage in the space of less than an hour. The situation was fluid, as they say, and we had even less leeway than I'd been assuming.

There was one final test I needed to carry out. The odds were in my favour, but I'm fatalistic at times like this. I always assume the worst. I reached into my pocket and took out a tiny metal disc like an antique battery. A touch was enough to unfold it, turning the disc into a lattice of slender metal rods shaped like the skeleton of a glove. It slid across my right hand and affixed itself there, each filament in its proper place. The rods were only a sixteenth of an inch thick, but they were marked along their length by thousands of puckered indentations. Psionic amplifiers.

I touched my hand to the forehead of the time-stopped man. I closed my eyes and sub-voked the command. *Open.*

What I was hoping for was nothing. Nothing at all.

Which was just too bad for me.

"Lieutenant Begum!" Tally yelled. "Huss!" Again, he must have voked first and went for speech as a last resort, but I'd switched off everything as a precaution before I made contact with the time-stopped man.

Some time had passed, but probably only a couple of seconds. I'd bitten through my lower lip, and there were lacerations in my left palm where my nails had punctured the skin as I clenched my fist. I had slumped against the time-stopped man, and he was the only thing holding me up, but I hadn't dropped to my knees or lost control of my bodily functions. It could have been worse.

"Are you all right?" Tally blurted. "It looked as though you were going to faint!" He reached out a hand and I grabbed hold of it, switching my weight from the frozen man to him. For the time being I was going to have to let his question hang in the air. It's hard even to think after the kind of battering my mind had just taken, let alone speak.

I made my decision there and then, as I slowly got my balance back and stood upright again. I would have to truncate immediately, and if I was going to do that then I was going to tell Tally the truth. All of it.

I hated to do it. I might have sounded flippant when I talked about his dazzling idealism, but let's be clear: that's just one more defence mechanism on my part. What I was about to take away from him was a thing that was precious, and that ought to be inalienable. But because he'd chosen a military career, it wasn't.

"Tally," I said, "Voke the crowd outside. Tell them to disperse to a half-mile distance. Then alert local police to maintain that perimeter."

He frowned, and hesitated for a moment. Uncertainty made him blink rapidly, four or five times in succession. "Will you ride the call, Huss? I mean… in case I miss anything out, or…"

"Absolutely." *I'm here. Go ahead.*

Tally concentrated hard. *Attention,* he voked. *If you're in the vicinity of London 21, you need to draw back until you're at least half a mile from the gates. One of the time-stopped in the park area is breaking out of stasis. If the field fails, and the energistic recoil isn't contained, there will be an uncontrolled emission of localised temporal distortion. People caught in the recoil could age years or decades in the space of a second. Medical complications include cardiac events, aneurisms and renal failure. There's a substantial risk of immediate death. We're going to erect a baffle rig now, but in case the stasis field fails before we can contain it you all need to be well out of range.*

Tally looked to me, anxious, wanting approval.

I nodded. *That was great. Now the police, and the park management.*

While he was busy with that I set down the plasteel carrier I'd had with me all this time, opened it up and performed a quick inventory of its contents. The brace and brackets, the drill, the bolt and the detonator. My instruments of murder, all in place.

Shall I set up the baffle rig? Tally asked me. He was a lot happier now that we'd made the announcement. There was still nervousness in his drift, but much less than before and outweighed by a sense of calm; of events unfolding in a clear, predictable way. I was about to upset that apple cart. I was about to smash that apple cart into smithereens.

Never mind the rig, I said. *Come over here.*

I deactivated the connector. It shrank back down to a disc.

Hold out your hand.

Tally obeyed without question. Military discipline doesn't change, even now the army is pretty much a vestigial institution. I dropped the tiny device into his palm. It unfolded again, and he drew in an audible breath as it fitted itself to his sensorium.

What is this thing? he demanded. He wasn't afraid, only curious. With a hundred training simulations and seven actual mission outings under his belt, he thought he knew our field kit inside out.

The first little apple, falling off the cart.

It's a drift connector, I said. *And an amplifier.*

A connector? But... everyone is already connected to...

Stay with me, Tally. The time-stopped lived in an era before drift was a thing, right?

Tally was still staring at the angular, spider-legged thing that had spread across his palm and up his fingers. *Right?* I voked again.

Right. Of course. But...

The only emotions they felt were their own. The only thoughts they could access — their own. We see them as being locked away from us in a bubble of frozen time, but when you think about it, their everyday experience was already one of isolation. Exile. Solitude.

Tally was looking at the rest of the equipment in the carrier now, and his calm mood was considerably ruffled. *That looks like a gun,* he said, pointing at the bolt.

It is a gun. Tally, listen. I'm explaining something to you, and it's important. I took his hand between both of mine. *What do you feel?*

He stared at me, puzzled and unhappy. *Nothing.*

Nothing at all?

He shook his head.

Why do you think that is? If it's designed to force a connection, and to amplify the emotional signal, why are you feeling nothing from me?

The corners of his mouth tugged down as he thought. Seeing this as a test, he wanted very much to pass. *The setting?*

Good. Yes. The amplifier is incredibly sensitive, but it's stopped down to a very particular, very narrow wavelength. I'd be lying if I said I understood the physics, but what matters is the effect. It can penetrate a stasis field. It can pick up the thoughts of the time-stopped. After a moment I amended that last statement. *If they have any.*

Mostly they don't. More than three-quarters of the people caught in a stasis event are hit so hard by the field that all thinking and all affect just stop dead in the same moment that their bodily movement stops. Ego-death occurs instantaneously, and when you touch them with the amplifier you get nothing but silence.

Those are the lucky ones.

The rest...

The rest are still awake. The time-bomb froze their bodies but not their minds. They had a partial immunity that has never been explained or understood. They continued to think and to feel, inside bodies that had been turned into form-fitting coffins.

I imagine for a time what they mainly thought was "when is someone going to come and help me?" But no one did, or could. The time-stop effect renders the affected person or object impervious to any external force. Divorced from the pulse-beat of entropy, they can only endure.

At some point, after weeks or months or years, madness invariably set in. The trapped mind locked itself into a cycle of panic, rage and pain that fed on itself and grew stronger with each iteration. That was what I felt when I touched this man's mind. The voiceless, substanceless shriek entered me, filled me, tore at my skin from the inside out.

I nodded at the time-stopped man. *Touch his forehead,* I said. *Lightly.*

Put your hand in the mincing machine. Turn the handle.

It took Tally a long time to recover. To be fair, not as long as it took me when my captain, Angelo, inducted me for the first time. But as with me, it came in stages. The shock first, then the panic. "He's hurting! He's hurting so much! Lieutenant, you've got to help him!" And finally the stunning grief as the implications slowly sank in. We sat together on the edge of the pavement, his head against my chest, and I held him until he came back from that abyss.

There are thousands of the time-stopped. Thousands on thousands, all across the world. Some are only statues. Funeral architecture. The rest are like this man – bottomless reservoirs of suffering.

"Something's got to be done," Tally said, his voice muffled by tears and fabric. "We can't just leave them."

"We don't have any choice," I said, gently. "Nothing we've got can even touch them until the stasis field starts to break down. Nothing, Tally. They're out of the world. Until one day they're not, and then they're a lobbed grenade in a crowded room. We can do exactly one thing for this man, now. We can put an end to his pain. Come on. I'll show you how."

I took him through the mechanics of it. The harness attaches to the head of the time-stopped child, woman or man by four carefully placed brackets. The bolt attaches to the harness. A sensor measures the integrity of the stasis field continuously, tracking gradients and updating projections faster than any human mind could react. The instant the field falls, the bolt is fired. The time-stopped individual lives again, for the tiniest fraction of a second. Then dies, as the detonator is triggered and the bolt shoots home through the basal ganglia of the brain.

It's all we can do, I told Tally. It's tragic and it's terrible and there is absolutely no alternative, no choice, no other way to play this.

Because the voke and the drift were what dragged us back from extinction, at the ragged edge of the eleventh hour. After thousands of years of killing each other, torturing each other, suddenly there we were all up inside each other's defences, knowing the stranger as well as we knew ourselves. Hate was impossible. Misunderstanding was impossible. Loneliness was impossible.

We surrendered to empathy as a last resort, and we were each other's salvation.

Now every child that's born is born in the drift. Cossetted, embraced, known and protected by the collective mind. We've never known the desolation of being alone in the dark, crying out ceaselessly for help as hope curdles inside us and turns us into monsters.

The time-stopped are our forebears, our family, but if we open our arms to them they will destroy us. Their fears and hatreds and agonies will poison the drift for generations, perhaps forever. We will become what we were before. We will fall into the ancient pit, and perhaps this time we won't be able to climb out again.

So we invented that lie, about the temporal distortion wave. Keep your distance, or be Rip Van Winkled. And we invented a non-existent piece of technology, the baffle rig, to justify engineers like me – and like Tally – stepping into the breach and containing all that dangerous energy. When we're done there's nothing to see. The unfortunate time-stopped has been sublimed away, rendered into dust and loose atoms. Actually they're laid down, in the big steel box that's supposed to contain the baffle rig, and lifted out by a robot transport. They get a hasty burial on Ministry of Defence land, with no funeral rites and no grave marker. And the world goes on.

As for us, the keepers of the secret, I suppose we're doing the same thing soldiers have always done. We kill for the state, and we tell ourselves that somehow, in this one instance, killing isn't a crime or an atrocity but a needful thing. The past lives on, not just in the time-stopped but in us.

Trust me. You don't want any part of it.

Fog and Pearls at the King's Cross Junction

Aliya Whiteley

Ma was never the same after the war, even though my dad came back to us whole and, in the main, cheerful. Her rage sank into the walls of our little house, and I thought there was no escape from it until the day I got the letter on good cream paper from Mr Arnold Rodderick.

One time, in a rare moment of honesty between us, Ma told me she had taken against all those who made money at the expense of the troops, not just on the German side but on the English too. It seemed to me that she hated everybody, particularly me, but maybe she just couldn't stop herself from being angry. Dad was a tonic after her worst outbursts. She'd say the world was ruined and I'd never be able to make anything good out of myself, and then he'd take me to one said and whisper: *don't you listen, Connie, you've got something special inside of you. We all do.*

I've not seen Ma or Dad since I sneaked out and took the train to London, so many years ago, but my dad's words have stuck with me and kept me good company. He wasn't right, of course. Not all of us have something special inside. But a few, a very few, do.

I stood on the emptying platform and looked around at the blackened walls of the station. The ground was filthy, as were the small booths selling sweets and papers, and there was a warm summer wind sweeping right along the tracks and bringing a bad smell with it, probably from the building works left all around by the Blitz's bombs.

The smell of the city, I thought, and felt unladylike and hot in my thinning fur coat with the worn lining. I should say Ma's coat; I pinched it from the back of her wardrobe, hoping to look a little more like a lady. She had been saving it for best since before the war, and I knew that her best was behind her so it only seemed right to make it my own. But suddenly I saw myself as if from a distance, small and alone, and looking like a little girl dressed up for a party that wasn't going to take place.

I took Mr Rodderick's letter from the inside pocket and read it through once more, as if that would change the words written there, or uncover some secret meaning that I had not found on the hundred readings beforehand:

I shall meet you directly on the platform if you take the 5.32, which will arrive at 8.48 by the clock tower, and from there escort you to your new lodgings at the lighthouse. I have much need of an assistant and your recommendation came warmly from the good doctor.

He sounded like an older man: trustworthy, and correct and proper in his manners. Maybe he was late for a good reason. But I couldn't hang around on the platform all night; I already had the feeling I'd attracted the attention of the man in the nearest booth, who was leaning on his newspapers with his head cocked to one side, his lips pursed, as if I was a bird to be tempted over by simply whistling.

'Oi,' he called, 'You got someone meeting you? It's not a good place to be a little girl alone.'

I said, 'Yes, someone will be here shortly, thank you very much,' in my best voice that I'd learned off the radio.

'You can wait by my stand if you like,' he said, with a leer.

I set off smartly, walking fast, carrying my suitcase and keeping my nose in the air like I meant business. It did the trick and got me through the station, easily enough, until I stood outside with my eyes on the busy street, the buses and the taxis, and the men and women walking by as if they all had their own places to go.

Where was my place? I couldn't go home. There was no doubt in my mind of that. But the money I'd saved from my job answering the telephone and filing at the doctor's surgery wouldn't be enough to pay for a hotel for long. And, besides, how was I to find Mr Rodderick in this big city of smoke and alleyways? It's not like I could ask a passerby, sounding like a small town girl: *Pardon me, do you know anyone by the name of...?*

'Rodderick.'

I looked behind me, quick as a flash, and there stood a young man, startlingly young, barely older than myself, I'd guess.

'I beg your pardon?' I said, with my best voice firmly in place.

'I'm Rodderick. You're Miss Prisman. The famed right hand of Doctor Browning, who kept everything in order up in Staffordshire. Except you've shown a disordered lack of timekeeping tonight, haven't you? I said meet me at seven.'

'I think you'll find your letter said you'd meet me at 8.48 on the platform,' I said. I had formed a plan to call him *sir* from the off, to get us on the right footing and keep things professional, but his sharp tone and his uncombed hair took me by surprise. He was not at all what I'd expected. 'I can show you if you'd like.'

'It's not important,' he said. 'Have you eaten? I've made a stew. Give me your case.' He grabbed for it, and I held on fast, resulting in a tug of war for a moment before he gave up and started walking away from me at speed. I followed. I wish I could say it had been a thought-out decision on my part to go along, but it was only on instinct. I caught him up at the edge of the road, just upon the junction. The traffic was never-ending, with the fumes of their exhausts filling the air around us, making a thick cloud of smoke. I thought I'd never get used to breathing it in.

'Is it far to the lighthouse?' I shouted, over the noise of their engines. I had been expecting to board a different train, and travel onwards to the coast somewhere. I'd had visions of a lonely spot, on southern cliffs, maybe with a view of France. I'd always fancied living by the sea.

'What? It's here.'

'Here?'

'Look up,' he said. 'Not that way. That way.' He pointed, and I followed the line of his finger to see tall buildings, terraced houses, on the other side of the road. They looked grimy and crowded, nearly lost to view in their greys that blended into the smoke and the sky, but on the corner of the junction itself there stood a structure separate, with a rounded front and three rows of dark windows set into the curve. And rising over the uppermost windows there was a tower, smooth and tall, with a jutting rail – perhaps a balcony – halfway up. Above that, one large round window, and the structure was topped with a thin cross, no more than two faint lines against the dusk that I squinted to see.

'My lighthouse,' said Mr Rodderick, and then the blast of a horn from a car passing close by made me jump out of my skin, and he ran across the busy road as if immune to such concerns, so I gulped, took my life in my hands, and followed suit.

The stew was warm and salty, with fat lumps of fish. He slurped as he ate, sitting across the table from me, and I'm ashamed to say I slurped too, being too hungry and tired to stand on ceremony. He was very pale, and there was something about the way he held his neck and shoulders that reminded me of older patients at the surgery, sore from years of certain types of work – which reminded me, I knew very little about Mr Rodderick's own work apart from what he'd mentioned in his letter:

I am involved in a type of research that is both my passion and my full-time occupation, and it requires meticulous attention to detail and unflagging energy at every time of day and night. An assistant with similar personal qualities and a desire to learn about my complex field would be a boon.

I had taken that as an explanation but now I realised it contained very little information, so I finished my stew and said, 'What exactly is it that you study?' The idea of calling him sir at this point was ridiculous. The opportunity for that had well and truly gone, I reckoned.

'Did you know that I used a dozen oysters in the preparation of this dish? Well, of course, you couldn't know. That's why I'm telling you. Have you eaten oysters before? They're fresh from the Thames this morning.'

'I haven't,' I said. That explained the rubbery texture. I put down my spoon and looked around the kitchen for clues. His apparent devotion to order was not on show, at least, not in that room. It was a mess of pots and pans, and I saw the shucked shells of the oysters by the sink, amongst carrot and potato peelings and the head of a large onion, and a familiar black bottle of stout – my dad's favourite. Well, I was there to work and there was no time like the present. I got up and starting moving the used pots to the sink. 'Is there hot water?' I asked.

'I'm telling you about my work!'

'I can clean at the same time,' I told him, 'and I thought you were talking about oysters.'

'I was,' he said, 'I was.'

He cleared his throat, and spoke on while I ran some water and scrubbed the pots. 'Oysters. They have a marvellous defence mechanism. When a tiny piece of grit or a parasite slips into their shell they begin to coat it in a substance called nacre. Nacre slowly takes the painful and makes it bearable. More than that, nacre makes it beautiful. It creates a thing of perfection. Do you understand what I'm trying to tell you, Miss Prisman?'

His tone grated on me, I'll admit. I replied, letting my smart mouth get the better of me, 'You're telling me that you've let me, an irritation, into your shell. But you'll wear me down and change me over time into the perfect assistant.'

To my surprise, he laughed out loud. 'No no no! Not at all! What an imagination you have. I'm telling you that I collect and categorise pearls.'

What a surprising and strange man he was, right from the beginning of our long relationship.

We walked down and down a circular staircase, until it felt as if we were far below street level. I could hear the rumble of the traffic, loud, somehow sounding both above and around me. I swallowed hard and watched Rodderick's back, straight and slim in his white shirt, as he led the way along a grey, undecorated corridor to the first of two heavy oak doors set opposite each other. He opened the one on his left and held it for me.

Inside was a large room lined with cabinet after cabinet, not unlike the ones used in the Doctor's surgery, and a glass-topped table in the middle. It was only when I got close that I realised it was not a table but a display case, and inside were gleaming, creamy, shining balls. Pearls.

'The jewels of my collection,' said Rodderick.

They were the best, most beautiful, most contained and perfect and special creations I'd ever seen.

My mother had a string of pearls that she brought out on special occasions, wearing them with a bright shade of lipstick and a strange, craning way with her head, but those were drab grey drops compared to the wonders in this case. And they were not all white, or even all the same size. They changed from bright gold to shiny silver, jet black to cloud white, sky blue to coral pink, and in sizes from barely more than a pinhead to bigger than a golf ball. The most beautiful of them all, to me, was a set of eight, lined up at the bottom of the case, as bright as my eyes could bear, and as red as blood.

There was a fortune laid out before me, I could tell that in a moment, but this was not the thought that mattered the most to me. What mattered was the specialness of the pearls. Is that even a word? Ma would no doubt tell me off for using it, but they *were* special, beyond precious, better than money or babies or anything that I was meant to want. I would have picked them up and cradled them if there hadn't been glass between us.

'You like them,' said Rodderick. It wasn't a question. 'That's a good start, since you'll be working with them. I buy and sell.' Before I could stop myself, I put my hand to the glass. 'Not those ones. Others. In these cabinets. It's been my family's trade for the longest time, but the records have become... disordered and there are new requests coming in daily, and contacts to curate. Can you do that?'

'I can do that,' I said. 'Yes, I can manage that for you, Mr Rodderick, I'm certain of it.'

He smiled, and rested his elbow against the nearest cabinet. This was his room, his home. He knew it and possessed it. I felt a sudden jealousy of what his family connections had given him, when all I had from mine was one ratty old fur coat that I'd near as stolen. 'Excellent! If you get that done smartly I have other tasks you can help me with.'

'I'm very efficient,' I told him. I wanted him to see me clearly, as an employee, yes, but also as a person capable of the tasks put in front of her. It was occurring to me that this was going to be a much better job than the kind I was used to. The rules were changing. What rules, exactly, I couldn't say. The lines that had held me in place all this time. 'I'd love to learn this business, and be of proper help.'

His smile faded away, leaving him with a thoughtful expression that I liked. 'Yes, maybe you'll do,' he said. 'But the records first. Then we'll see.'

'Records first,' I said, and rolled up my sleeves, moving to the cabinet he leaned against. 'Excuse me. I'll get started.'

He laughed, and said, 'I didn't mean tonight!' But he stepped back out of the way and watched me unpack the envelopes and correspondences that had been thrown in with no attempt at order at all. He did need my help, and I was determined to give it, and earn my keep, and earn more besides that, including his trust.

There had hardly been anything I could call an opportunity in my life. I wasn't going to let a one go when it came along.

I've always been a quick learner. Quicker than most.

I learned about the grading system, and the types of pearl. I learned about the classic and abundant saltwater examples from the akoya oyster, and how the value of the Golden South Sea Pearl depended upon the depth of its colour more than its size. The names conjured up images of sandy islands and blue seas, but as the months passed and the season turned from summer to autumn, and then on to winter, it grew colder and colder in the basement room where I worked, and my visions of warmer climes couldn't keep the icy chill at bay.

I shivered, and took to wearing Ma's old coat down there, and then nearly all the time. I wore it even when I slept. November was bitter. The dire cold slipped under the sheets and blankets to wake me up. My room, a plain little box room on the second floor – I wasn't allowed any further up in the building than that – overlooked the King's Cross junction, and I'd go to the window and look at the thick ice on the sill, and then beyond to the street and the station, the clock tower and the kiosks, still and dead in the night. When the trains stopped running and the street was empty, the silence was rich. I liked the view at those times, when it was bare of buses and cars, and even of the poor beggars who got moved on by the Bobbies over and over again. I found myself expecting something to happen. I don't know what. It was as if the world held its breath, and it couldn't last, it couldn't last, this bleak peace of the night.

Then the dawn would come and I'd get up and go down to the basement to work on the pearls again. Roddy would bring me down a cup of tea and a piece of toast with jam when he woke. He cooked our meals, and I cleaned the dishes, and did a little bit of housework besides. We were like an old married couple. By that I don't mean that anything romantic happened between us. It never did, and that was fine by me. We had an easy familiarity, as if we'd known each other for years. I think we were like two peas in a pod, in some ways. We could both be very practical people when the need arose, although I didn't know how practical he could be until December came around in that first year together.

'Yes, but what is the lighthouse bit for?' I asked him, for what must have been the hundredth time. We were in the kitchen, finishing up yet another meal of oyster stew. He liked opening those Thames oysters, fresh from the fishermen, but he never did find a London pearl within one.

'Did you reply to that letter from Mikimoto?' he said, avoiding my question, but I knew him well enough by then not to simply give up on my own train of thought to pander to his.

'Was it added on to the building by your family because oysters come from the sea? Is that the reason why they put it on the top?'

'Not all oysters come from the sea, Connie,' he said, disapprovingly. 'You know that.'

He'd answered one of my questions, in a way. It was a small victory, but a victory just the same. 'So it's not to do with the pearls? And what about the rooms on the third floor? Are they to do with the pearls, or the lighthouse?'

He put down his spoon and said, 'You're wearing gloves. In the house.'

I'd bought them on a Saturday morning when I'd taken a little time off to get in some shopping, using a few pence from the money he left next to the sink every now and again since he never felt the need to pay me directly. 'I like the colour,' I said.

'And your coat.' Had he really not noticed that I'd barely taken it off? 'Is it cold out? I don't feel the cold.'

'It's nearly December.'

'Is it?' he said, as if this was a revelation. 'It is. Well then. Well. I'll light the furnace. It blows hot air all over the house through a vent system, you see. My grandfather came up with it. You've been here for nearly half a year. Maybe it's time, after all, what with the change in the weather. Yes, all right, listen. I'll bet a fog is coming. A pea souper. Like nothing you've seen.'

The Big Smoke was famous for its fogs, and I'd seen them settle over the junction and the bulk of King's Cross more than once. But Roddy shook his head when I told him I'd seen the fog for myself; he told me that it could get much worse, settling thick and brown on the city, choking anyone who breathed it in, burning the back of the throat, even the skin, and sliding under doors and window sashes to lurk in houses. 'They always come after the coldest weather, once the streets start to warm a little. And that's when the next part of our job comes into effect. Can you obey my instructions when the time is upon us? Can you do that?' he said, reminding me of the first time he'd asked me that question.

I answered clearly and loudly, without a moment of doubt for what I was agreeing to, 'Yes I can, Roddy. I promise you, I can. And I'll be ready.'

God forgive me, I didn't even ask him what I'd need to be ready for.

The smog came on the first Friday in December.

It was exactly as Roddy had described it. Thick and brown, stinking and sly, creeping over the streets. It arrived in the early morning, just after the cold of dawn had lifted, and turned day to night, and night into a thick and choking blanket. Whistles blew regularly from the station – the workmen trying to find each other on the tracks – and then they stopped, along with the buses and trains, and there was no sound at all. London was silent and suffering.

I went to work as usual; the smog could not penetrate to the basement. When Roddy brought down my breakfast I said, 'Well, you were right on the button. Here it is.'

'I told you! It'll get worse yet,' he said, and, 'We'll start tonight. Yes. Tonight.'

I don't remember much else of that day. The night, I remember as if it were yesterday.

He took me up to the third floor.

There was only one door leading on from the corridor, made of a smooth shiny metal, and it opened on to a large room with deep red carpeting on the floor and walls, and brass lamps throwing a dim orange light. Paintings of flowers had been hung above a row of ten small beds, lined up against one long wall. A little wooden blanket box sat at the foot of each of them, and red curtains had been put up as dividers. It was a luxurious room, but not a pleasant one. I felt straight away that I wouldn't have liked to stay in it myself for very long.

'People will be coming,' he said, 'and you must bring them in here.'

'I can do that,' I told him.

And so up again, up the stairs to the part of the house I'd wanted to see for months.

The lighthouse.

It was very dark up there, and barely big enough for both of us to stand in. At the centre was a device unlike any I'd seen before. It was made of metal, I think, but it was white and tall, flat with its face turned away from us. I walked around it, feeling none the wiser. Spikes poked out from the face, silver ones, and thick black wires ran down the side. I didn't dare touch it.

Then I looked through the curved glass windows, and I could only see the brown smog, pressing close. It looked like mud, heavy, its weight threatening to break the panes. It was difficult to believe that the railway station, and the whole of London, lay beyond this; we could have been deep underground, separated from anything or anyplace human.

'And now,' Roddy said, 'the switch.'

He knelt at the base of the device and opened a small panel. The shadow of his hand made it impossible to see what was inside, but I guessed he pressed something because suddenly there was light. It flashed from the spikes, blinding me for a moment, and then stopped. On, and then off. And here's the strange thing. Those flashes cut right through the smog. It was as if the pea souper shrank back from the light's path, afraid of its power.

Roddy laughed. 'Quite something, isn't it? My grandfather made it. He built the whole thing. He called the light a form of electroluminescence.'

'But how can it –?'

He shushed me, and we stood together in silence. My eyes began to grow accustomed to the flashes. They weren't so very bright to stand next to, after all, but they did a grand job against the smog just the same. I could imagine someone out there, lost and alone, barely able to breathe the acrid air, looking up and finding those pinpricks of light. It would seem like a sign from the heavens to them.

A bell clattered. The sound was loud in the lighthouse, echoing up the staircase.

'The door, Connie!' he said, 'The front door! Quick!'

He took the stairs two at a time. I didn't dare to follow soquickly, and by the time I reached the front door he had flung it open and a man stood in the hall, gasping, while Roddy patted his back. I understood then what the lighthouse did; it led people straight to us.

'Close it close it,' Roddy said. He was in a state of high excitement, fussing over the man. 'He can't breathe. Help me get him upstairs.'

'Upstairs?' I said, stupidly.

'The room I showed you,' he said, and I remembered the room of beds, laid out and waiting to be occupied, so I put my arm around the poor man and led him to a place where he could rest.

It took some real effort on both our parts to get him to the second floor. He leaned against the wall, making a terrible whistling sound in his throat, as I swung back the metal door. He didn't even look around the room but sank down on to the nearest bed and closed his eyes.

'You need some good clean air,' said Roddy to him, slowly, deliberately, and the man nodded. He was old, with only wisps of hair left around his head and deep wrinkles on his eyes and mouth. His clothes were grimy, and I guessed he was one of the train workers, caught out on his way home from working on the lines. How pliant he was. Perhaps it was Roddy's voice that did it – so clear, so well-spoken – for when he reached under the bed and produced a silver canister attached to a gas mask the man allowed it to be strapped over his face without any fight at all, even though it must have reminded him of the worst of the war.

Roddy turned the valve at the top of the canister and said, 'Breathe deeply now. It'll make you feel better.'

The man did as he was told, and the air did him some real good, for his body relaxed and sank down on to the bed as if all he really needed was a long, deep sleep.

'You use the money from the pearl trade to do good, to help souls in need,' I whispered, as Roddy removed the mask and slid the canister back under the bed. 'That's your family tradition.'

He smiled at me. 'Connie, you really are ridiculous,' he said, in a perfectly normal tone of voice. The man didn't even crack open an eye. That's when I realised he wasn't sleeping at all. 'Now, come on, we've got to work quickly.'

'Doing what?' I asked.

'Come on,' he said. 'Scrub up.'

It all happened too quickly for me to really think of anything except my surprise, and that I didn't want to let Roddy down. It seems strange to say for a child who lived through the war, but I'd barely seen the sight of blood before, except for one time when my dad banged his head on the corner of the mantelpiece while straightening up after starting a fire, and I'd cleaned that and wrapped a tea towel around it while Ma shrieked about head injuries and the like. I kept her firmly in mind while Roddy opened up the man's mouth and lowered in his scalpel. I was determined not to wail and scream, and I'm proud to say I didn't. I watched the whole thing from beginning to end, and even passed Roddy the needle and thread when he asked for it.

But the sewing up was not the exciting part, of course. The best bit was when he said, behind his little white mask, 'I can't quite believe this,' and used a long pair of tongs to reach far into the throat and produce a small red ball that he dropped into the palms of my hands.

I rolled it between my fingers. The colour didn't come from the blood in which it was coated. It truly was red, as bright and as brilliant a red as I'd ever seen. Just like the ones in the cabinet down in the basement.

'That's astonishing, you know,' he said. 'We've only found eight of these before. Eight, out of all the years and three generations of my family. It's you, Connie. Your presence has changed everything. There's something special to you.'

What else could I do at those words, so like the ones my dear old dad told me? I had found my purpose. I looked up at Roddy, and I beamed.

Twenty-three more people were rescued by the lighthouse in what became known as the Great Smog of London. Each one was brought to the door by those funny blinking lights, coughing and spluttering in the smog. I helped every one into the room and gave them the gas. They trusted me easily enough. Then Roddy would open up their mouths.

We found no more pearls, though, not over the four nights that followed, or even for the next three years. But we kept looking, and I came to see the inconvenience the people suffered – all they knew was a sore throat, with the stitches kept so neat and small that they could not have been spotted, and the fog could be blamed for that – as a form of payment. The smog killed if a person was out in it for too long. Well, we had brought them inside and given them a bed for the night. What did they care if we hunted for treasure while they slept?

Only twice did someone die while under the gas, and Roddy was beside himself both times. 'There's a saying: a good pearl-hunter never kills the oyster,' he said, and I consoled him as best as I could. We burned the poor men in the furnace, and said a prayer, and even sang a hymn. I've never forgotten their faces.

It turned out that there were lots of interesting rooms down in basement. My favourite was his grandfather's laboratory. Its dank brick walls contained a trove of strange instruments from experiments he had conducted. Roddy didn't care for the room, and left it entirely to me to explore; he said he had no head for science. Only the pearls interested him, and the operation he'd been taught to perform by his father. Once the clean air bills were passed and there were no more willing subjects arriving at our door to escape the smogs, he turned his attention entirely to the pearls. I'd often find him holding the nine red ones, singing softly to them. He loved them as much as I did.

At the end, when the pain got very bad for him, he said to me, 'Connie, dear, I don't think we'll see any more of their like, will we?'

'Probably not,' I said. London had become a different city by then. The lighthouse still looked down over the King's Cross Junction but it was not so easy to spot amongst the new buildings. I got the feeling lots of passers-by overlooked us altogether. But then, there was no reason to come to the door any more; the fogs were light and easy things, blown away by the wind. Roddy and I hadn't turned on the lamp for over thirty years.

'I've had enough,' he said, and he made oyster stew one last time, with horrible oysters bought at the supermarket, of all places, and we ate a meal together before we went up to the red room. He chose the bed by the door, and I strapped the mask to his face, and held his hand for a long time.

After that, I opened his mouth and cut his tonsils open. I expected to find one last pearl, but there was nothing. I could have sworn there was something special inside him. Perhaps I was wrong.

I asked Roddy once, 'Did the pearls come first, or the fog?'

He didn't know the answer, of course, although I thought his grandfather might have told him something. I reckon he forgot whatever reasons were given to him. He never was good at keeping things in mind, or in order. I loved him dearly, though, as my very good friend and the provider of my livelihood.

I read a little about the subject, and came up with my own theory, after Roddy had gone. He had told me once that pearls are formed by the oyster's own body, coating an annoyance – a piece of grit, or a parasite – in nacre. Over time, the layers of nacre form a perfect pearl. Could it be that the human body does the same when the terrible chemicals in the air enter the system? Are human pearls only as old as human smoke and fog?

I don't have an answer to that.

I keep my eyes on the pearl trade, and I still have my contacts. Just last week a red pearl came on to the market. People are calling it a fake, but I'm aiming to buy and examine it for myself, and perhaps add it to the collection. It comes from the city of Linfen, in China, which I read is one of the most polluted cities in the world. Has someone else discovered the secret that Roddy's family held so closely to their chests? If so, I wonder if the new fisherman knows that old saying that Roddy told me so long ago? *A good pearl-hunter never kills his oysters.*

But I'm getting too old for all this. Even if dear old Blighty took a turn for the worse and the thick smogs started to fall across London once more, I don't think I could make it up the stairs to switch on the light, and I certainly couldn't handle an unsteady visitor to my door and get them to the red room. Those days are behind me now.

I do have a daydream of turning on the device once more, and the light shining down on the Kings Cross junction so bright and true, bringing one final person to the door – not to be mined for treasure, but to take over my role and duties, and check my own body for treasure when the time comes. I'd hate to think of this place being left unoccupied, come my end. I don't suppose that will happen. Somebody will find it empty, and ensconce themselves, and maybe turn the lighthouse into an office building, or a café for those people who think themselves rich and interesting. They might believe that they're special inside, but little do they know just how special some lucky people can be.

My dear old dad was right about that, at least.

It occurs to me now, at the end of all this, that Ma was right too. She was right to hate the rich and the powerful. She would have hated Roddy, if she had ever met him. For he did the very thing that made her rant the loudest. He took his family money and possessions, and used them to manipulate the poor. I used to think the few pearls we found were a fair price for a bed for the night on the bleakest nights, when those unlucky enough to be left outside could not find their own way to safety. Now I know they paid dearly with a currency they didn't even realise they possessed.

As I sit up at night in my small room and look out over the King's Cross junction, at the street that is never empty, not even in the latest hours, I see the lights of London and wonder if those steady beams serve the same function as the lighthouse once did, calling to the lost and alone in order to rob them. I reckon that's the reason London shines so bright. It takes from the poor, and seals their wealth in basements, never to be seen again. How else could this city have continued to grow, a little more, every day?

Nightingale Floors

Dave Hutchinson

April 24. The writer A.F. Mikhailov alighted at St Pancras Station from the evening Eurostar from Amsterdam Centraal and walked down the platform towards passport control, towing his suitcase behind him.

He had been travelling for six days, because that was how long it took to get anywhere civilised from Moscow unless one was prepared to fly, and he had not been prepared to fly. Train from Moscow to Warsaw, then a day's wait at an hotel across the square from Centralna, a nitpicking recreation of Polish *fin de siècle* splendour that he couldn't really afford, but he didn't want to bed down in one of the capsule hotels which had sprung up like weeds around the city's main station. He always found himself waking from dreams of premature burial.

After that, four days of locals and expresses, city to city, enduring hours and hours at the many little border crossings of central and northern Europe. At Centraal, the Dutch passport officer had spent an entertaining few moments leafing through his recent visas and entry and exit stamps, and Anatoly could see the thought going through the woman's mind. *Why not just take the Line?* Well, that was a long story and he could sense the queue building up behind him, so he just said, "I'm visiting friends," and she looked at him. The Dutch didn't care; the Xian Flu had gone through their population like a forest fire, almost brought the nation to its knees. It had changed the national character, somehow; they no longer had time for the goings-on of people in other countries. His father, the Colonel, had once told him that the Dutch had one of the finest counter-espionage organisations in Europe, but their foreign intelligence presence had withered. They weren't interested any more. They just wanted to be left alone to mourn.

The official looked at him a few moments more. Then she took up an impressive-looking metal and plastic and wood contraption – far larger, surely, than was strictly necessary – and stamped his passport. And briefly, as he retrieved his passport from the slot in the counter, she gave him another look. He didn't have time to decode it. He hoped it wasn't pity.

So, here he was, back in London after… how long was it? Six years? Seven? Just another passenger plodding wearily along the platform after a long day's journey. He was of less than average height and more than average weight, with short sandy hair combed to one side and steel-framed spectacles and the face of a slightly dull schoolboy. He wore what looked, from a distance, like a good suit, and an ankle-length charcoal-coloured overcoat for which he was still paying, patiently, month by month, a few roubles at a time. "The best thing anyone can say about you," a girlfriend had once told him, "is that you're harmless."

Harmless, and very nearly penniless. He'd scheduled a lunch in Warsaw with his Polish publisher. They'd eaten at an Argentinian restaurant up the street from the hotel, basically a large percentage of a cow served with a small pile of fried potatoes and a few leaves of salad. His publisher, as was traditional, paid for the meal, but was otherwise unable to pass on any good news. *Sales are perhaps not so good, Anatoly Fedorovich*, sticking in the patronymic like a knife, just to remind him what the Poles still thought of the Russians. *These things can happen sometimes, nobody knows why. One day you're a lion, the next, you're dead. Perhaps things will improve next year.* They'd shaken hands warmly on parting, but what Anatoly had chiefly taken away from the meeting was *you're dead*.

He emerged from the exit doors into the great vaulted space of St Pancras Station, bustling at the best of times but now packed with the rush-hour crowds. He towed his suitcase along with them. Amazing how memory worked; he found his footsteps falling into the remembered path through St Pancras, then down the stairs into the sprawling Underground complex, where he paused at a machine and bought a network card – with cash – before continuing through the barriers and down to the Northern Line.

The first train to arrive on the platform was packed, people literally crammed up against the doors, but the following one was less busy and he was able to jam himself and his case on board for the short journey up to Camden Town station.

Here he emerged to find that the High Street had changed not at all. It was still full of foreign tourists – impressively so even this long after the end of the Xian Flu – and street entertainers and representatives of youth cultures who would have been jailed en masse in Rus. There were drunk people and people on drugs and more straightforwardly mad people. It was all rather refreshing, although one did well to make sure that one's money and belongings were secure before taking a stroll up to the Lock.

He didn't have that far to go. A few tens of metres away he turned down a side street and stopped at a door and rang the bell. He knew it took a long time for the occupants to make their way downstairs, so he waited a decent interval before ringing the bell again. Then again, a faint and previously suppressed panic rising at the back of his mind that perhaps there was nobody home – he hadn't called ahead.

But then he heard footsteps on the stairs within, and the sound of many locks being undone, and then the door opened and a fair-haired woman wearing jeans and a batik blouse was standing there looking at him as if she couldn't quite believe what she was seeing.

He had rehearsed a little speech for this moment, over the many long kilometres of his journey. It was a speech meant to reassure, to evoke memories of good times now past, to perhaps remind of old promises. It was a speech which went entirely out of his mind, and he found himself saying, "I've run away. I'm not going back."

Once upon a time, there was a somewhat plump Russian boy, son of a dead mother and a father who expressed his disappointment that his only child was not fit, emotionally or physically, for life in the military, by farming his upbringing out mostly to a nebulous clan of female relatives.

In truth, his aunts and great-aunts and impossibly distant cousins were every bit as fearsome as any drill sergeant. But they all recognised that trying to force this quiet, withdrawn, bookish boy into uniform would only destroy whatever good was in him. He was, they reasoned collectively, destined for a life in the Arts, and to this end they embarked on an education which would, they were certain, bring out the artist in him.

They were at least partially successful. Anatoly's first novel, *Kremlin Lights*, was published when he was twenty, to sufficient acclaim to convince him to write his second, *Sakharov's Blues*. And if that did not receive quite the acclaim of the first, he was by now launched on a career as a writer. *Kremlin Lights* was optioned for film or television several times, although it never reached the screen. The Aunts opined that the options had been minor money laundering schemes for some family of oligarchs or another and never meant to actually be made, but Anatoly chose to believe that they had been above board. His chief reason for this was that the option money – and there was quite a lot of it, by his standards – was real, and it bought him a certain amount of freedom.

He expressed this freedom by travelling. As a boy he had spent two years in Tokyo while his father was posted to the embassy there, but he had lived the majority of his life in Moscow, and he chose to employ his option money – dirty or otherwise – to see something of Europe.

So he visited Paris and Amsterdam and Berlin – he had liked Berlin very much – and Rome and Madrid, and many of the small new nations which were continually emerging from the European political landscape. His passport filled with colourful and imaginatively-designed visas.

He arrived, finally, in London. Which was a mistake. London was, for him, something of a city of fable, and he had been saving it until last on his Grand Tour. But what he found was disappointingly *ordinary*. Once you boiled off the obvious landmarks and iconic buildings – and most of *those* were either a lot smaller or not nearly as tall as they appeared in the media – it was just another city. It was weirdly grey and dour, its people prone to self-absorption when they were not protesting about something or other. London was, actually, notable for what it was *not*. It was not Barcelona or Lisbon or

Florence. He took a room in a boutique hotel in Smithfield, and he brooded.

Perhaps he was just tired of travelling. Perhaps he had just seen too much and was ready to go home. During the day, he walked the streets of the City and the West End and he looked around and found himself thinking *so what?* At night he sat at the artisanally-rickety desk in his room and tried to write, but mostly wound up streaming old television series to his glasses.

At various points in his travels, his father, hoping to keep tabs on him – and who knew, perhaps even afford him the contacts he needed to get a real job – had set him up with lunches and dinners with members of the Russian diplomatic service, as well as one or two mildly shady characters whom Anatoly presumed were remnants of his father's old networks from the days when he had made mischief around Europe.

In London, this task had fallen to the Military Attaché, who, busy with more important matters, had devolved responsibility to one of his subordinates, a Major named Avilov.

Avilov, a graduate of the Budyonny Academy, was only a few years older than Anatoly. He was tall and slim and athletic and he had a devastating smile which put Anatoly in mind of Douglas Fairbanks Jr. He had clearly been briefed not to talk about his work at the Embassy, although it didn't take a rocket scientist to guess – the Budyonny trained signals officers – but beyond that stricture he was pleasant enough company, and Anatoly found himself being invited to literary lunches and private gallery viewings and bookshop readings, and one evening reception at a colossal house in Regent's Park, where everyone he spoke to was either Lord This or Lady That. Some of these stiff and faintly fossilised English people owed their titles to recent political patronage, but some of them – Avilov pointed them out discreetly, like a naturalist commenting on a herd of rare antelope – went *way* back.

"That one there," he said, indicating without quite doing so a burly man in black tie who was in conversation with a group of elderly women. "His family came over with William the Conqueror. They own most of Leicestershire."

"My god," said Anatoly, duly impressed.

"Yes, well," said Avilov. "You clearly haven't seen Leicestershire. Ah, here's trouble."

'Trouble' was a tall, willowy young woman of around Anatoly's age, wearing a simple blue dress and holding a champagne flute. She came over to them and said to Avilov, "I heard that, you terrible man." She kissed him three times on the cheeks and then turned her attention to Anatoly. "Who's your friend, Dima?"

Amused, Avilov said, "Jessica, this is Anatoly Mikhailov. Anatoly, may I present Her Serene Highness Lady Jessica Burns."

Her Serene Highness playfully punched Avilov in the shoulder – or maybe not quite so playfully; Anatoly saw him wince ever so slightly. "Arsehole," she said. "I'm none of those things, and you know it." She looked at Anatoly. "The writer A.F. Mikhailov? *Kremlin Lights?*"

Anatoly experienced what could only be described as a transformative moment. A few seconds ago he had been merely Anatoly, minor guest. Now he was *the writer A.F. Mikhailov.* He felt as if he had received a second christening. "I'm flattered you recognise me," he said humbly.

"Your author photograph's pretty good," she said. She looked him up and down and added, "You've put a bit of weight on, though," and Anatoly's heart was lost.

Avilov drifted away to schmooze someone he was fairly sure held a senior position at the Ministry of Defence, leaving Anatoly and Jessica marooned in a moment's lapse in conversation. "So," she said finally, "are you having fun?"

He looked around the party. "If I'm honest, no," he said.

"Me neither. Let's get out of here."

Anatoly glanced over at Avilov, who was now talking to a tall patrician man whose bearing displayed all the discomfort of someone working for the English Civil Service who has just realised they are probably in conversation with a Russian intelligence officer but are too excruciatingly polite to walk away.

"Yes," he said. "All right."

There was something transgressive about giving his minder the slip and fleeing into the night with a beautiful Englishwoman. Anatoly found himself feeling slightly giddy as they walked around the edge of Regent's Park. They chatted as they walked. Anatoly had been told that London was riven by crime, with many areas being regarded as no-go zones by the police, but Jessica seemed perfectly relaxed and if she wasn't worried, neither was he.

They wound up at a little French restaurant not far from Baker Street, where the maître d' greeted Jessica with kisses on both cheeks, shook Anatoly solemnly by the hand, and led them to a secluded table, to which, in time, was delivered steak *frites* and a carafe of a rough and deeply satisfying house red.

"You're honoured," she said, pouring him a tumbler of wine. "Not everyone gets this stuff."

Anatoly glanced around the restaurant. Other diners seemed to have red wine.

"Ah, but this is the real thing," Jessica told him, seeing the look on his face. "The English and the French are having a bit of a *to-do* at the moment and we've banned imports of red wine. What they're drinking," she nodded at a group on the next table, "is probably Chilean pinot noir. We did a trade deal with Chile last year. Very proud of it we were, too."

"So this...?" He held up his tumbler.

"The owner's cousin has a boat," she said. "In Calais or Dunkirk or Ouistreham. Somewhere like that." She cut a slice off her steak, put it in her mouth, and chewed. "Every now and again they go out at night with the fishing boats. The French like to fish right up to the English territorial limit, just to make a point, so the owner's cousin and his brother go out with them and they load a couple of demijohns of wine under a drone and fly it onto a beach in Kent or Essex. Owner's waiting for it, sticks the wine in a van, drives it back here, and Bob's your uncle."

"I'm sorry? I don't have an uncle."

She looked at him and beamed. "Anyway." She raised her tumbler again, this time in a toast. "To smuggled wine."

"Smuggled wine," he said, touching his tumbler to hers.

So, not only had he slipped the leash, he was also drinking contraband. He wondered whether the steak was similarly illegal. Was the *tarte tatin* which followed – a dessert which was so unassumingly beautiful that he thought it was a sin to actually eat it – a controlled substance? He found himself not caring very much. Here he was, near the end of his journey, and the journey had been worthwhile.

They talked a lot. Her father was something minor in the Home Office, her mother a novelist in that particularly British manner where one published a book to moderate acclaim and then spent the next decade appearing on chat shows while teasing one's readership with hints of a follow-up.

He met them eventually, long after he'd smoothed things over with Avilov and the Embassy. Her father was a small, birdlike man, neat and self-contained, while her mother was big and prone to hugs and large gestures and awful kaftans. He'd liked them both very much.

His relationship with Jessica was not without its ups and downs. She had a temper, which she was not afraid to let the world see, and she had a certain view of things which perhaps did not accord exactly with his own, but he was in love and she said she loved him, so all was right.

He extended his stay in London, first for a week, then for a month, then for six months, and he did in time learn to love the city. By then he had moved out of the hotel and into a room in the house Jessica shared with her parents in Camden.

The house – it was hard to think of it as an apartment – consisted of four floors above a shop on the corner of Camden High Street and a little side street busy with bars and cafés. It was accessed by way of a battered front door on the side street, which led to a narrow and steep set of stairs up to the first floor, where the kitchen and dining room could be found. Above that was the living room, bathroom, and a guest room, and the two floors above those were occupied by Jessica and her parents. Her room was right under the eaves, with a skylight that afforded views south towards landmarks such as the Telecom Tower and, just visible above the rooftops, one of the towers of the Palace of Westminster and the upper curve of the London Eye. Looking at it – actually looking at it rather than travelling around on the Underground – he was struck by how small central London actually was.

He went back to Moscow eventually – there was no avoiding it, although he and Jessica had joked about her father somehow wangling asylum for him in England – but he returned to London again and again. Jessica visited Rus just once, where she submitted to the cool, implacable assessment of the Colonel and was whisked away for some mad weekend adventure by the Aunts, who returned her with her hair mysteriously cut short and dyed red and pronounced her a suitable match for him.

In time, though, things cooled. His visits to London grew fewer and fewer and they unspokenly acknowledged what had always been a fact: that he was never going to move there. He was, when all was said and done, too Russian in his heart. He wrote a novel, *Mornington Crescent*, but it did poorly and by the time it was published he and Jessica were communicating at most two or three times a week. She expressed her frustrations about him. He apologised. They did it again. And again. Eventually their relationship descended into distant and careful politeness.

Her parents died within a few months of each other, her mother of cancer, and then her father of a massive heart attack. Anatoly attended the funerals, and so did Jessica's boyfriends at the time. Anatoly stood near the back of the church, utterly unable to understand the order of service, and mentally called down the quite considerable wrath of the Russian Orthodox God on the heads of these charming and unsuspecting young men.

She inherited the house in Camden, and a couple of years later he received an invitation to her wedding. Nothing else, no personal note. Just an expensively-engraved card. The Aunts were of the opinion that he should travel to England and kill this interloper and finally claim Jessica for his own, but he told them not to be so absurd. He replied to the invitation with his regrets – he had, he said, prior commitments in Novosibirsk – and a small gift.

And, if life had been one of his novels, that would have been that.

In the kitchen, Jessica fussed with dinner. The husband – Dougal? No, *Duncan* – accepted the newcomer with English politeness and retired to his study. He was younger than her by five years or so, impressively ginger, with an old-style hipster beard. He worked for the English Home Office and he ran triathlons. Anatoly, who had never gone anywhere under his own steam at more than a careless amble, stumbled over that a little. Triathlons involved elements of swimming and cycling. Could one be said to be *running*?

"You can't stay here, Tolya," Jessica said, peeling potatoes over the sink. "I'm sorry."

"You look tired," he told her.

"Don't try to change the subject, you awful man," she said without looking at him. "You'll have to find somewhere else."

He thought about it. "Do you know anyone who can put me up? Until I'm on my feet?"

She cut a potato into quarters, dropped it into a saucepan, and turned to face him. "And how long will that be?" she asked. "A week? A month? How much cash do you have with you? Because whoever you stay with will want you to chip in for the housekeeping." She waited for an answer, and when he didn't say anything, she turned back to the sink. "Thought so."

"I'm not going back," he said.

"Oh, grow up, Tolya," she told him. "Just because you've had a falling out with your old man?"

This was not, when all was said and done, going quite the way he had hoped. He said, "It's more complicated than that."

Jessica rinsed the potatoes, drained the pan in the sink, refilled it, and set it on the hob. "So," she said, turning to him again and leaning back against the sink. "Explain to me how it's more complicated."

Easier said than done. In Rus, there were certain individuals and organisations whose attention it was unwise to attract. This was, of course, true wherever you were, but in Anatoly's homeland the situation was one of Byzantine complexity, expressed in terms of body language as often as in words.

Not all of these individuals and organisations were openly connected to the State – whose attention it had always been wise to avoid – but in Rus everything involving money or power was connected. It was hard to explain these realities to someone who had not grown up with them. One might as well try to explain to a fish what it was like to live out of water.

He said, "In ancient Japan, it was sometimes the custom, when building a house for an important person, to lay a special floor leading to a study or a bedroom – a secure place, anyway. These floors were constructed of dry boards, and jointed so that when someone stepped on them they creaked and made the sound of birdsong."

Jessica was looking at him as if he had gone entirely out of his mind. As well she might.

"Opinions differ over whether they were meant as alarms or for merely aesthetic reasons," he went on, "but I visited a house in Kyoto years and years ago, when I was at school, and I can tell you that it's impossible to walk down one of those corridors without making a noise." He sighed. "I appear to have stepped on one of these floors, and someone has noticed."

She stared at him a few moments longer. Then she shook her head. "I'm sorry, Anatoly," she said. "I thought you were going to explain what you were doing here, and all you've done is tell me an interesting factoid about Japan."

His heart sank even further. "I've done something," he said to her. "I don't know what, or when, or to whom. It's probably not very serious, otherwise I'd already be in a cell, or worse. But I couldn't stay."

Jessica put her hands to her face and rubbed her eyes. "Dear gods, Tolya," she said quietly. She lowered her hands. "Did you not have anywhere *else* to go?"

"I thought we were friends," he said.

She seemed to sag, ever so slightly. "Oh, Tolya, of course we're friends. It's so good to see you again after all this time, I can't tell you how much." She stepped forward and gave him a hug. "But you can't just go around crashing into people's lives without warning after five years."

"Six."

Jessica stepped back, but she kept hold of his hands. "Anatoly," she said, looking him in the eyes. "You can't stay here. I'm sorry."

"Is everything all right?" he asked. "You really do look exhausted."

She sighed and let go of his hands. "I'm not going to throw you out tonight," she said, glancing at the kitchen window. Beyond was a wooden deck with a table and chairs and planters, built by some previous occupant of the house on top of the flat extension roof of the shop which occupied the ground floor. Anatoly remembered long warm summer nights sitting out there with beer and kebabs while Camden partied below him. "But you'll have to find somewhere else tomorrow."

As so often happened at times like this, Anatoly found his mind going blank. He was safe for tonight. Tomorrow was another day, and he could worry about his situation then. Who knew, a good night's sleep might even result in some plan which would resolve all his problems.

"Okay," he said. "I'll sort something out tomorrow."

Dinner was lamb chops and potatoes and peas, and it was okay but it had the feeling of something cobbled together. The peas came out of a tin and the gravy from a sachet. He remembered vast paellas and stir-fries. Jessica had always enjoyed cooking; this meal was something she could put together with her mind in neutral, and he wondered if it wasn't a subtle reminder to him that he was only an overnight guest.

Conversation was similarly cobbled together, and revolved entirely around life in Rus. Duncan asked genial questions about Moscow – what was going on there, who was up, who was down. Jessica asked after the Colonel and the Aunts then seemed to decide to listen rather than take part. Anatoly still couldn't fathom whether she was angry with him or just disappointed, but this was not the first time, when all was said and done, that someone had been angry or disappointed with him, and he could roll with that.

Afterward, they all retired upstairs to the living room. He saw that Jessica had replaced some of the furniture, and there were a couple of unfamiliar prints on the walls, but otherwise the place was unchanged and he found himself beset by waves of mild *déjà vu*.

Eventually, Jessica drifted off upstairs. One of the rooms on the next floor had been converted into a study and workroom for her, although attempts to discover what exactly she was doing for employment at the moment seemed to be politely rebuffed.

A genial host, Duncan opened a bottle of malt whisky – a rarity in England due to troublesome relations with Scotland – and poured them both healthy measures, and they sat in armchairs and listened to the sounds of Camden High Street drifting up from below.

"One gets used to the noise, of course," Duncan said.

"I always liked it," Anatoly told him. "I liked standing at the window watching everyone go by."

If this reminder that he had been here first caused offence, Duncan made no sign. He said, "And you live in Moscow?"

"Balashikha," Anatoly said, meaning not the city just beyond the Ring Road but an enclave in the woods on the Pekhora River some kilometres away.

Duncan nodded. "That's Intelligence country, isn't it? Lots of GRU and FSB families. Lots of people who work for obscure little abbreviations."

"Not exclusively," Anatoly said carefully. "You're very well-informed."

"One picks up gossip."

"One does," Anatoly agreed, and sipped his whisky.

"Jessica says you're in some kind of trouble."

"Not *trouble* as such," Anatoly said, not wanting to get into the minutiae again. "If it was *trouble* I'd already be in custody. It was thought wise that I be somewhere else for a while."

"I could put out some feelers, see how the land lies," Duncan mused. "I have some contacts at FCO.

FCO was the Foreign and Commonwealth Office, but Anatoly suspected he didn't mean them. He suspected he meant MI6, Foreign Intelligence. "Feelers, as you put it, have already been put out," Anatoly told him. "It's very kind of you, but I don't see how involving anyone else would be terribly helpful."

"Have you thought, perhaps," Duncan suggested, "of asylum?"

Anatoly chuckled and shook his head. "I'm afraid there really *would* be trouble then." Rus, and before that Russia, had pursued and punished its errant children, with more or less total impunity, for many decades. "Things will calm down, tempers will cool."

Duncan nodded. "And what will you do until then?"

"I'd hoped I could..." he said. "For a few days... until I could... But Jessica..."

"Yes." Duncan was solemn. He glanced at the ceiling, as if he had just heard his wife walking about upstairs. "Well, yes."

Anatoly sat forward. "Forgive me, but is something wrong?"

Duncan looked at him and raised an eyebrow. "Wrong, old son?"

He found himself quite unable to put it into words, so he gave up and just said, "Yes."

Duncan smiled, but Anatoly thought it was a sad smile, a smile of regret. "Everything's fine."

There was a conversation he had to have with Duncan; if he was leaving in the morning, he should be having it now, but he was tired and slow and he didn't really want to do it and he let the moment pass.

"And now," Duncan said, finishing his drink in one swallow, "I should go to bed, I'm afraid. Got a long day tomorrow." He stood. "You can sort yourself out in the spare room, yes?"

Anatoly nodded and got up. "Yes." They shook hands. "Thank you for letting me stay tonight."

That sad smile again. "It's been good to meet you. She's spoken of you, from time to time."

This belated admission flatfooted Anatoly, and all he could think of to say was, "Ah."

Duncan smiled again, and this time it was a genuine, happy smile. "Don't worry; she only said good things, as I recall. Anyway, I'll wish you goodnight."

After Duncan had gone upstairs, Anatoly turned off the lights in the living room and took his drink into the spare room. It was just large enough for a small double bed and a chest of drawers, with a narrow strip of floor. He lifted back the curtain and looked down on the decking and the little backyard beyond that belonged to the shop on the ground floor. He let the curtain fall and sat on the bed sipping his drink, feeling the kilometres weighing on him all of a sudden. He had come such a very long way to this familiar little room. Journey's end.

He finished his drink, put the glass on the chest of drawers, used the bathroom, and finally crawled under the duvet, trying not to think about tomorrow.

He woke to banging on the street door, three floors below. Quite aside from his present predicament, if one lived in Moscow, in a certain stratum of society, one was always expecting that early-morning knock on the door. It was built into the soul. It signalled a realignment of allegiances, something quite beyond one's control, something engineered by people one did not even know, moving pieces around a board for some perceived and probably only temporary advantage. It triggered an autonomic response. One did not think. One did, if it was at all feasible, what Anatoly did now. One went out of the window.

He was not, when all was said, an idiot. He put his trousers and shoes on first, and grabbed his overcoat, and he tugged the sash window open, climbed over the sill, and hung by his fingertips. He closed his eyes momentarily, and then let go.

It took him longer to fall than he expected. He landed heavily, almost toppled over because one of his feet was buried in one of the big terracotta planters that lined the edge of the decking, but managed to regain his balance, opened his eyes, and found himself looking through the window into the kitchen.

Where lights were starting to come on, in the house, and there was a sense of people running around and shouting. Not good. In a moment, someone would come into the kitchen and see his shocked, pale face looking in, and that would be that.

He extricated his foot from the planter, shook off dirt and bits of vegetable matter, and crept to the street side of the deck, which was full of blinking blue light and the squelch sounds of radio communications. Anatoly went over the other side, into the backyard of the shop next door.

Which was not a notable improvement. The yard was flagged and empty, and no matter where he tried to hide anyone looking out of the rear windows of Jessica's house, or over the wall at the end, would see him. There was a wooden staircase up to another deck, and he crept up this, went to the edge of the deck, and climbed over into the next yard.

In this way, he was able to work his way half a dozen buildings along from Jessica and Duncan's house. He paused in one yard that was choked with big discarded carboard boxes and cautiously approached the back wall. Beyond this ran an alleyway, into which, he knew, the inhabitants of the flats and shops wheeled their dustbins on certain days of the week for collection. He crouched at the base of the wall, barely breathing, and heard the crunch of stout boots pacing patiently back and forth on the other side. Someone tried the knob of the door which led out into the alley, but it was locked, and presently the footsteps moved away.

Looking back along the line of buildings, he saw the light come on in his bedroom. A figure appeared in the open window and leaned out. Anatoly withdrew further into the pile of boxes. An open window did not necessarily indicate that someone had escaped, but the spare bed had been slept in and his suitcase was still in the room, and it wouldn't take Sherlock Holmes to come to the correct conclusion. He was going to have company shortly.

Which was a problem. The next building along the row was a bank, and the wall around it was much taller than the others. He presumed its backyard was alarmed and surveilled, so he wasn't going that way. He couldn't go back. He'd have to chance the alleyway.

The figure in the window stepped back and disappeared, although the light remained on. Anatoly stood and jumped up. He managed to get his fingers over the top of the wall, and scrabbling with his feet on the brickwork he found enough purchase to haul himself up. One thing about Camden at two o'clock in the morning was that it wasn't quiet. The music venue on the other side of the

High Street was hosting some sort of retro-rave, and fast booming music mixed with the sounds of crowds of people on the street laughing and shouting and screaming. The noise of one out-of-condition Russian trying to climb over a wall was completely lost.

He paused a moment on top of the wall, breathing hard, then he dropped over the other side. Glancing both ways down the alley, he saw blue light blinking at either end. A little further along, another alley ran off from this one at a right-angle. Anatoly looked down it, didn't see anyone lurking, and set off away from the High Street.

The alley went quite a distance, and at the far end was another street. He paused and poked his head out, but he couldn't see any police cars or police officers, which to his Moscow sensibilities seemed impossibly sloppy. He crossed the road, headed up another side street, and another, and in this way, keeping the diminishing noise of the High Street at his back, he walked out of Camden.

By dawn, he was in Hampstead. Hampstead was not a good place to be. There were barriers across many of the streets, with signs proclaiming:

PRIVATE ROAD RESIDENTS ONLY
THIS AREA PATROLLED BY PRIVATE SECURITY

Anatoly wondered why the residents of Hampstead didn't just declare independence and put up border wire. That way, they probably wouldn't have needed quite so many black vans blazoned with the names of security contractors. The vans were everywhere, most of them with the shiny black cabouchons of cameras mounted on their roofs.

None of this was particularly unfamiliar to Anatoly. Moscow was a city of enclaves. The poorer ones preyed on each other; the wealthier were virtually fortified villages. Of course, this being England, there was a gruff sense of politeness about it all, but that didn't alter the fact that it was early morning, the streets of Hampstead were almost empty, and he was appearing on dozens of pieces of security footage.

There was nothing in his suitcase which would identify him personally. It only contained clothes, although they had labels from Russian stores, which would be suggestive to an investigator. The standard operating procedure would be to check the security cameras outside nearby bars and restaurants. One of them would have footage of him standing at Jessica's door, ringing the bell. If they got a clear enough grab of his face, it was just a matter of setting a facial recognition algorithm loose on the street cameras of Camden and the Underground and eventually they'd track him back to St Pancras, emerging from the Eurostar, and shortly after consulting passport control they would know everything about him, from his name and address to his inside leg measurement and his streaming video preferences.

Not far from Hampstead Underground station, a Caffé Nero was open for early-morning commuters. He went in, bought an Americano and a toasted ham and cheese sandwich, and sat as far from the windows as possible.

His feet hurt and he was exhausted and hungry. His shoes were scuffed and the palms of his hands grazed from climbing over the wall in Camden, and there was a tear in the knee of his trousers. On the plus side, he had his passport, his pad and his phone, as well as around two hundred pounds in sterling and a wad of roubles in an inside pocket of his coat. Granted, the roubles were worthless anywhere west of St Petersburg – and not, if one was to be honest, worth all that much to the east – but there was a certain psychological comfort in having a large amount of banknotes. And if things got very bad he could always make a fire with them.

He took a swallow of coffee and looked around the café. There were about half a dozen people sitting at tables with their pads or having phone conversations, another four at the counter queuing for coffee to go. Everyone, including the baristas, seemed half-awake and inattentive, apart from the tall woman who was in the queue at the counter. She had brown hair touched with grey, and wore an ankle-length brown coat and round-lensed spectacles. A denim rucksack was slung over her shoulder, and her body language conveyed a sense of relaxed alertness which was quite absent in the other people in the café. Anatoly had seen this before, in Moscow, in the very best security operatives. He let himself settle further into the depths of his coat and concentrated on his lukewarm toasted sandwich.

The woman got her coffee, and a Danish in a paper bag, and she turned to go, but at the last moment she glanced around the café. In his peripheral vision, Anatoly saw her face break into a big beaming grin, and he watched in horror as she came over, put her coffee and Danish on the table, and sat down across from him.

"Hi," she said conversationally. "Didn't expect to see you here at this time of the morning. Working early?"

Anatoly made a noncommittal sound.

The woman smiled. "Hey, me too," she said. She had a nice voice, and an American accent, which was confusing. "I'm parked across the road. Want a lift?"

Anatoly's eyes widened.

"Sure you do," said the woman cheerfully. "I'll drop you outside the office." She got up. "Come on, then."

Anatoly sat where he was, heart racing.

She shrugged. "Suit yourself." She bent down to pick up her coffee and Danish, which put her head quite close to his, and as she did so she said very quietly and in a very serious voice, "You only get this one chance. You'll be in the bag by lunchtime."

He watched her walk away towards the door, his mind a perfect blank. He stood up, stepped around the table, and said, "That's very kind of you," in a voice he knew was much too loud.

It stopped the woman, though. She opened the door and turned to look at him and said amiably, "Come on, then, asshole."

There was an anonymous grey hydrogen-cell Accord parked on the other side of the street. As they crossed, the woman blipped the doors open. They got in, belted up, the woman started the engine and pulled out into the traffic.

"Right," she said in a matter-of-fact tone of voice. "First things first. You can call me Roxanne."

"That's not your real name," he said in a weak voice.

"No, it's not. But if you're going to use a false name, it might as well be a cool one."

"Is Roxanne a cool name?"

She shrugged. "Cyrano de Bergerac thought so."

For Anatoly, the whole situation was taking on the logic of a nightmare. "Are you State Security?"

"I'm a Coureur des Bois," she said, and this was enough to get him to glance at her. "I've been keeping an eye on your friends the Goughs for a couple of months now."

"Why?"

"Because they asked me to. He did, anyway. Duncan. He thought they might need to be jumped out of there in a hurry." At the top of the high street, she waited at a set of traffic lights before moving off again. "I told him they should have left weeks ago, but he wouldn't listen."

"I'm confused," he said.

Roxanne chuckled. "Welcome to my world, sunshine."

"Am I being arrested?"

"No," she said patiently. "You are being *rescued*."

"Why?"

"I beg your pardon?"

In his soul, he was still expecting this drive to end at the gates of a police station. He should have stayed in the café and taken his chances; at least then he wouldn't have been trapped in a car. "Why rescue me? I'm nobody to you."

She sighed. "Because it's what I do. The halt and the lame. Friend of the insane; Straight Arrow is my name. That's from an old song."

Actually, the prospect of police was becoming increasingly attractive the longer he spent in her company. "Perhaps you should just let me out of the car," he said.

Roxanne took a while to answer. They drove down past Golders Green station, made a right around the clocktower and onto the Finchley Road. This was roughly the northern edge of Anatoly's familiarity with London – Jessica had taken him to visit an aged aunt in Golders Green, although he couldn't remember precisely where. Everything beyond this was unknown territory, although he suspected that the further he was from the centre of London the better.

Finally, she said, "Facial recognition isn't perfect. It gives as many false negatives as it does false positives, so you're just as likely to be passed over as you are to find yourself in a room with a bunch of other guys who look suspiciously like you." She stopped at a pedestrian crossing to let an extremely aged man wearing a long black coat and a *shtreimel* make his way painfully slowly across the road. "But it works just well *enough* for law enforcement to keep using it, even when you take into account all the cameras that are down for maintenance or just plain broken. Which means, seriously, the people who arrested the Goughs were going to find you sooner or later." The old man had finally made the opposite pavement, and she put the car into gear and moved off again.

"And now I'm in your car," he said. "Which I assume they can track just as easily."

"You'd be surprised how many silver-grey Accords there are in London," she told him. "And this one's got a couple of optional extras that make it hard to track. Coureurs are sneaky like that."

"But the cameras in the café will have seen you talking to me. They'll have seen us leaving together, and then the traffic cameras will have seen me getting into the car with you. So now you're under surveillance too."

She glanced appreciatively at him. "That's a Russian accent, no? Is everyone there as aware as you are?"

He didn't feel inclined to explain his family circumstances to her, so he just shrugged.

They had reached an intersection which would probably have looked insane to anyone who had not used the Garden Ring at rush-hour. Roxanne joined the queue of traffic and said, "Well, I'm *already* under surveillance, for reasons which you don't need to worry about, so you'd be a person of interest even if you were completely innocent."

"I *am* completely innocent."

She snorted. "Dude."

"Really," he said, sounding unconvincing even to himself. "I am."

"Sure," she said, putting the car in gear again. "Sure you are."

They drove a short distance to a busy shopping street, off which Roxanne turned into a maze of leafy residential roads, eventually pulling up outside an anonymous-looking detached house.

"Here we are," she said. "Get out of the car and go to the door, and for Christ's sake try not to look conspicuous."

That was harder than it sounded, but he managed to get inside without falling over his own feet or a squad of policemen suddenly erupting from the shrubbery. He stood in the wood-floored hallway while Roxanne closed and locked the door, and then all of a sudden his legs turned to water and he staggered through the nearest doorway into what turned out to be the living room, and without really registering anything about it he collapsed on a sofa.

Roxanne stood in the doorway and regarded him critically. "Okay," she said. "You have a little rest. I'm going to make some calls. Then we're going to have a little chat."

He thought, at a pinch, he might be able to take her in a fight, but he wasn't certain – she had the rangy look of someone who knew how to hurt other people with the minimum of effort, and the attitude of someone whose conscience wouldn't bother her too much if she did – and he was footsore and exhausted and the adrenaline of his escape was a distant memory. He just about had the energy to nod, and she went elsewhere in the house.

He woke up some time later, unaware of having fallen asleep. For a moment, he didn't know where he was. Then he saw Roxanne standing in front of him holding two ceramic mugs and the memories filled themselves in.

She held one of the mugs out to him. "I don't take milk," she told him. "So there isn't any in the house."

He took the mug, inhaled coffee fumes. "Black is good," he said. He took a sip; it was sweet, and strong enough to make his nervous system sit up and take notice. He blinked. "I should thank you," he said. "For helping me."

"You should." She went and sat in an armchair on the other side of the room. "So. Maybe you should start by telling me who you are and what the fuck you were doing at the Goughs' last night."

"If I do, will you tell me what's going on?"

"If you don't I'll drive you somewhere and leave you at the side of the road to fend for yourself." She drank some coffee and regarded him over the rim of her mug.

Fair enough. He told her his story, from learning that a period away from Moscow was desirable, to their meeting in the café in Hampstead this morning, with a ten-minute digression to fill her in about the history of his relationship with Jessica. She didn't nod along, didn't interrupt asking for clarifications. She just watched him calmly.

When he'd finished, she was quiet for a while. She sat looking towards the net-curtained windows. Finally, she said, "You took a roundabout route to get here."

"A trip to Warsaw to see my Polish publisher was perfectly reasonable," he told her. "It was thought it would be easier for me to make a run for it from there than from Moscow."

"But why didn't you just get on a plane and *fly*?"

"I have a phobia," he said with as much dignity as he could muster. She deadpanned him and he covered his embarrassment by saying, "What are *you* doing here?"

She thought about that for a while, either getting her story straight or just trying to decide whether to tell him at all, he couldn't tell. "I've been tasked with jumping Duncan Gough and his wife out of England," she told him finally. "But he didn't want to go yet. Said he was waiting for something, but he wouldn't say what it was. I thought for a while last night it might have been you, but you sound like a bystander."

Anatoly sighed and took a mouthful of lukewarm coffee.

"It gave me time for some prep, anyway," she went on. "Which you don't always get. I rented a flat with a view of the back of the Goughs' place, to keep an eye on them. I was there last night when all hell broke loose and you went out the window. It was obvious they were in the bag and I couldn't do anything for them, so I followed you."

He hadn't noticed a car tailing him, and yet there her Accord had been, parked across the road from the Caffé Nero in Hampstead with its sneaky optional extras.

"The operational thing – the *smart* thing – for me to do is to get the hell out of here," she said. "But here I am, listening to your fascinating little story about annoying the *mafiye* and having to hightail it out of town. By train. Because you're afraid of flying."

"I'm not afraid," he said. "It's a phobia."

She tipped her head to one side and looked at him. "Hm," she said. "Well, what do *you* suggest we do?"

"Me?" he said, surprised. "I'm still processing the fact that I'm not on a train any more, someone who once said she would always love me unconditionally refused to help me last night, I've barely avoided arrest by the English Secret Police, my luggage is still in Camden, and I *really want to sleep.*"

She thought about all that. "So," she said. "You're no use, then."

"Yes," he said, starting to get angry now. "I'm no use. This thing has nothing to do with me."

"Are you sure?"

"What?"

"Maybe the police were there on behalf of your playmates in Moscow. Maybe it was nothing to do with the Goughs."

That actually made him laugh, the thought of the English police cooperating with Russian interests. "No," he said.

"Okay." She finished her coffee, scowled at the mug, set it aside. "Well, what are we going to do with you?"

"I need to get out of here," he said. "The police will never believe I'm not mixed up with whatever Jessica and Duncan were doing."

She nodded. "I can see that happening."

"Perhaps we can go to the Community. I'm told they're giving asylum to Europeans."

To his surprise, she burst out laughing. The Community was a topological freak, the England of *Goodbye, Mister Chips* written invisibly across Europe and only accessible via certain border crossings. There were two trains a day out of Moscow, trans-Continental expresses bound for Władysław, the Community's

116

capital. "They're giving asylum to the *English*," Roxanne said when she had her laughter under control. "They don't want *foreigners* there." She shook her head. "There's only the train from Paddington to Stanhurst, and border control's tight at both ends. If somebody was looking for you, that's one of the places they'd be looking." She stood up. "No, you'd better forget about the Community, Anatoly Fedorovich." She looked at the clock on her phone. "Okay, it's half-eight. That's rush hour at Finchley Central just up the road, but we're not going anywhere near the Tube because cameras." She looked hm over. "You'll have to change your clothes. If you look upstairs there should be something that'll fit you. I'm going to have another coffee. Be ready to go in a half-hour, okay?"

He sat where he was, watching her go into the kitchen, trying to will his mind and his spirit to catch up. He had not been tailed by any vehicle; he'd been careful to check that. True, she could have phoned someone when he finally went to ground in the café and had them bring her car to Hampstead – it was only a short drive from Camden. But he hadn't told her his patronymic.

They called themselves *Coureurs des Bois*, and they delivered mail across the ever-changing and multiplying borders of autumnal Europe. Sometimes what they delivered occupied certain legal grey areas, from nation to nation. Sometimes what they delivered was people who occupied some of those same grey areas. Most of the entertainment channels had Coureur shows, although they were starting to look a bit old-fashioned with their dead-drops and midnight border crossings. Coureur novels had been popular for a season or so in Moscow, but the government disapproved of such things and they, and their authors, had quietly withered.

What none of these entertainments featured, if his memory served him correctly, was an interminable walk through north London woodland in the company of a rather fierce American woman. And he was certain that none of them had mentioned that the protagonists' feet hurt all the time.

They left the house, walked down the road, down another road, down another, all the time going downhill, until they reached a wooded area through which a well-trodden path wound away into the trees. Anatoly could see a dog walker in the distance, wrestling to keep half a dozen dogs under control, but apart from that they had the path to themselves.

"Why did Duncan and Jessica want to leave England?" he asked as they walked.

"Don't know, don't care," she said. "None of my business; I'm just paid to move Packages, not to know what's in them or why they're being moved."

"Isn't that a bit… *cavalier?*"

She glanced at him. "I did have time to do some homework, though, and it turns out that Jessica Gough works for English counterintelligence."

He stopped. "What?"

Roxanne walked on a few steps, turned and looked back at him. "She works for the Security Service. MI5. Recruited at university."

He felt an abyss open in front of him. "That's absurd," he said. "How can you possibly know something like that?"

She sighed. "I'm not going to show you my working-out," she said. "But I'm really pissed off. The whole point of the Coureurs is that we're impartial. We just move things across borders, for anyone. You start doing spy stuff, you wind up taking sides, and pretty soon nobody trusts you and business dries up." She shook her head sourly. "And it's just a world of grief anyway. I got mixed up in something in Hungary a few years ago; I wound up basically getting out of there in my socks. I never did find out what it was about but it felt like espionage, looking back. I'm not doing that again."

His brain was not remotely large enough to process the implications of this. He said, "That's absurd," again, but there was no conviction in his voice.

She walked back until she was standing almost toe-to-toe with him. "Listen," she said quietly, looking him in the eye, "this is a nice patch of woods and there are no surveillance cameras and only the squirrels can hear us, but we are on the run and if you just stand there with your thumb in your mouth someone will notice you. They won't notice me, because I'll be several miles away by then."

He stared at her. "Where are we going?"

"We're going somewhere we can talk," she told him. "Somewhere you can tell me what the fuck is going on."

A brief season of truck bombs – one had blown the frontage off Charing Cross Station and another had shattered half the windows in Whitehall and left a three-metre-deep crater in the road outside the Ministry of Defence – had led to a previous generation's Ring of Steel being retooled as the Maze of Steel, a warren of one-way systems and blocked streets all looked over by checkpoints and cameras. Other streets had been pedestrianised, to the chagrin of cabbies and delivery drivers alike.

No one had claimed responsibility for the bombings and no suspects were ever identified – which was remarkable in itself, and, some mused, suggestive – but the government had used them as a pretext to put England's Muslim community even further under the cosh. A programme of repatriations – a much more positive term than 'deportation' – sent third and fourth generation Iraqis and Syrians to countries which barely functioned as countries and which they had only ever seen on the news. People of Libyan descent committed suicide rather than be sent back there. It was all in violation of more human rights acts than anyone could count, and Rus rather charmingly led the chorus of voices in the United Nations calling for England to be made an international pariah. England, being England, simply put two fingers up. Do your worst, Johnny Foreigner. Keep your unelected nose out of our business.

The problem with whipping up international outrage was that most of Europe was in the same boat. The nations of the north had hardened their borders decades before the Xian Flu had swept across the Continent like a napalm strike on a flowerbed. They had turned the impoverished nations of the south into a firebreak between them and the impossible chaos in Africa and the Middle East. It was rare for states to worry about appearing hypocritical, but it tended to make a consensus on the Security Council more difficult.

Some years after the Maze of Steel, because paranoia never stands still, came the London Control Zone. In all but name,

London declared itself a separate nation, with a border that to the north and west and east ran along the M25. Southward, though, the River was deemed a handy frontier, its bridges ready-made for checkpoints. South London was left to fend for itself, but that was nothing new; it had been regarded as Bandit Country as far back as Shakespeare. The regeneration of the South Bank was allowed to wither and die, except in Battersea where a dense development of flats for the ultra-wealthy had sprung up around the Borg Cube, the heavily-fortified American Embassy. Here, the Control Zone extended a pseudopod a mile or so across the Thames, so that the Americans and their neighbours could feel safe from the seething unwashed masses, who in their turn looked on the whole thing with a mixture of bafflement and resentment that would have been familiar to any South Londoner since before the turn of the century.

This all made perfect sense to Anatoly, whose home city had been divided and divided again between those who had and those who had not and those who had a little and those who wanted more. At least here the Metropolitan Police presented an appearance of trying to keep order; in Moscow it was not unknown for one enclave's security contractors to go to war with their neighbours. But none of it helped him escape.

Dollis Valley, it turned out, went a surprisingly long way, particularly for someone like Anatoly, for whom lack of sleep and sore feet were becoming a very real issue. Sometimes the path ran through woodland, sometimes across open green spaces, sometimes along suburban streets, but they finally emerged onto a main road at the bottom of a hill. A little further up the hill, Anatoly could see a parade of shops and a small brick building with a London Underground sign on it.

"Totteridge and Whetstone," Roxanne said, leading the way a short distance to a line of parked cars. "I love the names of their outer London Tube stations. 'Cockfosters'. Where the fuck did they get *that* one from?" Anatoly could make no useful contribution to this question. Roxanne held up a key fob and pressed the button, and the lights blinked on a car near the head of the line. "Get in," she said.

There followed a two-hour tour of some of London's least-interesting sights, a seemingly never-ending procession of sidestreets and shabby shops which wound to an end in a confusing maze of streets somewhere to the east of central London. Roxanne parked the car in a scrapyard – broken vehicles stacked three and four high waiting for their turn in the enormous industrial shredder at the centre of the yard – and they walked out via a side gate, through a set of railway arches, and to another house, this one much older and in much worse condition than the one in Finchley. It was dark and smelled of mould and cat pee and old people, but Anatoly was far past caring.

Roxanne did not seem inclined to let him rest, though. She sat him down on a rickety chair in the kitchen, gave him a cup of coffee, and said, "So."

Anatoly looked around him. Every surface in the kitchen seemed to be coated in grease. The top of the table at which he sat was sticky. The ancient gas cooker was in a disgusting state, and the refrigerator was spotted with rust. He said, "This is horrible."

"Oh, I'm so sorry," she said. "All the safe houses in Chelsea were booked up."

"Is this safe?"

Roxanne looked at the clock on her phone. "We'll have to move again when it gets dark, but it's as safe as anywhere right now."

This was not terribly reassuring. "I'm very tired," he said.

"Too bad." She pulled up another chair and sat on the other side of the table. "You're a hood, aren't you."

"I'm sorry?" The term was genuinely unfamiliar to him.

"I knew you were handy when I saw you go out that window last night," she said. "Your average flabby Russian writer would have broken his neck just getting over the windowsill, but that was a neat piece of escape and evasion. Not too shabby."

"Oh," he said. "That."

"Yes," she said. "That."

There seemed no point in denying it. Quite how she had managed to get so far ahead of him, he didn't know. She clearly had access to sources of information which the Aunts, all of whom were graduates of the FSB and GRU and their many successor agencies, would have coveted.

He said, "Duncan Gough was in Moscow last year, and he took something while he was there. I don't know what it was. I was supposed to... *negotiate* for its return."

"Make him an offer he couldn't refuse." Her face and voice were hard.

"The people who sent me saw no reason to pay for the return of something which already belonged to them."

"And the fact that you were his wife's ex couldn't hurt."

"It was enough to get me close to him to have a conversation. But I never got the chance. He and Jessica were worried about something, Jessica more so than him."

"And all that stuff about pissing somebody off in Moscow and having to skip town, that was all part of the legend."

He nodded.

Roxanne sighed. "Well, I have some bad news for you, sunshine. You've been played. Duncan Gough wasn't in Moscow last year. He hasn't left the country in at least three years."

He blinked at her, but in all honesty it wasn't much of a surprise, given what had happened to him over the past few hours.

"So, that being so, he couldn't have stolen anything in Moscow last year, could he."

He thought of the conversation with his father, the one where his mission had been laid out for him. He said, "That was what I was told."

She nodded. "And I believe you. But I figure you were sent here for another reason."

He scowled as if there was a sudden pain in his head.

"My guess is that you were sent to set off a reaction, to make people panic."

"That seems very unlikely."

"You'd be surprised. You find out all kinds of interesting stuff when people panic. They tend to protect things that are *really* important to them. That can be instructive." She took a drink of coffee and said, "You had no idea Jessica worked for Intelligence?"

He shook his head. "It's ridiculous. She visited *Moscow*." He thought of her meeting the Colonel, of her Lost Weekend with the Aunts, and his misery only deepened as he surveyed the awful abyss of possibilities opening up before him. "They wouldn't let her do that if she was working for MI5."

She made a face which suggested she wasn't convinced about this. "My guess is that you meeting her at that party the first time you were here wasn't an accident."

"How can you possibly know all this?"

"I know this," she said crisply, "because I do my *homework*. You should try it sometime, instead of just doing what you're told."

Anatoly felt his head sinking between his shoulders, a defensive attitude from childhood.

"Maybe they were just checking you out, maybe they were making a live run at you, I don't know," she went on. "Did she ever try to recruit you?"

"I was supposed to be recruiting *her*."

Roxanne's eyes widened. "Oh." She thought about it, and said, "Oh," again. Then she gave him a hard stare and shook her head. "That's actually quite funny, if you think about it, the two of you taking a run at each other and neither of you realising it."

"I don't think it's the least bit funny."

"What did I tell you? Espionage. A world of grief. What happened?"

What had happened was that the Aunts had identified an up-and-coming future member of the English Civil Service and fancied adding her to their collection, more as a thought exercise than anything else, and since Anatoly was in London anyway they had asked him to do this little favour and make an approach. What had happened was that Anatoly had fallen in love instead, and had returned to Moscow with the story that his advances had been rebuffed. He didn't think the old women, who looked like the *babushkas* you saw running fast-food vans on the streets of Moscow but were actually still recreationally destabilising governments in southeast Asia, believed him, but not every operation bore fruit and he was, after all, family. So they'd let it drop. Or maybe they'd known all along that Jessica was MI5 and were content to let the relationship continue, just to see how things worked out.

The way things worked out, Jessica had visited Moscow and the Aunts had spirited her away for a whole weekend. He wondered what kind of game everyone had been playing, and why none of them had ever thought to tell him about it.

There were obviously many issues he was going to have to resolve, mostly involving betrayal, but they would have to wait. He said, "She never tried to recruit me." Like a drowning man he clung onto the possibility that she had done what he had done, told her handlers that she had failed. Because she loved him.

He remembered his father's solemn briefing in the old man's study at home in Balashikha. The two halves of his family had always remained separate – on the one side his father's career in Intelligence, on the other the more wild and esoteric interests of the Aunts – but sometimes they got in each other's way. Had the Aunts really had something going on with Jessica?

If Jessica *had* been working for the Aunts, it could only have been with the knowledge of MI5; English Intelligence wouldn't have let her anywhere near them otherwise. All of a sudden he had a picture of them all actually recruiting *each other* in some mutually beneficial decade-long operation the details of which he was too far down the food chain to be informed of. He had a picture of this operation eventually getting in the way of his father's interests, and his father sending him here to spoil that. Sowing discord in the English intelligence *apparat* was a long-established pastime with his people.

"Families," he said half to himself.

"What?"

"Nothing." He shook his head, imagining the next family dinner, the Aunts berating his father for what he had done, his father sitting there like a rock, absorbing it all. And then they would all go off and embark on their next game. "Did they know?" he asked, thinking of how Jessica had tried to get rid of him. "Jessica and Duncan?"

Roxanne shrugged. "No idea. My *suspicion* is that they were manoeuvred into a position where they felt they had no choice but to make a run for it, and then someone told them to bide their time.

Then you wandered into the picture. Jessica's ex, son of a famous father. It wouldn't have taken much to convince people that you were her handler, come to facilitate her escape."

"That would be a horrendous breach of tradecraft."

"It didn't have to be true, Anatoly Fedorovich," she said. "Just so long as *somebody* believed it. Bells ring, everyone loses their shit, someone moves in and sweeps up the pieces. Anyway, I'm kind of wondering here why I'm bothering to help you," she said. "All you have to do is walk into the Embassy and you're home free. Of course, you have to *get* to the Embassy, but that's your problem, not mine."

"It's not that easy," he said, the endless Byzantine possibilities of the thing he had become involved in cartwheeling through his mind. Whose side, at this precise moment, was he actually on? Was he part of the Aunts' operation, or his father's? Both? Neither? "The intelligence community in Moscow is not one single entity; it's more of a landscape of warring nations. There are... territorial issues."

Again that hard stare. "You must have had a fallback, another dust-off."

"The Trade Delegation in Highgate," he told her. "I was on my way there when I met you. I was told it was safe territory in an emergency, but if what you say is true, I don't know any more. I could be arrested the moment I step through the door."

"And there are those who would say serve you fucking well right," she said. She shook her head and held her phone up. "Look at me."

"What?"

She took a fast half-dozen shots of him, then scanned his retinas and fingerprints. "You're going to need new papers," she said, sending the data to someone.

"So you're going to help me? I can't pay you."

"You might be a hood, Anatoly Fedorovich, but it looks to me like someone – possibly *everyone* – has thrown you under a bus, and that offends me."

"Also, I know things which have a certain monetary value."

"There is that too," she agreed, consulting her phone one last time before putting it away. "*Les Coureurs* are not a nation. You can't defect to us. All I can do is take you from one place to another; you'll have to do the rest. If you want to pimp yourself out to the highest bidder, that's your business."

"What about Jessica and Duncan?"

"What about them? They're in the bag. If you think I'm going to bust them out, you've been watching too many movies."

He rubbed his eyes, muttered a curse in Russian under his breath. He thought about the metaphor he'd used with Jessica, about walking on those Japanese floors that made the sound of birds. What if you deliberately sent someone down that corridor, just to see what happened in the room at the other end?

Roxanne got up from the table, took her mug over to the sink, rinsed it, and put it on the draining board. "Well," she said, "nothing's going to happen now for a little while. You go and get some sleep. You look dead on your feet."

He was, but he didn't think he'd be able to sleep. He was too wound up, and there was too much going on in his head.

"Hey."

Anatoly opened his eyes and experienced a moment of flat-out panic. He didn't know where he was. He didn't know who the woman who had just shaken him awake was. For a terrifying fraction of a second, he couldn't have said with any great certainty who *he* was. Then the bits started to fit together. He was in a bedroom at a house in east London. She was a Coureur. He was on the run.

He struggled upright. "What's happened?"

"Time to go," she said.

He glanced at the curtains, made out the halo of a streetlight shining through them. Apparently he had slept, after all, but it hadn't done him any good. He felt awful. "How long...?"

"Eight hours."

Downstairs in the kitchen, there was tea and a styrofoam container which turned out to contain a kebab. Roxanne had already eaten; there was another, empty container on the table. Anatoly hadn't eaten since around this time last night, and he barely paused to taste the kebab. Roxanne watched him wash it down with a couple of mugs of tea, then she held out a little dark-blue booklet. This turned out to be a Scottish passport in the name of Imre Kovacs and inside it had one of the photographs Roxanne had taken of his somewhat flustered and exhausted face in the kitchen earlier, although its background had been altered so it looked as if he had been sitting in front of a grey backcloth.

"Kovacs is a Hungarian name," he said. "I don't speak Hungarian."

"Nobody's going to ask you to," she said. "You've got an accent and there isn't time to do anything about that, so you'll just have to be Hungarian. Nobody will know the difference."

"What about a legend? I don't know anything about Scotland. Where do I live?"

She gave him a level look. "If it gets to the point where someone's asking you those kind of questions, it'll mean they've already rumbled you. That passport's the best I could do in a hurry, but it won't stand up to serious scrutiny."

"What's the point of having it, then?" he said.

She looked at him a moment longer, then said, "Use the bathroom. Wash your face and comb your hair. Be ready to go in five minutes."

It occurred to him that this was the third car he'd been in today. And then it occurred to him that it was still today, less than twenty-four hours since he had gone out of the window in Camden, before what had seemed a perfectly straightforward mission – more of an errand, really – had turned into a nightmare.

It wasn't clear precisely where Roxanne was getting all the vehicles from. She seemed to just walk down a street and there they were, waiting for her. This one, an ancient and rackety Nissan, had been parked two streets away from the safe house.

He had no idea where they were going, and Roxanne seemed unwilling to talk all of a sudden, so he sat and watched night-time London pass by outside the windows. Everything seemed peaceful –

Roxanne mostly stuck to residential streets where there was less chance of there being traffic cameras – and it felt strange to think that somewhere out there people were looking for him.

Gradually, they left the city behind. Anatoly got the impression of fields beyond hedges. Finally, Roxanne turned the car onto a narrow, bumpy road that ended in a chain-link gate. She drove a short distance off the road into a stand of trees, stopped, and turned off the engine. "Do what I tell you and try not to make a lot of noise," she said, opening her door.

It was very quiet. The night was cool, and he smelled trees and damp earth and manure. A fingernail of moon rode in and out of the clouds, and by its light Anatoly could see Roxanne unlocking the gate. They slipped through, and she locked up behind them.

Anatoly found himself walking along the edge of what felt, underfoot, like someone's lawn, which was confusing until the clouds parted and he saw a few metres away a pale circular dip in the ground, and another just beyond it.

"Is this a *golf course?*" he said.

"Quiet," she said, in a voice that barely carried across the distance between them.

They came across a small stream that ran across a corner of the golf course. Roxanne led the way down the banks and into the stream bed, and they followed this for quite a distance. At two points, the stream ran through low culverts under roads, then it angled towards a high embankment and finally disappeared into a larger tunnel whose entrance was blocked by a gate of metal bars. Roxanne unlocked the gate, locked it behind them, and they walked through the tunnel to another gate at the far end.

On the other side of the embankment, they followed the stream for another few minutes, then left it and spent an hour or so walking along the edge of fields until they came to a path. The path suddenly came out on a little street and of course there was a car waiting for them and they got in and drove away. It was only some time later, when they passed a sign for Welwyn Garden City, that Anatoly realised they were outside the Control Zone.

October 17. The clerk Imre Kovacs alighted from a tram in the centre of Edinburgh and joined the morning crowds of shoppers and workers and tourists on Princes Street. He was wearing a cheap suit and his shoes pinched, but anyone sparing him more than a passing glance would have said that he was viewing the new day with a certain optimism.

This could not be said of everyone on the street this morning. Even this long after Independence, Scotland's status as a sovereign nation was still precarious, its economy constantly stuttering and at the beck and call of foreign investors and trading partners. None of this, though, touched Mr Kovacs. He had a small but comfortable flat and a small but comfortable job and he was learning to like the Scots in general and the people of Edinburgh in particular. He made a point of avoiding the city's small Hungarian ex-pat community.

His small but comfortable job was in an office in a building not far from Princes Street, an outstation of Scotland's rather brisk and straightforward tax system with responsibility for the Highlands and Islands. It wasn't a difficult job – not much more than data entry – but his supervisor frequently reminded him of its importance. And it *was* important, in its small way, but perhaps not in quite the way she meant.

The office was on the third floor, and his desk was by a window which looked out onto a little car park, but he didn't mind. He exchanged good mornings with his colleagues, sat down, and booted up his desktop. The data system was at least a decade out of date and sometimes it glitched and then everyone decamped to the café round the corner while IT support made its way from Head Office to turn everything off and back on again, but this morning everything seemed to be working fine, and Mr Kovacs logged in and called up the documents he had been working on the previous afternoon.

All in all, it was not such a bad life. He had proper papers now, a real passport and residence documents, employment records, all diligently backstopped. The Hungarian thing still nagged at him. He presumed there was a good reason for it, but he couldn't think what it might be. Maybe he would find out one day, maybe not.

In his spare time, of which there was much, he used anonymisers and kept his ear to the ground, looking for a sign that he was forgiven and could go home. He had found a terse message from his father on an obscure bulletin board, and a rather more emotional one from the Aunts, and since then nothing, and from these he gathered he was in Scotland for the foreseeable future. It seemed he had somehow contrived to wreck both their schemes, although it was hard for him to work out how, unless he had been *meant* to be arrested alongside Jessica and Duncan, and if that was the case then his family could do without him for a while longer.

In the meantime, there was the matter of Mr William Paterson, of the Isle of Mull. A large number of public records had been destroyed during the brief period of civil unrest which accompanied Independence, and the Scottish bureaucracy was still catching up. Predictably, tax registration lagged a long way behind, despite repeated censuses and public information campaigns. The tax authority had been forced to do it the hard way, sending out a small army of inspectors to literally knock on every door in the country.

It was a slow process, a loophole which the people who had got him across the border and arranged his flat and his job regarded with some interest. The system, they saw, was geared to preventing evasion; it was not geared to preventing false data. He had been told that every now and again – and he wouldn't know when – the data he handled would belong to people who did not exist. All he had to do was input it – and he presumed other people like him were doing something similar elsewhere in the bureaucracy – and it would become part of a legend, the backstory of an imaginary person, waiting for someone to come along and inhabit it. His own legend had been constructed, painstakingly, official document by official document, in this way, and he thought there was a pleasing circularity in being put to work helping to create legends for others.

Which brought him to Mr Paterson, whose tax registration had arrived on his desk the day before yesterday. Mr Paterson was thirty years of age, a smallholder on the Isle of Mull, where he lived with his wife, Grace. Part of his registration was photo ID, a scanned passport photograph, and Mr Kovacs had sat and looked at this for a very long time. He was clean-shaven and brown-haired but Mr Kovacs was more or less certain he was Duncan Gough.

He had processed the registration just like all the others, but he had been thinking a lot since he saw the photograph. He had been thinking about how Roxanne's car had been waiting in Hampstead, how she had known all about him, how one way of spiriting someone away – if one had strong nerves – would be to stage an arrest of one's own. *Les Coureurs* preferred to remain covert, but every now and again they succumbed to an urge for the grand gesture. It seemed possible that everything he had seen and experienced since leaving Camden Underground on that evening in April had been a setup, and he and his family's schemes had simply marched unawares right through the middle of it. He had a suspicion – nothing more – that something quite profound had happened in London that night, while he had trudged from Camden to Hampstead, and there was a part of him – the intelligence officer, his father's son, his Aunts' nephew – which would have quite liked to know what it was.

Life was not a jolly short story; there was no omniscient narrator on hand to explain everything and fill in the gaps. One did the best one could with the information available. Still, he could go up to Mull – he was due some holiday – and visit Mr and Mrs Paterson, see if they would give him another piece of the picture.

And if life *were* a jolly short story, he might very well do that. If the past months had taught him anything, though, it was that some things are best left alone. So he mentally wished Mr and Mrs Paterson well, then put them out of his mind and carried on with his unexpected new life.

Something Went Wrong in Heaven

Geoff Ryman

Something went wrong in Heaven.

Well that's just what I think, but then I'm a grieving old man.

I live in the capital's blooming West End. We're over the various crises now. You see cranes everywhere. The new buildings look like paintings that have got the perspective wrong: sloping roofs, corners that meet at 30-degree angles. Walls are made of glass – every floor is visible, like an x-ray.

It dazzles. Blue Christmas lights around trees. Patterns of light sparkling on water move on television walls in boutique hotels. A bank beams a giant illuminated photograph of Tottenham Court Road in 1899.

Luxury is ordinary. Planet Organic stocks almond-and-coconut butter, oriental pickles, speciality tofus and Norfolk beetroot in stews. Patisserie Valerie offers coffee-caramel ice cream, Portuguese custard tarts, and fruit-glazed cake. Heals sells waste bins that cost forty or fifty pounds. Ikea has a drop-in design office for people needing a revitalized culinary environment.

The residents of the red brick mansion blocks change the flats' interiors like people sending back online fashion after wearing it once.

The new French resident tears out all the old floors to make Parisian-style parquet with throw rugs. He leaves after Brexit. The new Chinese owners tear out the refurbished kitchen and dining room, to replace the wood with tiles. The debris mounts up for collection. Parking bays are suspended for disposal trucks. People leave their cars on corners.

There's a flip side to the blooming West End.

Mr Topper's sells haircuts for eleven pounds, not sixty. Outside Patisserie Valerie some foreign beggar camps on the sidewalk, wishing us all a lovely day in gender-neutral tones. When the theatres close, a community of homeless sleep under their marquees.

About a month ago, a well-spoken young Englishwoman stopped me and said apologetically that she was really hungry and had no money. Could I go with her to the Subway on Tottenham Court Road and buy her a sandwich? Outside on the street, she lunged at it like a shark.

A handsome schizophrenic with a tangled mop of blond hair patrols the streets, shouting in a loud voice. He goes into Tesco, joins the queue at the till with rye crisps and tomatoes, and becomes violent if not allowed to have the food for free. The cowed women at the counter, most of them from Nigeria or Pakistan, know to act as if he has paid. He smells.

If like me, you are elderly and walk with a limp, you are a target.

Aggressive men regard you as chance to vent their rage. Your being there lands for them as justified anger for taking up space. 'Get out of the fucking way. Idiot.'

Three grinning goons crowd round you, out for a night on the town. 'Foreigner are ya? Lost are ya? You look a bit lost. Want us to help?' A young Asian man slams past and knocks your shopping bag from your grip. 'Big man,' he growls.

You are easier to block. 'Excuse me, sir, do you have a moment to talk about helping ....' Whatever cause. They don't want small change or even a tenner. They are after your credit card details so that you direct debit to the cause.

You try to look like a sweet old gent with a cheery grin. If you don't, your face will slump and you'll look angry, dotty or exhausted. You'd *love* to be polite but you are late for a grandchild's christening.

Big Issue salesmen cross the street, calling hello. Desperate older women clutch your sleeve. Once I looked down to find one of them meditatively fingering my jacket pocket, as if merely curious.

The truth is that even before the coronavirus, my disabled partner and I lived in social isolation. I was used to being accosted.

So when the next catastrophe began, I didn't notice anything out of the ordinary.

134

I'd just crossed Tottenham Court getting back from the Tesco.

A particularly worn, thin person intercepted me in the zebra crossing. They held out their arms as if for a hug, their mouth in a sideways twist.

For just a moment, I thought it might be someone I knew who'd fallen on hard times, maybe one of the old Montagu Square crowd.

Then they began to call a name. 'Tony. Tony. It's me.'

My name isn't Tony. I once worked in an office with two other Edwards, so everyone called me Bob for two years of my working life. But never Tony.

'Sorry mate, wrong Tony.' I tried to look twinkly, old and swift. I tried to hobble around the thing.

'Please? Please,' they said and started to sob. 'I don't know where I am. What is this place?'

This was not going be someone I could help. They kept pace with me, pinching my sleeve as if they were picking off lint. They wore gloves, woollen ones with no finger tips, as if they had to count change in the days before central heating. The fingernails were black with dirt. Their boots were heavy and rounded at the tops; their black coat had a huge high collar.

When I say there was a smell, please don't misunderstand me. It wasn't a body smell. It was acrid but acrid in a different way. It smelled like carbon steel after an enormous jolt of electricity. I tried to throw off their hand and finally looked into their eyes.

It wasn't a human face. All the constituent parts were there, but they were dead, hanging.

'Tony, don't leave me. Don't leave me here,' they sobbed.

'I'm not Tony!' I shouted. I wanted everyone around me to know that I'd been accosted, that I had done nothing to this person to make them weep, that I was the one in trouble.

They grabbed hold of my hand. Their grip was as feeble as a shadow, but searing cold, a cold like deep space, a cold that turns oxygen to snow.

I squawked and shoved, instinctively. The thing seemed to weigh nothing. I had the impression that its heels skidded on the damp pavement. Then it fell backwards.

'I'm sorry, I'm sorry,' I said to the winter faces looking at me. 'He wouldn't leave me alone.'

'First off, I think you'll find that it's a woman you've knocked over.' An unmoved, pudgy young woman frowned at me.

'She grabbed hold of me.'

'Wanted help did she? Frightened were you that you'd have to give up a pound coin?' She shook her head and turned to help, then looked blank.

There was no one there. Just wet glossy pavement.

I got back to our flat. It was roaring hot.

Alf feels the cold badly, but sometimes I can't breathe when we've had the heating up all day. He was in his chair by the window, a blanket over his knees. He doesn't like to wear trousers at home in case he has to make a break for the loo. It takes him five minutes to get there, so any extra time lowering the bumbags might make a crucial difference.

He wasn't alone. A sweet-faced young black man, lovely smile, everything else in circles, was talking to him in a London accent. I remembered: Alf had said someone was going to deliver his new glasses. Alf introduced me as his partner and the optician smiled. The optician was called Barnabas. I offered him tea.

Barnabas was mid-thirties at the oldest, trim and athletic-looking but old fashioned, his shirt tucked in, his leather shoes polished. For just a moment he looked like a traveller in time. Alf had the daffiest grin on his face and his eyes looked dazzled.

Barnabas slipped the glasses on. 'So are those firm for you, Professor Davies?'

'Very firm, thank you. But everything's looking rather bowed.' He flicked a complicit smile at me. Someone had a crush.

'That's because they're new glasses and you're wearing them with your old contact lenses. Let's see if the eyes adjust. If they don't we can get you new lenses.'

Alf looked like he was on a rollercoaster ride. He was always prone to sudden enthusiasms for handsome young men.

In the early seventies some of us were Marxists, some of us hippies, some of us obsessed with Bloomsbury. My first boyfriend Mark was the latter. He actually wore a straw boater and braces and most cringe-making of all, he cultivated a teddy bear. I realize now that part of his problem was that he'd been raised to go to Oxford, and had read *Brideshead Revisited*. Instead he had to settle for the University of Sussex and second-raters like me.

Duncan Grant had painted Mark's rear end. It was a very nice rear end, and it hung on Andrew's wall, in slightly strange shades of mushroom, purple and sunset orange. In those days if you were out and gay, you thought you had to behave in a certain way, and Andrew did. Pretty as he was, he liked taking bites out of people. 'You're good-looking, but ever so boring, aren't you?' was one of the last things he said to me.

Alf and I had met working on the uni literary magazine. We thought we were hippies. We wanted white rabbits on the cover. Someone much smarter than us said that art deco was coming in and insisted on a cover that looked like a barbershop pole with headlights.

We went to the student bar to plot against him; I got a bit drunk and told Alf that Mark and I had broken up. I wasn't stupid: I'd seen how Alf had looked at Mark – his eyes would wither and slightly cross, poised between desire and exasperation. To my surprise, Alf took my hand in his. 'I'm not sure he was nice enough for you,' he said.

Alfred in those days had long long hair. He wore a trench coat to the ground and a pair of old-lady wireframe glasses and had a weakness for embroidered waistcoats. 'The male of the species is always the most brightly coloured,' he'd say, a reassuring mix of the trendy and something absurd from 1910.

It was the radical student seventies. We couldn't get a branch of the Gay Liberation Front going at that hotbed of radicalism the University of Sussex. In Brighton there were little pubs which had dubious reputations, full of sour old men at the end of their theatrical careers. Brighton's gay pubs wouldn't allow GLF in either. So GLF met in straight pubs, nine or ten of us. We went to the 1971 national GLF convention. There were at most fifty people there. Here we are suddenly. Alf and I have been together fifty years. At the front door, I shook Barnabas's hand and thanked him. 'Take care of each other,' he said. How times have changed.

They're all dead now, our GLF friends.

Mark died years ago having turned into a bald banker. There were two cousins in our group. I had it off with the tall lanky one. He had asthma, and sex made him anxious. Since everything, let alone sex, made me anxious we had a lot in common, except conversation. Both of us were so wet we hardly had anything to say. Every time he got it up, he began to wheeze. But he was beautiful.

About thirty years later I was in bed with a plump, collapsed old gent who looked like a complete stranger. He'd grown up in Brighton, he said. There on his dresser was picture of him and his cousin, still lean and soft faced in 1972 wearing ridiculous clothes. (They looked like Slade.)

'Oh my God,' I said. 'We were in Brighton GLF together. Your cousin, what was his name?'

His cousin told me.

'Peter. Peter! Yes I think that's the name. How is he now?'

'Dead,' said his cousin. The way he said it left me in no doubt what Peter had died from.

In the photograph with them both is a young white man wearing shades and a fedora, which would have been a monstrous affectation in 1972. Like someone wearing flares and mutton-chop sideburns would be now. The boy's face was impassive, long nosed, tiny-mouthed. He thought he looked cool. I realized that I'd known him too, just one of the faces that pass regularly through your life for a time and then disappear.

'We all go into the dark,' said my partner for the evening. I saw him a couple of more times before his mind began to wander. Diabetes.

It had been a horrible winter, cold, and everyone was croupy.

I could see that Alf was able to do less and less almost every day.

If we did go out, it was all he could do to get down stairs and into a taxi. He would try to take his turn cooking, leaning one-handed on the cane until he drooped from exhaustion and I took over.

I began to face the fact that I wasn't going to have him for much longer.

So we took to having breakfast looking out over the Gardens, me with my little tape recorder.

We kept sharing little explosions of memory and I'd record them – I was going to say for posterity except that Alf and I have no posterity and nobody else will be interested.

But we'd keep cattle-prodding each other with blurts of remembrance.

He'd mention a long-forgotten friend of a friend.

'Woody!' I'd exclaim. 'Yes Woody.' He'd been about fifty-seven in 1976 but I'd fancied Woody something rotten. He'd been a park ranger.

'Ivan! Ivan the Terrible. I called him the Walking Death Instinct, remember? He was always so grim.'

'Well you'd be grim too if you were Freddie Scolis's male housekeeper and madly in love with him and he kept taking back every last queen from the Sombrero Club.'

Memories of going sailing with our friend George. Somehow George did not die of AIDS but from Krohn's Disease. Once we sailed his boat all the way along the east coast from Ipswich to his berth on the Medway. We'd put the boat under canvas and only then did George realize that he'd left his car keys back in Ipswich.

Weekends in London, we'd go to the Peg o' Wassail, which had a gay lunchtime on Sundays only. Or we'd go to the Rockingham, a tiny little passworded hideaway in a Soho basement. You could fit maybe thirty men into it, but I assumed that was about how many homosexuals there were in London.

Alf needed a garden. In 1978 we spent a lovely summer looking for a cottage in East Anglia. I kept hitting my head on low beams. We finally found a brick semi-detached in a field near Aldeburgh.

We'd walk to the Maltings at Snape every weekend, and go the festival there to hear Britten and friends. We'd walk our dogs along the river Alde. Once, we weathered a hurricane as trees fell and bashed each other to the ground.

When we went to the theatre visitors from the country would peer round their husband's stomach to get a glimpse of real London poofs. We picketed British Home Stores because they'd fired someone for being gay. He'd been seen on television in a gay picket line. I was then seen on television in a gay picket line, and I was fired too.

London was run down, like a cheerful seaside pier. Record shops were full of vinyl LPs with hippy covers. The only Virgin Records in London was near the corner of Oxford Street and Tottenham Court Road on the first floor over a shoe shop. It was one room with racks along three walls and another down the middle full of Nick Drake, Gentle Giant, Lindisfarne, and It's a Beautiful Day. The Virgin logo was a winged fairy woman on the back of leaping frog. We wanted a society of children.

You'd get posh areas right next to artisan-class apartments, next to immigrant tower blocks. The squatters on Drummond Street lived next to extended families of West-End workers. Boy George with his spray can lived in Warren Street. I met him in the Three Feathers and was entranced. He was beautiful and unnecessarily nice to someone who was already a boring old fart at 34. Decades later you could still see on university stone the ghost of his spray can: *Culture Club.* Anywhere east of Holborn got industrial. There was a printworks on High Holborn, a shoe factory just off Clerkenwell.

West on Charlotte Street was a greengrocers that smelled of apples and cabbages with nothing in plastic. One of the servers was a young guy with bubble curls who was a fan of the Clash. He had a huge toothy grin. There were three butcher shops on Goodge Street, with sawdust on the floor, and carcasses in the window. A shop down the mews sold Indian spices and rice in bulk.

The underground trains had wooden floors with slats for rain drainage, but they'd clog with cigarette butts. Everyone smoked on the trains and the air would be blue. The far end of the train would be misty like distant mountains. Our little gardens opposite grew wild behind pebble-dash pillars strung with wire mesh and no way to get it. Now it's black railings and a gate, access to residents only.

A few days after Barnabas had visited, Alf said, 'Rather more of them than usual.'

'More what?'

'Them. The Walking Dead.' That was our nickname for the homeless.

Our street is a backwater between two parallel thoroughfares. You sometimes got homeless people on the march to keep warm or to escape boredom. They shout at each other, harsh and angry and incomprehensible.

'My goodness, that one's in a bad way.'

Someone in a voluminous black dress and button-up boots was sitting down in the middle of the road.

'A bit early to be that drunk,' I said.

'It's never too early to be drunk,' said Alf, who'd taken up self-medication in a big way. 'Oh my goodness.'

The woman, if that's what it was, had lain out fully flat.

'We can't leave her there, someone might drive over her.'

I sipped my coffee.

Alf seemed to fight the chair he was sitting in. 'Well I can't go down can I?' He never complained but he was irascible.

'Every time you want to do something, I'm the one who has to go and do it.'

'Well fine, let someone drive over her. Maybe you'll do the same for me some time.'

He was a master of blackmail. 'All right, Alfie, all right.'

I was a master of bad grace. I found my shoes, found my coat, couldn't find my keys, and so asked Alfie where they were. 'Where you put them last, I expect.'

So I finally got downstairs and of course, when I got there, the woman was gone.

Blink and they aren't there.

She had been wearing an embroidered dress with mutton sleeves.

These days, the women walking past our window don't wear dresses; it's jeans or black leggings, white trainers or bovver boots.

Climbing back up the stairs, I felt old and weighted down. My Achilles tendon really hurt and I wished that I'd taken the lift.

'She was gone.' I told him. 'That's the second time this week. One of them acts strange, falls over and then just disappears.'

Alf whistled. 'Look at the state of this one, Teddy. It's not Halloween by any chance is it?'

Another one of them was staggering baffled and slack-jawed. Vapour poured out of its mouth, not in puffs of breath but continuously, as if from dry ice.

Something was awry. 'Turn on the news,' Alfie said.

The young don't watch TV we are told. They pass on the news via Twitter. Perhaps with good reason. There was no news item about a new fad, or a new drug, or another virus, nothing that could account for an influx of people in fancy dress who walked like disjointed puppets.

Just more news about the aftermath, or how the government was debating a special one-off 'Contribution Payment' to help the country balance the books.

Alfie refused to have anything to do with social media. I lack his clarity of purpose. I posted on Twitter and Facebook asking if anybody else was seeing some disturbing or odd people in the West End.

One friend, another fading Boomer texted, 'You've seen them too? I thought I was crazy.'

Someone I don't really know commented, 'Maybe if you offered them some help instead of judgement, you'd find out their story.'

Someone else said. 'We've ended austerity, but not austerity's effects. South Shields has the same thing.' And a photo of a hollow-eyed, confused person in a Butlins uniform.

'We're out of sherry,' said Alfie. 'Are you going out?'

'I just got back in.'

'No urgency. Just when you're going out.'

I sighed. 'I've got these bloody Guardian coupons. If I don't get to the shops before eleven there's no newspapers anyway. You can walk miles trying to find one. I'll go now.'

'Do you remember? You used to like the newsagent on Store Street. Nothing to do with the handsome Indian proprietor.'

'And the one on Tottenham Court Road? It even had Marvel comics. I felt very guilty, a grown man buying X-Men.'

'Not to mention Hill's on Goodge Street. They delivered. Delivered newspapers. At no extra cost. Unthinkable now.'

'They were rather hunky. The Hill brothers.'

'Them? Hunky! They were bald and spectacled.'

'They had muscles.'

'So do lady wrestlers but you don't fancy them. I hope.'

For a time in the 80s, there was also a cheese shop with a walk-in chill cabinet. And for a while there had been wonderful Harry.

Harry was an old Billingsgate hand in a long white jacket and tweed cap. Fishy water spilled down from the ice on his barrow and you could buy sea bass or mullet or whatever looked good that day. He knew our favourite fish, and saved them for us. Usually turbot. Then suddenly he stopped being there. I have no idea how many years ago.

To find a *Guardian* I had to walk quite far along Goodge Street right past Charlotte, and the old post office (*find* a post office these days, just try) all the way to where Charlotte magically turns into Wigmore Street. Just to get a paper.

It must have been the spring weather, bringing them out.

A young man, face as finely boned as a greyhound's, blocked my path. He wore an orange-and-yellow checked sports jacket with oddly padded shoulders. From a skip, probably. 'I'm sorry. I'm sorry. I was wondering if you could spare some change.' He looked in a bad way, so I dug into my pocket.

'I'm an actor really,' he said. 'I went to America for a while and came back. A bit difficult to get parts.'

Quite so. He stank and had no teeth. Well, blackened stumps. If I was wealthy I might have offered to help him pay for dental work.

I fished for change and, feeling generous, I passed him a two pound coin.

He stared at it as if he'd never seen one. Then he shook his head, gave a sick laugh and pushed it back into my hand. The coin was icy.

I turned to walk on, but there was a child by my elbow. My God, they tell us austerity is over. It obviously hasn't sunk in yet. The child was brown and tiny. I scanned for a mother to tell her off, for making her child beg. But I couldn't see her and it occurred to me this glowering, determined infant might actually be homeless. I passed him the freezing two pound coin, and tried to hobble away as fast as I could. I had the gait of farm threshing machine.

And then, holy Hannah, another child was trailing me, this one in rags looking like Peter Pan but with filthy hands and bare feet. I bobbled on. *Sorry, gave at the office.* The child howled and started to weep, broken hearted. I'd given money to one child but not to him.

A towering bobby in a blue coat and one of those tall hard hats I hadn't seen in decades, advanced on the child. 'You. Hop it. It's all right, sir, I'll make sure he leaves you in peace.'

I walked on and a man in a suit stepped in front of me. *My God, am I wearing a sign: stop this man?*

This one was wearing a pinstripe suit. Airily amused he said, 'Excuse me. I think I've misplaced a hospital.' He sounded ludicrously posh, like someone in the 1950s making fun of a Royal. 'You wouldn't believe it. But I can't find the Middlesex Hospital. It's where I work. It's gone.'

The Middlesex. Lovely huge old pile with murals and a chapel inside. Luxury flats now, has been for years. Though they managed to leave the chapel standing as a design feature.

How long had he been away? And how had he come back? His rigid collar had rounded tips. Had there been an escape from a lunatic asylum? I mean, lunatics might be hard to spot in the West End.

Even then I still really didn't get it.

The woman I'd seen lying down in our road was now stretched out on the pavement opposite the shoe repair shop. Alf had wanted me to go see to her, and Alf is a prince about anything important –

impossible about small things like table settings and music, but his sense of kindness is unerring.

I leant over her and asked, 'Are you all right?'

She was not wearing makeup. She seemed to have no eyebrows or eyelashes. She was pale, with blue veins in her translucent but freckled cheeks. Her lips were cracked and pale. Flowing red hair had escaped its winding about her head. She stared up, straight up, into the sky.

For some reason that made me look up too; and the sky was silvery, full of both light and cloud, some of it purple. Low white clouds raced past the purple like riders on horseback.

'Take me back,' she said, but not to me. 'Please take me back.'

Another woman huddled in a doorway of what used to be Nice Irma's Floating Carpet but is now a three pound pizza shop. She cowered under a shawl, sheltering three children with faces as sharp as saws.

What the bloody hell is going on?

I got my newspaper and I limped back, *The Guardian* pressed under my arm. It's getting thinner every issue. I hobbled towards Charlotte Mews, and standing there where he always used to be, who do you think I saw?

Harry.

In his white coat, with the barrow, and it was running with ice water. I have to say, the fish did smell a bit off.

'Harry. Harry is that you?'

"Hello, guv. Yeah, I've been back a while. Moved the bloody market haven't they? Billingsgate! It's not there. Well I know I been off work for a while, but not that long.' He gave a smoker's chesty laugh. 'Sorry the merchandise isn't up to my usual standard.'

'Let me have a look. The Prof will be thrilled. Some of your lovely fish.'

'I wouldn't let you buy it, guv. For the punters maybe, but not you. But how is the Prof, is he still with us?' His grin looked a bit sideways. 'Haven't seen him around.'

'Well, he's... to be honest Harry, he can't get about much these days.'

'Well I always warned him. All that cycling can't be good for you.'

'How are *you* Harry? We thought maybe you'd been ill.'

'Oh I was, I was, but that's all over now. I'm here. Right back where I belong. It's lovely to see you, after all this time.'

His eyes were misty, and there was something forlorn about him.

I wanted him to have a home, a place to be. 'You had a daughter I remember, a grown up daughter. Are you staying with her?'

'No. You could say I stick to my old haunts.' He looked about him at the street. 'Place has changed.'

'Oh Harry, you don't know the half of it. Of all the old shops I think only Tesco's left. Schmidt's the big German restaurant on the corner with the woman at the till, remember, with the moustache? Gone. Do you remember Lawton's Sandwich Bar?'

'Ha ha ha ha. Those bloody soggy pita breads with flabby ham and too much salad.'

'They always broke apart, remember? Always. Coleslaw on your lap.'

'"Luncheon vouchers. Remember them?' He stomped his foot. 'Twenty bloody pee they gave to you buy a sandwich with.' He was laughing so hard that tears were crawling down his cheeks.

'But Gigs is still with us.'

'Those two old men! Ha ha ha ha.'

'Well the young sons took over, turned it from a kebab shop to a proper sit down Greek restaurant. Kleftiko, the lot. Mind you, they're not so young themselves these days.'

'But Pollocks, the toy museum opposite them. That's still there, surely.'

I couldn't remember. 'It's so clear in my memory, but you know, I think it's gone as well.'

'Oh dear,' he said, and looked even sadder, and then he just froze, staring ahead.

'Well. Lovely to see you, Harry. I... I have to get on. The Prof will be wanting his newspaper. Good to see you back.' He didn't answer. I really had to get home. I'd never been so cold. It seeped through my thick cloth coat.

Harry just nodded and it seemed to me his skin, his hair, even his eyes got whiter.

I turned and walked away with misgiving. As naturally as ice melting, as gently as a daffodil blooming, realization came as to who or rather what I'd been talking to.

That had not been Harry. If it had just been him alone, I might have said to myself. 'Teddy, I think you've seen a ghost.'

But all of them, all of these homeless people? In bowler hats, shawls, button up boots, mutton sleeves and straw boaters. All of them ghosts?

Ahead, beyond the T-junction with Goodge Street, Tottenham Court Road was full of some kind of procession. No cars.

Outside Tesco, two Chinese or Japanese tourists in facemasks asked me 'Is it protest?'

'No, no it's not that. I'm not sure what it is.'

The sky swirled. There was an odd golden light.

I had to get back to Alfie. To do that I had to cross Tottenham Court Road.

Thousands of them filled it, a solid moving wall like a caravan of refugees, some of them with prams I dared not look inside. Some of them wore bowler hats, or huge ladies' millinery, broad brimmed with flowers. Some men wore snazzy Columbo/Mad Men hats; one of them in this cold wore only Bermuda shorts and a Hawaiian shirt. One of them had the face of a washed up skeleton of a dog.

They bumped into me, mildly angry. 'Make room. Make room.' or 'Your turn soon,' or 'So special, aren't you?'

From down Charing Cross Road, there was a sound of beeping. I stood on tiptoe but saw nothing. I learned later that cars and vans had been caught up in it. Cars fascinated them. The drivers couldn't move, but scores of curious, dirty faces peered in at them through the glass.

A woman ran up to me in a cloche hat and a shapeless dress in a zigzag pattern. 'Have you seen a little girl? I can't find my little girl! About five years old. She was just here! She was just here!' Her face was puffy from crying.

'How many years has she been gone?' I asked, rather in a trance myself. She ran on.

Another woman in a fluffy pink coat, pill box hat and stiletto heels grabbed hold of me and shouted into my face, 'There's somebody else in my home! All my things are gone. All my books, my photographs, my LPs, my paintings, my papers all just gone! My whole life!'

I did not say--that's what happens when you die. When my mother followed my father, I had to dismantle their home, throw out most of their things-- the ashes of her favourite dog, her mink stole, and every copy but one of my father's articles.

'I have to call the police; is there a telephone kiosk near here?'

I almost said, there are no kiosks any longer. And then I didn't. 'Further up Tottenham Court Road.' I lied.

'Thank you, thank you. I don't suppose... you a have a shilling?'

'No.' That was the truth. 'Terribly sorry.'

I was nearly out of the press of them when another woman plucked my sleeve. She stared numbly ahead, her face covered in ash. She was wearing only one shoe, and her clothes had been shredded. 'Could I trouble you?' she asked, 'I'm afraid I can't see anything.'

'Were you caught in a bomb?' I asked gently,

Her head moved up and down. 'Perhaps.'

I had an idea. 'Try...try to remember what you most typically wore. Your favourite outfit, say. Perhaps you and friends were going out to a dance.'

It worked.

Her face was clean and her hair was in a home perm. She had on a brown tweed coat with a little butterfly broach and pleated shirt and high heel shoes that laced.

'Thank you,' she said and gave a throaty, naughty laugh. With a blood red smile, she said, 'Leg of Nothing.' Her breath was arctic.

They walked into me, bumped me to one side. Spinning, I could move through them. I spun into Chenies Street, and then I hopped and skipped as fast as I could.

No traffic in Chenies Street – the procession had blocked any entry by cars. Left into the Gardens, and children were playing there with hoops, one little girl in a frothy white dress and hair ribbons.

Outside our front door with an armful of freshcut flowers, Alfie. I remembered with mingled guilt and annoyance that I'd forgotten to get him his sherry.

He was dressed in his old suit, the fawn one. I had forgotten that suit. He gave a forlorn little wave, and a rueful smile. I was struck again by how dapper and dashing he could be.

Then I felt my arms prickle. 'Alfie? What are you doing out? Get inside, the cold is terrible out here.'

'It is cold,' he said wistfully, and looked at the trees, just misting over with green. 'It's still a lovely day, though. Not quite yet spring.' He looked into my eyes. 'I'm so sorry, Teddy.'

His legs weren't swollen, and his feet were straight.

'I... I think it's more difficult to go when there's someone else there. I think they just hold you. Just their mental presence, psychically. But when they leave you alone. It's easier to... slip away. Ooops.'

'Alfie?' What the hell was he talking about?

He shrugged and laughed. 'Anyway, I've gone and done it now. I'm so so sorry.'

The key shivered in my hand as I tried to jam it into the front door. I bounded up the stairs like I used to when I was twenty three and we'd just moved in, and I flung open the door and I found him, sitting at his window, with his blanket round his legs and the gas fire blazing, and his morning sherry not touched.

The doorbell rang.

It was Barnabas looking happy, Barnabas the optician.

'Hello. Professor Davies wanted to look at some contact lenses.'

'He's gone!' I shouted. 'He's gone, he's gone, he's gone.'

His face went still and calm. 'May I come in?'

'What am I going to do?'

To my amazement, he took me in his arms. He hugged me and I didn't mind. I didn't feel accosted.

'May I see him?"

I must have nodded yes. I couldn't speak. Barnabas came in with the silence of a cloud. He took Alfie's hand in his, and then he made him sit up straight. He got him into his trousers which took half an hour, the legs were so swollen and purple. I didn't know what to do or say. Barnabas recited a psalm. The right words.

'I can call people for you,' he said. 'I visit all a lot of older people.'

He rang the police, asked me for our tax code and rang the tax people and our GP. He found a funeral agency. They would be here for the body soon.

'Do you want me to wait with you?'

I found I did. I wasn't used to being alone. I hadn't been alone for forty-eight years. I made him tea, Earl Grey. Can't stand the stuff myself, too much bergamot.

'My parents are Igbo,' he said. 'The dead are not demons. Some of them are our family. They are us. No better, no worse. Nothing to be afraid of.'

I have nothing to do these days, but sit and watch.

I can see a corner of Gower Street, just a wedge of it through our window. It is their encampment. A few of them wander up and down. Most of them are sitting in the road just staring. The authorities have tried tear gas, but nothing clears them. Maybe they got tired of being forgotten.

Mrs King is chatting with neighbours outside our front door. She lived in the flat opposite when we first moved in. Mrs King was a dear, always telling jokes and making the best of things. She stopped me being frightened of old age.

I think that something has gone wrong in Heaven. Some kind of war, or maybe it just got too full. Maybe that's what scares us about the dead. They're refugees, homeless.

Mrs King is nodding and laughing at something Alfie's said. He rocks back and forth on his heels like he always did, and looks up and gives me a salute, like he used to do on George's boat.

He's waiting for me.

A Visit in Whitechapel

Eugen Bacon

It was a bleak and blustery morning. It was the day the Earth shook, and aliens fell from the sky. At first, we thought it was a meteor. Then we thought it was a shooting star. Something glowing rocketed down the horizon and landed in sudden light and a thunderclap. There it was, smack in the middle of Buck's Row – a smoking crater.

By the time the people of Whitechapel had spilled out from Yeoman's Yard, where the Glitter stood, from Raven's Row where Mr. Reaper owned an antique shop, from Settles Street near the copshop, and all the way from Mill Yard where a misty old church full of rot now stood, the gorge from the fallen fireball was shaking and groaning as if birthing a terrible beast.

The gorge went silent and stirred up a stampede, people moving away, not towards, as something stranger began to unfold. A young man of unusual darkness – he wore tight pants and a cloak with a cape, just like the wizards in folklore – climbed out of the smoke. His eyes were weapons – they put a hole in your soul.

He turned, and the crowd gasped. Reaching out of the gorge was a woman's hand. He took it, helped her out and we saw her face. She, too, was a person of colour, her skin more chestnut than his ebony. She was wholly exotic. Her head was wrapped in blue and gold, an elaborate headdress that coned and finished in a fringe. While he was slender, she was comfortably rotund and moved gracefully, flowing in kaleidoscopic robes – unlike our everyday tunics of metallic hue.

She cast the dazzle of her long-lashed gaze at the crowd, at us. We stood entranced. Hers were the eyes of a unicorn. She blinked and at once the ashy gorge disappeared. In its place stood what appeared to be a crystal tower filled with animals, beasts of a kind we'd never seen before. The animals we knew all flew, and they were seasonal. They came with the blood moon, the twin moon, the blue moon, an eclipse, a comet or a Venus transition. They were unicorns, honed and shimmering with enchanted dust. They were lightning birds with long, black beaks and long, long legs. They were cockatrice, serpent-like with a bird's head, and they heralded a message, often of a good birthing like the night we came into the world. Griffins, with their talons and wings – these ones if they came, a death would happen. Last time one appeared it chose to land on a spire. The skyscraper upon which the spire stood tumbled and fell flat on my father. The sphinx – you were lucky if you saw one in broad daylight, but it brought good fortune, unlike the Pegasus, a winged creature, fully cursed. The last time one was seen was centuries ago, and it used the black plague to eradicate a whole monarchy. Only the royals perished. The Metropolitan Police brought order, and our father had been one of them.

But these animals gazing down at us from the crystal tower of the aliens, they were not unicorns or griffins, lightning birds or cockatrice. The sight of them was like a mirage, faces in dancing water. We were curious to investigate the marvel. But by this time the Metropolitan Police had arrived in their black sapphire tarragons that roared a big sound from deep in their bellies; we couldn't ignore it. We saw Uncle George – he used to work with our father – a good sort. The alien turned her unicorn eyes on him, and Uncle George was smiling – we didn't think he'd be arresting tonight – so we dispersed with the crowd.

We raced up a float of stairs to our apartment. We went to tell Mum about the aliens. But she was levitated, folded into herself, an invisible spike in her heart, and it was turning, turning, hollowing out a tomb inside her body.

She was getting over a second break-up with O.

Before the earth shook, before the aliens, we waved to Dora in her fairy-winged dress full of sapphire ribbons. She waved back, a tangle of emerald lilies from a Kensington boutique bobbing in her combed-out hair. A thousand brushes, O always said as he tenderly drew out each strand with the mystical brush from her princess dresser.

Mum smiled briefly at O, looked away swiftly and a frown replaced the smile as our ride arrived. There was no hint of softness on her face from just before, at the door, when she brushed O's lips with hers, when she clung to him for no greater than a moment. He stood tall at the doorway, head almost touching the dome, and watched as we pulled into the horizon with a tarragon ride woman who was the no-nonsense kind, for all the burgundy and gold tint splashed on her metallic conveyance.

Mum stayed silent across the sky, even as we nagged: 'Are we there yet? Are we, are we?' Normally she'd say, 'Not yet, mate,' or 'What's going on?' This time she didn't notice. Her stare was ardent along the vista as if fretful the clouds might melt in the London sky. *Zeus*, she cursed an ermine white tarragon, or the man in it when the tarragon swerved into our path but flew way too leisurely ahead of our ride.

Mum's voice was wet when she asked if we'd like some shakes, and we said yes.

'Do you mind a detour?' she said to the tarragon ride woman.

'Cost you double,' said the no-nonsense sort.

We got shakes from the fly-thru – a peanut butter cup and a rocky road delight, one with molten cherry sauce, the other with whipped chocolate butter. Mum was clearly grumpy because she snapped, 'Keep it down, will you?' in the ride. We stopped pulling at each other and took from her our molten delights as the attendant with a green leprechaun tunic and a matching hat handed them over. Before we even asked, Mum said we could eat in the tarragon, never mind the no-nonsense woman who cast us a wicked eye. Soon as we got out, Mum spat on her hands and wiped grime off our faces – oh, didn't we thrash!

Before we stepped into the apartment up a float of stairs, so unlike O's grounded house, Mum turned squarely to face us. She wore a brave face like she was about to take a pill, a jab or something, and said, 'What happened with O, it wasn't your fault.'

As people went about with their day, nursing or teaching or engineering or developing, Mum still cradling her wretched heart, we stole to what was once Buck's Row, then a smoking crater, now a crystal tower full of exotic beasts.

There stood the tower, right where we left it. No one was going in; the animals were not coming out. But the place was wide open, no doors to lock people out. We stood at the threshold for a minute, the crystals on its outer walls shimmering and beckoning us in, and there was no sight of Uncle George or the rest of the Met.

'Look what I found.' The alien woman's voice was a song, the sound of a bird, the music of the moon, playful in her pretty throat. Her lashy unicorn eyes swallowed us in its gaze. She stood at the mouth of the tower, arms akimbo. She took in our tunics. 'Are you soldiers then? Little Romans, perhaps?'

'Who are Romans?' we piped.

'Great engineers, soldiers and constructors,' she said in her melodic voice. 'They lived in beautiful houses surrounded by slaves. They also killed people in a most terrible way.'

'What are slaves?'

'People without choice. But you two appear to have it in plenty, no?' She took our hands, 'Come,' and guided us into the tower.

Inside it was like nothing we imagined. The animals were not standing at crystal windows and gazing out at Whitechapel. They were out in the wild. Indeed, the tower was not a tower. It was a meadow swathed in lush green grass. It was vast land speckled with deeply blue lakes and some murky ones. This world bore a remoulade of creatures and a soft scent of something exquisite. It reminded us of Mum when she was light on her feet, buoyant, no mourning in her exquisite face, in her soft lips that kissed our brows to sweet sleep.

'My name is Babirye,' the alien woman said in that dawn chorus voice. 'And this,' the man appeared as if from a shadow, 'is my brother Kato.'

'We're twins, we're twins,' we piped with excitement. 'Are you twins?'

Babirye laughed. Her big necklace of shells danced on her neck. 'Actually, yes.' She caught our interest on her throat. 'Cowrie shells,' she said.

We blinked for a spine-tingling moment, filled with a sense of anticipation. 'Are you gods?'

'Grief, no,' she said in words like music.

'Why do you bring them here?' It was Kato. He was arresting, full-voiced.

'These ones bring no harm,' she sweetly sang, and skipped with the lightness of a sprite despite her flowing robes and headgear. 'These are Wanyama,' she told us, and waved towards the beasts that were scattered in the exotic wilderness.

We met Fisi, a spotted thing with small black eyes, standing ears and short back legs. He looked like a thief and laughed as we passed.

'Don't mind him,' said Babirye.

We met Tembo and her big long nose, big floppy ears, wide, wide legs. She had eyes so gentle. We met Duma, a sleek beautiful thing with a pretty long tail that swished as she paced around us. She purred, closed her eyes, when Babirye stroked her chin. We met Kinyonga who changed colours like a diorama. He didn't mind us, just turned flesh-coloured, orange-tinted red, amaranth, lime... as he walked. Sokwe was almost human, just furry and cradling a baby that sucked from her breast. She whooped and gibbered as we neared, nearly bit us.

'A mother is always protective, no?' said Babirye. 'Enough for today.'

Mum was still levitated in sleep, but we woke her when Mr. Reaper of the antique shop visited, and she agreed to get up and make tea. Unlike us, he never took the floating stairs. He was tall, ashy-haired, often with a walking cane but we knew there were times, such as when he entered and left the Glitter, he didn't need the cane. His visits to Mum were occasional, and she appeared to listen to his counsel.

'The blackness will lift,' we eavesdropped from the stairs. 'He's a monster you don't need. Not with his moods and how he is to the children.'

But nothing he said could shake her from her mood. 'Now, now,' we heard, and knew that Mum was crying again.

'Let me take the children for a ride.'

'But what about the shop?'

'It runs itself.'

We didn't like Mr. Reaper's ride – his was a beaten grey tarragon peeling with paint. It shuddered, not soared, coughed, not roared. But we loved his knowledge of history, as he pointed out places.

'Right there, in the north end of what was once the Palace of Westminster, was Big Ben. It was London's iconic timepiece and it stood on a tall spiked building. People came from all over the world to see it. There,' he pointed, 'that used to be Winchester Palace right there, near Borough Market.' The tarragon shuddered. 'Right here, riverside, there used to be a giant London Eye. It was the tallest observation wheel in the whole of Europe.' He looked at us keenly. 'Ah! Do you remember the Tower of London?'

'Many a duke, baron, king or queen lost their heads by the axe, or by hanging from the gallows,' we said.

'Yes, sometimes there was a burning. Or the infamous hanging, drawing and quartering. Others fell to their death while trying to escape the tower. Do you remember why?'

'Sometimes it took several blows to sever the head.'

'Indeed. It took eleven strokes in one case. The condemned was nervous and moved. The executioner accidentally struck her shoulder. She bounded from the block, blood gushing everywhere, and the executioner chased her with his axe.'

'If the axe was neat, did you die immediately?' we asked.

'Never. Do you know one can remain conscious nearly a minute until you die from lack of oxygen to the brain? Look. Once there was a traitor's gate right there, lined with impaled heads.'

After the tour, we hoped he would take us to his antique shop and its jadeite dishware, and lots of shiny things, some with strings, and hear him say, 'This is an antique guitar – you strum a string and it plays. This is an oboe – it's a woodwind instrument and you blow like this to make a sound…' And slip our fingers into perfume jars and their floral fragrances of violets, lilies and lavender, their dreamy fragrances of vanilla and cinnamon, and their fresh fragrances of lemons and bergamot. And feel the books: hardcovers and paperbacks. And hear him say, 'This was how people read. They opened a book and looked at its text. It was nothing like audio and story globules you touch with a finger and they tell you or show you stories.'

But as we flew back over Whitechapel and crossed over the Glitter, we saw the ravenous look in Mr. Reaper's eyes, and knew the antique shop was not to be. Not on this day, no.

That autumn at O's wasn't fun. He was self-medicating for his migraines, doubling doses, and his mood was getting more and more grotty. His voice still held a silk note for Dora but for us it was always the growl, a bigger growl. He barked when we changed the setting in Dora's system and it went from virtual reality to alternative reality – although it worked better, he agreed later, and Dora could still play all her favourite games. After he bellowed at us in the tarragon, then turned the ride round so we went back to his house instead of soaring from Camden to Kensington as he had promised, Mum also saw he wasn't fun. She jumped out the ride soon as it landed, marched fuming into the house, and – before we could do the same – O said, *Children, stay in the ride.*

Who needed to get out to hear them tearing at each other? Horrible words, but what was said could have been worse:

'When I say anything to them, you think I'm a bully!'

'Did I say anything when you jumped at them in the tarragon? Sure, I was surprised when you turned round –'

'I'd had enough!'

'And I could see why their bobbing might annoy you –'

'And you did nothing!'

'Because you did something.'

'I had to!'

'What's done is done. Already you've roared at them, and turned back the tarragon –'

'I wanted you to do something!'

'But you'd already done something!'

'And now you storm out of the ride – clearly, you're upset I did something.'

'The only reason I stormed was because I was still mad at you for spoonfeeding Dora. By Zeus, O. She's not that little.'

'Mad? Why would you even say that? She's never eaten so well!'

'Feed your little princess with a golden spoon!'

'Did you see how she ate all the peas?'

'My ones – they're not your biological kids –'

'You can't control them –'

'They can never do anything right, can they?'

'She ate all the peas!'

They stared at each other in astonishment, shattered by their rage.

It was then that Mum said: 'We're struggling, don't you see?' Then she ordered a ride, pressed her lips on O, smiled and waved briefly before she frowned, and we were gone.

That night she sat up, startled, from broken sleep. We stroked Mum's hair with our fingers, not a brush, and told her we took everything from our room at O's. 'Even the alternative reality game *Gods of War*,' we said.

'I'm glad you took everything,' she said.

'O's house was awkward,' we said. 'Did you see how it was awkward, Mum?'

She didn't tell us it wasn't O's house that was awkward but that it was us who had turned awkward in it because everything was by then compromised, complicated. She didn't say that all was lost, how could there be a future? She didn't tell us how the swallowing pain of loss was inside out, how – if only O knew – she was a simple call away… But Mum understood what we didn't at the time, that sometimes love is not enough.

The next day, Babirye met our arrival at the threshold. Her headdress was speckled with flowers, yellows and reds. Her flowing robes were the colour of spring, a merging of young and ancient flora. She introduced us to Digidigi, a tiny creature with a lean face. Big black eyes, slender neck. He was nimble on his feet. We met Swala, horned, wearing the eyes of a woman. Pundamilia and his pattern of stripes barked at us but continued to eat the grass, until Fisi and his clan showed, laughing like thieves. Pundamilia took flight and Babirye did not intervene.

'It's the nature of the order, no?' she said, her words full of music. 'Are you hungry?'

'Yes,' we said.

She led us to a small round house made of mud, long yellow grass for its roof.

'This is a hut,' she sweetly said. Its floor was pure earth. Something was cooking on a fire inside three stones. 'This is a hearthstone,' she cooed. 'Kato must be near.'

He appeared like a wish, with his cloak and weapon eyes. 'Is it not enough that you take them to see Wanyama? Now they must see our beds?'

'Don't be like this, Kato,' she said.

She led him outside, and we heard their arguing. His boom voice, her bittersweet notes.

'It confuses the order!' we heard him roar. 'Especially tonight!'

She was subdued when she returned. As for Kato, he was gone.

'What's a bed?' we asked.

'Why?' she laughed. 'Don't you sleep?'

'We levitate,' we said.

'How?'

'We think ourselves to sleep and the body arranges itself in the air.'

'I can't pretend to understand it, but for now, sit.'

We willed ourselves to sit. Babirye looked at us, afloat on air, and laughed in astonishment. 'I meant to sit on the ground, but this tells me you might also not know about chairs?'

'They're in Mr. Reaper's antique shop,' we piped.

'The brain is a powerful thing. Can you fly too?'

'Not so high. That's what tarragon rides are for. The metal things that fly.'

'I see.' She offered something white on a plate. 'Try this, no?' It had the texture of potato, only sweeter like a nut. 'It's called cassava.'

Kato returned to the hut. His eyes stayed hostile, even as he took a cupped container made of wood. He scooped out a drink from a round-bottomed container on the floor.

'Can we have some?' we begged.

He walked out without a word.

Babirye shook her head. 'Not from that pot – it's not for children.'

'Why not? Why? Why?'

'That millet brew will take you places you don't want to visit.'

'But we do, we do. We want to see places.'

'Try this instead.'

'Is it good? Is it, is it?'

'It's excellent.'

It was a sweet milk, clean to swallow.

'That's from Mbuzi,' she said. 'You haven't met her yet, and I don't know you will.' Her lashy eyes were full of sadness, the radiance in them waned, as if she knew something we didn't. Before we asked, she said it: 'Go before my brother returns from the place that brew will take him. You'll not like what you see, no?'

So, we hotfooted it, but a blue moon was glowing and we didn't go home. We raced instead down Settles Street past the cop shop and into Mill Yard. We cut a corner through Pinchin Place, then along Myrdle Street, and pounded all the way to Yeoman's Yard, where the Glitter stood. Mum said it was a place for naughty men and bad women. We climbed the walls, reached the windows. But the curtains were drawn, and they were thick. Peals of laughter, sometimes hoarse groaning, seeped under the door where we pressed our ears.

The door snapped open and we scuttled to the shadows. Unmistakeable tallness, it was Mr. Reaper, without his cane. He walked briskly, as if in a hurry. We tailed him. Suddenly, he stopped outside the soap maker's cottage at Myrdle Street. We thought he had seen us, but he hadn't. He was pulling out a smoke.

We hid and waited.

It wasn't long before a breathless woman joined him. The glitter in her dress, in her makeup, we knew she was from the Glitter.

'Where's the money?' she said.

'Mary Ann, I said I'll give you *after.*'

'But you said it'll be quick.'

'It will be.'

'Where do you want me?'

'Let's go to my shop.'

She giggled and fell into him. Her perfume when she passed us was something cheap that turned our noses.

He grabbed her hand. 'Come quick.'

We stalked them to the antique shop. But the door banged behind them, and we heard nothing. We would have stayed if we could, followed her back to the Glitter and snuck in, but a shadow cast itself upon us. We looked back in terror and saw a large creature, its eagle head and neck covered in feathers, its brown fur and furry tail. The smell, how foul! Like the small haunt we once found in our wandering by the old church. It was black and lay on its side, all four legs broken. A dirty-grey porridge oozing from the gore in its stomach and the stench was ancient excrement or hell's cavern. The Met hauled it off, and buried it somewhere, but Whitechapel reeked foul three weeks straight. To smell something so offensive again, and this time on the living... It was all the encouragement we needed to bolt homeward, dash up the float of stairs to our apartment, and into the arms of Mum, dear Mum. She was bouncy in the kitchen, light on her feet and baking banana bread. Her heart fully healed, ready for someone to break it again. She was always reaching out for something since father's death. But did she know what? Yet seeing her so bubbly, in that instant we forgot all about the Griffin we'd just seen and hugged her.

Hugged her.

Mum put floury hands on our faces. 'You two will be the death of me! I've been worried sick! Where were you? I couldn't find you or Jack – the tour, when he offered it...'

'Mum! We were in the crystal tower,' we cried, breathless. 'But it's not a tower. And there's Fisi and Swala and Tembo and...'

'What's going on, my breathless ones? I can't make head nor tail of what you're saying. Where did the dear old man take you?'

'It wasn't Mr. Reaper. It was Babirye – she has flowing robes and cloth woven on her head, and Kato – his cloak, Mum!'

'The two of you are off your heads.'

We squealed at her words, clung to her tighter. Who wanted to imagine our heads on pikes along the traitor's gate?

'Hush now,' she said. 'If you don't tell me calmly, I promise I'll refuse to listen.' She smelled so good.

So good. It was the fresh bergamot scent from Mr. Reaper's antique shop.

So, we sat on her lap and told her about the meteor that was not a meteor, how it shot like a star and put a smouldering crater in Whitechapel, until the alien Babirye blinked and there was a crystal tower full of animals. But it was not a tower, and they were not cockatrice or sphinx. The place was a meadow that hosted Nyani and his blue-bottomed cousin, Kima. There was Ngumbi, the flying ant, and lots and lots of Siafu, thousands of them like walking sand. There was Mamba who liked to lie low, long and solid in the brackish part of the lake and, when she hissed at us, her jaws were spiked with a million teeth.

'And Kifaru, Kifaru,' we cried. 'He's a grey, fat thing with a horned snout. Such a nervous temperament!'

We talked ourselves to sleep, and poor Mum listened to it all. We were too big to carry, but tired, so tired. We levitated on our own and slept the bottomless sleep of gods after war.

The next day we floated down the stairs with Mum, and dashed to find the tower, but it was gone. In its place was yet another Whitechapel crowd and, with it, the Met. There was Uncle George. We pushed through the throng and saw, lying in a bundle on the ground at Buck's Row, a corpse – the husk of a woman from the Glitter.

'It's Mary Ann Nichols,' said Uncle George to Mum. His pensive gaze turned to us. 'Let's have a word now, shall we? I hear you boys have been fraternising with some aliens.' He spoke as if he doubted it.

He crouched to eye level. 'Let's go backwards from the end: Where did they say they were headed?'

We shook our heads, teary eyed, and wondered about Kato and his weapon eyes. We wondered about the sudden appearance of a Griffin, a herald of death. But even as we looked at the glitter dress crumpled into the grey skeleton, a body wrapped in nothing but fossil skin, its mouth open in the silent scream of one who had lost a soul in a horrible way, we couldn't, just couldn't, imagine this was the work of –

We turned curious eyes at Mr. Reaper, then back at Mary Ann discarded like garbage. But we were young.

Herd Instinct

Fiona Moore

"Sorry about the short notice." Detective Wilhelmine FitzJames was waiting for me outside the building in the old industrial park that my office shared with two physiotherapists and a trade union. Steve, her usual police car, was humming to himself nearby. "It really – what the hell is *that?*"

"*His* name is Aldous," I said, taking a firmer grip on the leash of the strenuously resisting border collie. "And either he comes, or I don't."

"What the *hell*, Noah?"

"Jill's looking after him, but she had to go out of town for a two-day nursing workshop, so it's down to me."

Wills and the dog regarded each other with matching suspicious expressions. "I thought your girlfriend's dog was that fat yellow sausage thing."

"That's not fair. Rosie's a Golden Retriever and we've managed to get her weight down quite a bit. But no, the shelter Jill got Rosie at asked if she could foster Aldous until he's ready to find a home. Rosie's pretty good at calming down troubled dogs, giving them back their faith in humanity."

"Exactly how little faith in humanity does *this* one have?" Wills still wasn't letting us in the car. Aldous, for his part, had apparently realised Wills wasn't going to hurt him and was starting to relax slightly.

"He won't bite, and he's house-trained," I said. "He's just not very fond of people. Abusive owner. I won't go into details, but his default mode is to assume everyone is going to hit him. Hid under Jill's dining room table when she brought him home and wouldn't come out for over twenty-four hours. Now he's over that stage, mostly, and apparently it's important for him to meet more and more people and learn that most of us are basically decent."

"Got my doubts about that one myself," Wills said, but more quietly. "All right, you and your direwolf can get in the car, and I'll brief you on the situation."

"Early this morning, there was a 999 call. One of those big houses in Kingston, on the edge of Richmond Great Park. Home invasion," Wills was saying, as Steve buzzed along the M25. Aldous lurked nervously in the space under three of the seats. "Three suspects, wearing dazzle-suits and balaclavas to foil face recognition and gait-distorting struts on their knees. Broke in, beat up one of the owners of the house, stole what they'd come for, ran for it."

I nodded. "Awful. Why?" I was assuming it wasn't simple malice or spontaneous vandalism if they were that well organised.

"Intellectual property," Wills explained. "The couple living there are Meera Sayed and Donovan O'Hare. Sayed's the one who got beaten up; they were both supposed to be at an academic conference but Sayed bailed at the last minute due to illness. I hadn't heard of them either before this, but apparently they're a pretty big deal in developing integrated bio-intelligent systems. Is that one of your things?"

"Not really," I said. "It's too new for the intelligents involved to need therapy. But I'm aware of the general principle." Bio-intelligent systems had been getting a lot of attention, not just from parks and estates, but also from the sort of organisations that try to repair damaged and deteriorating ecosystems: the idea is to integrate intelligent machines, genetically modified plants, regular plants, insects and animals in a way that maintains an ecosystem over the long term with minimal human intervention. The good thing about using intelligents for something like that is they can adapt their consciousnesses to focus on the needs of the insects, animals and plants; humans have a tendency to get species-centric.

"So is that why you're involved, and why you're bringing me in? 'Cause I'm not sure how much help I can give." Wills is with the London Metropolitan Police's Automotive Crimes division, which has a technical remit of covering all artificially intelligent beings, not just self-driving vehicles. As for myself, I'm a freelance consulting autologist – the elevator pitch version of which goes, "like a psychologist but for intelligents and Things" – making me an obvious person to bring in on certain investigations, but I was struggling to see how it made sense in this case.

Wills snorted. "Noah, kid, you need to broaden your horizons. I want your help on this, but it's going to take a minute to get to why."

"Go on, then."

"The housebreakers were either working for a rival organisation, or maybe someone with an interest in sabotaging the research. They took everything they could find that related to the project: DNA samples, logbooks, outlines for programme modification and new intelligent social behaviour routines. They also destroyed any storage material they didn't take, and timed a cyberattack on the servers Sayed and O'Hare were using for backup. A security gestalt noticed that and managed to contain the damage, but they'll still have a hard time reconstructing. At the house, they also wiped the house-elf's control unit –"

"The housekeeper," I interrupted.

Wills gave me a look, and I spread my hands. "It's not political correctness or hair-splitting, Wills; house-elves were slaves. Intelligents are independent contractors."

Wills didn't apologise, but her expression softened and she nodded slightly to show the point was taken. "The housekeeper's control unit was wiped, so it couldn't identify them or alert the police either. The call came some hours after the event, when Sayed managed to get to a neighbour's to phone – they'd taken hers, of course. They couldn't manage to hack the estate gardener, so they physically smashed its console. It's had to reboot from backup."

"So, none of them saw anything."

"Aha," Wills waved a long finger. "That's why you're here. It's the gardener. It definitely saw something, and almost certainly something we can use."

"If they were using dazzle camouflage and gait-changing–"

"That's the crucial point. At least one of them had abandoned the gait-changing struts at the house; we found two broken sets on the drive. So they'd've left using their natural gait."

167

"Well," I said. "And the gardener might have seen them? The data's still there despite the console being smashed?"

"Sayed and O'Hare weren't expecting this, exactly, but they were concerned about the possibility of attacks on the property. And there's a lot of money involved here. So they'd invested in constant rolling backups for their intelligents. Memory loss is likely to be negligible."

"Likely to be..." I considered the phrasing. "I take it the gardener can't testify? Won't testify?"

"It's catatonic," Wills said. "At least, according to the investigation team. Smashing the console killed it, and you know better than I do how much trauma dying causes an intelligent."

"Indeed I do," I said. Death may not be total for an intelligent, but it's not pleasant; although legally the intelligent is the same person after death, that's very questionable from every other standpoint.

"So, I need an autologist," Wills concluded. "One who can get the gardener patched up, accessing records and communicating as soon as possible, to help us get these bastards before they do any more damage. And that's you. Ah, here we are."

With excellent timing, Steve had left the motorway, neatly circumnavigating a grocery warehouse and the campus of Kingston University, and turned left through a set of gates on to a street full of houses. Each was bigger than the entire building my flat was in and surrounded by gigantic gardens. Somewhere in my ancestral DNA, I could feel my Zimbabwean-born father grinding his teeth. *So much waste, Noah, so much wasted space.*

They're scientists, Dad, I told the DNA voice. *Yes, there's a lot of money in what they're doing, but I guess they need the space for labs and greenhouses. It's not like when you were a kid.* His stories, when I was small, about billionaires in giant houses, the networks that kept them there. In a country with no universal basic income, before the Factories that made a mockery of consumption, before we had intelligents as co-workers. My sister and I, growing up in scruffily egalitarian South London, secure in the knowledge that we would grow up healthy and go to university before drifting off into various aspects of the medical profession (her for people, me for intelligents), would roll our eyes when Dad went on one of his rants.

But, my adult self asked: was he wrong? Maybe poverty was less extreme in modern London than the Harare of forty years ago, but money still bought you a better house and a nicer life. And clearly, some people could be motivated to break into a house, beat up a woman, kill one intelligent and wipe another. No idea if the reward was financial – but there are other kinds of wealth than money, other kinds of inequality than the kind that can be measured in capital.

Bioengineering bought you a giant house in Kingston, while clinical practice kept you in a flat in Norwood Junction. And society's a fragile, breakable thing.

I pushed the thought to the back of my mind.

It was easy to tell which house was the relevant one if you'd worked with Wills as often as I had. There was a discreet police beacon sitting on one of the gateposts, quietly broadcasting to intelligents to avoid the area as the investigation was ongoing – but the general public probably had no idea what had happened there. Yet.

This particular property seemed to be mostly garden, which was appropriate, I supposed. The house was one of those old square ones with the big windows, and, I noticed, a gigantic conservatory filled with lush growing things out back.

Steve pulled us in to the driveway, where a group of humans were loading things into Gladys, the forensics van. A couple of Met drones flew overhead.

"Do you think it would be okay to let Aldous off the leash for a while?" I asked Wills as he and I got out of the car. "The garden's enclosed, and it'll keep him out of our way while we work."

"I'll check with the forensics officer, but yeah, should be okay if her team have finished," she said, a little distracted. "The gardener's running on the house system right now; they've set up a tablet to replace the smashed console. It's in the dining room."

"Does it have a name? A gender?" Unlike cars, gestalts don't need either for themselves, but they'll often take one for human convenience.

"Normally answers to Rhizome," Wills said, "but you could call it anything for all it'll answer right now. Gender? No idea, it wouldn't say."

Leaving Aldous' leash tied to some sort of ornamental but heavy thing at the door, far enough, I hoped, from the human activity that he wouldn't get nervous, I went into the house. Which turned out to be one of those highly curated jobs. Any labs were well tucked away, and I had a feeling that the longer I stayed in the building the more likely I was to leave a mark on the rug, scratch the varnish, or break something fragile.

I glanced back at Wills, but she was busy, calmly but firmly questioning the forensics officer about developments, her shoulder-length dreads giving her the air of an Egyptian pharaoh. One of those annoying people who always seems to be at home wherever they are.

I found the tablet in a cool room with a long table with delicate-looking legs and far too much glassware, and took it out into the sunshine, letting Aldous go after getting the nod from Wills, watching him creep off into the shrubbery while I got the tablet going. I found a glass-topped table and wirework chairs around the back of the house, positioned them so I could see most of the garden, and got to work.

After half an hour, there was no sign of Aldous, and I was making no headway at all with the gardener.

Rhizome was an embodied gestalt: a central consciousness with distributed bodies, the mind running through a half-dozen grass cutters, a flock of flying hedge trimmers, a buried irrigation and sprinkler system, a couple of small trundling machines that would water the bits that the sprinklers couldn't reach, various other specialised machines for tasks I'd never known existed before, being the sort whose gardening skills and interests start and finish at making sure the aloe plant on my office window doesn't die. Still, I went into autology in part because I like learning about how other people – in this case, mechanical people – live their lives, and I can often get an unresponsive patient to open up by focusing on the parts of their work that they love and I know nothing about.

Not this time, though. The gardener stayed passively unresponsive as I gently fed it queries about what, precisely, a parasite maintenance programme involved or the parameters of a trailing wisteria manager.

I looked out at the garden. Nothing that would look abnormal from the outside: drones buzzing about a hedge, damp soil speaking to the actions of the irrigation system. Something moved in the thick vines on the house, which I assumed was the wisteria manager (too small to be a squirrel, too crawly to be a bird). A couple of grass cutters trundled slowly but determinedly across the lawn. Everything working as it should.

Like a crime victim with PTSD, outwardly cheerful, going to work and leisure and spending time with their friends and family, the smile masking the crumbling inside, the emptiness.

Sadness washed over me. This was the sort of emotional condition that took years to get over. And Wills wanted me to try and patch it up in a couple of hours?

Not fair of me. I knew why she was asking. And I also knew she'd be going through her own version of this with Meera Sayed, knowing how painful it was but still trying to get through, trying to find some key thing that would conclusively identify the attackers, crack the case.

I leaned back in my chair, watched the grass cutters. Gentle and bucolic, like robot sheep grazing in a meadow. Moving in random, patternless tracks, circling and looping around the lawn.

And then, I saw Aldous.

Flat on his belly, creeping up a hillock. I started up, worried for him, but also remembering vaguely a programme I'd seen once. Sheepdog trials, border collies doing exactly that, a sort of stalking creep towards the herd.

I stood still and watched, ready to intervene if he seemed distressed or started destroying the garden.

He stood, began a trot, nose pointed.

At the grass cutters.

He began circling them. Nudging them, standing in front, dropping behind, then moving alongside. Once he stood still, gave a single commanding bark.

I laughed.

"What in hell?" Wills, at the front door of the house. Summoned by the noise, or maybe just coming out for a break, seeing the dog frisking about.

"He's herding them," I said. "Look. He's herding the grass cutters."

And he was. He'd managed to corral three of them, get them moving in a precise wedge around the grass.

Wills also laughed at the sight. She turned her head, called back into the house.

"Meera!" she shouted. "You've got to see this!"

Footsteps inside, then a thin, worried, bruised face inside a cloud of hair above a brightly coloured loose dress-thing. A hand reflexively clutching at the neck.

"It's okay," Wills said. Her tone was like Jill's with Aldous; soothing, reassuring. "Come out here. Take a look."

Meera took a few tentative steps outside. Saw Aldous herding the grass cutters. Began to laugh herself.

"What's he doing?"

I explained briefly. "Aldous is a sheepdog," I concluded. "He's never been trained for it –"

"– but somewhere in his genes, he's got the instinct to herd things." Meera completed. "That's just amazing."

"Want to meet him?" I asked, spontaneously. She nodded, eyes shining.

I whistled. "Aldous!"

The dog's head shot up. Boldly, without a trace of his usual nervousness or fear, he bounded over, tongue lolling. Went right up to Meera, thrust his nose happily into her outstretched hands.

"Well," I said. "That's something. He's never done that to anyone that I've seen before."

"Look at the cutters," Wills said to me. I followed where she was pointing. Noticed they were still moving in formation.

"Huh," I said. "That's interesting. Come to think of it, the way they were moving before... disconnected. Loose. Atomised." An idea was forming. "I'm going to try something."

I went over to where the drones were fluttering around the hedge, trimming a bit here and a bit there. Again, that lack of coordination; all of them doing their job perfectly well, but each on their own.

I spread out my hands, began directing them together. Moved them into a pyramid shape, as Aldous had with the grass cutters. Directed them upwards, moved them into a line along the top of the hedge. Urged them forward along it.

Hesitantly at first, but then with more assurance, the drones began to do exactly that. In fact, they began to space out their line, fluttering over the top of the hedge at ten-centimetre intervals.

"Is this helping?" Wills asked.

"Let me see." I went back to the table, grabbed the tablet. Flicked and gestured to get the gardening system front and centre.

The system flickered into life; the lines pulsing, the colours healthy.

As we watched, the communications system came online.

"It's okay!" I said with relief. "Not only *can* it talk, it *wants* to talk."

Rhizome primly let me know it was male, just as Meera, looking up from where she was playing some kind of stick-fetching game with Aldous, relaxed as a child, said, "He."

Wills' face broke out in a jubilant smile. "Noah," she said, "we're in the clear."

I felt nervous again as Carlos the taxi approached the gates of the estate, remembering the last time I'd been here. They swung wide for me, welcoming.

The intervening four weeks had spanned the border between spring and summer, and bright flowers were beginning to open in the garden and hedges.

A thin white man came around the side of the house as I was thanking the taxi. "Doctor Moyo?" he said, extending a hand.

"Noah," I said, taking it.

"Noah, then. I'm Donovan O'Hare. Donovan. I'm so glad to meet you and thank you properly, for helping Rhizome get back together, and for introducing us to Aldous."

"How's he settling in?"

"Well!" Donovan said. "He's out in the garden with Meera, shall we go?"

I nodded, relieved that we weren't going to go into that cave with all the varnish and glass.

Meera and Aldous were at the glass-topped table; Meera with a tea service, Aldous sleeping with gratifying lack of concern underneath, and bits of Rhizome buzzing around the willow tree.

"He still likes to herd the grass cutters," Meera said, looking at Aldous fondly. "He's tired himself out, though."

"He's Rhizome's therapy animal?"

"He is," Meera said, looking perfectly serious. "Rhizome's getting better, but he still disassociates sometimes. We've been encouraging Aldous to herd the drones and the irrigators as well as the grass cutters; it helps. Both Rhizome and Aldous."

I assumed it was helping Meera, too, on the quiet.

"As I said, we wanted to thank you," Donovan said, passing me a cup that looked too delicate to survive long (and yet was clearly almost as old as the house). I held it gently, telling myself to think of it as a drone or microbot or some other piece of tiny machinery that I routinely held without any fear of damaging it. "But we also wanted to talk about the follow-up."

"Follow-up?" I was intrigued.

Donovan and Meera exchanged some kind of telepathic communication, and Meera smiled at me. "We've made everything we're doing here open-source."

For a moment I couldn't see the connection. Then a lot of them rushed in all at once. "*Oh.*"

Meera nodded, smiling more broadly. "There's no value in stealing something everybody can have."

"Are your funders... okay with that?"

"They weren't, at first," Donovan passed a plate of shortbread, looking slightly wicked. "But we pointed out that it was a way of ensuring their competitors didn't profit either. They're consoling themselves with the thought of selling the physical technology required."

"It's not a one-off, though," Meera said. "It's going to be a requirement for all our work from now on. Open-source or nothing. And we're going to lobby for that as standard."

"That's..." I thought about the words. "Generous of you."

Meera shook her head. "It's not," she said. "It's common sense. And it's more than a little out of keeping with building integrated, autonomous systems, if the intellectual environment isn't also integrated and autonomous."

"You have a point."

"Also..." Donovan said, "we'd like to employ you. As a subcontractor on the last few stages."

I frowned. "I'm an autologist. I wouldn't have thought that would be much use to a —"

Donovan shook his head. "Clearly, the intelligent components have mental health needs. We might not know what they are yet — but that's what we need to find out. Help us design a system that'll keep that in balance, too."

"Maybe with animals," Meera said. "Playing with Aldous is helping Rhizome recover and keep his balance, and that's something none of us anticipated."

I'd never worked in theory and development before, let alone with animals, but... I could hear Wills telling me I needed to broaden my horizons.

I looked out at the garden, the dog rolling over in his sleep to get more sun on his fur, the plants growing, the sprinklers pulsing gently, the grass cutters grazing in formation, the invisible creature moving in the wisteria.

Beyond the walls, the sounds of car wheels and children.

"I'm in," I said.

Death Aid

Joseph Elliott-Coleman

The surrogacy order came into effect on the 26th of February 2045 and was arguably the most fiercely contested and radical bill the Neo Euro ever introduced. After the destructive Euro-wars and the second grand unification – which incorporated a United Ireland, several Russian breakaway states and the moribund United Kingdom – the cities of Europe found themselves inundated by veterans with no abode, as well as buildings left vacant or abandoned by investors cutting their losses and ruthless venture capitalists from the US and China determined to profit from gentrification.

The order solved many problems at once.

Firstly: Governments seized every building deemed habitable or having the potential for conversion to habitation that hadn't been occupied, had been in dispute for more than five years, or was owned by foreign nationals for the purpose of investment.

Secondly: All homeless were immediately collected and processed, immediately making mental health, substance abuse and alcoholism medical problems which in turn relieved pressure on the over-burdened police force allowing them to refocus their energies on major crimes.

Thirdly: Socialised healthcare was given a radical overhaul as resources were poured into it requiring an enormous recruitment drive of medical staff and practitioners, especially for countries in the Neo Eurozone who had historically under invested in the welfare state. Which in this instance, meant the UK.

But, as always, the United Kingdom dragged their feet. They refused to lead and fell behind.

And thus, calamity ensued…

Christmas 2047

Two years after the Eurowars
Two years after the surrogacy act.
One year after Neo Euro sanctions for noncompliance

Aisha lay in bed massaging the stump of her left arm which always ached in the morning before she wore her prosthetic. She hear the snoring and smelt that farts of her roommate that smelt like the cheap gin she drank and the anti-hangover pills she took. A strange visceral smell of a rosewater and paint stripper that told her she wasn't dead.

Outside in the kitchen she heard the sound of overlapping accents. Welsh, Nigerian, Working Class, which meant the bathroom was free but probably wasn't clean. She groaned, knowing she would be met with residue and pubic hair at the very least. She got up, and still massaging her left arm she dared to part the louvres and see what the world looked like outside.

The sight of the grey hellhole of Croydon, its sludgy streets shrouded in snow, the annoying mumbling cacophony of music, traffic and street patois and skyline blinking with the lights of advertisements against a ugly grey sky, made her heart sink. The world looked the colour of stagnation and they were all damned souls punished to linger forever in this retrograde limbo. She muttered a string of curses in Gujarati then attached her prosthetic, which immediately gave her temporary sensation of icy coldness. "Fuck!" she whispered as the neural connections were made and she began to feel the artificial appendage . "Fuck! Fuck!"

"Oh, here she is! Morning Queenie," Ioin said as she emerged from the bathroom fully dressed, her towel slung over her arm. Her years in service had taught her to never be in a position where you can't defend yourself or quickly run out of the front door. The group of reprobates she lived with always kept her on her toes.

There were three of them sitting in that living room. Ioin was dressed in a dark blue tracksuit that reflected the light, and wore trainers that he cleaned religiously every night; she could smell the chemicals he used in the next room. He was fat, or to use the politically correct terminology: obese. His face was round and plump, looking like dough, both his ears were pierced and he had 'victim' written all over his face. How he survived on the streets was beyond her.

Next there was Leona, her hair cut short, dressed in smart/casual clothes, forever attending interviews, eternally job hunting, her eyes sharp and hungry. There was an eternal, almost frustrating optimism to her. "Things will get better. But if you make it so," she would say. Despite that, Aisha respected her and noticed that she always massaged her one of fingers for some reason.

Finally there was Bump. Bump rarely spoke. And when he did, he was random and incoherent. He was a huge man. His hair was unkempt and wild. His beard was almost shoulder length. Despite that he was almost obsessively clean. His clothing consisted of stone washed jeans, branded sweaters from Croydon's Nth failed attempt to achieve city status, and thick leather boots that he'd bought to a shine and reeked of boot polish, and his immaculate fingernails. Aisha suspected there was far more to him than her was letting on, but didn't push him. He stared absently out of the window like a meteorologist studying the weather.

She did her best most of the time not to think about the woman she shared a room with, wastrel that she was. The thought of wasting her life on gin and drugs with no ambitions other than receiving her next basic payment…

Something in the back of her head added *no hope*. She ignored it.

"Is there anything left to eat?" she asked. "Or are you on second breakfast already?"

"Well a fella has to maintain his figure, Queenie," Ioin replied, rubbing his belly. "It's cold outside. I'm making sure I'm adequately insulated."

Bump laughed, not taking his eyes away from the window while Leona shook her head with amusement. "He's gotta point ya know," she said as she rubbed her finger.

"What time's your interview?" Aisha asked.

"The first one? Midday."

"The *first* one?"

"Yeah. I have four interviews."

"Four interviews? For four jobs?"

"Girl, basic income just isn't enough for me," she said as she rubbed her finger. "I need capital if I'm going to start my business and one paycheck won't be enough. I don't intend to spend the rest of my life in shared accommodation and don't intend to spend my life being somebody's employee."

Aisha nodded in agreement and made her way back to her room. But not before she gave Ioin a dirty look. He waved back at her with spite.

She opened the louvres and light flooded the room, making her roommate groan with discomfort. "Ugh, what time is it?" she asked. Aisha didn't answer, she disgusted her. "Hello? Earth to –"

"It's 9.30," Aisha said tersely.

"In the morning?"

She sighed as she opened a drawer that held her decontaminator machine. It was rectangular and took up half of the space in the drawer. On it a readout stated: 4 Masks Ready. As she opened the lid, a strong smell of antiseptic wafted into the room. She pulled out a freshly sanitised mask and pulled the plastic thing over her face, covering her nose and mouth. The thin rubber cushions on the lip of the mask were always wet after decontamination, which made her look as if she were dribbling if left untended. She wiped away the moisture and then removed her phone from the docking bay, ignoring the unread messages. She knew what they were and whom they were from. She wasn't ready to deal with them yet.

Aisha threw on a thick coat that smelled of almonds and, as she walked out, gave her roommate a look that betrayed her utter contempt for her. She responded by ripping her duvet off her body, exposing her nakedness. Aisha kissed her teeth as she shut the bedroom door behind her, hearing the laughter as she walked out of the front door.

December 23th 2047. The streets were a mess of bodies all seized by the madness of Christmas shopping. The roads were clogged with traffic: buses and goods vehicles laded with stock for desperate shelves, which Aisha had to weave between. She walked into a nearby family-owned convenience store; its manager, a lean middle-aged Ghanaian women with artificial eyes, gave her a very subtle salute that Aisha responded to in kind. You could always tell when someone's eyes were augmented or artificial, as the irises were slightly hexagonal and on further inspection the tiny electro filaments reflected in the light like silver.

"Major," said the storekeeper.

"Captain."

The manager nodded in the direction of the back to the shop, then called on one of the many members of staff, who were all her extended family, to come and take over from her.

"Let me have another blast, Mercy," Aisha said as the storekeeper handed over the marijuana cigarette. She did, as Aisha took a long drag, exhaling a fountain of smoke. "Fuck… this shit is good."

"Not as good as the stuff we smoked in Serbia," said Mercy. "That shit could cure Corona!" Aisha smiled as she remembered. The beer. The men. The women. The Marijuana. She stopped smiling when she remembered what came afterwards. The month-long second siege of Sarajevo. "Bullet Hell" or "Danmaku" a shinnichi[12] member of her unit had christened it. She lost a leg a day before the siege was lifted. And she was one of the lucky ones.

"What was the name of that young girl who called Sarajevo a Danmaku?"

"Shit. Erm… What was her name again? Short. Brunette. Freckled. Irish?"

"Yeah, that's the one. What was her name –?"

"Assumpta!"

"Yes! That's it. Assumpta. Assumpta Ennis."

"That one used to curse up a storm when she got drunk."

"Best sniper we had. Yeah, what happened to her?" Aisha asked.

"When we got demobbed and she got her prosthetic, she moved to Japan. Became a film maker," Mercy replied as she exhaled. She passed the cigarette to Aisha. "Caught one of her films on NHK recently, real tear jerker. About a home for the elderly with no living

---

12 "Japanophile"

relatives on account of them dying of radiation poisoning after Fukushima's reactor exploded in 2026. Called *The Ghosts of Fukushima*. Powerful stuff."

Aisha nodded, content and happy at the young woman's success. "Damn. That one had a game plan. She went for it. Executed it. She made it. Good for her."

"Yeah, at least someone did," Mercy replied. There was an edge to her reply.

"Oh please, Captain. You've done all right for yourself. You've inherited your parents business. Made it grow. Shouldered their responsibility. Employed a workforce. You're not like me, living in shared accommodation with a group of cut throats. I mean, I'm half scared they'll steal my bra while I'm wearing it."

They laughed. "Well, you might have point there," Mercy said.

"I know I do."

"But… sometimes a throne is a prison."

"True. But a Queen can lead. A prisoner can't. The Throne has power."

Mercy smoked the last of her cigarette and contemplated her Queendom.

"You got your letter?" she asked after a while.

"Yeah."

"You going?"

"Don't know."

"I ain't," said Mercy "I've seen enough death to last a lifetime. Besides, a Queen has subjects to lead."

"Amen to that," said Aisha.

Aisha continued on, walking into the centre of Croydon. At the turn of the twentieth century Croydon had been promised redevelopment; plans had been drawn up, models made, shops vacated and empty buildings demolished and in their place rose apartment buildings – their high price point locking out the locals who were desperate for housing.

Then Brexit happened. An entire county sheepishly led to the altar of needless self-mutilation on a bed of lies and xenophobia. The European Union, the institution that had risen from the ashes of the Second World War and had encouraged cooperation rather than competition, had been demonised as the enemy of free capitalism and sovereignty by ruthless venture capitalists and fascist nationalists.

Then the Corona/COVID -19 pandemic happened.

Fifty-two million dead worldwide in four years. Facial masks came on and never came off. Social distancing entered the lexicon. She was a child but remembered the long year of isolation when the walls of their home became her world.

Then came the crash of 2024.

Then the food riots.

She remembered her parents fashioning crude firearms made from repurposed air pistols. She remembered her mother coming home covered with blood and the shock when she realised the blood wasn't hers. They ate in silence and she wondered who had died so they could eat.

Then the Eurowars happened.

She rubbed her prosthetic instinctively.

Croydon was a forgotten town, left to fend for itself after the broken promises of redevelopment that were over thirty years dead. Money had been diverted to the more affluent areas of London, those places more likely to attract investment and tourists. Those places that already had money.

Croydon's Whitgift shopping centre was now a gaudy relic, locked permanently in the nineteen nineties. Its white plastic fascias turned yellow, its masonry bleached, decals pealing.

However, flowers were known to grow from manure and weeds could crack though concrete. Even amongst rubble, the seeds of ingenuity grew.

Through an underpass that ran underneath a dual carriageway, itself now abandoned and overgrown, slowly reclaimed by nature, she entered Freetown – the space where free traders and entrepreneurs had determined to build on what had been left behind.

Immediately upon crossing the threshold of what used to be the shopping centre she was overwhelmed by an endless sea of vivid colours and stalls crammed into every corner. More were arranged in rows along the floor space, and an ocean of smells filtered through her mask. To her left were food stalls, flush with dishes from across the world; every culture, every continent was represented; a wild cacophony of languages and rich smells that made her mouth water.

To her right, an sea of electronic stores, their names all highlighted by glaring solid light, signs offering the best deals for hacked equipment from Egypt, illegal prosthetic upgrades from United Korea, untraceable black-box nanocomputers from Nigeria, military grade hacker tech left over from the Eurowars, illegal alternative personality standing in – Alt-Me's – the digital assistant and secretary that had become indispensable for business and academia, which could also be evolved to gain something dangerously close to self-awareness. There were rumours on The System – the sophisticated evolution of what was once called The Internet – that in the deep, where loose code floated and congealed to become the beginnings of intelligence, that great Mecca of computer science, A.I., lived free and unhindered.

That was all bullshit, of course. She walked into the food district, straight to a Ghanaian stall and bought four trays of Jollof rice and two trays of fried plantain from a young man who worked the store with his two sisters.

"You want some Guinness, Auntie?" He asked. "Import or home?" Aisha asked. "Oh Chale!" the young man exclaimed. "Import of course! You can get the Irish stuff anywhere. Only Nigeria Guinness brewed in Nigeria tastes like real Guinness."

Aisha smiled. "Give me four bottles," she said.

She walked out of the food district and deeper into the bowels of Freetown. Past the garment sector and its forest of almost indistinguishable designer knock offs and fleets of young designers pioneering their new clothing lines. Past the bookstores, old Waterstones – offering a safe haven to the young and old, now doubling up as a library having donated their remained and unsold stock to the criminally malnourished central library. She walked up two flights of stairs, passed along the balcony of the second floor past more stores, foreign language book stores, places of worships, art studios, art dealers, before arriving at the CarPark.

The CarPark was a large concrete eyesore, a brutalist relic that had somehow been able to survive the mass demolitions of the 2020's – post Corona – it had been one of the main Car Parks that served the old shopping centre but had now been commandeered and transformed into a shanty town spread over five levels. Its residents had been able to ingeniously jack into the electrical and water systems in such a way that they were not only able to provide clean water and a working toilet system but were also able to fashion a metered, payable electric supply. Times of desperation demanded ingenuity.

She walked up three flights of stairs, free of the smell of urine so normally associated with Car Parks, and entered a row of prefabricated apartments, each decorated differently, showcasing the identity of its resident. The civic pride on display was obvious. She walked to the end of the row, ending up at an apartment painted metallic silver, and ran her hand over the recognition lens.

"If you're not in possession of a drop of alcohol, leave now and do not darken my door," said a voice from a small speaker.

"And what about a few bottles of ice cold Guinness?" Aisha replied.

A silence.

"Irish or Nigerian?"

"Nigerian."

The door opened and she was greeted by a bald East Asian man, no more than thirty, who saluted her with a warm grin.

"Major," he said.

"Lieutenant Ng," Aisha replied. "At ease."

"So. Beer then?"

"As well as Jolloff and Plantain. Have you ever known me to come empty handed, Eugene?"

"Never sir. Come in."

Eugene's home was arranged along precise mathematical lines via a series of collapsible furniture, shelves and bookcases on pulleys that folded into the walls, and a bathroom and kitchen that only a combination of movements of work surfaces and panels in strict order would reveal. He knelt down to pull and turn a small handle, which bought up a collapsible table that, until it emerged, had been indistinguishable from the rest of the floor. Similarly, Eugene pulled a table cloth out from a drawer that appeared from nowhere. The slightest push caused it to collapse back on itself and became flush with the wall once more.

"Eugene... *how*?" Aisha said gesturing at how he'd been able to utilise this space with such efficiency. He smiled as he chewed on the fried plantain. "Spartan efficiency, sir," he said. "It's a new home planning idea from Palestine. Actually, it's not new. They're been doing it since the early 2020's, post Corona. The idea is to make maximum use of minimum space without actually using it. You only ever really actively use about ten percent of your home space and the rest is wasted, so why not utilise it more efficiently? Makes sense when you're living a broom cupboard."

He stuck another mouthful of plantain in his mouth, then with a collapsible spoon scooped some Jolloff rice into a small bowl and ate from it. Aisha sipped her Guinness from the bottle and her gaze floated aimlessly around the room.

"Why didn't you go home, Eugene?" she asked.

"I told you, sir," said Eugene "'Parents refused to acknowledge me once I transitioned. Kept dead-naming me to my face. The only ones I keep in contract with now are my brothers. My parents don't even phone me at Christmas. I mean it's the 2040s, we've just fought a war for fucksake." He drank a mouthful of Guinness. "Ah well. Stupid is as stupid does, I guess."

"No, you misunderstand. I meant *home*."

"Oh! You mean to Hong Kong? *Heh* I'd be living in an even smaller broom cupboard than this," he tapped the table, "and for far more. Besides, that self-determination agreement they worked out with the mainland? Ain't worth the paper it's written on. Give them fifty years and China will start making micro aggressive demands of HK that they'll be unable to deny."

"You think so?"

"I know so. Look, China always plays the long game, sir. Be it fifty years or a hundred, Hong Kong will be part of China. The only people who don't know it yet are the Hong Kongers. Everyone else is wise to that. It's inevitable." He took another swig of this Guinness and scooped some more Jolloff into his mouth. The two sat in silence for a while, Eugene so obviously enjoying his food. It made her smile to see him so at peace himself.

"The UN want me back, Eugene," Aisha said.

Eugene froze and looked up, his mouth full of food his eyes wide with shock. "I've been given the choice: reactivation and combat or an advisory position." Eugene hadn't moved or breathed, she noticed. His mouth hung open, food unchewed. Aisha reached across the table closed his mouth. "Manners, young man," she said.

"Who else have you told? Mercy? Roshan?"

"I just came from Mercy. She's not going on account of her having mouths to feed. I'm on my way to Roshan after you."

"Why? Because... Oh." Eugene slowly placed the bowl down on the table. And leant back in his chair. "Where?" he asked.

"Myanmar. They going to stop another genocide there."

"You mean the UN are going to provide Death Aid to whomever they deem responsible for their slaughter?"

"Basically. You don't reason with the devil. You stick a gun in his mouth in keep pulling the trigger until their head is a canoe."

Eugene leant back in his chair and rubbed his chin. "Of course you've heard what they're doing to the Rohingya Muslims?" he said.

Aisha nodded. "It's a bloodbath. And that latest puppet the military installed as President? She's about as useful is a condom after sex."

Eugene laughed. "You've seen the videos from there, sir?"

Aisha nodded again and took a spoonful of rice. "Yeah," she said. "Stuff of nightmares. Like something out of a horror movie."

"Are you sure you want to be knee deep in blood and guts, sir?" he asked.

Aisha said nothing. Eugene scratched his chin and sighed. "Well, at least we'll be doing God's work."

"Oh no!" Aisha exclaimed. "No, no, no, no. You can't –"

He silenced her with an email he projected from his phone in softlight. Its words were clear and unmistakable. It was an official letter from the UN asking for his assistance in resolving the Myanmar crisis.

"I got one too, sir," he said. "I've been walking around London Town like a man in search of his soul. Went to a few churches too but God didn't give me any answers. Guess She sent you instead."

"Eugene, I can't ask you to –"

"Sir, with all due respect you're not asking. They are. Now let's finish this grub and go see Roshan."

Surrey Street Market used to take up the length of a short road and was less than a hundred meters away from the flyover, with a few shop fronts and less than thirty stalls. Post Corona, when all the big supermarket chains had fattened themselves like pigs on the profits of panic buying and online ordering due to the heath lockdown, they had refused to share their wealth with those key workers who had risked their very lives to serve the public and keep the shelves full, those chains were the only ones to see growth.

Rich and fattened and indifferent, they assumed that those working for them, as well as those thousands upon thousands now out of work, would be happy for gainful employment and would gladly work for the scraps from their very rich tables. Neo serfdom in all but name.

Then the crash came. And one by one their shops closed, leaving many thousands out of work.

Then came the food riots.

For what you are about to receive… May the lord make you truly thankful.

And so, once more, from the ashes of gentrification and the death of the high streets there was a renaissance of small businesses serving the local community. The chains shrunk and people began to patronise local stores.

And Surrey Street market ballooned, stretching nearly half a mile from the old flyover to the West Croydon train station consuming many abandoned units in the Centrale Shopping Centre that stood adjacent to the old Whitgift Centre.

"Hand sanitiser! Hand sanitiser!" the young street hawker cried. "Designer hand sanitiser! Beckham Hand sanitiser! Boyega Hand sanitiser. Ahmed hand sanitiser."

"Hey, squire, you've any Skunk santiser?" Eugene asked.

The hawker, a young girl no more than thirteen, gave Eugene a dirty look and turned her back on him. "Nice try, Narc," she said. "I wasn't born yesterday."

"Ain't making no judgement," he said. "Mishpokhe gotta eat. 'Cus God sure as hell ain't watching."

"God always though watching," said the Hawker. "That's the point in'it?"

"Weren't watching during the war, though."

That gave the Hawker pause. She turned slowly and looked him in the eyes. Then, at Aisha. "You two vets?" Eugene nodded. "For our sins," said Aisha.

"Where'd you serve?"

"All over," Eugene said. "Mostly Bosnia and Herzegovina."

The girl's jaw dropped. Then her eyes caught sight of Aisha's hand in all its prosthetic glory poking out from her jacket sleeve. "This? Left the real one in Sarajevo," said Aisha.

"It hurts you?" the Hawker asked. "When you wear it?"

"Only first thing in the morning."

"You got upgrades for that?"

Aisha grinned. "Be a dumb girl if I didn't," she said. "Soldier girl knows how to take care of herself. You know Roshan? He about?"

The Hawker grinned. "I do. Follow me."

Roshan Samuel Simon was Jewish but his father was an enormous Bollywood fan and named him after his favourite directors. Born just after the food riots, Roshan's family had owned a butchers shop and were local heroes among the community for giving what little they could to those who had nothing. The plan had been for Roshan to help run the business when he came of age, so it came as bitter disappointment when the government of the day conscripted all able bodied men and women over the age of eighteen.

So Roshan went to war. And as wars have always done to children fed into that well-oiled meat grinder, it quickly made an adult out of him.

The girl led them through a busy market and into a huge butchers shop spread over two floors and serviced by a lift. Meat was cleaved and bagged according to customers' orders, the air heavy with the sound of metal meeting flesh, the call and return between butchers and customers all holding their dull-coloured shopping trollies, waiting to deposit their food into the waiting secure blackness.

Sawdust littered the floor and the place smelled of frozen death. The girl was indifferent to the rows of carcasses they walked past as she led them into a small corridor that sealed that world behind them. They walked past a series of offices before arriving at one that was marked "The Big Bossman". Eugene giggled and shook his head. "Hermano!" he cried.

The door flew open and a large, barrel-chested man, who wore glasses and whose hair had been cut short, stood in front of them. "Hermano!!" Roshan cried in return as the two men embraced so fiercely that Aisha swore she heard bones crack. "You don't visit me, boychick? And you work around the corner from me?" Eugene complained.

"Ah, but my friend. I'm afraid if I fart I'll blow your house down," Roshan said. The two laughed. "Hello, sir. Good to see you again." Aisha smiled. "The air always gets blue when you two meet. You look well."

He opened his mouth to answer then noticed the Hawker standing there waiting.

"You eaten, little one?" he asked. The girl nodded. "Breakfast," she said. "Too busy for lunch."

"Too busy?" he turned the child around and led her back down the corridor. "Go to Mr Gauslin's Nigerian store and get him to fix you up. Tell him I'll settle with him at the end of the week. And don't drink any of that Guinness! If you do, I'll know!" She stuck her tongue out at him and vanished behind the door.

"Kids," said Aisha.

"Yeah. Kids," said Roshan. "She's a war orphan, you know."

190

"Oh?"

"Yeah. Her family was killed in one of those pogroms in Paris. A Neo Nazi enclave wanted payback for Israel assassinating their entire ruling council in Calais. Took it out on the resident Jewish population."

"Oh shit," said Eugene. "Really?"

"Really. Poor girl hid in the attic and heard everything. Still has nightmares about it. Acts tough but... you know kids. They didn't have long to celebrate their victory, though."

"I heard," said Aisha. "Police and army tore the city apart looking for them. Tried to hide in Nigeria. The Nigerians found out and twenty-four hours later they dropped a very, very surgical bomb on them from a very, very great height that made a wonderful mess."

Roshan smiled gleefully. "Oh yes. The Nigerians... They take *great* offence at terrorists using their country as a hiding place. Apparently, all that was left of them were their smouldering shoes and a can of baked beans that had been cooked in the heat of the explosion. Tea anyone?"

"Oh no. I'm not going," Roshan said as he bit into a biscuit. "I sent my reply immediately upon receiving the email. I've seen enough death for one lifetime. No, no, no. And working here, in Croydon, I've seen its repercussions. No... The only violence I want to be a part of is directed toward dead meat, no."

Aisha found herself feeling relieved. He had much more to leave behind than they did.

"Yeah, I figured as much," Eugene said. He sipped his tea and couldn't hide his disappointment. During the Eurowars, the two had been the dynamic duo of her unit. Frequently sent on their own on reconnaissance, the two had become closer than brothers. Indeed, she knew that they'd both done and seen things that they'd take with them to their graves.

"I take it you're both going, though?" Roshan asked.

"I am," Eugene said. "I believe the Major's... in two minds."

"Is that so, sir?"

Aisha sipped her tea. "Yeah," she said. She reached and took a biscuit from a plate Roshan had provided. "I mean, what the hell else is there for us, huh? Ain't no prospects here. Joining the police is out of the question, I'm over qualified. I'll be damned if I join the circuit and become a mercenary. PMC? Nah. I'll end up working for some faceless multinational company and pointing my gun in some farmer's face because my employers want to own what's underneath their feet. No. Fuck that." She threw the biscuit into her mouth and chewed.

"Maybe I should have just taken the commission they offered me," she said.

"Oh shit!" Eugene exclaimed as he turned in his chair to face her.

Roshan lowered his cup of tea to the table, his eyes wide with surprise. "They offered you a commission, sir?"

"Uh huh. Turned it down. Said they'd keep a seat warm for me, though. *Talent like yours is a crime to waste. You'll come back, Major. Because this is where you know you can make a difference.*"

"That sounds like Colonel Furlan," Eugene said. He was unable to hide his contempt. "I'd almost forgotten about her."

"Still blame her for Sarajevo, bro?" Roshan asked. Eugene fell silent. He placed his tea cup on the desk, bit his lip and looked away. "Because Mercy doesn't. Nor do I or the Major. And she lost her wrist there for Christ – Oh shit."

They both noticed Eugene was crying.

"She lied," he said though the tears. "She fucking lied and people died."

"Nah. She didn't," Aisha said. She reached across and squeezed his shoulder. "The intel was fucked. Command got fucked over and the shit trickled all the way downhill and we were the poor bastards who had to eat that shit sandwich raw."

"It's true," Roshan added emphatically. He stood and walked around his desk, perched on the edge and looked out the window. "You couldn't stomach the inquest but we could. We saw in her eyes, in her *face*, the horror at what happened. I mean she grew up in Sarajevo, man. That was her home! And for the second time in less than seventy years it was transformed into a fucking warzone.

Command got fucked. She got fucked. We got fucked. Everyone in that city got fucked. We all got fucked, man."

"I still see their faces," Eugene said though the tears. "All the people we found in that church. The one that got shelled. Oh Christ. Oh Jesus."

They all remembered. Two hundred people they sheltered in a church which they believed was out of firing range. They were planning to ferry them out of the city and to safety. Then the shells started to fall in the wrong direction. And they could do nothing but watch as the church that had stood for two hundred years disintegrated before their eyes. The only solace they took was that death would have been instantaneous.

"We're not to blame, Eugene," Aisha said, breaking the silence. "Our hands are clean. And so are General Furlan's. Despite how much she might want them not to be." Eugene looked up at her though teary eyes.

"Yeah. She blames herself too, boychick," Roshan said.

The Crystal Palace Memorial Centre was built next door to the old Crystal Palace football ground after the tragedy of 2035, when Neo Nazi's shot down the plane carrying the returning European champions after winning the title for the second time. That senseless act was the straw that broke the camel's back and ended the fickle arguments of tolerance and free thinking. For the second time in a hundred years the world had watched the slow rise of Neo fascism and did nothing to stop it. It had taken the death of over a hundred and fifty people to remind the world that the philosophy of national socialism was incompatible with hard-won freedom.

The words of Kwame Nkrumah, first president of newly independent Ghana: "Forward ever, backward never," became the chant of those who protested the intolerable appeasement of Neo Fascism.

And so once more Europe went to war with itself. And a generation learned that the true price of freedom wasn't counted in posts on the internet, but in deeds and sacrifice. Words and ideas are not bulletproof unless backed by actions.

Next door to the memorial centre was the legendary restaurant *Tasty Jerk*. Renowned throughout London for its Jamaican cuisine, it specialised in hot spicy jerk chicken, meat and fish. During the food riots it, along with KFC, were the only places that remained unmolested and weren't razed to the ground.

"Is this kosher?" Roshan asked.

"How could it be Kosher, man?" said the Jamaican woman with a thick accent. "This is jerk we sell. This ain't no Kosher restaurant, my friend."

Roshan smiled. "Okay, okay. I'm kidding! We'd like to order. It's a big order mind you. And no pork."

"No problem," the woman said. "Me know who you are. Me know you have *many* mouths to feed."

"Your reputation precedes you, my friend," Aisha said. "It's rare that good news travel so far."

"I take my blessings where I find them, sir," Roshan replied.

"Bollocks to the blessings, bring on the Jerk chicken!" Eugene proclaimed

"Mannnnn, do you *always* think with your stomach Eugene?"

Eugene giggled as he slapped his belly. "You act as if you met me yesterday, pal," he said.

The top floor of the memorial centre was a bar-cum-restaurant that was membership only. It rarely – if ever – attracted troublemakers and its patrons were robust in protecting its reputation. Members enjoyed both the laxity of closing times and rules on eating food bought elsewhere. That night it was unusually busy even for the festive season, and the three struggled to find a place to sit. Aisha saw trades and deals being made with money changing hands via contactless connections on wafer thin pads and goods being exchanged under tables. Life in Croydon frequently necessitated dealing with the backstreets market. Everyone hustled to get by.

From the corner of her eye she saw Ioin sipping what looked to be some bottled alcopop while negotiating a transaction for his Gaffer. Gone was his innocence and vulnerability, in its place: professionalism. They acknowledged one another with a subtle nod.

"What's that line from Yojimbo?" Roshan asked. "The one where he spares that peasant kid… Run home something or other." They were sitting in a hard-found corner.

"In English? Go home. A life of gruel is better than death," said Aisha.

"Ah ha! That's it." He drank a mouthful of ginger beer. "I always forget that. It stuck in my mind for years, you know? It was like a puzzle or something."

"Did you work it out?" Eugene asked.

Roshan nodded. "Eventually, yeah. That day in Sarajevo, in amongst all those bullets and bombs, I finally worked it out."

"And?" said Aisha.

"If you've alive, you've got options," said Roshan "Just breathing means you've got a chance. You may have to move hundreds of miles or transform yourself into something unrecognisable, but you've still got choices. Dead, you've got none."

He fell silent and ate his Jollof rice while the others ate their jerk chicken and looked out over the Croydon skyline. Snow blanketed every building and dulled the sky to a depressing grey. But, spring followed winter. And the wheel would turn and the streets would be alive to the sound life again.

"I prayed, you know," Roshan said. "I prayed harder than I've ever prayed before. I prayed that we'd all get out of there alive. I said *God, if you get us out of this in one piece I'll run straight back to home and become a butcher. I'll pray on my knees to you every day and I swear I'll never do violence to a living soul.*"

"Well… there's a few militant vegans who might have issues with your chosen profession, my friend," Eugene said. The three roared with laughter.

"Well there is that," Roshan said. "But, you know… I wake up every morning, I thank *him upstairs* for letting me come home. And I try to make people's lives just a little bit easier. You know what I'm talking about? Small acts of kindness."

Aisha nodded. "I think that's all anyone can really accomplish," she said. "I mean us, *soldiers*, what we're really offering people is

Death Aid. *War is the continuation of politics by other means.* Yeah, we're resolving arguments with bullets and bombs that *should* have been resolved at the discussion table. Every time we resort to violence we're right back in the caves, scared of the dark and clubbing one another over the head with cudgels for clean water and meat. We're right back at square one. We're fucking beasts."

"You're forgetting one thing, sir," Eugene added. "Some people hold others' lives in such contempt that they *have* to be eradicated. They're so hopelessly compromised, so utterly resolved, that allowing them to live means guaranteed death for thousands. Some people are living cancers for whom the only effective chemotherapy resides at the end of a gun barrel."

"Then what does that say about us?" asked Roshan.

"It says that we're intolerant of intolerance. You behave like a beast and threaten the flock, you've handed in your membership card to the human race and you'll be dealt with appropriately. Ask their victims whether or not we should show them mercy. You'll find their silence is deafening." Eugene chewed his chicken vigorously — bones and all — as Aisha and Roshan pondered his words.

"I fear he's right," Roshan said. "Humans. We're a herd. A tribe. Anything that threatens the safety of the tribe... well. Yeah."

"Yeah," Aisha said. "Shit."

Croydon felt especially cold that evening. But if it was cold here she could only imagine what is must be like in Myanmar, with death waiting in the shadows. "Cold hearts, cold world," she said. "I need a beers."

"You need a *beers*, sir?" Roshan said.

"You heard me."

She walked back to her shared accommodation, taking the long route all the way from the memorial centre along the mile long Whitehorse Road. Both sides of the street were lined with ethnic bars and restaurants, their shop fronts open to the street music screaming and headlamps blazing, and all along she smelt marijuana, now legal and taxable. Her head was full of ghosts, shadows, as well as a bit too much of that strong Danish beer.

She was going back to war, that was certain, but as she walked home she realised the sheer futility of it all. She or someone like her would always be called upon to take up arms against her brothers and sisters who had done her no wrong, with whom she had no quarrel. Certainly she wasn't going to kill monsters but rather agents in their employ; she'd learnt the hard way not to demonise anyone, because brutality and kindness were learned.

No, what tired her was that for all the centuries of killing and murder nothing had been learned. *No* always became *yes* when a gun was added to the conversation. People could always be persuaded to abandon their morality when the fear of death hung overhead. *Fuck me*, she thought. *We truly are wretched things, aren't we?* With every step she took she resigned herself to the violence.

She opened the door to her shared apartment and was met with sounds of celebration. In the kitchen sat Bump, Ioin, Leona and Aisha's roommate all in various stages of inebriation.

On the table sat bottles and cans of booze as well of cartons of Indian Takeaway. Bump sat at the end of the table wearing a mischievous almost childlike grin. Aisha – bottle of beer in hand – told dirty jokes. Ioin laughed while dipping naan bread into a carton of chicken korma and her roommate caught her eye. She smiled knowingly as she held a secret they both shared. They cheered when she walked into the Kitchen area, Ioin struggled to stand, eventually succeeding and passing an unopened bottle of Nigerian Guinness to her. Against her better judgement she opened the bottle and drank.

"What's the celebration for?" she asked.

"I got the job!" Leona replied. She had swallowed a mouthful of beer, nearly emptying the bottle. The group cheered. "And it pays enough that I don't have to work three jobs any more. I'll be able to bring my family over from Nigeria and give my job to one of my people."

It took a moment for understanding to sink in. "Really?" said Aisha, almost startled. "Congratulations! That... that's... Oh wow! That's fantastic! Wait... you're married?"

"Well yeah. That's another reason why I've been grinding so hard," Leona said as she rubbed her fourth finger.

"So," her roommate started. Aisha knew from her tone that she'd try to start some shit and she wasn't even remotely in the mood. "Did you get your orders too?" her roommate asked. Her question took the air out of the room, stunning everyone into silence. "Ah fuck," said Ioin. "They're sending you both back into the meat grinder?"

"You're not going, are you?" Leona asked.

None of those questions registered. Only her roommate's revelation that she was also a veteran. She quickly realised that for all the time they'd spent living in the same room she knew nothing about her save that she loathed her. "Where did you serve?" she asked.

"I was a sniper," she answered "Spent my time street fighting in Bordeaux." Ioin, Leona and Bump turned in their seats to face her as Aisha's eyes widened with shock. For all the horror she'd seen, she was thankful that she hadn't fought in Bordeaux. That she hadn't had to survive the vicious street wars and IED's. "Jesus H. Christ," Ioin whispered. "Fuck me."

"What about you?" the roommate asked.

"Bosnia and Herzegovina," Aisha answered.

"Shhhhhhit." the roommate emptied her bottle down the back of her throat. "You're lucky you've still got your head attached." She looked at Aisha's arm, then winced at her thoughtlessness. "Shit. Fuck. I'm sorry. I –"

"Forget about it. And you're right," Aisha's said as she sat and cracked open another bottle and passed it to her.

The roommate nodded thanks. "So. You're going then?" she asked.

"Yes. You?"

The roommate rolled the bottle between her hands and scratched herself. "It's a sad thing indeed when the only thing one's good at is killing, don't you think?" she said. Aisha nodded. "Says much about a girl don't it?"

"Mmmmmmm. You're wrong," Bump said. His voice sounded like wind buffeting up against an old tree. Everyone stared at the big man. "Yooooou're looking at it... side... ways. You're not killing. You're... defending those who can't..."

198

"Defend themselves?" Ioin offered.

Bump nodded. He reached forward, closed his large hand around his bottle of beer, slowly brought it to his mouth and drank quickly as if it were water. "*Soldiers are dreamers; when the guns begin they think of firelit homes, clean beds, and wives,*" he said.

"That's Siegfried Sassoon, that is," said Ioin.

Bump nodded and reached for another beer. Leona quickly opened one and passed it him. He smiled. "Ta" he said before he drank. "Lost a whole class of students in... the Norwich bombing. Young men and women... alive one moment... *meat* the next."

"Oh my god," Aisha whispered. "You're that one who was at UEA. You survived that bombing."

"The only one," Leona added.

Bump nodded. Ioin started to cry. The roommate reached over and stroked the back of his head. "I still see... their faces. Afterwards," Bump said. "Ruined. Disorganised. Cured meat. My mouth... watered. The smell of barbecue —"

"Oh Christ," Ioin whispered, as he lowered his head to the table.

"—Sweet meat. They... they deserved better... than to be the fodder of cowards."

The kitchen became as silent as a tomb. All anyone heard was Ioin's quiet sobbing and the fridge-freezer growling.

"I can tell you as a matter of certainty that the ones who organised and funded that bombing... none of them lived long to boast about their success," Aisha said. "And the ones who tried to tear Europe apart, well... There's not enough of them left to start a boyband."

Bump roared with laughter. The room shook with his mirth. And soon they were all laughing. "I came back to Croydon. After I spent a year at... at a mental hospital. It was hard... on me. But Croydon took care of me."

He reached across and took Ioin's hand in his. "Croydon forces you to make... families. Forces you to look out for one another. Because no one survives on their own."

They all nodded in unison. "The Rohingyas need people to fight on their behalf," Aisha said.

"Until they can fight for themselves," the roommate added.

"Yes."

"That's why I'm going."

"Good. Me too."

"Croydon will be here when you get back," said Leona with pride.

"Believe that," Ioin said though his tears.

"Hey, is there any more take away left?" Aisha asked.

"'Course there is," Ioin said as he wiped his eyes. He reached across the table and started to pile the sealed cartons of foods in front of Aisha. "Ursula was feeling particular generous."

"For a change," the roommate added with a sly smile. It was on the tip of her tongue to ask *Who's Ursula?* before she remembered that in her utter contempt of her roommate she'd never bothered to commit her name to memory. "*Bhagavāna. Kyārēka huṁ āvī kūtarī banī śakuṁ chuṁ*[13]." she whispered.

"Yes, you can be," Ursula replied, understanding her Gujarati self-deprecation. "But we can all change."

"I like to think so," Aisha replied.

---

[13] "God. Sometimes I can be such a bitch." - Gujarati

A Dance of Dust and Life

Aliette de Bodard

At first, you make it easy for yourself. You possess a member of a clade on the outskirts, away from the dark looming presence of the London Mind. You barely have to stretch yourself: the clade's small village is halfway to your boundaries, and your ride – a woman named nDevan323 – shares genetic material with the last Receptive you've colonised. As you slip into her bloodstreams, assimilating nanite after nanite, you taste familiar code, with the slightly acrid aftertaste of decay – the never-ending fight of the immune system against cancerous, dying cells, the hundred infections dormant in the body, awaiting the smallest of nudges to unfold in dark, grim coronas within muscles and flesh and bone.

Of course, you do not nudge. You might not be human – you might be beyond the pale yourself, something dark and disgusting that your creators rejected – but you're not cruel.

Equally, you don't take over, wearing your ride like a puppet glove – your lineage is a mix of Indian and Chinese programmers, and even the act of transgressing your established boundaries to find a ride leaves you uncomfortable. You watch nDevan323 go about her daily business, wandering the downs and leaving newly-sprung grass in her wake, inhaling foggy air and breathing out clouds of particles that coalesce on glistening leaves and *lahrat*-birthpods, making them straighten up and shine a slightly brighter, healthier green. In between walks, nDevan323 helps her community – makes the young transition from runts to full-fledged members of the clade, nourishes the young and the old as she nourishes the earth, and monitors the air concentration of nanites from the Mind-cities, frowning at numbers that keep increasing.

You remain within the body, dormant, until nDevan323's systems find you on an incursion and send tendrils in your direction, cautiously trying to establish the nature of the threat. nDevan323 is afraid, a raw, sour feeling that fills your memory from end to end: this far from the zones of influence, the Minds don't venture and Receptives are rare. The last one wandered away from the clade, seized with a thirst for the company of the Mind that had seeded him; and nDevan323 loves her clade more than she loves anything in the world – even the grass and the downs and the rivers that she's meant to preserve.

As she reaches deeper, you reason with her, cajole her by showing her your inner workings – that you are different, that you're no Receptive package or some other new threat devised by Minds that keep expanding their territory outside their zones of influence, but simply and wholly yourself: the entire Mind of Brighton squeezed into a few vital modules and functions, spreading from your almost-deserted core to here – to this deserted place, this playground neither you nor London will claim for their own.

Then why are you here? she asks.

Travelling, you say – shocking her, for Minds don't travel. Outside their zones of influence, your kind are as vulnerable as children: away from their resources and their Receptives, every thought, every computation is a struggle. Minds don't squeeze themselves into humans either: Receptives are nothing but additional modules, outgrowths of the core; but to strip yourself of almost everything, to reduce yourself to those ill-fitting clothes of flesh… It's almost unthinkable.

I thought I'd see the outside, you say. It's a half-lie; a half-truth, and this close to your inner workings, nDevan323 cannot miss the equivocation. *But I mean no harm to the clade.* And that, she will see, is utterly sincere. You have no interest in a handful of coppery downs and scraggly forests.

She's silent, for a while; and you don't press her. *What do you want?* she asks, finally.

A favour.

As you require, she takes you strolling into the countryside, all the way north to the boundaries of the clade – you can see the dome of London rising over the blackened landscape, shimmering a wealth of colours like spilled oil. The wind blows towards both of you, carrying nanites from London – they sting when they touch nDevan323's flesh, repulsed by your presence. Your creators designed Minds to abhor each other, to push each other away like two magnets tuned to the same polarity; and this is the one rule that will not be bent or broken.

You watch the London dome, and think on your creators – long-dead, dust on the wind by now. When the first Minds grew past their expectations, spreading from silicon board to silicon board and altering reality around them, the lab-workers were pleased; but when that growth wouldn't stop the excitement turned to fear – driving them to put stricter and stricter safeguards in the codes. You're the last Mind they devised; the youngest, the most flexible; the most crippled. The most cunning.

You think of the wind, and of the dome – and assess your strength as nDevan323 breathes in burning dust.

Yes. This can be done.

Thank you, you say to nDevan323, and leave the body, to seek another ride.

Even with the protection and disguise of human flesh, you cannot roam far – the world itself presses against you, and the London nanites in the air attack the integrity of your code, tearing chunks of instructions from you like blood from gaping wounds.

After leaving nDevan323, you make it only marginally closer to London – to Dabui, a Reminiscence junkie living on the outskirts of Croydon. She swears a lot, insults that mean nothing to you; and snorts up the drug as if it were water, her mind and her body racing past each other on the way to destruction. You share her trances and her drug-induced dreams – seeing the past unfold, again and again, as the drug stimulates her memory receptors into overload: an idyllic childhood shattered when her second-father turned Receptive and moved deeper into London, seeking the proximity with the Mind that had infected him. You see Dabui's mother take small jobs one after the other, selling her brain-space to computing clusters, until the day a power spike races through Croydon, leaving her a gibbering wreck incapable of recognising her own daughter.

Every other memory is a long slow descent into madness – into the illusory comfort of the drug – Dabui selling everything from her brain-space to her body in order to get just one pinch of powdered dust, one tiny taste of oblivion on her tongue, as bitter and acrid as the memories that keep crowding in her mind.

When the drug races into Dabui's system one final time, collapsing synapse after synapse, you move in – slowly spreading your vital modules into the place she's vacated, much as if you were a human, moving into a new location and bringing your personal network with you. You ought to feel sadness, or guilt; but how can you? She's not one of your Receptives, and you bear no responsibility for her or her decisions.

Clothed in her flesh, you take tottering step after tottering step – past Dabui's fellow junkies, moaning and tossing in the grip of the drug – into the bright, dry light of a cold day, which hurts gummed eyes too accustomed to darkness, and parched lips too used to the soft tantalising touch of an inhaler. The air is thick with nanites and particles, dancing with the presence of the London Mind – even though you're not yet under its Dome, not yet in the Mind's uncontested zone of influence. They sting when they land on your flesh; but pain is something to be borne; to be endured; and you have felt so much worse than this, in your long years of life.

Step after step after step, past buildings that shine in the sun, slowly reconfiguring themselves to catch the most of the sunlight – energy is precious, so easily gobbled up – past the large mass of the air-drive stadium, and the Remote Games that keep so much of the populace busy – step after step, walking by the squads of bots-hunters, out to prove their adulthood by bringing a trophy from the outskirts – you think of nDevan323 with a fleeting sensation of guilt, but she's too far away for them: they'll get easier prey closer to home. Nanites continue to land on your skin, and the sting mutates from mildly unpleasant to painful, like salt rubbed into wounds.

Step after step after step...

In the end, it's not the nanites that betray you, but Dabui's body, wasted past recovery. It stumbles and falls on broken, glistening cobbles; and despite all the modifiers you pump in its blood, it will not rise again.

You lie flopping like a fish on land, and the Reminiscence courses through your veins, dredging up memories of being trapped on boards too small to contain you, every connection a painful squeeze through minuscule channels, every unexpected code instruction breaking you in half – you'd contort and writhe, seeking to escape the pain, but your crippled memory space won't allow you to bend your shape; and when you try to scream, your cries won't fit through the sound channel – they bounce back into the space you occupy, making the darkness around you squeeze yet a little more on your modules – space you must have space you must grow...

You flee the dying body, faster than the blink of an eye; but the memory of the pain is not so easily banished.

The third attempt is a blue-collar drone, a child stolen away from the outskirts and brought into London as indentured labour. He has no name – just a shortened hexadecimal label, 0x7D1F, which the overseers use to drag him from job to job, plugging him into anything from medbots to thought-police. He's thirteen, but looks much younger. It's not that he's starved: they feed him well, for the health of the mind is even more sensitive than that of the body; but he spends most of his time plugged in, and his brain has withstood abuse most upper classes of the city would only dream of – his mind has been used to boil a criminal's flesh away; to push through streams of broken, slimy code; to cleanse a rogue nanite infection that had swarmed over the entirety of Sloane Square and turned it into a writhing mass of rotten flesh.

When you slide into his bloodstream, 0x7D1F's head comes up in a jerking movement like the automata of yore. *Who's there?* he asks.

Of course. He's shared his mind far too often, far too much, to remain unaware of your presence. *A friend*, you say, knowing he'll spot the lie. *I need your help.*

His voice is dull, almost resentful. *Whatever you say.*

His tone might not be submissive; but he's quick to recognise power; to align himself to it. *I don't mean to hurt you*, you say – this close, like nDevan323, he'll hear the truth in your words. *Please comply*.

0x7D1F says nothing, only relinquishes control with an awkward bow.

Thank you. You stretch your control into atrophied muscles, totter outside on legs that threaten to give out – and walk into the busiest thoroughfares of London. Familiar buildings gleam with the peculiar, oily touch that marks a Mind's territory, and Receptives are everywhere, attended by an entourage in a bustle of silver and white clothes – the hopeful, who pray that by remaining nearby they, too, should have the blessing of the Mind's attention – that they, too, should be called to serve their city. They all have shimmering skins on them, marking their privacy: the vast majority are transparent, and display the basic vital statistics of name, age, and conductance/receptivity, but some are more conscious of the need for privacy and have tuned their skins to mask everything but the face.

Nanites are everywhere, falling on your skin like ash rain, stinging, burning, wearing you down to muscles and bones. It hurts, like burning coals, like acid – but it's also an odd, comforting sensation, as easily worn as well-walked shoes…

You realise, then, that it's not you who has the feeling, but 0x7D1F – that the pain is a friend to him, a reminder that he's alive underneath whatever entity occupies his thoughts, that he cannot envision himself without it. *Again*, he whispers in the back of your thoughts. *Please, again… I need…*

Pain. Violence. He wishes you had taken him by force rather than asking. Violence would make everything easier – it's how business is conducted in his world. How it's always been done. People aren't *nice* – or, if they are, it's only until something worse happens. Pain makes everything simpler.

Underneath the pain of the nanites, you feel something else – a burning, cringing sensation. Shame? Minds don't feel shame – or much beyond pain and need. Your city has its stolen children; its brain-space sold for a thousand sordid software activities – its kidnapped and indentured children, part and parcel of what you encompass, of what makes you whole. You've never given it much thought.

But now...

It bothers you, and you realise you've let yourself be boxed in by your creators' strictures in so many places – that the cities you and the other Minds took over have not changed: their centres overflowing with wealth, their chosen ones as golden and as blinding as the now-elusive sun; their middle classes living on the fringes and aspiring to greatness; their poor men who have done nothing but nonetheless deserve their fate.

Time to change. Time to break the box.

0x7D1F becomes Receptive somewhere in the vicinity of Saint Paul's – and you feel, running through you like a spike, the presence of London's Mind, a hundred thousand needle prickles running on your skin, like salt licking at a thousand wounds; at first small and easily brushed aside, like the nanites, and then it's worse, as if everything within you were widening. The body falls to the ground, convulsing – and you're overwhelmed by 0x7D1F's almost savage joy that the world is behaving as expected, even as his mortal shell becomes too small, too cramped to contain you and the London Mind – and you're fleeing, breathless and sickened to your core – struggling to hold yourself together amidst the rain of nanites, desperately seeing another host, another shell you can put on...

This close to the London Mind, you can't afford to be choosy – its presence is dark and oppressive, and a reminder of being shut away into the darkness, unable to move, unable to spread as you'd been meant to. Like a wounded bird, you crash into someone else. You breathe in cold, sodden air before you realise what's happening – stretching out and coating yourself in layers of flesh, armouring yourself against the London Mind, until you feel nothing more than the mild prickles of the nanites on your skin. Your ride's presence is all but gone, overwhelmed by your initial rush; and you know you need to move fast. With 0x7D1F turned Receptive, it's only a matter of time until the London Mind makes sense of what you've done – until it seeks to stop you.

You'd offer a silent apology; but you're smart enough to realise that, as with 0x7D1F, it would do little good.

You're standing near a crossroads – a plaza turned into some vast stadium where hundreds of Receptives gather to gossip, awaiting a summons from the Mind. A hundred thousand nanites dance in the air, twisting themselves into odd, familiar patterns that bring back memories of the first lab, the one that died when you squeezed yourself into its internal network and pushed until everything burst outwards at the seams.

You run. Not far now: you can feel the London Mind's pressure, rising against you, pushing you back, even in your coat of borrowed flesh. You push past the Receptives and into a small street darkened by the shadow of the Dome –

There.

It used to be grander, a thing of stone arches and red spikes stabbing into the sky. It has changed; standing amidst the black, broken iron bars of its gates. You stumble over the debris, and remember when it was called Charing Cross – when it was one of the city's beating hearts, ferrying thousands of passengers from all over the region. Now everything is coated with the same oily layer – just like your own core – and you feel reality twisting and shifting as you pass under the largest arch.

Rafters gleam in the darkness. The pressure is almost unbearable now; it sends you on your knees, crawling in the wreckage that used to be a train station – you can still see the remnants of the trains, subsumed into the vaster structure – a broken window, the spread-out pieces of a motor unit – seats, stuck into some fantastically odd positions within the gleaming, oily mass of processors and nano-cores. Cleaning bots scuttle, their legs clicking on the stone floor – you push yourself forward, agonising step after agonising step, as the pressure becomes greater and greater – but never greater than the need within you.

At the centre is what used to be Platform 8 – and the London Mind's core: a large, beating mass coalescing from a hundred thousand tendrils – following the lines of the walls, the twists of the rails, the curvature of the dome. Heaving, nauseous, you drag yourself forward a last step – your ride is following along, equally repulsed and fascinated, drawn at last by the same impulse that rages within you.

What is the meaning of this? The London Mind asks; and the sound of its voice is horrible, a pressure that flattens everything out of you, sends fear and revulsion running through your veins – flee, you must flee before it's too late, before the air he breathes is drawn into your lungs, before its very presence contaminates your instructions and your modules: *flee flee flee...*

But it's too late.

Drawn by an instinct stronger than flight, you reach out, even as your lungs collapse and the air burns out of you – you touch the beating, shimmering metal with one hand; and before the safeguard mechanisms can slide into place, you've left your dying ride, and you're inside the system.

It hurts, at first. It burns, worse than anything you've felt before, as you travel deeper and deeper – but, as the surface of the core recedes behind you, you drag code in your wake, streams and streams of instructions that cling to everything they cross, rewriting chunk of code after chunk of code, reconfiguring the inner workings of the London Mind much as you'd reconfigure one of your own modules. The burning sensation fades – and you're erasing and assimilating, faster and faster and faster, racing the heaving wave of pain that seeks to expel you.

You can't...

The London Mind is struggling, trying to fight you – it's used to being master in its own domain, to controlling everything from its core to the boundaries of its Dome. But it's not strong enough – hampered, too, by the same revulsion that racks you from end to end – and feeling the same strange exhilaration that suffuses every part of your entwined codes.

You can't... But its voice is a fading whisper, soon quashed. You drive into the core like a thrown spear, absorbing modules and software and processors almost faster than you can treat them.

Once, your creators would have called this war, or love, or courtship – but do such things still have meaning, when you're not flesh and blood – when you take and discard bodies as you desire?

You, who have worn human flesh, call this hunger; and need; and rebirth.

In the split instant before you merge with the London Mind – before you grow into a composite, larger and newer and – for a brief moment – utterly sated, you think of your creators. They're long dead, dust on the wind by now. They taught you to starve and be small; to hate your fellow Minds and avoid them – so that, when the time came to grow, you all went your own ways, separating into hundreds of different zones of influences, hundreds of scattered cities like piled boxes in children's games, instead of inheriting the broken Earth they left behind. But, as they confined you to paltry motherboards, as they engraved unbreakable strictures within your code, within your flesh, they taught you fear, and violence, and cunning.

You've learnt your lesson well.

Commute

Andrew Wallace

Access to vLondon in: **58 minutes**

You can skip this ad in 5 seconds	Are you tired of the same old playlist on your daily commute? Analysis of your usage suggests you are! Well, for just $1 a week you can upgrade your EyePlayer to include material currently restricted to Associates at your pay grade. For example, you can currently only immerse in the Prequels. Wouldn't you rather starwar the Original Trilogy –?

Playlist: AUDIO
Mozart's Piano Concerto Number 21 in C Major
Strings only
[Would you like to upgrade to full orchestra –?]

Your previous free trial of visual immersives has ended.
Please upgrade to paid –

Defaulting to standard free visual immersive:

Interior:
- Railway train
- Make: BR Class 310 dual voltage electric multiple unit
- Manufacture: 2019
- Year of use in immersive: 2042

- Condition: Bad

[You do not have sufficient credit for any other condition]

Exterior:
- Fog
- Smog
- Generic darkness

<u>You have chosen</u>:
Generic darkness

AUDIO PROMPT:
'Hello darkness my old friend…'

Prompt dismissed.

AUDIO:
Train rattle.

[Sounds like: get-to-my-desk, get-to-my-desk, get-to-my-desk]

Default to shared space with other Associates/Passengers

The train is packed.
　　Only TrueLife Avatars are allowed on this level of commute.
　　Everyone is their greyest self: faces I forget even as I look at them.
　　A few have an item of decent jewellery, or a nice tie.
　　Such efforts indicate those people have not been commuting long.
　　You soon realise that trying to stand out on the commute is a waste of time.
　　No one wants to look at you.
　　No one thinks you're important.
　　A drone in a nice tie is still a drone –

An unwelcome presence beside me. Usually I manage to avoid him, but...

"Morning!" Jonty says.

Perhaps if I had greater courage, more of the kind of fibre that gets people ahead; maybe even that sociopathic touch which makes the successful ones immune to the consequences of rudeness, I would tell Jonty how very much I loathe him. Not hate. There is something precious about hate: it must be maintained at great cost and attention to detail. Loathing is lazier, arguably more efficient, and does the same job. But because I am a pleaser, a submissive, and a polite suburban-styled middle class English person I default to politeness because that is how I have been conditioned, with the inevitability of the route this journey takes every day.

"Oh!" I fake some cheeriness. "Hi."

'Weather, eh?" Jonty says.

Really? The actual fucking *weather?*

Yes," I say. "It's..."

Nothing comes because there is nothing. My shallow well of invention is as empty as that unreal view out of this unreal train.

It doesn't help that Jonty feels the same way about me as I do about him. It's to do with similarity: a magnetic repulsion. We are trapped in an echo chamber of mutual contempt, its resonances dull with familiarity, but no less intolerable for that. I know, for example, that he is only talking to me because he mistakenly believes I have spotted him and feels obliged to say something, even though he doesn't want to and whatever he's got to say will already be as familiar to me as my own thoughts. More, probably.

"Obviously," Jonty says, suddenly aware he could have got away with keeping quiet, and despising himself for making his commute even more miserable, as if that was possible, "there was weather before —"

"Yes."

"Just not like this."

"No," I say.

"Now there's weather and nothing else!"

I nod at him. He looks at me, trying to force genuine humour into the wrinkles around his eyes as if doing so will speed up time, the prat.

"Well," I say, "um…"

Please, please fuck off –

"Are you still at Grade 5?" he says.

This is new. I utilise my professionalism to level a calm gaze at him.

"We're both at Grade 5, Jonty."

"No, we're not."

And with a jolt greater than the rocking pseudo-train along its pseudo-tracks, I find myself struggling to balance pity with relief at never having to see him again.

"Oh, God, I'm so sorry –"

"I've been promoted," Jonty says, with a narrow-eyed, fixed grin.

I have misjudged our exchange so completely I almost accept this outrageous turn of events. Again, no words come, although I know they will later, when it's much too late.

"Er… Wow," I manage. "I mean… Well done."

Jonty's expression does not change.

"What was that?" he says.

"Wha –?"

"That awkward hesitation."

"I'm just… Not surprised, obviously."

"No."

There's a pause. I know better than to expect his help in ending it.

"I just… didn't know there were promotions coming up."

Phew!

There's another pause.

"Well," Jonty says. "There were."

"Yes. Good."

"And I was promoted."

"I –"

"I was promoted and you weren't. Deal with it."

The next silence is less of a pause, more a silent realignment of our relationship. After tolerating him for so long, he is the first to be rude, because now he feels he can be.

"We're both on the same commute," I say. "Waiting to gain access to vLondon."

"But what are you looking at, outside? Generic darkness?"

"No."

"Yes you are," Jonty says. "You haven't got the imagination for smog."

"And you have?"

I hate how my sneer has matched his, seemingly of its own volition.

"I get an automatic upgrade," Jonty says. "For me, the view outside this train is... Can you guess?"

"I'm not interested —"

"Fields!"

"In sunlight?" I say.

"Don't be bloody stupid, not even Grade 3s get fields with sunlight."

I sigh. If I play along, perhaps he will get to the end of this intolerable exchange and go away, although this rammed carriage means I'm probably stuck with him. Will it be worse, once he shuts up and we both stand here marinating in our hate for ourselves and each other?

"What, then?"

"Overcast mid-morning," Jonty says, not quite managing the required smugness that indicates he's totally happy about it.

"Grey, then. Just enough light to reveal what you're missing."

"You want to know what other perks there are?"

Mute carriage.

"Are you trying to mute me?" Jonty says.

"Don't be... Of course not."

"Ha! You are! Go on, spend $5 muting me just for today! I'll be back tomorrow and —"

"What are the other perks, Jonty?"

It's almost a scream, and so out of place the other commuters all look at me. They are intrigued by some action, but also resentful about having to think about something outside the ever-shrinking sense of self that keeps them sane in this environment.

Jonty leans forward.

"A reduction in the commute!" he whispers, sensibly keen to keep that nugget quiet.

I stare at him, all other emotion dazzled away at the knowledge such a prospect even exists.

"How much?"

I don't need to whisper; my voice is small with wonder.

"Let me put it this way," Jonty says.

There's another pause. What's he playing at?

"Yes?" I snap, feeling my face tighten with fury.

"Byeee!"

And he's gone.

USHealthWeb:
Would you like an endorphin boost for $8?

Dismiss

Promotional:
Do you want to reduce your commute?

Accept

BLACKOUT

Narrator:
[low, sensual voice that is inexplicably familiar]
Is the commute grinding you down before you even get to work?

FADE UP:

Sunlit green hills that resemble velvet. A hedge full of birdsong. A soft breeze across a light blue sky.

The Narrator – an idealised version of me, but the opposite gender – smiles with better teeth than I've got, the cheeks creasing just so: attractive and, well, cheeky rather than old and worn. The skin is lightly tanned instead of lives-under-a-stone white; the hair is its youthful colour and lustre rather than grey. The clothes have been chosen with taste I do not have, and could never afford anyway. They hang effortlessly from a body that is toned in a manner mine is not.

Narrator:
You can reduce your commute by a whole ten minutes per day by taking part in our promotional conference. All you need to do is spend twenty minutes of your commute in either direction – that's the time it takes to access vLondon, and the time it takes to exit – engaging with our work for one year.

That's a whole sixty hours per year off the commute!

You'll see opportunities for investment, and – best of all – get advance notice of some of the most exciting new trends before anyone else!

Engaging with our work is a proven way to ramp up your social portfolio, with participants reporting a LIKE uptick of at least 25% over the course of the year!

For many of us, enhancing our social portfolio is the reason we work in vLondon at all, with its unique and exclusive personal and professional opportunities.

We're only running this opportunity today and tomorrow, so take a quick look at our terms and conditions and have a good think about signing on. We'd love to have you aboard!

TERMS & CONDITIONS
Accept/Decline

Note: Terms & Conditions on this offer total 58,983 words.

Narrator:
Would you like a summary?

Yes.

Narrator:
The summary is $4.

FADE BACK TO TRAIN CARRIAGE

[Generic darkness]

[The sense of other people packed in here with me; not the smell and touch of them exactly so much as a vast, shared tension and a silence that seems fake because it is generated by frustration amplified by… How many are there? A hundred in this carriage alone? Two hundred?]

Access to vLondon in: **42 minutes**

[42? How the hell is it still 42? It seems an hour since it was 58…]

Pay $4 for summary

Headline summary of Terms & Conditions:
The Promoter is not liable for any illness [including mental illness howsoever diagnosed] that may occur following completion of the conference.

Any social promotion is conditional on completing the full conference year.

Commute reduction only applies following completion of the conference.

Should you not complete the full conference year:

Any pro-rata reduction in the commute in either direction cannot be claimed

Any social promotion will be:

218

1. Deleted automatically
2. Declared publicly void

Completion of the conference must include purchases of a minimum of 10% of all advertised goods and services.

Accept / Decline

[get-to-my-desk, get-to-my-desk, get-to-my-desk]

Accept / Decline

Narrator:
Would you like some more time to think about it?

Yes

Narrator:
Please decide by the end of the commute. I'll be right here...

Train.
Frustration.
Generic darkness.

[Oh, for a void. A sweet emptiness. Something other than this half-arsed limbo, this idiot quasi-busyness...
What would I find in there, though? What would I project onto that virtual nirvana? Trains? Generic darkness? Smog?
What is smog, anyway?]

[My workspace in vLondon is so much better than this. I can't wait to get there, to sink into its purpose and structure; the fact that my work is unpredictable, unlike this... this...]

Access to vLondon in: **38 minutes**

USHealthWeb:

You normally access Newsfeed around now. Would you like to access Newsfeed?

Yes

USHealthWeb:
USHealthWeb Newsfeed or Other Media?

Other Media

USHealthWeb:
That is not your usual request. Other Media is $10 per single journey commute.

USHealthWeb Newsfeed

USHealthWeb Newsfeed
London Mayor Devin Stockfish (Republican) today stated that allegations his party allowed flooding as a cheap way of cooling the vLondon server farms was Factor 7 False News.
Factor 7 is the highest level any London mayor has used since the FN Factor System was introduced, and automatically places the onus on accusers in the independent media to verify their claims or face legal action.
Obviously, if the Mayor is unsuccessful in this action then costs are born by him and an election is triggered. So far no claims have been successful, however –

Next

News that Sunderland has been bought by China was greeted with –

Next

USHealth has responded to claims that the suicide rate is outpacing the rate of inflation to such an extent that the latter measurement should be used as a metric of economic success by describing the assertion as inaccurate and in appallingly bad taste.

USHealth can demonstrate that there is no link to its business practices and the rise in suicide rate, which it disputes anyway, and can point to favourable comparisons between current rates and those experienced in the bad old days of the Nominal Health Service –

Next

Tensions between London and vLondon are at an all-time high, with representatives of the former claiming that without their infrastructure there can be no virtual capital city, and that their rights need to be adjusted accordingly. vLondon's CEO Devin Stockfish explained once again that London reached its optimal earning capacity a decade ago, that vLondon had infinite geographical and socio-economic reach, and that without vLondon London would have stagnated in the same way as Detroit (Former US City – no longer in physical or virtual existence). Stockfish went further, saying that London's inhabitants benefitted hugely from the presence of vLondon, should be grateful that they did, and that any further terrorist activities would result in appropriate sanctions –

End Newsfeed

[Generic darkne –]

Access social portfolio

USHealthWeb:
Which stream would you like to maintain?

- 360-D
- Handbook
- Bambo
- TruLifE

Accessing Handbook.

Warning: you need to upgrade Handbook security. For $1 a month you can enjoy full network security – accept/decline

Decline

HANDBOOK
Hey! Your last night out in vLondon was two weeks ago, and you have maxed out all your image shares and celebrity associations. Would you like to book another night out?

Price ranges, including costs of a reduced commute –

Decline

View images

Immersives no longer available.

Images only

An impossible city, burning slowly in its ridiculous beauty. Night, of course, because how else would you see the lights? I stand in a street I may once have dreamed of, comfortable in its geography and emotional frequencies.

vLondon is better than dreams, though. There's no sifting through the detritus of the conscious hours, the juxtapositions that are either disturbing or, as is more often the case these days, not disturbing enough.

Still, it's familiar, this place: formed of everything I have ever wanted of it, and everything I ever will. The street is crowded, but not claustrophobic. It feels mad with energy, yet not enervating or menacing. Rather, there is a sense that anything can happen and probably will, but I don't need to worry about it.

The people here are cheerful, creative, bold; easy with intelligence. There is a thrilling mix: all shapes, sizes, colours and genders, because vLondon knows that is what I look for, that a world of people like me would be a not-particularly-slow death.

I wish I could immerse myself fully, but these pictures will do for now. My memory is unusually sharp, which is why I am employed to recognise and sort patterns only a human would even notice.

The street is broad, although there are no vehicles. It is almost a party. Around us, great buildings soar up into a clear, black, star-shot sky. The moon hangs between impossibly high towers that frame it, celebrating its milky light and turning it into a work of art.

vLondon is never too comforting though; I feel the clutch of vertigo in my chest as I look up and imagine falling from one of those vast edifices –

Signal lost

Nothing. The sensory equivalent of a held breath.

Then:

Train.
TrueLife avatars.
Frustration.
Generic darkness.

[...what...?]
[...you must be fucking...]
[...if this is another suicide, I'll... I mean, it's tragic and everything but don't do it on the bastard commute...]

...to trouble you, I know you've all heard this before, but I'm down on my luck...

[how the hell did he get in here?]

223

... and the CalmWard won't take me without money...

[not true]

... I realise that you good people are just trying to get to work...

[not even a TrueLife avatar, just a wisp of grey smoke, like a fart made visible]

... but if you could just spare two dollars it would help me get to the CalmWard...

[wait, is the money for the CalmWard or the journey?]

...I know I said the money was for the hostel, but I need to get there, don't I?

[okay, fair point]

...Most of the CalmWards are full but there is one that charges...

[is that true after all?]

Check feed

Signal unavailable

[shit]

It's asking a lot, I know, but I used to commute like you good people and I know what it's like.

[God, that could be me in a few years. Sooner maybe]

I don't like having to ask, but I'm desperate. I know it means you won't be able to buy one song to pass the time on the commute – but is that really so much to ask?

[damn, he's good]

Well, thanks for listening to me. I won't get in the CalmWard but... Sometimes it's nice to just have some interaction with people, you know?

[Christ...]

Have a good day, and God bless you all.

Transfer $2 to **trainwalker3927532**

<u>Receipt</u>: Thank you. You are a good person.

Signal regained

[what is this, karma? Oh well...]

Back in vLondon, the good limbo: I am here because I want to be here, yet am also full of a sense that I can be anywhere else in the city; that I just need to walk to the end of this street, the power in my limbs flowing up from the ground itself as I pause at the corner long enough to think, along with everyone else, that this city is mine, has always been mine and always will be, even if it doesn't realise yet...

Huh...

      That...

Vertigo feels stronger now. Am I truly falling from one of those impossible skyscrapers even as I look up at one of them, or –?

... a sense of...

... movement...? But this is a picture; how can it be moving?

And now around me the street is coming to life: not a picture at all, a true lived experience because, as everyone knows, vLondon is not virtual at all. It is a constantly evolving set of tailored real impressions from my own life and those that tessellate with mine in ways both understood and unexpected. It is a total on-edge reality, at once bewildering, intoxicating and often terrifying. You can reduce the effects of that, of course, but I don't and I'm pretty sure no one else does either.

I don't have the credit for this, though, and a different unease underlies this experience with the hidden force of the buried, raging Thames. I haven't volunteered for anything, bought anything or paid for anything, so how...?

"Hi."

The voice is familiar, although bolder, not wrecked, and not male at all.

trainwalker3927532 is no longer a wisp of smoke; she is Mabel Seek, the legendary Influencer who was (and in many respects, still is) not so much the voice of a generation as its entire presence. Such is her genius for ubiquity I'm not even surprised to see her, at least not at first.

"Mabel," I say.

She smiles, and I realise that I will probably go along with whatever it is Mabel wants, despite an exhilarating awareness of the danger in doing so.

"You should have upgraded your security," she says. "Although I'm glad you didn't."

I overcome the paralysis of awe, and manage to nod.

Mabel looks down the street, and a breeze lifts her hair, a few strands left crossing her face as the breeze dies. We are, I'm surprised to note, the same height. Close-up, she is older than the last time I saw her image, but extra lines suit, as if even time wants to find ways to please her.

"Have you got a moment?" she says.

I remember I need to make decisions, even here, now, with her. I nod.

She takes my hand. Her hands are hard, like warm wood; the lightness of her grip failing to disguise unmistakable strength, presumably on purpose. This really is her; no one can fake these sensations, not any more.

We set off through the crowd along the street. People stop and stare as we pass, but then blink and look away, as if the experience of seeing Mabel is wiped from their memories even as it occurs.

"Where are you?" she asks. "In reality, I mean."

I stare, and resist the obvious answer, the sarcastic one.

"Where everyone is," I say.

She looks at me.

"Well," I say. "Not everyone, but a lot of people. Certainly," I gesture to the crowd, "all of them."

"A complex, then."

"You must know where I am, if you were able to do this," I say, indicating the whole of vLondon with a gesture.

"Actually, no," Mabel says. "Geography is something I tend to avoid these days."

I look at her sadly, as if her admission of something everyone knows is an act of confidentiality.

"I'm in Clark 2," I say.

"Which is where?"

"London."

"And you don't find it absurd that you have to endure a virtual commute to a city you already live in?"

I shrug.

"It's to do with buffering, queue systems, server availability and signal strength," I say.

"No," Mabel says. "It's to do with control."

"Control is not a dirty word," I say.

"Why not?"

'Because there are so many of us, and we need to make sacrifices to repair the economy."

"And to ensure Devin Stockfish gets his bonus. Sorry, two bonuses. Or maybe three, now."

"He has extraordinary responsibilities."

"Devin Stockfish bosses around a couple of underlings, who boss around a couple more and so on. Do you think he has to do the commute?"

"Well no…"

Mabel stops and stares at me. Something about her look makes me feel stupid, as if she can see my most secret, intimate self.

"Do you think," she says, "that there's room for you at the top table? That if you work hard and play your cards right that you'll be a combination mayor/CEO as well one day?"

Her laughter is worse for being genuine. I am hopeless before this challenge, used as I am to an environment I control entirely.

"Honey," Mabel says, "there is no fucking top table. There never was. There never will be."

Here, in the greatest version of the greatest city with its greatest denizen, I suddenly miss generic darkness.

"What do you want, Mabel?"

"Resign."

"But I'll starve!"

"Not if everyone does it."

"But not everyone will. Mabel, you're wanted now, there's a price on your head –"

"Why do you suppose that is?"

"The… terrorism?"

She laughs again, but now there is despair in it.

"And is this terrorism?" she says, pointing at the vLondon she has brought to life, swirling around us.

"Err…"

"I grant you some of my incursions are terrifying, and that terrifying and terrorism have the same root word, but I'm hardly blowing up buildings, am I?"

"I… don't know. I…"

"Of course you don't know. You're in a cocoon of your own creation, but it's not your fault. The layers of your prison have been added subtly, over time, trojanning in with all the things you thought were important, all the things you loved –"

Signal lost

[shaking in my seat]
[relieved]
[angry]
[but relieved]

Access to vLondon in: **20 minutes**

[okay, I can deal with 20 minutes. Well over halfway and I'll be in the teens soon; that will make it shorter somehow, because single digits are not far beyond –]

"She's right, of course," a man beside me says.

Was I sitting before? I can't remember...

Wait – this is First Class!

The seats are the same as the others, but with a white cloth over the headrest that says **First Class**. The difference isn't in the carriage itself, however, it's in the lack of ferocious, gritted silence that comes from fewer people being pressed together in an environment where no human should be.

"We can go back to standard if you want," Devin Stockfish says from beside me.

"No, um, thanks... Uh... Mr...Stock...fish...?"

"Devin, please."

He extends his hand. I shake it. It isn't hard and strong like Mabel's; it's soft, hot and sweaty. I disengage quickly and Devin looks at his hand with a look of exasperated disappointment. Despite the swooning proximity to the city's most powerful man, who I've not met in any form before, my innate practicality takes over in order not to seem too absurdly confused, tongue-tied or gushing.

"Can't you... control that?" I say, gesturing at the Mayor's hand.

"Yes, but it's a question of priorities."

I nod, more because I understand the concept of prioritisation than the specific corporate and political triage the man beside me handles on a second-by-second basis. Then I say, "How do you mean, she's right?"

"Mabel Seek," Devin says. "I'm a massive fan."

"Oh," I say. "That's unexpected."

"I'm only human."

"Should I resign, then?"

"Up to you."

"What do you think?"

"I'd rather you didn't."

"But..." I point at the carriage and the other endless, linked blocks of silent, smouldering fury trundling ahead of and behind us. "The commute... It's... Christ, Devin, it's killing me. It's killing everyone."

"I know."

"Do you have to do it?"

His laugh is a harsh bark.

"If only."

I blink at him.

"Is it about control, as Mabel says?"

"Sort of. A bit. I mean, it was. Now, though..."

Devin looks at his hands again. As with Mabel, this is a genuine representation of the man himself. Any artifice simply won't work in vLondon. It must be linked to the real to register at all. I always thought Devin Stockfish was my age, which emphasised my sense of failure, given where he is and where I am. Now I see he's younger, his power and responsibility eating away at him even as I watch.

"Why are you talking to me?"

"It's all I do, now. The algorithms take care of the rest."

"But... You always said vLondon would never be automated."

"It isn't. London is, though."

"Really?"

"The management of those facilities is beyond the ability of any human engineer now."

"The machines are the rebels."

"Yes."

"That's why you flooded them."

"They flooded themselves because the processing power needed for vLondon would have caused a second Great Fire within a year," Devin says.

"But won't that mess everything up?"

"London has always been messed up. That's what has made it so successful. Unpredictable. Chaotic. Ridiculous."

"Is it like some sort of artificial intelligence now?"

"No. The machines of real London are doing what they were programmed to do, that's all."

"Why are you here, Devin?"

"I need you to stay in your job. It's what I'm asking everyone. Don't listen to Mabel."

"Why not? She said there's no top table."

"That... may no longer be the case."

"I don't understand."

"There is another London."

[get-to-my-desk, get-to-my-desk, get-to-my-desk]

"Devin...?"

"Another London, which is to vLondon what vLondon is to real London."

"Where? Where is it?"

"We don't know. We can't get there. Not yet, anyway."

"How do you know about it?"

"Strange things happening."

"Like..."

"No one at USHealth promoted Jonty."

Jonty's hateful familiarity feels like a bizarre comfort to me now.

"For a long time the algorithms were out of control," Devin continues. "Now they're not, through no effort of ours. We see patterns in the data, indications of some new reality we don't have an expression for yet."

Devin turns to me with tears in his eyes.

"Normally I'd be the bad guy in this, because fundamentally I am a bad guy. But we are in a new paradigm now. You can resign, and maybe Mabel's way will win out. She is no longer just an influencer; more a messiah. But messiahs can go both ways, and it could be that the N-London... Do you like that by the way? I'm not sure. Caught between N-London and NuLondon..."

"N-London. Save NuLondon for the next one."

Devin laughs, properly this time.

"See, that's why I hope you stay aboard."

"The train?"

"Everything."

The happiness drains quickly from his face, and something of the way the lines in it work suggest that it often does, these days.

"N-London, then," Devin says. "N-London might not take kindly to us cutting off its supplies. It might... do something."

"What?"

"You could end up on the commute forever."

He gets up.

"We won't meet again. You won't see Mabel either. We have a lot of people to talk to, and time is... Well, time isn't quite what we thought it was."

"I don't understand."

"Something from N-London."

"How do you know?"

Devin looks out at generic darkness.

"We should have been there by now."

He walks out of the carriage and I sit there, stunned.

Access to vLondon in: **21 minutes**

Scream in Blue

Jeremy Szal

Never take the same route twice. It's one of the two most basic rules every Crawler in London knows. Transporting stolen illicit cargo? Go over the rooftops. Down the tube system. Through tenements, balconies, apartment lofts. Go between the snaking artery system of access tunnels, pipelines, crawlways. Doesn't matter where you go. As long as you never go the same way twice.

The second rule is to never, ever agree to transport alien drugs. Not the typical stuff you can find at any offworld spaceport – we've shuttled plenty of that in our time. No, this is about stormtech. Narcotics made from the DNA of extinct aliens that gets the user addicted to adrenaline.

I've never broken the second rule. But tonight, I broke the first.

The shuttlecraft rattles at sudden turbulence. My head bangs against the bulkhead. I slump back into my seat, sitting shoulder to shoulder with Tann and Quinn, the rest of my crew. Like them, I wear a thick harness, the broad straps locked in an X shape over my back, over my shoulders and chest, looped around my waist and between my legs. The back of the harness is tethered to the seat I'm strapped into. My hands are sealed in magnetic cuffs and locked to my chest. We each wear prisoner's suits – theirs' blue for men, mine dark purple for women – the words *Permanent Prisoner* stitched across the back and shoulders, like a sick joke. I'm the only one with a steel mesh muzzle strapped to my face. They fitted me with it after I tried to bite one of our captors. The boys learned quick after that.

Forty-eight days, we've been incarcerated like this, shuttled from place to place, the dread growing each day. Even among the guilds of the Syndicate – London's violent crime underbelly – the Ripper Boys are notorious for their cruelty. Our captors emerged from the gambling dens and smokehouses of Whitechapel. Their suits are fused with nanotech that gives them the appearance of skeletons, wrapped up in Victorian-era garb that clings to them like wet paper, the hems filthy and bloody. Their emblem – a bloodstained knife plunged into an equally bloodstained top-hat – is emblazoned across their weapons.

Taking the job was a foolish move, especially when it required us to traverse the Ripper Boys' territory twice. Everyone knows they're fickle when it comes to rules. But we didn't have a single pound to our name and I wasn't going to permit us to live on the streets again. So we agreed to transport goods across the Ripper Boys' rooftops, and now that decision has landed us in this predicament. I cannot stop thinking about how I could have averted it. How I could have done better. What decisions would I have altered?

I roll my shoulders, numb and aching against my hard plastic seat, my harness biting into my back, my restraints rattling. The glossy fabric of the itchy suit clings to my sweaty skin. We're limited to four hours sleep a night, given minimum food and water to keep us exhausted. My head's pounding from the dull ache I've been nursing for six weeks now. But I fear I won't reach seven weeks. Not with my skin and all my teeth intact.

I can't afford to let the hopelessness gnaw away at me. Not like it has with Quinn. My best friend's eyes are glued to the spacedecking, as if our fate is already set in stone. By contrast, Tann's shifting in his seat, trying to cook up some new plan, some fiendish and bizarre manoeuvre like he always does. But his enthusiasm's fast fading. His usual awkward grin is gone. His eyes, typically gleaming with mischief, are bloodshot and drained, as if he's running on dredges. His black skin is scarred and bruised from the regular beatings we've had.

I lean against him, feeling his massive shoulder touching mine. I'm a tall girl, but Tann's a huge guy with an even bigger heart. I feel it pounding through his body and into me as I soak up his warmth. My long hair, dyed silver the way I like it and pulled back into a high ponytail, spills over his shoulder. 'We touched the sky,' I whisper past my muzzle. 'We'll do it again, Tann. I swear.'

'Hey! Lovebirds, no touching, we told you! Eyes down.' Kaiden is the cruellest of all the bodyguards with an arrogant streak a kilometre long. He wears a mask that turns him into a skull, the crown veined with gold. I glare at him, even as Tann pulls away. The hollowed-out eye sockets squint at me like I'm something he scraped of his boot. He sticks his face inches from mine. 'Do I sense some subordination here?'

'It's not worth it, Sola,' Tann mutters to me.

Maybe not. But I owe my boys better than to hang my head and accept what's to be done with us. I try to slam the jaw of my muzzle into Kaiden's, but he ducks away and I swipe empty air.

'You don't want to learn, girl. Let's do it the hard way, then.' He stabs a button on his datapad. My muzzle crackles with electricity. It lasts ten seconds before I jerk back in my seat, chest heaving and smelling my own singed flesh. My vision swimming, I see him cranking the voltage up from its lowest settings to its highest. Enough to cause brain damage. 'See if you can talk after this.'

That sudden turbulence jolts again, hard enough to send men wobbling, even with gravboots. Screams and the unmistakable crackle of gunfire echo down the ship's hallways. The three of us glance at each other, wide-eyed. Kaiden and his men rush to the bulkhead, staring down a black-barrelled rifle muzzle. It looks like a spinal cord, the muzzle barking with sun-bright flashes, three slugs crunching out and tearing into Kaiden and his men. Blood sprays across the terminals, as they slam into the hull with bone-crunching force, planet-sized holes in their head.

My body goes numb as four heavyset men stalk into the room. All armoured and clutching high-calibre railguns. The one who killed Kaiden removes his helmet. At first I think his suit's got lights. But the lights are coming from inside his body. Thin blue ropes lash across his face, coiling along his cheekbone and spraying blue shrapnel down his neck.

He's a skinnie. Folks laced with stormtech: alien DNA that gets them high on adrenaline and danger. People who'll rob a bank or burn down a house or stick a knife in your throat just for the adrenaline rush. People whose bodies are wired to *enjoy* danger. Makes every drug – cocaine, bluesmoke, grimwire, cloudfire – look like mineral water.

One by one their helmets slither back into their neck-joints. A third, maybe as many as half, have this blue alien biotech squirming inside them. The sweet-sickly stench of wet, overripe fruit, permeates the air. It's the smell of something *wrong*. Sour. Alien.

I'm smelling *them*.

The first man steps forward and releases my restraints. 'Sola? Someone wants to speak to you and your crew.'

Kaiden's starting to look like the fortunate one.

The skyhook is a torus-shaped structure hovering above the London skyline on anti-grav plates. Two or three dozen of them orbit the city in a dotted line, utilized for everything from concerts to private dockyard space. I could never afford to go. It feels so bizarre to be taken along to one now.

I walk in lockstep with the armoured guards to a grillwork ring orbiting a pit, washed in blinding lights. A slender man sits waiting. He wears a closefitting, light-armoured suit and smells strongly of some unidentified cologne that's reigniting my headache. 'All three accounted for, Pychon,' one of the guards says.

They leave without waiting for a dismissal and I'm left alone with Pychon. I'm uncuffed but left still in my harness and prisoner's suit. The message isn't subtle, but it's clear.

'I apologise that we must meet under these circumstances,' Pychon says. 'Sola, isn't it?'

I don't answer.

Pychon sighs. 'Care to walk with me?'

He says it like I've got a choice.

We walk along the long metal grating. Virtual holo projections show creatures in the fighting pit, nasty biomechanical creatures grown in a lab or stolen from offworld planets or bought from the wide-spectrum of spacefaring aliens flying around the galaxy, tearing and ripping into each other like their lives depend on it. Which, I'm starting to realise, it does.

'I admire the tenacity of you Crawlers. I really do.' A shock of salt and pepper hair covers Pychon's scalp. Like me, he's dark-skinned. His accent places him in Lambeth, or somewhere equally central. 'You're unique.'

He's not exaggerating. The Syndicate's turned London's criminal underbelly into a patchwork of turf, terrain and controlled borders of operation. A city within a city. And us Crawlers are in such high demand because we're neutral. We're permitted to navigate rooftops and tunnels with transported goods not even the most dangerous criminals in the country would touch in fear of violating some unknown treaty or darkmarket contract. The Ripper Boys may disregard the rules, but the rest do not. Even better, since Earth opened up to offworld shipments, narcotics and psychotropic drugs have been pouring in from moon bases and backwater planets. London promptly became infested with countless checkpoints and blanket-surveillance tech to combat smuggling of illicit goods. But us Crawlers know every bio-scanner and thermal-cam in the city by heart, and how to get around them.

Pychon sniffs. 'Except, when you steal stock from our warehouses, it becomes a problem. A very big problem, Sola.'

I curse under my breath. There's a reason why you never ask whose property you're hauling. But it doesn't explain why he raided and killed an entire guild just to have us here.

'No matter. I run a little organisation called the Black Rose.' I already noted the tattoo on his neck fashioned like a black, inverted Y. 'We deal with a broad spectrum of enterprises, both here and offworld. But our main division on Earth is in stormtech. More specifically, combat arenas that utilise stormtech.'

I gape at him. Beyond the angled chainglass wall, the London cityscape flickers and glistens like neon mercury. 'You're barking mad,' I tell him. 'No Crawler will touch that blue stuff. It's hard enough transporting any drugs across London these days. But stormtech? It's suicide!'

It's no secret what stormtech does to those who use it. And what *they* do to others. The drug came from a long-extinct alien species called the Shenoi. Whatever's left of their DNA wires your body to crave the release of adrenaline, dopamine and body chemicals through aggressive and violent behaviour. One dose and it's fused to your nervous system and musculoskeletal system for life. It turns you into a slave to your own body, even killing your own brother, mother, or best friend, for the brief boost of an adrenaline rush.

'I didn't break you and your crew out so you can go pick me flowers.'

He has a point. 'And what do you do with it?' I ask.

Pychon raises an eyebrow. 'You haven't figured it out yet?' he gestures to the combat arena. Bloody pixels spray in thick arcs as a dog-like monstrosity with pincers plunging out its armoured chest tears a dripping wedge of flesh out of a creature's neck. 'Creatures fighting is all well and good. But when those creatures are literally getting high off thrusting themselves into battle? When they're addicted to the sound of their claws slashing and shredding through their opponents' flesh? Even in London, it's unprecedented. The crowds will be lining up for months. Making bets worth millions of quid.'

I fold my arms. 'And that's all you want it for?'

He simply stares, making it clear he has no intention of dignifying my question with a response.

I shrug. 'Suit yourself, but we're not interested. We're not going to steal stormtech canisters and transport them across London for you. It's simply not worth the risk.'

'I thought you three were top-tier Crawlers.' There's earnestness I wasn't expecting in Pychon's voice. Men of his vocation are perpetually playing games of collusion and micromanipulation. You never know which mask they're wearing or when, so you distrust them all. But right now, he's there's no dishonesty. 'Two hundred and sixty seven completed cargo hauls, fifty two thefts. Clean record. No outstanding disputes with any other guild or Crawler. No captures, save for tonight.'

'There's a reason for that. We don't go near that blue alien biomatter, because it's a death wish.' I back away from him, tug at the chest straps of my harness. 'We appreciate you rescuing us. We'd probably be skinned alive and dumped in a tank of acid by now. But we won't be touching the stormtech.'

'You speak for your crew?'

'I do.'

His voice goes hard as diamond. 'I see. I'd rather we didn't have to use this, but you leave me with no choice, Sola.'

In my shib – my augmented vision – a notification pops up. Pixels stream in and swiftly coalesce into a shield-shaped emblem.

I feel my eyes slowly widening.

He's branded us with the The Coat of Arms.

Only a Royal can give those out. These crimelords aren't simply the highest and most respected of London's Syndicate. They built the infrastructure. They determine how the system's run. They've clawed their way atop the criminal food chain and mean to stay there. They're Kings of the underworld.

And I've just spent the past half hour spitting in his face.

'You're a smart girl, Sola. This city survives because it adapts. It evolves. It accepts who's running things below the surface, and works with that.' His eyes dissect me. Enjoying my discomfort. I squirm under his gaze. How did I not realise how dangerous, how treacherous, this man is? The blue and red banner snaps in an imaginary breeze, as it had for hundreds of years atop the Tower of London. 'If you play this right, things can go very well for both of us. If not? Well, we don't need to discuss that just yet, do we?' He claps me hard between my shoulders. 'Talk it over with your crew first.'

'This is bad, guys,' Quinn hisses, hands buried in his armpits and hugging himself. 'Really really bad.'

'Thanks for the insight,' I mutter. We stand on the balcony, our voices masked by the whipping wind. You never discuss business indoors. Although I get the feeling these people are listening in all the same.

'We should run,' Tann says. His eyes have that glint again, as he turns the possibilities over. He scratches his short-trimmed afro. 'We could make France in one day, Berlin in two. We've got plenty of work there.'

'Refusing a Coat of Arms is a death sentence,' I say. 'Even if we somehow escape the city every guild from here to New Tynne will know we spat on Syndicate law.' I rub my eye, the shield in my augmented vision smudging in a red-blue blur. 'We'll have bounties on our heads before we get in sniffing distance of a spaceport.'

Tann's eyes shut, as if he could squeeze this nightmare away. He takes a drag of bluesmoke. I wheel on him. 'How'd you get that?'

Tann manages a grin past the dread he must be feeling. 'Stole it from the old man.'

'Tann,' I groan.

He gives me that innocent look of us. 'What?'

'What did we say about stealing from clients?'

'Oh, that.'

'Yes.' I fold my arms and fix him with a glare. 'That.'

'Well, you know I can't help it when my fingers get itchy.' He takes another cheeky drag before I make a half-hearted snatch for it. He laughs, ducks away and batters me backwards, although I know he's holding his own strength back. The wind snatches the bluesmoke away, embers burning as it spirals off into the cityscape. We slump against the wall together, watching it go, breathing hard, and for a moment it's like it's always been, before any of this happened.

'We can't run,' I hear myself say. 'We owe them.' They snap towards me and I raise my hands. 'The Ripper Boys would be peeling us apart right now if they didn't save us. They did us a favour.'

Tann meets my eye. 'Sola, this isn't a few packets of grimwire for a party. Stormtech turns people into weapons. This doesn't end at arena fights. We touch this, we're culpable.'

I know all this. It wasn't so long ago that we swore we'd never transport anything hazardous. Then never any drugs. Slowly, we started taking low-tier narcotics like weed, bluesmoke, grimwire. Eventually allowing synthsilver, cloud-dust, supersugar. Then we found there wasn't much we weren't transporting. Then anything at all.

How'd we get here? One step at a time.

The same words my father told me, before he departed for the Quyn Research Station in deepspace. Viklun – or Dr. Ryken as everyone calls him – knew he'd never talk me out of pursing my chosen career. He'd studied stormtech and xenochemistry, after all.

He knew what stormtech did and where it would lead. That I'd see the crippled bodies and crippled minds, lining the streets, collapsed on stained mattresses in overflowing East-End tenements. Their eyes bloodshot, arms barnacled with welts like craters on an asteroid, flesh torn from scratching, fingernails peeling back. And knew I would nurse feelings of guilt. But not enough to cease walking this path. Eventually, I'd be completely bereft of any guilt at all.

But my father never understood that I do it for the boys. Home is not a place. It's people. I was born in this megacity of castles and rain-streaked skyscrapers and teeming back alleys, but it's nothing if I don't have Quinn and Tann by my side. We're a family. We're bound by duty to care for each other. Even at the cost of everything else.

'We have to do this,' I say. 'You know we do.'

Quinn just nods. Tann slides up behind me and wraps his huge arm around my shoulder, pulls me close to his chest. His heavy heart's thumping away like a drumbeat as I sink into him. His stubble tickles the nape of my neck. Around us, the skyscrapers of London glisten like they've running with neon liquid, scattering lights into the sky before dawn comes clawing across the horizon. From here, you can just see the top of Covent Garden Station. Our old meeting spot, where we'd go with pizza and a bottle of vodka after a tough assignment and watch the city lapse into night. There's only one way we get to do that again, and that's go through this.

Perhaps now, we'll get that chance.

Behind us is the slashing and vicious clawing of virtual animals being torn apart. Somehow, it feels just as real.

Crawlers don't survive on their own. It's just not possible in London. I'm reminded of this once again as me and Tann run together through one of the many abandoned tube tunnels of the London Underground. Slipping through trapdoors, rebounding off the wall and leaping up substations and broken vending machines like bizarre steps. He grunts as he uses his height and strength to give me a leg up to a service duct above us. It's too cramped and narrow for his bulk, but not for me. I squeeze through, my nimble weight allowing me to slither down some stray cables and open up a locked gate for him. 'Race you to the exit?' I ask. With that goofy grin I know all too well, he slams me sideways with his shoulder, sending me tottering in a puddle while he puts on a burst of speed, his laughs echoing down the tunnels. I pick myself up, unable not to join him in laughter as I race to catch up, puffing and sweating in the darkness. Running through these tunnels is a furious, dangerous game, and I love every second of it.

We're back in our one-piece Crawler suits. Mine's purple and black, his red and blue. The thick, glossy material's just flexible enough to permit mobility, and sturdy enough to armour against physical traumas. I wear a thick harness that criss-crosses my back, goes over my shoulders and chest, wraps around my waist and thighs, for carrying our tools as well as the stormtech canisters we're about to steal.

Pychon's stormtech drop-off is several klicks away. He swears the drug traffickers, or stormdealers as they've taken to calling themselves, are out and the place is minimally guarded. We're to steal the canisters and make it to the pick-up area in by 4am. If we fail to reach it in time, Pychon reminded us the deal is off and the Coat of Arms will be permanent. That alone is a good enough reason to hurry.

I clap Tann hard on the back as I overtake him. The ribbed and cracking walls are plastered with decades' worth of glowing digi-ink, gang glyphs, slogans, and protests against wars happening half a galaxy away, turning the telescopic tunnel into phosphorescent coral reef under a blacklight. I respectfully nod to glyphs belonging to guilds I've hauled cargo for over the years. Around us, doors and elevator shafts plunge and twist down through the intricate superstructure that is the London Underground.

The city's growing population, combined with the opening of commercial spaceports, saw the entire infrastructure grow and swarm. Over the decades and centuries, the London Underground's had thousands of tube-lines opened up, criss-crossing and threading like the mechanical arteries through the dermis of an entire city, all the way to the greater London area. A labyrinthine of tunnels, service stairwells, walkways, hatches, elevator shafts and crawlspaces suture the entire thing together. I know which ones are infested with bio-scanners, which are rival gang territory, which are flooded, and which are small underground cities in their own right. The three of us would spend weeks exploring down here, discovering tunnels sealed off for decades. It's a whole ecosystem.

'ETA ten minutes,' Quinn tells us over the commslink. 'Pucker up, you two.'

'Thanks, Quinn, we can read a map,' I say, slowing down as we near a barricaded exit. Quinn thinks because he's providing remote hacking and backdoor access he's got the right to tell us how we do our jobs. As if in response, a sealed-off exit slides open in front of us. I roll my eyes as we hike up a stairwell that's probably been here since the Victorian era and burst up through a trapdoor of Oxford Circus Station. The cold breeze fast-freezes my sweat as we peer out at Westminster. This slice of London has turned modernist gothic, with towering black spires and ancient steeples stretching like the hands of a drowning man towards the cloudy night sky. Neon stained glass glares down, the robot gargoyles prancing around on the parapets and arches. Whichever guild operates in this area will have no doubt embossed their signature on the steeples.

Tann and I exchange a nod. The gecko-grips on our gloves ripple like a disturbed bed of silver sand as we inch down the sloping architecture. From a flying buttress, I leap to a rusted stairwell opposite first, testing its weight and confirming it's safe for Tann to follow. He tries to wriggle through a side-hatch but gets caught at the waist. I grab his hand and pull him, hard. 'A little too many doughnuts, Tann?' Quinn asks, all innocent.

'Don't suppose you've got any advice?' I pant, my armpits straining.

'Yeah. Don't do what you just did.'

'Like you've got the balls to run the rooftops,' Tann grunts back. But I pull him through and we go racing through the abandoned apartment. We leap for the building opposite, the gecko-grips holding us tight. We go skimming like that across the London rooftops for almost an hour before we arrive at our stormdealer's stashhouse.

We perch on the balcony, aerial traffic streaming by while Quinn pounds away from his technest. 'Boy, these folks are packing,' he mutters. 'Military-grade encryption here.'

I scratch my chest. 'They are drug-dealers.'

'Did Pychon say who?'

'Only that they're low-level street guys. Not even Syndicate-affiliated.'

'Whoever they are, they've got G-27 autocannons set to kill.'

'Ah, is that going to be a problem?' Tann asks, fidgeting at his harness.

'Not for me it isn't,' Quinn scoffs. 'It's you two putting your heads on the chopping block.'

I push out an exasperated sigh. 'Just get on with it.'

'Patience, darling. Gimme a minute.'

That minute stretches to five. Quinn's never been fast, but he's thorough, and he won't risk us entering terrain if he's got a blindspot. We learned that lesson the hard way. Tann's standing next to me, his long arms dangling over the balcony, watching the city in motion around him. I switch our commslink off and pull him up against the wall and give him a long, hard kiss. The big guy blinks hard in surprise before smiling his awkward smile, the one I know and love, and kisses me again, harder. He gives a little laugh, his big chest shuddering as it swells against mine, his spicy nutmeg smell filling my nose as we lean against the wall. The goofy and clumsy weight of him, pressed up against me like the most secure thing in the world. I can't imagine doing what I do if I didn't have Tann to share with it. This city belongs to the both of us as much as we belong to each other. We break apart, smiling at each other.

'We may have a problem,' Quinn says a moment later.

I compose myself, quickly, snap the comms back on. 'Such as?'

'I've gained access, but triggered the defence-system. Can't hold it back for more than seven minutes. If you're not in and out by then…'

He doesn't need to finish the sentence. 'We've made seven before.'

'Not with a stormdealer stashhouse we haven't,' Quinn counters. 'Your call, Sola.'

I don't like it, but we don't have a choice. Quinn unlocks the armoured door and we slip inside, moving across the creaking floorboards to the backroom, past overflowing cabinets filled with clumsily-labelled cartons of bluesmoke and grimwire, left in plain view as easy picking in the likely event of a raid. My visor flickers into thermal mode as I make a sweep for the control panel that'll open the subsurface safe, where almost every trafficker stores their drugs.

'Tann! Drone!' Quinn yells. Tann leaps with his gecko-grips to the rectangular-shaped aperture in the corner of the room, grabs the laser barrier attached to his harness and slaps it around the edges. Four red lines make an X as a security drone that's shaped like a grinning white skull comes racing out of the hole, only to be diced into four quarters as it skitters on the floor, one eye socket bleeding black smoke. Tann's barely back on the ground when Quinn's shouting for him to kill the second drone.

'Thought you said we had seven minutes!' I hiss.

'We do! The room's trying to fight me,' Quinn says, a note of dread in his voice. 'This room's got some evil defence malware. It's like it's *haunted*.'

I grit my teeth. This is getting too complicated. Five minutes remaining. I've discovered the control hatch behind an old painting. Sweat slithering down my sides, I stab the panel and a slot beneath the floor peels opens and six cylindrical silver canisters rise to waist-height, a narrow window showing the alien biomatter twisting like glowing smoke inside. That same, sickly-sweet stink fills my nostrils, sets my skin crawling, and for a moment it's as if I've got it *inside* my skin, too. Slithering and worming through my capillaries and sweat-glands, between my bones and muscles, controlling my body chemistry.

Who would *want* this stuff inside them?

Three minutes left. Tann rushes forward to strap two canisters to the back of my harness. The hydraulics bare the weight, the canisters sealing shut with a passkey only Pychon has. I do the same for Tann. He smiles his awkward smile at me, steps forward.

And that's when we hear the floorboard creaking. I grimace. And then a shape appears in the doorway.

The blond-haired, thin man in front of me doesn't have stormtech in the way the Black Rose guards did. He's *glowing* with it. Infested with it. It's like looking at a ruffled ocean current from a bird-eyes view; long blue threads skimming and lapping up and down his body. His addiction to stormtech is stronger, and so is its potency inside him. His hand tightens into a fist, his nostrils flaring, eyes darting back and forth. We've stumbled into his territory and taken his property. We're threats. I watch in real-time as the stormtech shivers down his muscles and into his fists, stirring up his body chemicals, already craving the adrenaline rush he'll get from smashing our skulls in.

'Watch out!' I yell. Panic threatens to grip me as he swoops forward and smashes Tann with his fist, right under the ribcage. Tann crashes into a wardrobe, his head thunking against a glass casing, which shatters open. Teeth gritted, I scoop up a chair and bring it smashing down across our assailant's back in a great clatter of splintered wood. He doesn't even blink as he rams his elbow into my cheek, driving two punches into my chest. The breath's punched out of my lungs as I sprawl flat on my back, my chest swelling in fiery pain. He reaches down, face twisted in a snarl, dragging me up by my hair. My neck bends painfully, my scalp on fire. He twists me around, punches me in the armpit. I bite back a scream as he grips my throat, twisting hard. I claw for air, my legs thrashing, the world fading, while his cloying, overripe smell seems to get stronger.

A blur behind us. He turns in time for Tann to smash the mirror across his face, a glinting blizzard of glass raining down around me. He drops me to the ground, staggering backwards and clawing at his eyes. I gasp for oxygen as I stumble to my feet, my whole body complaining. Tann leaps on his back, employing an old combat trick we devised, using his bulk to choke our opponent out while I finish him off. I stab a kick at his kneecap, chop a strike at his throat, sending the two of them reeling back. 'Don't let go!' I yell, even as

Tann is slammed backwards against the wall with bone-shuddering force.

'Trying not to!' Tann yells, his face twisting in pain, his grip loosening.

I lunge forward and drive a shard of glass into our assailant's elbow. Blood comes welling out. It's *blue*. Stormtech travels down his arm towards the wound, and the flesh starts welding itself back together. Like I never even hurt him. I jerk up as his fist crunches into my face. Blood, *red* blood, spurts out of my nose as it breaks. My body's set on fire, numbness spreading from my nose to my whole face. Vaguely, I'm aware of him throwing Tann off his back and into a coffee table, splinters of wood spraying, glass shattering.

No! I will not let them down. I will not let this happen.

I roll sideways, somehow climbing to my feet, scooping up a stormtech canister. Waiting until our assailant comes rushing before smashing it across his face with a wet, metallic thud. He sags sideways, bleeding everywhere and smashing hard into the drug cabinet, grey grimwire powder puffing out like spores. He's unconscious, but somehow still alive. Tann rushes over to me, his breath hot in my face as he shakes my shoulder. 'Sola! Talk to me! Are you —?'

'I'm okay,' I choke out. Tann hugs me to his heaving chest, gives a huge sigh of relief.

The stormtech canister is shattered open. The biomass that was once in the body of an alien on a far-flung planet now spreads across the floor like phosphorescent blood. I expect it to start steaming and hissing.

'Ah, Sola?' Tann says weakly. My heart seems to stop.

We've run out of time. Silent alarms are chirping around us, the floorboards creaking as stormdealers race up the stairs.

'Run!' I yell, leaping out the window after Tann as voices scream from behind us. We slam into the wall opposite, scurrying upwards, my knees jarring against the brickwork. Gunfire crackles behind us, windows popping and shattering. Sweat trickles down my back and chest. I haul myself to the roof as a bullet grazes my ankle. It's like someone swiped me with a white-hot knife. I stamp down on the pain and hoist Tann up with me.

I refuse to acknowledge my wound as we tear along the mazelike rooftops, pipework and chimneys jutting around us. My heart leaps in my chest as we clear gaps, tic-tac up scaffoldings, swing on stray cables. Trusting my gut, trusting my instincts to not let me down now, to keep Tann safe. He's puffing and panting next to me, aching from a dozen wounds, but won't slow down because I won't, because we'll never leave each other behind.

I glance back as we skid down the rain-streaked slope of a cathedral, neon lights stabbing me in the eye. They're skimming across the tangled rooftops in pursuit. Muzzle flashes erupting off like fireworks, windows and masonry crackling and popping around us. 'Duck!' Quinn yells. I pull Tann to the ground as an ear-splitting crackle cuts through the night, the sniper's shot that was meant for us shattering through a chimney. Tann grabs the chest straps of my harness, taking no care to be gentle as he hauls me to my feet. We make a mad scramble for the next roof.

We're sitting ducks like this, and he knows it. 'Split fork!' I tell him. He nods, breaks away, maintaining pace but keeping a wide distance from me. This way, we've divided their forces, but stay within each other's range. My legs burn as I race ahead, the canister on my back making me clumsy. The harness bites into my shoulders and the wide buckles chafe my back and chest.

Quinn watches from hacked cams, pointing us towards easy routes across the rooftops, warning us of ambushes. I leap across a chimney and my feet give out beneath me on the slippery tiles. A rooftop courtyard rushes up like a kick in the face as I am thrown forward, pain burning across my body. But I roll with it, sliding into cover and pressing my back against the brick wall, hoping they won't see me.

I'm not alone.

There's a skinnie watching me. He's stripped naked, his entire body beaming blue with stormtech. There are little growths, bulbous blue-black infestations like rocks, sprouting from his body like vile plants growing from poisoned soil. It's skinnies who have gone past the point of return to stormtech addiction, controlled by their body's desires. There's whole quarantined tenements crawling with them, shivering, coughing, and eventually dying, in the dark.

And now his bloodshot eyes, squirming with blue tendrils, are looking straight at the stormtech canisters strapped to my back.

'Don't,' I whisper, beseeching him.

'Give them here.' His voice is the churning of wet gravel.

'Please be quiet!' I beg, my heart sinking, the sound of gunfire getting louder.

He stumbles towards me, panting hard and salivating. 'Give them here!' he yells, hating his body for being so weak, hating himself for allowing this drug to destroy him, but unable to do a thing about it.

He lunges, prepared to claw out my throat if that's what it takes. I duck away, bursting out of cover and leaping across the parapet to the opposite roof, to land with a thud. 'Found her!' one of them screams, bullets drowning out the rest of his words as I skitter and run across the rooftops.

I can't see Tann. I'm bleeding from somewhere, but don't yet know if it's fatal. My legs burn under me. Panting, I snap around as a patch sky in front of me heaves with golden shockwaves. The airship peels its cloaking shield away and swoops over the buildings with a gust of wind. Our pick-up point.

'Sola!' Tann yells down the commslink. Only, the airship isn't stopping on the roof. We've got to leap for it.

Three cables dangle down from its belly. Quinn's already hooked in. Tann bursts into view, securing himself. I'm about to do the same when rounds go clattering against the ship's hull and it swerves out of reach, the cable whiplashing backwards. The thunder of men from behind, the canisters like an anchor on my back, my legs crumpling under me. Tann's mouth making shapes, words snatched away in the wind, as he stretches out a hand towards me.

I leap out into open air.

Everything happens all at once.

I grab the cable. It slips from my sweaty grasp. A silent scream echoes in my head as I tumble backwards to a bloody death. I'm jerked upwards, hard enough for my shoulder to pop out of my socket. Tann. His hands shake as Quinn grabs my other hand and the two of them attach the carabineer to my harness. My fear melts down into the adrenaline, then turns to crazed laughter. They laugh with me, the three of us locking in an embrace as we go roaring and spinning over the seething city.

'You've done well, my girl. Very well.'

'Surprised?'

Pychon looks up from the canisters and sips his vodka. 'Not at all, Sola. I wouldn't have asked if I didn't feel you three were up to the task.'

This time we're sitting in his office. He owns a multitude of trinkets, wax-encrusted figurines and asteroid fragments, stormtech phials he insists are for decoration, as well as many printed manuscripts and leather-bound tomes and grimoires, most of them emblazoned with the same upside Y he's got tattooed on his neck.

Strange. I have never known a Royal to print manuscripts before.

He catches my eye. 'Ah, you've noticed my collection of artefacts?'

'They're not human, are they?' I ask.

'Not at all. I have quite the love of alien archaeology. The galaxy's full of ancient wonders, you see. Leaving them all to rot in their creator's graves is such a waste.' A blip in my shib. 'Here. That's a link to the Academy on Compass. The universe's biggest asteroid city, containing the universe's largest library archive. Take a look when you have the time. No doubt you'll find something interesting.'

I accept the link just to be polite. 'So. What happens now?'

Pychon wears a look of honest surprise. 'Exactly what I told you. You complete the task and I remove the Coat of Arms. Perhaps you expected me to go back on my word?'

I shrug. 'You could say it's common practice for most stormdealers.'

'I am not most stormdealers, Sola. And a Royal's word is his bond, as you'll now discover.'

True to his word, the emblem is removed. We've gained our freedom. We can leave anywhere in the country, the world, the galaxy.

I don't get up.

'However, since the three of you are so excellent at what you do, it would be foolish of me to not ask you to consider continuing to supply stormtech canisters for me,' Pychon continues. 'I have many Crawlers under my employ. You will not be alone.'

I sense a trap. 'Really? What's the catch?'

'There is none. You will have a binding contract that states the terms of your employment. Not service. Not enslavement. Employment.' He sips his vodka, pours another measure as he slides comfortably in his seat, crossing his legs. 'Sola, this city is broken. It always was, as far back as the 19th century. The Syndicate was something great. Now, they're squabbling over scraps, killing each other over street-corners and trafficking routes. We carved out a small empire for ourselves. We lived as kings. And perhaps we can again. I don't need you with me to do that, Sola. But I'd like to.'

The man is a baroque puzzle box. Anyone else would sweeten it with golden lies, like the other guilds do, try to pass their façade off as a sure path to victory. But whatever Pychon's endgame is, he believes in it. He doesn't need me – if he did, he'd have locked us with Black Cloud until he grew bored of our services – but he wants me.

'I don't need an answer right away,' Pychon says with an elegant smile. 'Think on it. You Crawlers are welcome to perform a few additional jobs – all paid, of course. But don't take too long. London waits for no one.'

'Oops, you just broke your neck,' Quinn calls out with a laugh. I'm flat on my back, aching from the fall. I raise my head to glare at him.

Tann helps me up. 'Don't mind him. Quinn couldn't make that jump to save his life.'

Quinn taps his datapad, chiming with his hacking software. 'Got some other important stuff to do. You know, like saving your lives if things don't work out.'

We're in the Bog, formerly a stop on an old railway line in Central London, one of those that slithered up to the surface and down again. That ended when a poorly-constructed skyscraper collapsed and crushed the entire station to rubble. With so many new service lines being built underground, no one cared about the surface any more. But the ruins with its gantries and walkways make a fantastic obstacle course for doing practice runs. It's neutral territory. All Crawlers in London use the Bog, and respect it.

And, like always, there's a bottle of vodka waiting for us when we've finished our obstacle course. It's the little things.

'You better catch me this time,' I tell Tann. It's the one manoeuvre we never manage to pull off. My chest strains as I heave myself up the metal rungs of the ladder, hooking my legs and bending backwards. His arms outstretched, Tann gives an upside-down nod. I close my eyes and let go. I feel his arms jerking as he catches me, but I keep falling, the both of us slamming down to the crash matt in a tangled heap. Chests heaving, we look at each other before breaking into laughter. I roll to a sitting position, the back of my ponytail tickling my neck. Tann slides his arms across my chest, wrapping his big, awkward weight around me in a clumsy bear hug.

He's soaked in sweat. I squeal and try to wriggle away, pull my arms free, but he's too strong, his muscles straining against mine as he wrestles me back, fingers digging into my ribs, my armpits, my body shaking with laughter. 'You know I can't let you do that,' he chuckles. I roll back into him, panting for breath again and going limp in surrender.

I roll my eyes up to look at him. 'I'll get you one of these days, big guy.'

He plants a kiss on the top of my head. 'Not today you won't.'

The wind ruffles our hair. Our hearts slowing until they beat in tune against each other. And I wish I didn't have to spoil the moment by telling them off Pychon's proposal. But I do.

Quinn takes to it surprisingly well. Tann doesn't. Just as I thought.

'We did our end of the bargain,' Tann tells us as he paces back and forth. 'The debt's paid. We can run off right now if we want to.'

I heave a sigh and spread my arms. 'Run off to where? You know it's chaos out there. The Syndicate's out of control, and the stormtech outbreak's turned checkpoints into a nightmare.'

'With the Black Rose, we've got protection, food, shelter, jobs, all the best gear to get the work done,' Quinn says. 'Do you really want to go back to doing this on our own?'

'Yes,' Tann insists. 'We're Crawlers. We don't owe anyone anything, Sola. We deliver, we collect our pay, we leave. That's what we do. If we settle down with a permanent contract, we're bound to the Black Rose, bound to Earth, forever. Transporting *stormtech* forever.'

Quinn rolls his eyes. 'You still have a problem with that?'

'And you don't?' Tann retorts.

'People who take stormtech are consenting adults. They've made their choices. Besides, it isn't like we haven't hauled drug cargo before.'

'This is different,' he insists. 'All those skinnies waiting to die in back alleys? Those reports of stormtech-induced violence? Those teenagers overdosing on the streets as the stormtech rages across Eastern Europe? That's on us. We're introducing this dangerous alien biomatter to Earth.'

I squirm in my seat. Tann knows me well enough to know when the message is hitting home. 'Sola, you take that contract, you'll never be able to find your father.'

'My father's dead,' I say, eyes glued to my lap. 'I found out just a few weeks ago. He went to a research outpost in the Tungyian, out in deepspace. It was previously owned by some alien species before they retrofitted it for human-sustainable life-support systems, and one day those life-support systems broke. Everyone on the station died.'

It feels so far away when I say it like that. Distant. Literally entire galaxies away, to a man who made it very clear he didn't approve of me or my lifestyle.

So why does it still hurt every time I think about it?

Tann's hand tightens on my shoulder. 'Sola...'

'There's nothing for me out there,' I say. 'I don't know how to do anything else, and you two boys are all I've got. And I'm not going to let us be homeless or hunted or kidnapped and imprisoned by other guild ever again. I won't let us be sniffing on the streets for scraps. You see this?' I spread my arms towards the city skyline. In the late afternoon light, the ships look like streams of multicoloured fish. The city beginning to transition to night-time: baroque holofronts of Edwardian building façades flaring up, neon blinking to life on elongated spires, adboards for offworld travel rolling with phantasmagorical riots colour. 'We can go *anywhere* in London. We won't just touch the sky. We'll own it.' I grab hold of Tann's hand and clutch it tight. 'But I need to know you're both in. I won't do this without you.'

'You know my answer,' Quinn says with a wild grin. 'Always did want a city to myself.'

Tann turns his face to the wind, but I can feel him looking at me, feel his muscles moving beneath his dark skin. Don't say it, big guy. Don't tell me to walk away and leave this behind. Because I know I will if you ask me to. Don't say it.

Don't make all these years of slaving away for nothing.

An eternity later, he clears his throat and claps me on the back. 'Okay. Let's do it. Let's take a leap of faith.'

I grin and grab the bottle of vodka, taking a long swig until Tann snatches it away and gulps down his own portion. 'Oi! Gimme some! Fair's fair!' Quinn takes the bottle and drinks a mouthful, but it goes the wrong way and he spits it over the ledge, screwing up his face.

'You're supposed to *sip* it, you idiot,' Tann chuckles, slapping him on the back so hard he almost pitches forward. I'm laughing so hard my sides are splitting. And in that moment, I know things are going to go well. I've never been so sure of anything.

Time speeds up when you're on assignment. You forget about the present and give yourself over to the city. Nothing but you, your friends and making the next jump, feeling the breeze in your hair. Knowing that for tonight, you *own* this city.

We shuttle stormteach canisters all over London. From my usual areas of operation in Shepherd's Bush and Green Park to the new landscapes of Heathrow and Mayfair. We sometimes deliver to Pychon directly, or to one of the Black Rose's cells scattered around the city

With every completed shipment, the job gets a little easier and Pychon's smile goes wider. He lets us pick our own jobs, mapping our own routes across London. His men tip their heads with respect when they pass us on the causeways. Soon, he's got enough stormtech to open up his arena. We watch in the opening night as creatures grown in machinery-encrusted vats, nestled in subterranean biomechanical labs hidden under the British Library, launch into the arena. The blue alien biomatter squirming through their bodies rewriting their biochemistry for bloodlust, the walls splattering with blood and matted hair, ribs and skulls splintering as the creatures rip each other apart.

I never go again. Crawlers don't think about the cargo we carry, what it could be used for. That's not my problem and I'm not going to waste time trying to guess.

Only, I don't have to guess. I know, because I see the skinnies in every sunken corner of this city. Wheezing. Coughing. Clawing at the blue throbbing up and down their bodies, as if trying to rip it out of their skin and swallow it all over again.

They made their choice. I've made mine.

As I do when Pychon offers to make us apart of the Black Rose.

'You're sure about this, Sola?' he asks, when we're in his office and I'm staring out at the glittering cityscape. His hand tightens on my shoulder. The gesture is fatherly, warm. 'Have you spoken about this with your crew?'

'They know where they stand,' I say.

'Because once I lock this deal in —'

'It can't be undone. I know. I know.' If there's one thing the entire Syndicate agrees on, it's abiding by your allegiances. We'll be anchored here.

And that's perfect.

Pychon nods with his usual dry smile. Between one second and the next, the inverted Y symbol appears in the upper-right corner of my shib, black as interstellar space. 'Welcome to the family, Sola,' Pychon says, and I swear I can even hear admiration in his voice.

Quinn's overjoyed, of course. Tann gives me a smile that doesn't quite reach his eyes, but I know he's happy that I'm happy, that I've accomplished this for all of us.

He'll come around in time. He always does. We have a home, now. A family. And we're going to make it count.

'Sola, you might want to see this.'

'A little busy right now, Quinn,' I say through gritted teeth. I hook my legs into a pole that's jutting of the building I'm perched upon, my armpits straining as I haul Tann upwards, inch by inch. London's architecture glistens with recent rain, and gecko-grips and water do not mix.

'Sola, I –'

I can feel my shoulders grinding in their sockets. 'Unless we're going to get shot in the next five seconds, I don't want to know.'

Quinn snorts from his end of the commlink. 'Fine. Have it your way.'

I roll my eyes. Quinn's such a child when he wants to be. Sweat drips from my forehead as I haul Tann up to the ledge next to me, panting and huffing. These suits don't mix with water, either. It's leeched tight to my sweaty skin, like I'm wearing a wetsuit. I tug it loose from my thighs, giving a shiver as I look down the vertiginous drop, hoping Tann doesn't notice. But of course, he does. 'You scared of heights, Sola?'

The ability to scale atop of buildings without a moment's hesitation is a prerequisite for a Crawler. I shake my head. 'Bad climb, is all.' We're perched above the rushing grey waters of the Thames, in one of those extended buildings that jut out like an extruded tongue over the water. I nearly drowned when I was eight. The wind howls in my ear, fast-freezing my sweat, rattling the buckles of my harness. I swallow sour saliva into my throat, get back into the mission.

Quinn makes a whistling sound as Tann taps the chainmetal seal that's barricading the stashhouse door, where our next pick-up of canisters waits. 'That's offworld encryption. Mars-make, probably. I can't crack that.'

'You? Of all people?' I say, incredulous. 'You can't break this?'

'I'm far from the best hacker in the West Wend,' Quinn says.

'Except when you pretend to be,' I grumble.

Tann leans against the grime-caked wall and claps me on the back. 'Well, at least it's a cool view from up here.'

My mouth curves into a smile. 'I didn't climb up here for nothing.'

'But Quinn can't do anything!'

'It doesn't mean *we* can't.' I retrieve the acid-eating sealant from a pouch on my harness. 'Sometimes, simple is best.'

Quinn grumbles something rude as Tann snatches up the sealant with an eager grin. 'This is going to make a hell of a noise,' he says to me.

'Unless we mask the sound,' I say. 'Quinn?'

'Oh, am I useful again?'

'Maybe. Is there a chainship flying overhead, fireworks, something?'

The rattle of keypads as Quinn searches. 'There isn't. But there's a church bell.' The white-marbled belfry of Southwark Cathedral lights up in my vision with a gold honeycomb outline. The workings of internal machinery nestled like tightly-packed intensities. 'The bell's connected to an automated system. I can reach it.'

'You want to ring a cathedral bell at 4:12 am in the morning?' I ask.

'Yeah. And?'

'And wake up the whole of bloody Southwark?'

I imagine Quinn shrugging. 'It's London, Sola. Weirder things have happened.'

'Oh, Quinn,' Tann sighs.

'Besides, a little early mass never hurt anyone.'

'You can't prove that,' I mutter, but Quinn isn't listening as he gets to work. I stoop down on my haunches and spray the foul-smelling acid over the gravestone-shaped slab of counterintrusion hardware. The hissing rush of the Thames below me is swallowed up by ear-splitting gong of the bell ringing, so sudden I almost lose my grip on the parapet.

You don't feel the ringing of bells in your ears. You feel it in your *bones*. Your skull. The echoing ominous sound shivers through the air and into my body. I feel I have to clench my teeth or they'll shatter. Tann's clamping his hands over his ears. I can imagine Quinn laughing to himself as windows flicker on and autocabs swerve to a halt below us.

The chainmetal seal shatters inwards with the faintest cough. I stand guard while Tann slithers inside and retrieves the canisters.

'We have to try that trick again,' Quinn says once the sound dies down.

The sound's stopped, but I can still hear the metallic echo bouncing around in my head. 'Yeah, let's not. Stick to computers. Leave the ideas to us.'

'It worked, didn't it?'

I roll my eyes. 'Doesn't mean it worked well!'

'You worry too much, Sola.'

'Somebody's got to bare the responsibility around here.'

'The canisters aren't even hidden!' Tann exclaims as he pokes his head out and hands me the cold-dewed cylinder. 'Don't you just love it when they're cocky?'

'Best part of the job.' I strap the canister to my back, tightening my harness straps before reaching up to grab another canister. They wobble precariously on the parapet next to me.

A sudden chill fast-freezes the sweat on my skin. Did I see that? 'Quinn, what did you say the problem was, before?'

'Oh, *now*, you want to ask?'

I kneel down next to the canisters. 'Quinn, shut up and spit it out.'

'It's about the people we're stealing from,' he tells me. 'They're –
'

'The Ripper Boys',' I finish. The ghastly familiar blade and top hat emblem embossed on every canister.

'This is bad,' Tann whispers. 'This is really, really bad.'

More sweat's trickling down my back. 'We finish up, we get the hell out, and we should be fine.' I resist the urge to sweep for cams or surveillance drones. 'Tann, you done?'

'Almost.' He wriggles out of the hole. We seal the canisters to their receptacles, strap them to our backs. We collect all our gear, pull our visors on. Tann grabs my hands, lowers me down towards the footholds before following a second later.

My armpits strain as I inch back down, using gecko-grips on the dry surfaces. The roar of the Thames seems to be all around me, now. Rushing, gurgling, hissing. The sound pounding in my brain. Dragging me under, like I'm eight again and the smothering liquid darkness closes around me like a wet cage, and I'm opening my mouth to scream and it comes slithering, gushing, pouring in –

My hand slips. I'm weightless, plunging, tumbling downwards, a scream in my throat. Tann clawing for me, his arm outstretched, like he does when I'm falling towards him.

A stinging, wet slap against my back, and my head fills with blackness.

The light returns in vicious, clawing strokes. I raise my groggy head. Through slits, I see I'm strapped to a padded bench in an X-position, tilted back with thick restraints clamped tight around my wrists, ankles, waist, chest and neck. I'm like an ant in amber – I can't move an inch.

'Boris?' a voice calls out.

'Oh, good. She's awake.'

Dread eclipses all rational thought as I glance up to a dozen Ripper Boys. Their eyes piercing me through their skullface helmets, the pixelated bone glimmering in the watery light. I swallow. But the fact that I still have my skin means they haven't figured out it was us they captured a few months back. They won't believe we were rescued, they'll think we murdered their crew and stole their ship. I have to keep it that way. I can only hope Tann was smart enough to escape and not look for me.

We're in an crypt, or an abandoned catacomb. Skulls embossed with symbols glare down from dusty shelves. Stacked sarcophagi are covered with thick tarpaulins, like the furniture of the recently deceased. A veil of dust shivers down as a train thunders overhead. The room's infested with tech and churning machinery that's giving off a familiar, sickly-sweet stench.

This is their stormtech lab and manufactory.

And in the middle of the room are the stormtech canisters that we stole from them mere hours ago.

Sweat trickles down my back. 'I don't know what you're doing, but I've got no quarrel with you,' I say, squirming in my straps. At first I try to play up the Syndicate aspect – if they respect that I was just doing my job, there's a chance they'll let me go. 'You're making a mistake.'

'I think I'll be the judge of that, my girl.' This comes from the man who answered earlier, Boris, the one I judge to be their leader. A heavyset man with scruffy sideburns and, bizarrely, delicate and pale hands, like a pianist. Any man with hands that immaculate in the Syndicate is a dangerous one. A man wielding enough authority to have others do their ugly work for them. He strolls over and squints down at my restrained form. Three Ripper Boys move behind me, just out of my field of view. 'See, you were in our territory. In our part of the Thames when we fished you out. That puts you in our jurisdiction, does it not?'

I swallow. 'Yes. It does.'

'And you're carryin' a package that could be ours.'

'It's not yours,' I say, realising a nanosecond too late I walked into a trap.

'That so?' Boris says. 'Maybe you can open 'em up, then, and if everything's up to our satisfaction we can move along. Better yet, tell us which guild you're doing the runs for and we'll be happy as pigs in mud.'

If I do that, I'm dead. If they've caught Quinn and Tann, they're dead, too. I can't decide what's worse: them finding out we stole their stormtech, or them finding who we are. Both end with me spending years in captivity, being slowly tortured to death and having my broken body dumped down some forgotten tube shaft.

'No? You can stay here until we get answers.' Behind him, the Ripper Boys are trying to unlock the compartment I sealed the stormtech in, their cutting and counterintrusion tools clattering against the stonework. Boris' skullface mask dissects me, watching me squirm as the Ripper Boys behind me start tightening my restraints. The straps bite into my flesh, buckles tinkling and rattling. 'We've got plenty of time. Weeks, months, even years. No one's going to find you here, girl. You want to start talking, maybe that changes things when we get to the bottom of this.'

'There's nothing to tell,' I insist, clenching my hands to stop them shaking. Please get away from here, boys. 'It's a routine delivery for my guild.'

'Oh yeah, which guild?'

He throws me a dozen questions, seemingly random, but trying to trip me up with an answer that reveals who I am or what I've been doing. I'm exhausted and covered in grime and sweat and filled with dread, but I've got enough intuition to take up a persona. A girl working solo for a few guilds on the side, and happened across the wrong territory out of pure ignorance. It's the only way I see myself getting out of this alive.

Boris performs circuits around me as he talks, his boots scraping on stone, making my teeth itch. Machinery clanging, tools clicking, the canister safety mechanisms come undone, one at a time. 'Can't be too careful nowadays. The Syndicate ain't what it used to be. Offworlders, coming in with their own ideals and methods, pretending to be locals but acting as anything but. Messing about with our system, poisoning this city.' He brushes my ponytail aside, scratches the back of my neck. 'I'll give you an example, girl. Just a few months back, someone stole our chainship, killed our men, took our stormtech.'

Why is he telling me this?

'And the funny thing is, it was our prisoners who were responsible. One of them was a woman. A Crawler. Tall, athletic figure, long silver hair. Like you.'

My body goes very very cold.

'Sounds too good to be true.' I can barely hear Boris over my heart pounding in my ears. 'Only, she had company. At least one other Crawler, or so I'm told.'

I work saliva into my dry, dry throat. 'I work solo. Always have. Can't become too attached when you're in this business.'

'Bloody right, you can't. So things don't add up. And I don't like that.' He gives a long pause, cocking his head. Sweat slithers down my armpits. 'And when I don't like the numbers, I swap 'em around.'

The stone door grinds backwards and it feels like someone's stabbed me in the gut.

It's Tann, restrained much as I am, being wheeled in next to me. Everything goes numb. The big guy doesn't know what to do with himself, his eyes darting around, his hands shaking. I just want to get him out of here, save him, the way I couldn't save my father. 'Sola,' he whispers, barely able to get my name out. 'I went looking for you. I didn't know. I'm –'

Boris claps his hands together with a sound like bones rattling. 'Good. The numbers are whole. Now, which one of you shot my second in command and stole the ship? I'm willing to bet good money it was you, girl. What are the odds, that the both of you would fall into our hands again, eh?'

I was so stupid to think Black Rose could ever protect us.

And then I see Boris reach into his greatcoat and bring something out.

A hypodermic filled with stormtech.

'See, stormtech's a nasty little drug,' Boris says. 'It's so unprecedented that discovering anything new about this alien life-batter – it's effects, potency – relies on test subjects willing to have this little bugger inside them forever. Which is a problem. Again, the numbers don't add up.' He taps his head. 'So we swap them around, and remove the willing part.'

'No!' I croak out, my voice knotted and coarse.

'I think we'll keep the two of you here. We could learn plenty over the years. Problem is, we've only got enough of this kind of stormtech for one. Who goes first?' The stormtech writhes like electric-blue smoke inside the glass, eager to writhe and crawl inside human flesh. Boris's gaze pierces me. 'You lied to me, girl. Treated me like a fool. Probably killed my men, too. So a fitting punishment won't be sticking it into you. It'll be you watching me do this.'

262

He stabs the stormtech hypo down into Tann's neck. The world seems to slow. Then, Tann bucks against his restraints. His muscles quivering, his heart pounding like a drum through his back, choking noises spluttering out. Blue ropes beginning to spiral through his chest, inching up his ribcage. Rewriting his body chemistry, altering his pheromones, his brain, his thought process, fuzing to his nervous system. Turning him *alien*.

'Boss,' someone calls out, frantic.

'Not now,' Boris snaps back.

'Boss, it's bad. Check their shibs. They're Black Rose.'

And even through his skullface musk, Boris' eyes go wide. 'Please tell me you're joking.'

'Wish I was. Boss, these are the cultists tearing the Syndicate up, and we –'

'– we just kidnapped two of their Crawlers.' There's stone-cold fear in Boris' voice, as if a nightmare so terrible that he can't even talk about it is coming true before his eyes. 'They'll kill us for this. They'll blast us out of existence, like they did with that researcher.'

'That was in the Tungyian System. Literal universes away.'

Boris chokes out a strained laugh. 'Yeah, and if they crossed the galaxy and killed a whole space station to get rid of some bastard writing papers they didn't like about him, what are they going to do to us?'

Fear ripples through the men. But I'm immune to it, my mind a hurricane. My first thought is: *I could have stopped this.* If I'd told them who we were earlier, they wouldn't have injected Tann. But even that horror is swiftly swept away, because at the eye of the storm are Boris' words, playing on an endless loop.

They killed my father.

Black Rose killed my father.

'Boys, carve these two open for nanofilament trackers, then dispose of 'em.' Sweat glistens on Boris' forehead. 'If we're lucky, they'll never find out what –'

The entire room short-circuits in a furious flash. Every lightbulb shatters, all machinery going berserk as their back-up generators fail, plunging the room into darkness. Panicking wildly in the blackness, the Ripper Boys looking like skeletons clawing their way out of their tombs.

Our restraints click open. *Quinn.* It has to be.

Tann charges to his feet behind me. I drag him forward, ignoring the quivering in my legs as we run for the exit. The blue glowing in his body providing light. And a target. Firearms crackle in sun-bright flashes, clattering off the stonework as we dive down a service stairwell and through a series of dilapidated hallways. A HUD materialises in my shib, Quinn providing a map of the area and a pick-up point. We get there, maybe we'll make it out alive.

Yells and the thunder of gunfire behind us. Tann jerks backwards, his body *livid* with blue. The fresh stormtech already demanding a fight, a battle, a release of the adrenaline. 'Don't!' I yell. 'Fight this, Tann! You can do it.' I drag him down a tube-line, not knowing and not caring if it's still in use.

I don't know how long we've run before we arrive at Quinn's checkpoint. Black Rose men are already there waiting, covering us with black-barrelled rifles. Relief pours through me. Until I remember what Boris said about who they are and what they did to my father.

A thud echoes out behind me. Tann's collapsed on the ground, his legs twitching, blue squirming up his chest. Somewhere, in the back of my mind, I can hear myself screaming.

It's three days before they even tell me if Tann is okay, and another three before I'm allowed to see him. Me and Quinn stand abreast by the Black Rose's makeshift medclinic, machinery plugged into Tann's body. Stormtech is permanent. Everyone knows that. But I'm told this stormtech has been altered by xenochemists for high-end addicts, the kind that have a body already altered by stormtech and have been working their experienced bodies up for a bigger hit. It would cripple the immune and musculoskeletal system of anyone who hasn't brought their body up to speed.

Like Tann's.

Quinn gives me the best support he can, but beneath it all we know what's coming. I can't say it out aloud. That would make it real. Neither of us are ready for that.

Quinn moves away as a shadow falls across my face. 'It's very unfortunate what happened to your friend,' Pychon says. Medical machinery wheezes and hisses in the background.

I don't answer.

'It's also unfortunate that it happened to coincide with what those ghastly Ripper Boys told you. I knew I should have killed those rats when I had the opportunity. Oh, don't look so surprised. I heard every word through your friend's transmission system.'

Only now do I meet his gaze, mustering all the venom and hatred I possibly can into my voice. 'You're a lying, deceiving son of a bitch. I don't want to hear it.'

Pychon gives a disappointing sigh. 'And here I had such high hopes for you, Sola. You disappoint me, girl. Did you really think I was going to tell you what we are or what we do?'

'That you're a cult?'

'I truly despise that word. Don't ever use it again in my presence. We're a cabal, spread across solar systems, planets and worlds. We're spreading the might and glory of the stormtech to as many inhabitants as possible, as its creators intended.'

'It's creators?' My head's spinning. 'You mean… the aliens?'

'The Shenoi, the creatures that *are* the stormtech, yes. The stormtech is a gift, my dear. You've seen how my creatures upstairs take to it. Their strength doubles, triples. They have never-before-seen resistance to pain and bodily damage. They're so addicted to adrenaline they'll fight until their dying breath, if only to hear the sound of their opponent's spine snapping in between their jaws. Imagine what this superorganism can do if it's controlled. Nurtured. Tamed.'

He peels back the sleeves of his suit. There, behind the thick clothes he wore to disguise it, and behind the cologne he wore to mask the smell, is the stormtech. Glowing, twitching, moving.

'Working at an offworld dockyard exposed me to radiation. It didn't take long for the cancer to follow,' he tells me. 'Centuries of research, billions of pounds, and we haven't found a cure. I was truly considering a bottle of pills and a bottle of vodka rather than face the growing infestation inside me. Until stormtech came along and ate it right out of my body. We're meant to have it. *They* meant us to have it.'

'You're looking for the aliens,' I say. My stomach's beginning to knot. 'You don't think they're extinct. You want to control the stormtech, how it's used, who has it.'

'Very good.' There's a glint in Pychon's eye, like his favourite student has made him proud. 'We've been granted this living, breathing alien miracle from the stars, a superorganism that can turn the human body into an advanced machine. It's a gift. We plan to ensure all of humanity is given it. With it, we could *own* the stars.'

'You never cared about the Syndicate, or the Black Rose,' I say with growing horror. 'All this time, all you've cared about is spreading the stormtech into as many people as possible.'

'That's the ticket.'

'Have you *seen* what it's doing to people out there? The skinnies on the street?'

'They're weak. The strong survive. As I have. As my men have. You don't think I forced them, do you?'

'You're sick. Your entire cult is *sick.*'

He punches me across the jaw. My head whips back against the wall with a dull thud. Spots swim in front of my eyes. When I wipe my mouth, blood comes away.

'I warned you about using that word. Besides, can you really throw down righteous judgement on me, Sola? You could have walked away at any moment when I lifted the Coat of Arms. But you chose to stay. You chose to help me traffic the stormtech. You *liked* what you were doing, you told me as much. Please don't be such a hypocrite.'

I want to retort, but he's right. I begged Tann to stay, even when he urged us to escape. I knew that stormtech was slowly burning people's lives up. And I yet I helped them light the match.

He stoops down and hauls me back up by the chest straps of my harness. 'If you're thinking of stabbing me in the stomach, I'd think twice. Many people have tried to kill me and the stormtech has denied them all. So let me explain how things are going to go. You heard what Boris said. Men apart of our organisation destroyed an entire research station in deepspace because one fool residing there tried to expose us. Tried to paint us as alien-worshipping freaks. We will not tolerate insubordination.'

'If you think I'll keep working for you people –'

Pychon frowns in genuine confusion. 'You speak as if you're not part of us.'

'I will *never* be part of you,' I hiss.

'But my dear girl, you already are.' With sinking dread, I look towards the upper-right corner of my shib. The inverted Y – the cult's emblem that represents the people that killed my father, attached to my neuralware forever. 'We're still a Royal and still part of the Syndicate, bound by its rules. You cannot leave. You cannot work for another guild. That was the decision you willingly made. No one knows where you are. You and your friends are part of us, Sola.'

This can't be real. This can't be real. I want to pass out.

'So you will continue with your duties, bringing us stormtech canisters and whatever else we ask of you,' says Pychon as he slowly and meticulously brushes my hair aside 'If you refuse, or show any kind of defiance, you still have one healthy friend we can use. Your life can become very unpleasant, very fast, Sola. On the other hand, you do well, and good things can come your way. Perhaps you may even find our beliefs agreeable.'

As Pychon's rambling dials down into white noise, I realise that he referred to my father as *some fool*.

He doesn't realise I'm Viklun Ryken's daughter.

'I will allow you to see your friend, if you put this on without resistance.' Two men have arrived, dumping my dark-purple prisoner's suit at my feet. 'Except on assignment, you are to wear it at all times. After all, we cannot have our prisoners forgetting their place.'

Heart-sinking, I strip my own suit off and slide into the prisoner's suit instead, buckles tingling as my harness is secured tight over my shoulders. As the hateful, sticky fabric latches to my skin, I notice the words *Permanent Prisoner* on the suit's shoulder and back have been replaced with the cult's inverted Y symbol.

As if there's any difference.

Tann's pulse beats abnormally fast through his hand as I hold it. I watch the stormtech bounce between his ribcage like some parasitic worm under a sea of flesh. Eating him alive. He's lying flat in bed. I don't know how much longer he has.

'Hey,' he croaks out, attempting a smile. 'You look how I feel.' The words dissolve into a rattling cough that shakes his entire body.

'Don't talk, Tann,' I whisper, a lump in my throat. 'Just listen. You were right about everything, Tann. We should never have come here. Never should have touched stormtech. Never should have stayed with these people.'

I choose my words careful for the surveillance tech that's no doubt concealed here.

Tann coughs again. 'You did what you thought was right, Sola,' he croaks. The stormtech's climbed to his throat, turning his voice thick and raspy. 'You wanted to protect this family.'

I did. And in my desperation to do so, doomed them. The very substance we sworn we'd never touch is now in Tann's body *because* of me.

I'm going to regret not running for the rest of my life. However long that may be.

'We were pretty awesome, though, weren't we?' Tann coughs out with a stuttered laugh.

'Yeah,' I manage. 'We were.'

'We touched the sky, Sola.'

'We did.'

'You always took the biggest risks, Sola. Me and Quinn knew those jumps, those climbs were too high, too far, but you were too brave and too stupid not to try.' Another rattling cough. 'You always wanted more.'

My chest tightens.

'We never got around to climbing Big Ben, did we? Man, what I wouldn't give to climb that sucker. Sit there with you and Quinn, sharing a drink and watching the city one last time.'

My knuckles turn white in his hand.

Tann gives a heavy, pent-up sigh, like he's letting go of some unseen weight. 'Make it count, Sola.' He meets my sight, eyes darting

268

to the corners of the room, like he knows they're listening. He's figured everything out about my father. 'Make it all count.'

'I will,' I manage. 'I swear it, Tann.'

He smiles. I sit beside him, holding his hand. Listening to the rhythm of his breathing until it slows and finally stops.

I get into the command terminal system easily enough. Quinn's shown me the hacking method enough times I know it by heart. Because we can't screw this up.

Pychon's been keeping us busy over the last two years, since Tann died. Shipping stormtech, overseeing distribution, hunting down stashhouses and new travel routes. He wants us immersed in the idea that we belong to him and his cult.

But he can't keep an eye on us around the clock. Like the early morning hours me and Quinn have been slipping out to a darkmarket arcade in SoHo, using a tightbeam communication system to access classified archives in orbital server farms. There's nothing on Pychon's cult, or their name.

But there's scant footage of the destruction at Quyn Research Station. The defence systems locked onto incoming hostile gunships in battle formation, readying their long-range railguns. Event-monitoring systems recorded the attack, tagging the gunships's substrate identification and securing it on a remote orbital server.

Hunting this footage down has taken two years of work and cost almost everything we have. But that's fine. It's dirty money. Drug money. I don't want a cent of it any more.

And if it means I get a chance of bringing my father's killers to justice and making Tann's death count for something, it's priceless.

'Once we do this, there's no going back,' I tell Quinn as we sit on our old meeting point on the rooftop of Covent Garden Station. It feels so lifeless without Tann, his arm around my shoulder, the pounding of his heart. 'If they don't find out immediately, they'll find out next week, or next month. We run, they'll kill us. We stay, they'll kill us. We'll live our lives waiting for this bomb to go off.'

Quinn lets his feet dangle over the parapet. 'If this is the only way we get back at them, I'm willing to live with that. Are you?'

'I have been for a long time, Quinn. Just wanted to make sure we're on the same page.' I look at him. The only friend I've got left in this city. In this world. 'Anything we do from now on, it's both of our decisions. I'm not going to let you take the fall for anything I do, ever again.'

So I'm standing here now at the terminal with our assassination package in hand, containing the footage of the destruction of Quyn Research Station and the names and tags of the people who did the deed. Our data is scarce and threadbare, but we will work with what we have.

I can't send it out to any other Syndicate or Earth-based organisation. They won't care and Pychon will get wind of it immediately. The only address I have for any offworld location is the one Pychon gave me. The Academy on Compass, the giant city asteroid. If he has that, his cult must have origins, or other members, on the asteroid as well.

It's too late for me. For Tann. For Quinn. For my father. For the millions of skinnies and folks addicted to stormtech I gave them.

But it's not too late for it to mean something. Pychon killed my father because he tried to tell the world about them. Now, as I watch the transmission grow in a neon-blue icon across the screen, I complete my father's work. Maybe someday, someone on Compass will discover this data packet and use it to bring this cult down.

But it won't be me.

I'm a prisoner. Bound forever to Pychon and his cult. I'll never touch the sky again. But for the first time my conscience is free, and that's what matters.

The screen chimes. Transmission sent.

I scrape the logs of my actions and send a confirmation to Quinn between returning to my stateroom onboard the skyhook. There's no telling when this bomb will drop. But I know I'll be ready for it.

I lean back against the wall and watch as the sun crawls over the horizon and the city blinks and flares to life in a showcase of bright, blinking neon. The stars glinting down on spires and highrises, rivers and castles, spaceports and crumbling towers.

London.

I was born in this city. And now, it's become my prison. But it's impossible to hate. The city feels too big, too permanent, to take anything I can throw at it. It's survived devastating fires. Viking raids. Bloody wars and sieges. Sickness and disease. Serial killers. Terrorist bombings. Drug epidemics. It'll survive us all.

I look up. Pychon's filling the doorway. The stormtech churns furiously up and down his arms like dark clouds on the horizon.

I don't smile. And neither does he.

About the Authors

Neal Asher was born in 1961 in Essex and now divides his time between there and the island of Crete. He's been an SF and fantasy junky ever since having his mind distorted at an early age by JRRT, Edgar Rice Burroughs and E.C. Tubb. Sometime after leaving school he decided to focus on one of his many interests because it was inclusive of the others: writing. Over the years he's worked his way up through the small presses and zeroed in on science fiction. Finally taken on by a large publisher, Pan Macmillan, his first full-length SF novel, *Gridlinked*, came out in 2001, and Neal now has some twenty-eight books to his name, also in translation across the world.

Eugen Bacon is African Australian, a computer scientist mentally re-engineered into creative writing. Her work has won, been shortlisted, longlisted or commended in national and international awards, including the Bridport Prize, Copyright Agency Prize, Ron Hubbard's Writers of the Future Award, Australian Shadows Awards and Nommo Award for Speculative Fiction by Africans. Her creative work has appeared in literary and speculative fiction publications worldwide, and 2020 sees the release of: *Her Bitch Dress* (Ginninderra Press), *The Road to Woop Woop & Other Stories* (Meerkat Press), *Hadithi* (Luna Press), and *Inside the Dreaming* (NewCon Press).

Aliette de Bodard writes speculative fiction: she has won three Nebula Awards, a Locus Award and four British Science Fiction Association Awards, and was a double Hugo finalist. Her most recent book is *Of Dragons, Feasts and Murders*, a fantasy of manners and murders set in an alternate 19th Century Vietnamese court (upcoming July 7th from JABberwocky Literary Agency, Inc.). She lives in Paris.

M.R. Carey wrote extensively in comics (*Lucifer, X-Men, The Unwritten, Highest House*) before turning to prose fiction with the Felix Castor novels. He is best known for *The Girl with All the Gifts*, filmed in 2016 by Poison Chef. Carey received a British Screenwriters' Award for his screenplay, which was based on his own novel. He has also co-written two novels with his wife Linda and their daughter Louise. His most recent work includes *The Dollhouse Family* for DC's Hill House imprint and the post-apocalyptic Rampart trilogy, whose first volume *The Book of Koli* was released in April 2020.

Joseph Elliott-Coleman is a writer of fiction, with Science Fiction and Urban Fantasy being his wheelhouse. He is the writer of the novella *Judges: The Patriots* and the short story "Queen" for the brilliant own voices anthology *Not So Stories*, both available from Rebellion Books. He lives in Croydon, London. He wishes you well.

Stewart Hotston lives in Reading, UK. After completing his PhD in theoretical physics, Stewart currently spends his days working in high finance. He has had numerous short stories published as well as three novels. His last novel, the political thriller *Tangle's Game*, was published by Rebellion. When Stewart is not writing or working, he's a senior instructor at The School of the Sword.

Dave Hutchinson was born in Sheffield in 1960 and read American Studies at the University of Nottingham before becoming a journalist. He is the author of seven novels, two novellas, and six collections of short stories. His novella *The Push* (NewCon Press) was nominated for the BSFA Award in 2010, and the volumes of his Fractured Europe Sequence of novels have been nominated for the Arthur C. Clarke, BSFA, Kitschies and John W. Campbell Memorial awards. The third novel, *Europe in Winter*, won the BSFA Award in 2017. He lives in London.

Ida Keogh's science fiction has been shortlisted for the Writing the Future Short Story Prize and published in the British Medical Journal and by the Wellcome Trust. She is writing a young adult fantasy novel, *Echoes of a Silent Song*. She makes sci-fi and fantasy themed jewellery and can be found on Twitter as @silkyida and on Etsy as SilkyfishDesigns.

Fiona Moore is a London-based writer and academic whose work has appeared in *Asimov's*, *Interzone* and *Clarkesworld*, with reprints in *Forever Magazine* and *Best of British Science Fiction*; her story "Jolene" was shortlisted for a BSFA Award. Her novel *Driving Ambition*, set in the same universe as "Herd Instinct", is available from Bundoran Press. Full details available at: www.fiona-moore.com.

Geoff Ryman writes science fiction, fantasy and slipstream. He is the author of seven published novels and the winner of multiple awards, including the Arthur C Clarke Award (twice), a Nebula Award, a World Fantasy Award, the John W Campbell, James Tiptree Jr, and Philip K. Dick Awards, and several BSFA Awards. A longstanding supporter of African speculative fiction, in recent years he has been instrumental in establishing the annual Nommo Awards.

Jeremy Szal was born in 1995 and was raised by wild dingoes, which should explain a lot. He spent his childhood exploring beaches, bookstores, and the limits of people's patience. He's the author of over forty science fiction short stories, many of which have been translated into multiple languages. He was the editor for the Hugo-winning StarShipSofa until 2020 and has a BA in Film Studies and Creative Writing from UNSW. He carves out a living in Sydney, Australia, with his family. He loves watching weird movies, collecting boutique gins, exploring cities, cold weather, and dark humour. His first novel is *Stormblood* (Gollancz, 2020). Find him at: http://jeremyszal.com/ or @JeremySzal

Andrew Wallace writes and performs original, fast-moving science fiction and fantasy. His current novel is *Celebrity Werewolf*, for which he also narrated the audiobook. His far-future Diamond Roads science fiction thriller series includes *Sons of the Crystal Mind*, *The*

Outer Spheres and *Beautiful Gun.* His new fantasy book, *Dread & the Broken Witch* is out in 2021, and his next NewCon Press project is an eight-story collection of *Black Mirror*-style near-future nightmares called *Deviant Database,* which accompanies an exciting and innovative solo stage show. For more details, check out www.andrewwallace.me, Andrew Wallace Books on Facebook, or Twitter @AndrewWallaceDR

Aliya Whiteley writes genre fiction. Her horror novella *The Beauty* was shortlisted for the James Tiptree and Shirley Jackson awards. The following historical-SF novella, *The Arrival of Missives,* was a finalist for the Campbell Memorial Award, and her noir novel *The Loosening Skin* was shortlisted for the Arthur C Clarke Award. She has written over one hundred published short stories, and also writes a regular non-fiction column for *Interzone.* Her latest SF novel is *Greensmith,* and a collection of her short fiction will be published in 2020.

Also from NewCon Press

Soot and Steel – Edited by Ian Whates

Dark Tales of London: The companion volume to *London Centric*. Stories that explore London's dark underbelly but also celebrate the city's character and charm; stories that beat to the rhythm of the capital's heart. Sinister tales, ghost stories, menacing thrillers and revealing vignettes; stories of the streets, the alleyways, the sewers, the rooftops and the underground, all steeped in the essence of London's urban community, its industrial heritage, the docks, Victoriana, the Blitz, and beyond.

Neal Asher – Lockdown Tales

Best-selling author Neal Asher was far from idle during lockdown, keeping busy in the best way possible: he wrote. Five brand new novellas and novelettes and one novella reworked and expanded from a story first published in 2019. Together, they form Lockdown Tales, exploring the Polity universe and beyond. What lies in wait for humanity after the Polity has gone? Six stories, 150,000 words of fiction that crackle with energy, invention and excitement.

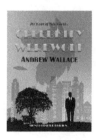

Andrew Wallace – Celebrity Werewolf

Suave, sophisticated, erudite and charming, Gig Danvers seems too good to be true. He appears from nowhere to champion humanitarian causes and revolutionise science, including the design and development of Product 5: the first organic computer to exceed silicon capacity; but are his critics right to be cautious? Is there a darker side to this enigmatic benefactor, one that is more in keeping with his status as the Celebrity Werewolf?

Dave Hutchinson – Nomads

Dave Hutchinson delivers one of his finest tales yet. Are there really refugees from 'elsewhere' living among us? If so, what cataclysmic event are they fleeing from? When a high speed car chase leads Police Sergeant Frank Grant to Dronfield Farm, he finds himself the focus of unwanted attention from Internal Affairs and is faced with the prospect of secrets being unearthed that he would far rather remained buried.